The beginning of the end…

"Hello?"

Jennifer could hear her husband's voice crackle electrically from the cell phone.

"Hello?"

"Brad…" she gurgled through the mouthful of blood, spilling the phlegmy mixture from the corner of her mouth to drip from the steering wheel of the car.

"Jennifer? Is that you? I can't hear you. I can't—"

"The baby," was all she could manage to croak, the force of her voice ripping through the membranous walls of her windpipe. "Baby."

"Where are you, Jennifer? Are you all right? Answer me!"

Her eyes lolled upward. A gust of wind rocked the car on the wheels, blowing the door shut and pinning her left hand between the seat and the metal door.

"Jennifer!"

Her eyes stared back at her from the window, a phantom reflection in front of the rising red dust. The same yellow growth she had seen on Debbie encircled her own lids, thickening in her lashes.

"Baby," she managed to scrape out of her throat. "Help…baby."

Sputtering bursts of air lurched from her opened mouth, convulsively spurting waves of blood across the dash of the car, dotting the window, obscuring the speedometer. Her eyes slowly glazed over in the window, the pupils widening to a fixed, waxy circle nearly as large as the entire iris. Jaw falling slack, no longer impeding the flow of blood, there was a final hiss of air escaping her body, like carbonation from a cracked two-liter.

The yellow fuzz about her still lashes slowly degenerated into a score of miniature, wriggling squiggles, sliding back under the lids and disappearing into the sockets.

"I've got to hang up, Jennifer," Brad sobbed from the cell phone. "I have to call for help. I love you…please, God, hang on!"

Click.

SPECIES

MICHAEL MCBRIDE

Black Death Books
An Imprint of
KHP Industries
www.khpindustries.com

To my family...for always believing...

Your support and encouragement mean the world to me. Without you, this never would have come into being.

With special thanks to Rob Wallace and the staff at Black Death Books, Karen Koehler, Tim Lebbon, Mort Castle, Monica J. O'Rourke, Matt Schwartz, and Steve and Lesley Mazey at Eternal Night.

SPECIES
by
Michael McBride

Black Death Books
is an imprint of
KHP Industries
http://www.khpindustries.com

This is a work of fiction. Names, characters, places and incidents are either products of the author's imagination or are used fictitiously. Any resemblance to actual events or locales or persons, living or dead, save those clearly in the public domain, is purely coincidental.

Species Copyright © 2004 Michael McBride

All rights reserved. No part of this work may be reproduced or transmitted in any form or by any electronic or mechanical means, including photocopying, recording or by any information storage and retrieval system, without the prior written permission of the Publisher, except for short quotes used for review or promotion. For information address the Publisher.

ISBN: 0-9747680-4-9

Cover art by KHP Studios

Printed in the United States of America

10 9 8 7 6 5 4 3 2 1

Prologue

Ten years ago

"I'll be back before you even miss me."

Debbie hid the twinge of jealously by staring out the passenger window into the thin woods, the trunks of the pinion pines rising from the red sand in defiance of nature. Tufts of buffalo grass and yucca plants drew the last remainder of water from the eroding hills that rose and fell to either side of the carved road. The pink asphalt shimmered and sparkled beneath the droning sun, waves of heat rising from the surface, the occasional oncoming car appearing from the hovering rift in reality as though driving straight out of a mirage.

"Yes. I promise I'll take it easy."

Jennifer shifted the cell phone from her right ear to her left, bracing her elbow on the armrest in the door. Her right hand rested atop the steering wheel, no more than holding it in place on the arrow straight road, though she could just as easily have accomplished the same with her enormous belly, pinned uncomfortably behind the bottom of the wheel. Even little William or Madeline—she and Brad favored surprise to a conclusive ultrasound—took exception, kicking at the vinyl-coated ring through the spread muscles at the front of her stomach. He or she, which was her preference, had only recently begun announcing her presence with her rapidly developing soccer skills, though she managed to find a way to sit right on top of Jennifer's bladder no matter what position she was in. They had already stopped three times to quell the pressure in the two and a half hours on the road, once at a Texaco, the other times on the shoulder behind whatever shrubbery was available. Nothing like the morning-fresh feeling of wiping with a handful of leaves.

"I know it's not ideal being this far from a hospital, but we've still got a good three or four weeks. We've been over this. We'll both be through with grad school before this little girl...okay, okay, or guy, decides to come out."

"Mile marker 210," Debbie said, her head turning on a pivot to read the small green sign which quickly fell behind the old, rust-devoured Scout. "Two more miles."

"I have to do this. You know that. My thesis is dependent upon it."

The rolling hills to the left leveled off, cresting waves meeting the foaming shore. A canyon slowly took shape in the distance, rugged cliffs stabbing from the broken earth. Tall stone outcroppings, chalk-red like the final light of the sun setting behind the Rockies, rose at violently impossible angles, haphazardly planted tombstones left to teeter and collapse into the unseen chasm time had all but forgotten. The once mighty Rio Grande, now but a trickle deep in the bottom of the towering walls that stood testament to its former glory, flowed as crystalline as glass, allowing every smoothed stone, every sparkle of fool's gold, to be seen with uncommon clarity.

Even a gentle breeze could raise the fine-grained sand from the silt and swirl it into the air, exposing the element-hardened ground beneath, the openings to the various rodent warrens, now occupied by the western diamondbacks digesting the sharp-clawed former inhabitants. Venom and three-inch fangs were one thing versus a prairie dog, another entirely versus the cars seeking shortcuts around the cop infested highways, as evidenced by the squashed carcasses spread out across the road, the curled whips on the shoulder of the asphalt belonging to those fortuitous enough to be able to slither off to die. Night brought the coyotes, from where Jennifer could only guess, as she had never stumbled across any bone-riddled domicile. Two small moons to the side of the highway, a reflective flash from the headlights, and those scurvy mongrels, rail thin with balding, clumping fur, would bound over the shoulder, their scavenged meal flopping from their mouths like a four-foot, scaled sausage.

The last human dwellings had fallen into their rising dust thirty miles ago, all but the abandoned-looking trailer far off to the left atop an infantile mesa. The white paneling was stained a permanent red from the ceaseless barrage of sandstorms; the screens forsaken in favor of plywood paneling as the glass was no match for the sudden hammering of sand granules that assaulted it as though fired from a shotgun. An oversized-antenna, the kind that could have served dual usage as a futuristic clothesline, dangled from the roof by the cords that formerly serviced it, clacking back and forth like a tethered tumbleweed. None bothered to re-mount it, as there was no signal to be gleaned from anywhere nearby.

"I thought you said your husband gave you the idea for this anyway," Debbie said, rolling her eyes to the roof of the car.

"Indirectly," Jennifer said, covering the phone. "But don't tell him I said that. I let him think he's vastly superior. It's all part of my master plan." And removing her hand from the microphone: "We're almost here now."

"I hate all of this dust! It forms this crust inside my nostrils…" Debbie said, hoping to justify the unsightly picking.

"I love you, too," Jennifer whispered, the left corner of her mouth rising into a smirk. "And don't worry."

"Next left," Debbie said, removing her finger from the rim of her nose long enough to point through the windshield.

"I'll be careful. Promise."

Jennifer eased back from the gas and flipped on the turn signal, though there wasn't even a hint of an approaching car on the infinite horizon.

"Gotta go now. Love you, too."

The Scout eased from the pavement and onto the loose gravel, the back tires first skipping to the side before catching with a lurch and propelling them forward with a kick like a mule.

"I promise! We'll be watching Leno together in bed tonight. All right? Sheesh…I know, I know. I'll call you on the way home…Love you, too. Bye."

"Getting a little possessive, huh?" Debbie said, licking her lips and then rubbing them together. They already showed signs of peeling in strands.

"He says he's got a bad feeling about this trip."

Gravel fired from the undercarriage and wheel wells like a rifleman sniping tin cans from a fence post. A cloud of dust like a hand rose behind them, swirling into an angry fist in preparation of smiting the heavens.

"You bring the antivenin?" Debbie asked.

"Of course."

"Then he's got nothing to worry about."

"I think it's just that we're getting closer to the due date and the reality of it all is starting to set in. You should have seen the look on his face the first time she kicked him. He had his head on my stomach while we were watching a movie in bed and he just bolted upright with this pale-faced look of horror, and said 'There…there's really someone in there!'"

Debbie laughed, clapping her hand over her mouth and nose to keep the dried flakes she had loosened from firing out. She had short black hair only recently shaved back to the skull, but kept it beneath a navy blue do-rag. Long silver crosses swung like pendulums from her large lobes in time with the bouncing of the car on the washboard road. She wore no make-up, her eye-sockets taking on a bruised, sunken appearance. Her tanned cheekbones looked like stretched leather. With the flannel shirt, faded Levi's, and dusty, worn cowboy boots, she looked as though she could have been equally comfortable wrangling cattle and working as a roadie for a bar band.

"Don't ask me how he hadn't fit that piece into place yet," Jennifer said, pulling out the empty ashtray and setting the cell phone inside. She moaned uncomfortably, shifting as much as the cramped confines of the driver's seat would allow.

"Don't tell me you have to go again."

"You try sitting with a bowling ball on your bladder on a gravel road."

"Fun as that sounds…"

The short pinion pines fell away as they neared the trailer, leaving sparsely more than the bare red sand and yuccas. Pockets of sage clumped from the nothingness, sharpened thorny branches rife with tangles of hair from the passing mule deer trying to nibble at the tender leaves within.

The Scout ground to a halt, the tires locking up long before the growling vehicle rumbled to rest. A cloud of red dust, the very same that had been trailing them from the tires, finally caught up, engulfing the car before dissipating on the thin breeze. Even with the windows rolled up, the dry, dusty texture settled upon their skin and parched their mouths.

Debbie was out the door and slamming it shut before Jennifer was able to loosen herself from behind the wheel and swing her legs out.

"Looks like they're already down at the dig," Debbie called, cupping her hand over her eyes to block out the sun and the dust.

"Go ahead on down," Jennifer said, making a beeline toward the back of the trailer. "I'm right behind you."

Debbie was too excited to even make the token gesture of waiting. She hit the path at a skip, hopping excitedly from one stone to the next on her way toward the lip of the canyon. Her master's thesis would be easy enough to prove. Heck, she already had the school newspaper and a handful of hungry editors at various journals awaiting her paper. All she had to do was write the blasted thing and she'd be a professor in no time. Was an Apatosaurus colonial? Duh. Find any vegetarian life form that isn't colonial. How many cows do you see defending their territory on the open prairie? So long as they unearthed more than two distinct fossilized remains, how could the claim possibly be refuted?

Jennifer rested her back against the trailer and relieved the pressure onto the nest of crumpled tumbleweeds lodged against the trailer's skirt. Though it felt as though her bladder had swelled to the size of a watermelon, she trickled no more than the contents of a shot glass. It felt better, however. For the moment, anyway. It felt better.

Her own theorem would be much more difficult to corroborate. Yes, Brad had unwittingly provided the spark she had needed to formulate her work, and he beamed like a proud papa, though he really knew little of what she was trying to establish out here. He was definitely brilliant in his own right. Even his professors envied his architectural skills, but doubted anyone would ever outright commission him to construct his wild flights of fancy when suburbia was becoming the definition of mass production, matchbox houses for the disposable computer market. "Someone had to buy the first Frank Lloyd Wright," he would say, ever the optimist.

Jennifer had been beating herself up, racking her brains for weeks to come up with any idea valid enough to base her whole graduate education upon, but had come up with nothing even remotely close until that one afternoon.

Brad had been sitting there on the couch, like he did every Sunday in September, watching whatever football game he considered himself blessed enough to watch. He had just finished off an entire bowl of popcorn and tossed it onto the coffee table, freeing all of the uneaten kernels to skitter across the table and onto the floor. She had no more than drawn the breath to vent her frustrations at him when he turned around and looked at her over the back of the couch, saying simply enough, "So you say that dinosaur bones are hollow like those of birds, eh?"

"The evidence supports it," she remembered saying impatiently, staring at the kernels on the carpet like they were coals spit out of the fire.

"Even the big ones like the T-Rex?"

"Yes. Even the big ones."

"Don't buy it," he said, drawing a swill from his beer.

"I'll alert the scientific community."

"You mocking me?" he asked, raising an eyebrow, but turning quickly back to the television as the commercial ended.

"With your vast experience in paleontology? Heavens, no."

"Joke all you want—"

"Thank you for your permission."

"All I'm saying is look at all of those houses in Hollywood built on those steep hillsides. They need stilts to hold them up."

"And this is pertinent how?"

"Well, I can't imagine using straws to hold up all that weight... you?"

She cocked her head to the side and just stared at the back of his head, framed by the green on the television set.

"Those big ol' dinos like the T-Rex and Brontosau...excuse me, Apatosaurus, weighed several tons each, didn't they?"

The fossilized bones were hollow. Of that there was conclusive proof...but there was just something about what he was saying that made the most simplistic, primitive sense.

"You ever heard of a hollow column? I wouldn't even use dinosaur femurs to support a deck. Tell me how those things—especially the T-Rex—could walk around on hollow columns without them folding like an accordion—Touchdown!" He leapt up from the couch, tossing a fountain of beer from the top of the bottle and proceeded to dance around the coffee table.

That was when Jennifer forgot all about the kernels (for the time being, anyway) and let the wheels start churning to see where they would take her. Fact: dinosaur bones were in the same format as bird bones, hollowed, lighter to help to maintain flight, leading to the now common assumption that dinosaurs evolved into birds rather than the prior speculation that they became modern day reptiles. How did they then support so much weight? It took all of about two pounds of pressure to snap a bird's wing like a twig. Granted, the tail helped not only to balance the creature, but also to help distribute the weight as well, but still...

Look at the structure of a human body. The long bones, especially the femurs—the weight bearing structural component of the skeletal system—are made of dense, compact bone surrounding a medullary cavity filled with marrow. Within the compact bone is a layer of spongy bone, a webwork maze of cavities like Swiss cheese, filled with arteries and veins supplying blood flow to the marrow. Structurally far more sound, but put a human beneath the weight of a car...

It was somewhere following this line of thought where the foundation of a theorem started to come together. The bones were hollow, not necessarily like straws as Brad had suggested, but more like Swiss cheese. True. Could there be another reason for them to appear as they did other than by birth? Could it be possible that decomposition altered their structure? Could the tissue have simply dissociated into some sort of festering goo and slipped right through the ground and into the shale? Could another organism have caused such results through some sort of infestation? Here! Here she was onto something. Some microscopic organism, say some sort of prehistoric roundworm for example, could have entered through the bloodstream, accessing the core of the bones through the arteries, consumed all of the available resources and then found itself trapped.

What then would it do? Why, eat its way right through the bone, of course! This could most certainly explain the lack of vascularization within, the absence of marrow and pulpy endothelium. It was a stretch. She could accept that. But there was also that certain amount of simplistic Brad logic to it that almost made it reasonable. The compact bone was hollowed both inside and aerated like a whiffle ball throughout its structure. It could... just possibly, be achieved by some sort of aggressive microorganism exiting from the inside.

That's why this dig was so important. Fossils already exhumed from the earth were of no theoretical use. She needed the ground intact. She needed some well-preserved trail exiting the dead animal, some sort of fossilized, chitinous exoskeleton right around the fallen body... some sort of prehistoric maggot.

Jennifer hurriedly stood, tugging her elastic waistband as high as the bulbous belly would permit, and waddled quickly toward the path.

Sweat beaded on her forehead, the lingering dust particles in the air clinging to the dampness, powdering her face, thick at her hairline like a red ring around her parched features. She held her arms out to either side like a tightrope walker, though the path was more than wide enough for the deer that had carved it through the years on their way down to the base of the cavern for their life-sustaining trips to the river. Approaching the rim of the canyon, the opposite side drew further and further back, exposing nothing but air between. A solitary hawk shrieked, circling high above the unseen river far beneath, its fantastically acute eyes scanning the crystal clear water for the first sign of an unsuspecting trout to run through with its talons and spear with its hooked beak. The tips of its feathers curled skyward, the updrafts making it rise and fall like a kite. It screamed again, the blazing sun glinting from its eye, and dropped like a stone toward the bottom of the canyon.

From first glance, the canyon appeared to fall dead away at the rim. One had to almost walk right over the edge before seeing the small path that wound carefully down the canyon. She sat down at the edge of the chasm, careful not to brace her hands in the multitudes of yuccas and cacti that lined the rim, and swung her legs down to the path. It wasn't nearly as steep as it looked from above, the walls slowly dropping in levels like irregularly spaced stairs carved by the ancient gods worshipped by the Indians that eventually made this canyon their home. The occasional shielded rock wall still paid homage to their artistic skills, pink and white childlike-etchings of speared deer and coyotes baying to the moon.

All the way down near the bottom, where until only recently the river had risen a good twenty feet up the straight walls, fossils could be clearly seen directly in the stone face. There were all sorts of beaked fish frozen in time as they had died. Triops and horseshoe crabs, fanged trout and immortalized sea grasses, captured by time like an old Roman foil rubbing.

Jennifer eased down the path, gravel slipping away from where it had managed to rest for eons and skittering over the edge. She braced her right arm against the wall, keeping her center of gravity low so that if she fell, she dropped no further than to her knees. Her eyes danced from the ground, and her gingerly planted feet, to the wall, making sure that she didn't slip her fingers into a crevice concealing a diamondback, basking in the heat-lamp sun. Horned Toads raced along the smooth, powdery stone, spiked and spiny, tails bowed up toward the sun, snapping up red ants as quickly as the unsuspecting insects crawled out of the fine fissures on the formative rock. Her ankles wobbled and trembled, but she crept onward, knowing that only a few more steps down the hillside, the others would be pouring in awe over their most recent find.

Bizarre, twisted trunks grew from cracks in the rocks, skeletal wooden manifestations serving no function other than to house the mounds of sticks that served as nests to the predatory birds that patrolled this lone sanctuary in the red sand. What few needles grew from the dead-looking appendages drew a sole mouthful of water before drying to a parched yellow and littering the thin path.

By the time she reached the end of the cut slant and slid down to the next step, she could see the others. Dr. Amos Montgomery, who had served as both her paleontology professor and ethics instructor, caught her eye first, with his sun-leathered skin visible from beneath his khaki shorts against his blinding white socks. He wore a leather Indiana Jones hat, and thought himself the part. All he needed was a whip and a revolver, which, as he often cocked his head and looked dreamily up into the sky, wiping the puddling sweat from his brow, she fancied him imagining.

His assistant, a graduate student by the name of Brooke, whose prime asset was waving to Jennifer, attached to a pair of long, slender tanned legs, leaned over the excavation, framed by a wooden bracket driven into the earth to keep the sandstone from crumbling away. Her long blonde hair was a shade lighter than Jennifer's—through the miracle of peroxide—but even in the middle of nowhere held all of the bounce and form of a stripper on a pole. With that Panama Jack hat and the Gap-bought khaki shorts and vest, she looked about as out of place as a clown at a funeral.

Brooke stood upright and turned to Jennifer, cupping a hand over her brow.

"Jen!" she called, waving a hand high over her head.

Jennifer. For the love of God, it's Jennifer! Jens spend hours in the mall with their girlfriends. Jens leave keggers with their underwear in their pockets. Jennifer! JenniferJenniferJennife—It's not even eleven in the morning in the middle of nowhere. Is she really wearing makeup?

Jennifer waved back, slapping her hand quickly back to the wall for balance.

Debbie arose from where she had been mesmerized, fingering the exposed end of some fossilized remain just out of sight. Eyes alight, her smile stretched so wide it flashed with molars. She blinked at Jennifer as though recognition had failed her, and then hurried toward her, scrambling up the rocky slope and to her side.

"You have to see this!" she gasped, grabbing Jennifer by the hand and nearly wrenching her right over the edge of the stone step and down to the next level.

"I'm coming! I'm coming!" Jennifer snapped, plopping her rear end immediately to the ground to preserve her balance. The excitement rose right up from her fluttering stomach, the baby suddenly flopping and kicking as though she too could taste the adrenaline, the anticipation. "What is it, Debbie? What'd they find?"

When Dr. Montgomery had called the night before, he had downplayed the discovery. He had exhumed so many fossils that by now it was surely old hat, right? But she could hear it in his voice… tremulous, eager. He was already fantasizing where to place the feather in that weathered leather cap of his.

"I think we found something that may be of some interest to you, Ms. Morris."

"Missus."

"Of course. My apologies."

There was the tinny hum of static across the miles of silence.

"The discovery, doctor?"

"Oh, yes. Hmm. I think perhaps you'd be best served seeing it with your own eyes."

"You're not going to tell me?"

He had just laughed, a raspy, throaty chuckle parched by years in the elements.

"See you bright and early, then?"

"My husband's going to kill me, you realize that."

"You can thank him in print."

"That good?"

"You'll have to judge for yourself."

She had hardly been able to sleep last night, between the anticipation and the baby's restlessness.

Jennifer looked down, her brow furrowing. Was that...? Was it really? She looked up from one face to the next; all of them focused on her.

Dropping to her knees, she leaned all the way over what appeared to be the intact skull of an Apatosaurus, vertebrae trailing off into the ground. At first she hadn't seen it, her attention focused on the brownish skull, the eye sockets filled with red dirt, the worn teeth ground nearly back to the mandible. And then she saw it, her heart trilling with excitement.

"None of you touched this, right?" she barked.

"We thought maybe we'd chiseled them by accident, but we cleaned them up and they were still there," Brooke said, smirking like she was in on the gag.

Jennifer gently reached past the crest of the cracked cranium, and ran her fingertips across the smooth sandstone that had hidden the decomposed carcass for so many millions of years. It could have been remarkably easy to overlook them, had they not been what she had been looking for from the start: small trails that could mistakenly have been drawn through the rock with the tip of a knife, leading from the skull and spine to a single point where they just terminated in a tiny dot. And there were hundreds of them, all disappearing into a single, hardly visible fissure.

"You can see the crown of another skull right over here," Debbie said, clapping and then pointing to the top right corner of the framed excavation. "Two of them, girl! How does this sound: Professor Deborah Beecham? Got a nice ring to it, doesn't it?"

Jennifer leaned carefully over the first, clearly defined Apatosaur, her belly dragging across the dinosaur's face, and studied what looked like a clay bowl buried upside down in the ground. There weren't nearly as many of them, but there were still a good dozen or so trails frozen in time there in the rock...and they all extended to the exact same point as those from the first.

Her mind began wildly racing with speculation. Were these the tracks of something that crawled from that fissure into the carcasses or were they something exiting the decomposing creature in search of a nest?

"I need a camera," she spat, hardly aware she had spoken aloud.

"Way ahead of you," Dr. Montgomery said, nodding his head to the right where there was a digital camera sitting on the ground next to a small, portable battery pack and a monitor.

"You sure you got these trails?" she said, not even looking up, already sifting through the pile of tools for a chisel and a small hammer.

"From every possible angle."

She lined the slanted edge of the chisel up with the fissure, immediately hammering the already chipped and flattened handle. Fragmented rock flew in all directions, the stone cracking and splintering away from the point of impact. Red dust rose with each strike and Jennifer immediately brushed the rocky particles to the side to keep her field of vision clear. The fissure reached downward into the rock like a fat vein, growing smaller and smaller until it resembled a crack in the rock less than a hole drilled by some sort of miniature auger. Maybe a quarter of an inch wide, it constricted to less than a couple of millimeters by the time she was four inches beneath the original excavated level.

She could only imagine what she would find...if anything at all. Perhaps there would be a small contingent of fossilized insects burrowed in the earth. Or perhaps there would be nothing. It would be naïve to think that whatever insect may or may not have infested the Apatosaurus would have an exoskeleton that would survive the millennia encased in rock. Maybe when she got right down to the bottom of this time-old fissure she'd find nothing but a hollow space. Maybe she'd find a pocket of shale. Or maybe, just maybe, she'd find precisely what she was looking for.

"Do you see anything?" Brooke asked.

"Don't mess up my Apatosaurs," Debbie chastened nervously.

"I can't see any—" Jennifer started and then stopped.

She had grown so accustomed to the swirls of dust billowing up into her face that she didn't notice immediately when the red faded to something of a polluted gray. And it wasn't rising at the beckoning of the chisel, but appeared to be blowing from beneath like gas trapped in a mine. There was a smell on it, a rancid stench like rotten eggs, not the tomb-enclosed scent of decomposition, but more like she had unearthed the secret tunnel to a long-lost, primitive hen house. It was a vile stench, overwhelming in magnitude, immediately summoning both the tears from her eyes and the contents of her stomach to her lips.

"Sulfur dioxide," she heard Dr. Montgomery say over her shoulder. "Toxic. Better back off and let it dissipate..."

All Jennifer knew was that sulfur dioxide was the chemical byproduct produced by burning crude oil still in the wells. They had made a big deal out of that on CNN during the Gulf War when the Iraqis were burning their own oil fields. But right now, that was completely inconsequential as the excitement of the whole thing overwhelmed her.

She started to choke, the air tightening in her chest, dampness streaming down her cheeks. Holding her breath and turning her head to the side, she raised the hammer one final time, and smote the handle of the chisel.

The ground crumbled immediately away, opening a pocket in the earth that none could even see as a swell of murky white smoke plumed upward as though issued from an industrial smokestack. Small particles exploded into her face on the steam like bats erupting from a cave.

Jennifer jerked her head back, the inertia toppling her onto her hindquarters. Furiously batting her eyelids, she tried desperately to clear the debris that felt like shattered, balled glass grinding beneath her lids and against her eyeballs. Each panicked breath drew with it the terrible, thick smog until she could no longer inhale at all, but coughed spastically, unable to evacuate it from her system. Her throat grew dry and raw, each retching exhalation tearing at the lining of her trachea. She couldn't breathe…couldn't pull…oxygen from…the air. Euphoria swirled through her head, only the intense panic, fear, holding her to anything resembling reality.

Coughing surrounded her, choked, blistering.

"Can't…breathe," Montgomery gasped through the useless collar he had pulled over his mouth, falling to all fours on the rock.

Uncontrollable tears tried to free the particles grinding beneath Jennifer's eyelids, allowing her to see in watery spurts that refracted everything around her like a carnival mirror. She could only vaguely make out Brooke's form, her hair shining like the rays of the sun itself, collapsed to the ground on all fours. Her back arched with the unproductive heaving that produced nothing but a raucous cough and a strand of saliva that connected her parted lips to the sand. Dr. Montgomery was little more than a khaki blur, and Debbie was completely out of sight.

Jennifer tried…tried to push herself to her feet. *The baby! Dear God! The baby!* Her instincts, both maternal and self-preservative, gripped her form, urging the muscles to action. She crawled forward, her fingers curled to claws, the knuckles peeling back to blood-induced red mud, until she found herself against the rock wall. Protesting mightily, her body shook and trembled, but allowed her to jerkily find her feet, clawing her way up the rock, her nails bending back and snapping, her fingertips splitting effortlessly to leave smeared arcs of blood across the rock.

It was all she could do to cast one final glance back, the surface of her eyes no longer shielded by a coating of tears, but by a thin crimson veil, its warmth streaking down her cheeks. Brooke had found her way to her feet as well, swaying there like a drunk, her fingers clawing at her throat. Jennifer had but time to see the blood explode from Brooke's eyes and nose like a levy breaking. Vest flagging, hands still carving marks into her prominently veined throat, Brooke didn't even scream when she toppled backward from the ledge and into the nothingness.

Montgomery lay deadly still, faint twirls of smoke drifting out of his mouth and into his nostrils. Vomit spattered his chest, encircling him in a vile-smelling ring, crusting his hair and his cheek to the ground.

The baby! Please God! Save the baby!

Jennifer clawed her way upward, knees and elbows rent and bloodied, forearms riddled with cactus needles and thick with dirt and small pebbles crusting into the fluid. All she could see was her hands—her dirty and bleeding hands—dragging her across the rock and upward toward the blinding, yellow glare of the unrelenting sun.

Her lungs felt as though they were shrinking, collapsing, threatening to ring themselves like a wet towel and shrivel right up. Hands trembling, muscles fluttering, all she could think was to climb...climb...

Pressure around her ankle...prohibiting her progress. She kicked at it...kickedkickedkicked...but to no avail. Whirling, she looked right into Debbie's face. Both of her arms were wrapped around Jennifer's right ankle, cradling it to her chest. Blood ran like tears from her unblinking eyes, trickling from her nose in parallel streams that rounded her lips and spilled down her chin. Splotches had opened up on her forehead and cheeks like abrasions, countless nicks and cuts from a razor, as if each microscopic pore had simultaneously yawned wide and begun absolving itself of its contents. But there was something else, rimming her eyelids, the rings of her nostrils, growing at the corners of her mouth. It was yellow, patchy, like the unpollenated stamen of a tulip.

"Help...me," Debbie gasped through her uncontrollable wheezing, bloody spittle spurting from her lips and freckling her chin.

But the baby...her own gift from God...it was still in her uterus...still.

Mewling, head throbbing, Jennifer turned and drove her tattered fingertips into the sand and gravel, the muscles in her arms screaming in protest as she defiantly pulled herself upward. Debbie sloughed off, taking Jennifer's sock and shoe with her. There was the thump of dead weight, the grumbling of sliding gravel.

A startled hawk screamed shrilly, its airspace violated by the limp form bouncing pall mall from the rock, clothing snapping in the wind, appendages flailing, accelerating toward the rocky banks of the crystal river.

Cresting the lip of the chasm, Jennifer dragged herself forward, through cacti and yuccas, clothes tearing, skin opening in seams. She could feel nothing but the convulsions in her gut, the tightness and cramping, driving channels of blood through her grated teeth. Time both stood still and became devoid of all meaning at the same time, her sole focus on reaching the car, the phone, her husband.

So long as she stayed the path...so long as her shaking arms could drag her forward...

The front right tire came into view when she racked her knuckles against it. With uncontrollably shaking fingers she latched onto the tread, urging herself upward. The chipped and rusted wheel well gouged into her shoulder, but by now she was well past the point of feeling it take a fleshy bite from the muscle. Slapping a wet trail of blood along the car door, she found the handle and yanked it wide, falling back down into a sprawled heap in the dust.

She lie there...momentarily staring up into the cloudless sky, the blazing sun baking her unblinking eyes. There was nothing but the relentless aura of pain to define her rag-doll form. She couldn't control her legs to make herself stand, couldn't so much as will herself to her elbows to prop her from the ground, from the stone that pressed mercilessly into the back of her skull. She was going to die now. She was going to die—

Her stomach visibly flinched from the force of an internal kick.

The baby.

God... the baby.

Jennifer didn't know she was doing it until she was on her feet, leaning across the driver's seat, spreading a layer of muddied blood like jam across the vinyl seat. Her fingers curled around the console, pulling her up and off of her stomach. Palsied, uncontrollable, her hand flopped toward the ashtray, finally taking loose hold of the cell phone and bringing it to her lap.

The blood from her peeled thumb covered the display window, but all she had to do was press the one button...just hold it down long enough for it to trigger the memory response and it would dial home...dial Brad.

The tone from the phone lingered long and loud in the silence, until finally her finger slipped from the button and she collapsed forward onto the wheel.

"Hello?" she could hear her husband's voice crackle electrically from the phone. "Hello?"

"Brad..." she gurgled through the mouthful of blood, spilling the phlegmy mixture from the corner of her mouth to drip from the wheel.

"Jennifer? Is that you? I can't hear you. I can't—"

"The baby," was all she could manage to croak, the force of her voice ripping through the membranous walls of her windpipe. "Baby."

"Where are you, Jennifer? Are you all right? Answer me!"

Her eyes lolled upward. A gust of wind rocked the car on the wheels, blowing the door shut and pinning her left hand between the seat and the metal door.

"Jennifer!"

Her eyes stared back at her from the window, a phantom reflection in front of the rising red dust. The same yellow growth she had seen on Debbie encircled her own lids, thickening in her lashes.

"Baby," she managed to scrape out of her throat. "Help...baby."

Sputtering bursts of air lurched from her opened mouth, convulsively spurting waves of blood across the dash, dotting the window, obscuring the speedometer. Her eyes slowly glazed over in the window, the pupils widening to a fixed, waxy circle nearly as large as the entire iris. Jaw falling slack, no longer impeding the flow of blood, there was a final hiss of air escaping her body, like carbonation from a cracked two-liter.

The yellow fuzz about her still lashes slowly degenerated into a score of miniature, wriggling squiggles, sliding back under the lids and disappearing into the sockets.

"I've got to hang up, Jennifer," Brad sobbed from the cell phone. "I have to call for help. I love you...please, God, hang on!"

Click.

1 | Night on Fire

I

"Has he always been like this?" Dr. Grunwald asked, nodding his head to the corner of the room. With the gray beard and thin features, he could have been a stunt double for his obvious idol, whose bronze bust rested on the corner of the desk at the back of the room between a flourishing fern and a box of tissues. There were matching pens in an inkwell: how Freudian is that? All he needed was a mug, conspicuously labeled "World's Greatest Mom," filled with pencils. The first thing Brad noticed was the kindness, the patience, in this man's bespectacled eyes. Framed by crow's feet, they had a certain warmth, a roundness magnifying the empathy within. Rather than a suit, as all of the others had worn in support of the walls covered with framed lambskins, this man looked much like he remembered his own father looking. Comfortable tan slacks with loafers, a short-sleeved button down with a pen in the pocket, equally suited to the casual demeanor of the office as to an afternoon seeding the garden.

The room wasn't crowded with bookcases brimming with every psychological tome thought for a second to be law, but rather spacious and empty. The entire front wall of the Victorian house that had been converted to the practice of Wilhelm, Grunwald, and Frank, was nothing but windows, staring down on the green lawns, warped from the massive roots of the fragrant elms that towered over the silent street. An occasional car honked from nearby downtown, yet still the chickadees chirped from the gutter above the second story room, ushering in the slanting rays of sunshine that spotted the floor, dancing with the otherwise unseen particles of dust lingering in the stale room. Posters of waterfalls and jungles, balmy coasts with turquoise waters, and meadows filled with streams and wildflowers were tacked to the walls between tall, potted plants that looked like miniature palm trees. There had been no stereotypical Freudian couch or armed chair from which the doctor could scribble his notes onto a yellow ruled pad. Rather, there was a couch at the back of the room with a loveseat perpendicularly to either side. They were comfortable, not sterile, with multicolored pillows stacked haphazardly atop the cushions. The doctor had been forced to pull the coffee table that serviced all three from the middle of the room so that he could even see William, hunched beneath the end table next to the couch, drawing with the nubs of crayons in that sketch pad he carried like others his age might tote a football.

Brad was encouraged by the way the doctor looked at his son, not the way the others had: distanced, inquisitively, like William was some sort of case study yet to be cracked. Dr. Grunwald looked at the boy with a kind of sleepy curiosity, tilting his head from side to side, breathing in the entire picture, and then got down on all fours and crawled along the loveseat, propping himself up against the couch. His red and gray argyle socks peeked out at odds with his tan pants and brown loafers.

"The others think he's autistic," Brad said, sighing.

"You disagree?" the doctor asked without looking to Brad, instead focusing on what the child was drawing.

"He's not slow in any respect. If you talk to him, you'll see the recognition in his eyes: not just identification of your voice, but of your words. He just doesn't talk is the problem. People seem to think that since he doesn't talk he's somehow, you know…"

"Stupid?"

"Not a big fan of that term, doctor."

"Let me tell you, Mr. Morris. From my experience, I've learned that it's not the silent ones, but those who talk all the time that prove themselves stupid."

Brad let out a nervous chuckle, relaxing just enough to allow his crossed arms to drop to his sides.

"And as for autism? I've seen it used as a 'catch-all' for a hundred different psychological maladies. Autistic children are cut from different cloth long before birth. They see things through an entirely different set of perceptions. They're not all your standard 'Rain Man-drop-the-marbles-in-another-room-and-the-child-will-tell-you-how-many-there-are-by-the-sound' type. Autism has as many different faces as the children it affects. There's no Mongoloid appearance or given affect. These are normal children whose brains function in fantastically different ways. To say your child is autistic as a knee-jerk diagnosis is irresponsible at best, and potentially detrimental to his developing psyche. There is a negative connotation to the word, and whether children understand it or not, they have no trouble interpreting the message."

Brad smiled cautiously and eased into the room. Leaning against the arm of the opposite loveseat, he watched the doctor carefully extract one of the well-used crayons from the yellow plastic, *Harry Potter* lunch box William carried them in.

"Are you a single parent?" he asked, watching William's expression to see if he had gotten away with borrowing the crayon or if the child merely hadn't seen.

"Yes, my wife di—"

"You and I can discuss that alone, away from sensitive ears. For now, you and I can have a simple conversation. All right?" His voice was hypnotic, melodic, both hollow and filling the room at the same time.

Brad nodded. All he could see was a portion of the pad behind his son's knee, the left hand scribbling back and forth with blinding speed as it always did when he colored. The child's fingers were stained light blue from the crayon, wax embedded all the way up the fingernails.

"Early life tragedy?" the doctor queried, his tone in contrast to his words. He sounded more like he was coaxing a free balloon from Mr. Rogers than verifying that he had just heard that the boy's mother was dead.

"Yes."

"Healthy child?" He had now brought himself to shading lightly on the side of the page.

"Extremely."

"No hospitalization?"

"No. He's never come down with anything worse than the common cold."

"Does he ever talk?"

"Yes. Well, occasionally. Nothing conversational. We'll be sitting there and he'll just say something completely out of the blue, but when I ask him about it, he just looks at me and smiles like he's teasing me with it."

Brad chuckled and rubbed his eyes.

"Is he hiding underneath the end table because he's nervous?"

"He does it at home, too. Had to buy him bunk beds so he wouldn't sleep under the living room table."

"Do you work outside of the home?"

"I'm an architect. I have the luxury of working from my home office. I think he draws all the time because he sees me doing it."

"Does he go to school?"

"Yes."

"Public?"

"Home school."

"That's quite a burden on a parent."

"It was daunting at first, for sure. But it's really amazing how much I enjoy it."

"Are his studies age appropriate?"

"As opposed to those parents who claim their ten year olds are doing college coursework?"

The doctor looked at him and smirked.

"Yeah," Brad continued. "He reads at a junior high level, but we're still just working on the fifth grade."

"Does he have any socialization?"

"He plays soccer in the fall and spring, but hasn't really made the social contacts I'd hoped for."

"So it's just the two of you, then?"

"It's the best I can do."

"I'm not passing judgment, Mr. Morris. There are, quote unquote, parents who leave their children to their own devices, trust the streets to raise them. The dream of the nuclear family went the way of *Mr. Ed*, and right about the same time. I choose to define family in a way the census bureau can't turn into a statistic: love."

"I try to do right by him."

"I'd know in two seconds if you didn't."

William ripped the page he had been furiously coloring from the book and set it off to the side. Without even looking, he replaced the blue crayon—the paper frayed back from the dull tip like the peel of a banana—and grabbed the red.

"Would you mind stepping out into the waiting room so that I can have some time with William here?" Dr. Grunwald asked, turning with something of a placating smile. "I promise the magazines are from the last decade or so."

"Sure," Brad said nervously, though he tried to mask it with a full-lipped smile and a pat on the arm of the loveseat. He looked to his son, hoping to catch the boy's eyes to reassure him that he'd be all right and that Daddy was going to be just down the hall, but William was far too involved with turning the white sheet bright red.

He walked slowly to the door, looking back over his shoulder with that same, now absurd looking smile.

"I'll just be right outside," he said, but William continued coloring without any sign of acknowledgment.

Brad turned the knob with a squeak and stepped out into the hallway, closing the door softly behind him.

Dr. Grunwald listened for the creaking floorboards in the hallway. All he could hear was silence for a moment, and then finally, the loud groaning of the warped boards moving in the opposite direction.

He smiled warmly and looked at William.

The boy's dirty blonde hair was shaggy, curling over the tops of his ears and hanging down to his eyebrows. Freckles dotted his cheekbones and the bridge of his nose, but he was otherwise unremarkable. He was so involved with his artwork that his tongue hung out of his mouth, his brown eyes narrowed and focused. A rather toothy Tyrannosaurus Rex roared on the front of his yellow shirt, the design making it appear as though the beast was tearing right through the fabric. The denim shorts, manufactured rather than cut-off, made his pale legs look pasty. Sitting on his knees, Nike's tucked under his rump, he hunched over that sketchpad, shoulders pressed against the underside of the table, he was completely absorbed by his creation.

"You're quite an artist," Grunwald said, tucking his head beneath the table to inspect William's design. He had colored the page red, top to bottom and side-to-side, uninterrupted red. "What's this masterpiece you're working on?"

William didn't show any signs of even hearing the doctor's words, but rather placed the red back into the box and produced the orange.

"My name's Dr. Grunwald. My friends call me Abe. Would you like to call me Abe?"

William's tongue slipped in and out of his mouth like a lizard, his hand guiding the orange in hardly discernible diagonal streaks across the red.

"It's all right. You don't have to talk if you don't feel like it."

The boy dropped the orange back into the box and rummaged until he found the yellow, making similar, parallel streaks to the orange.

"I think we have a lot in common, William. I'm a listener, too. In fact, it's my job to listen."

William peeked at the doctor from the corner of his eyes, plopping the yellow back into the box and grabbing the seamlessly colored blue page.

"Some people are better at talking. There are even some who do it all the time. But I've found that you can learn a whole lot sometimes if you just close your mouth and open your ears."

The boy pinched small sections of the blue page, tearing them out like long teardrops and dropping them to the floor. He whispered something in a voice so small that had Grunwald not seen those little lips move in conjunction, he might have thought it the rising of the wind outside.

"I'm sorry, William. I didn't hear what you said. Would you mind telling me again?"

"I can't hear them if I'm talking," he whispered, nervously checking the doctor again from the corner of his eye. The edges of his lips curled downward, but he just continued tearing those streaks from the paper.

"Can't hear who, William?"

William brought the blue page to his face, looking through the dozens of diagonally torn holes.

"You said 'I can't hear them if I'm talking.' What does that mean?"

"There aren't very many of them now. Not yet. I have to listen very closely or I can't hear them at all. Their voices are so small, so weak."

"Who are they, William? Them. Who's this 'them'?"

William aligned the torn blue page over the red page with the yellow and orange streaks. The bright colors showed like fire through the slanted, stretched teardrops.

"They're coming," he whispered, dragging the blue page diagonally down the colored one beneath. The movement made it look like meteorites streaking across the night sky.

William turned and looked the doctor dead in the eyes, their unblinking weight unsettling. Grunwald eased backward, tilting his head back on his neck with an open-mouthed look of discomfort.

"Can't you hear them?" William whispered softly, pleading with his eyes.

"No, William."

The child looked at him a moment longer, his face reflecting a sorrow that should by all rights have been outside of his range of emotion, and then dropped his attention back to sliding the blue page across the other.

"They're coming," he whispered in a frightened, barely audible whisper. "They're coming back."

II

"No," Shannen moaned, planting her palms on Brian's shoulders. She shoved at him, but the way he had his face buried in her neck, sucking hard enough on the flesh that it felt like blood would soon spurt to the surface, she wondered if he had heard her, or if she was really sure that she wanted him to. His left arm was beneath her, holding tightly around her waist, his right hand, creeping like a spider beneath the waistband of her jeans. The top button popped open against the pressure of his knuckles, the zipper slowly easing down the track.

He didn't relinquish his leverage, his fingertips sliding beneath the smooth rim of her silk panties. The warmth against her skin sent goosebumps across her tight stomach, all the way up into her shoulders. She bit at her lower lip, trying to slow the rising of her heartbeat, the production of the warmth that was the destination of his hand.

"We can't, Brian. I told you…we can't."

"Why?" he murmured, allowing the mouthful of skin to snap elastically back into place.

"You know why. I told you, mmm…before we even left."

"Your parents think we're at the movies. We've got hours."

"It has nothing to do with that and you know it!"

Shannen freed her left arm from beneath his weight and brushed her long, blonde bangs from her azure blue eyes. Sweat beaded on her forehead, glistening in the moonlight that filtered past the pines and through the back seat window of the car. Were it not for the buckle of the seat belt stabbing into her shoulder blade, binding her to her senses, she might have eagerly succumbed to his advances…regardless of the consequences.

His warm breath penetrated her sweater, damp, steaming against the swell of her breast.

"We have to wait until you have a…you know."

"Condom?" he whispered, sliding his lips back and forth over her erect nipple through the sweater.

"Yeah," she moaned, clearing her throat of the rising knot of lust. She ran her fingers through his short, dark hair, finally forcing herself to tighten her grip and yank upward.

"Ow! Ow, ow!" he grimaced through gnashed teeth, allowing himself to be led by his painful roots. Jerking his hand from her pants, he snatched her wrist and squeezed until she let go. "Christ, Shannen! What the hell was that for?"

She scooted herself up against the car door and immediately zipped and buttoned her pants, pulling her shirt down tight so her headlights weren't quite so prominent. Folding her legs Indian-style, she brushed her hair back behind her ears. Her lipstick covered her face from her chin to her nose, the make-up transferred to Brian's eager lips leaving O's along the side of her neck, ringing the rapidly bruising skin.

She couldn't look at him or she'd find herself doing the same thing again. Instead, she studied her hands in her lap, lacing and unlacing her fingers.

"We already talked about this," she whispered, shaking her head. She looked up just enough to see his tight jeans—one section appearing far more constrictive than the rest—and the bottom of his black and gold letter jacket. She flinched when his right hand fell atop hers, but she couldn't bring herself to tear it free.

"We've been doing it without condoms for months while you were on the pill, and nothing happened then."

"But I can't take the pill anymore. We've been over this. What did you think, once we started to, you know, that I'd just forget?"

"That was the plan."

She yanked her hand free in disgust and turned so that she was looking past the passenger seat and through the front windshield. The crescent moon shimmered on the wavering black water of the lake, straight ahead and through the gap in the trees. Starlight reflected back up into the sky from the duck-riddled lake, bills tucked beneath slumbering wings. Only the occasional drowsy quack announced their presence.

She loved Brian, in all of her teenaged wisdom she was certain of that one fact. Why? It was the depth of his eyes, the tone of his voice in her ears when he was atop her, the way he made her feel, there beneath the endless sky, like there was no one else on earth other than the two of them.

"I just don't get why it's such a big deal all of a sudden," he said, leaving his hand on her knee. "You know I love you, babe."

Shannen rolled her eyes, shaking her head gently from side to side.

"We'll get one for next time, you know. No sweat. We'll just be careful, right?" Brian said, easing closer. He tilted his head into her way to try to secure her attention with those big blue eyes of his.

"It has nothing to do with being careful. What part of this don't you get? I could die, Brian. That's the risk here. I could die." She enunciated those last three words very slowly and deliberately, looking to him and searching his face for any potential reaction.

"You're still alive now, aren't you?"

"You're a jerk," she spat, crossing her arms over her chest and pulling her knee back from his hand.

"All I'm saying is, what's one more time? We're careful from here on out—"

"What part of 'I could die' was unclear?"

"I think you're overreacting."

"I thought you'd care more about my life than your Johnson."

"I do, babe. You and me, we're in this for the long haul, right?"

"I can't tell if you're sincere or opening negotiations."

"Look," he said, taking a long breath and relaxing his tone. "I pull out early, no harm, no foul."

"You did have sex ed, right? That's no method of contraception."

"You could always just, you know…"

He mimed like he was bouncing a basketball in his lap.

"You could always just, you know," she retorted, making a certain up and down motion with her right hand.

"That's cold," he said, his faux, comforting smile growing as icy as his cold blue eyes. "Hostile."

Shaking her head, bottom lip pursed angrily out from the upper, she threw the door open and climbed outside. With a screech of frustration, her hands fisted at her sides, she stormed around to the front of the car and sat down on the hood between the rays from the headlights, stretching from the Mustang's eyes across the rutted, dirt road leading downhill to the lake.

She heard the car door open behind her, but unless there was some sort of impending apology involving dropping to his knees and kissing her feet, she wasn't quite sure she wanted to hear it. Staring at the flaxen moonlight sparkling on the infantile waves, she listened to the approaching footsteps over the rustling of the pine needles on the soft breeze.

Brian sidled up beside her and eased onto the hood. He looked over to her, clasped hands kneading between his knees, feet propped on the bumper, and laughed dryly.

"How come our nights seem to be ending like this more and more frequently?" he asked.

"You tell me."

Brian slipped out from his letter jacket—the big C covered with silver pins from both football and baseball—and draped it over her shoulders.

"It's not that I don't want to," she said. "Believe me. That's not the issue here. I'm just, well, you know—"

"Scared?"

"Yeah…scared."

"I didn't mean to push."

"Yeah," she said with a smirk, finally bringing herself to look at him from the corner of her eye. "You did."

Brian laughed. "Okay, maybe I did…a little." He slid his hand along the hood of the black car until he found hers, and laced their fingers together. "I just, well…I don't think I understand why everything has to change so suddenly."

"It's not really so much that this all happened so suddenly. We've just been incredibly lucky so far."

"Lucky that you're not dead?"

"Well…yeah."

"That's about the last thing I want."

"Blood's made its way back to your head now?"

"Funny."

"You were willing to sacrifice me a few minutes ago."

"That's not true. I guess I just can't seem to grasp how taking the pill could end up killing you."

"You understand that what the pill does is it makes your blood clot more easily, making it so that the ovum can't attach itself to the uterine lining, right?"

"Okay."

"That's why you have a period—"

"I don't have a period," he smirked.

"You want to hear this or not?"

"You know how I love hearing about all that female junk. Please continue."

"So what your, excuse me...what *my* body is doing, is expelling a large blood clot containing coagulated blood, an ovum, and the shed uterine wall. If for some reason, that clot became lodged up in there, it would hemorrhage and I could bleed enough internally that I could die."

"Then how come so many other girls can take the pill all of their lives?"

"They have normal blood."

"And you don't?"

"That's the problem."

"I don't understand."

"Remember when I had that clot in my leg and I had to have it removed?"

"I brought you flowers. We did it in your bedroom while your parents were getting ice cream."

"Yeah," she said, smiling. "I remember that."

He squeezed her hand and inched closer, allowing her to lean her head against his shoulder.

"So they tested that clot, which isn't a normal thing for anyone under sixty, let alone seventeen, and found out that I had this Prothrombin II mutation. Factor V, the doctor called it. It makes my blood clot like twenty-some-times more easily than most everyone else's, even without exposure to oxygen. You see, blood shouldn't clot inside of your body. It's the same as a scab. Say you have a cut... it takes exposure to oxygen to trigger the clotting agents to coagulate, but my Prothrombin II, this clotting agent in my blood, can just all of a sudden start clotting up. It could start in my leg like the last one, and then boom! Right up and into my heart, forming an air pocket, or up into my brain and I just drop dead right then and there, or best case scenario? Vegetable city."

"So what then? Your blood carries more oxygen than mine?"

"I don't know...maybe. It's one of those new things that the doctors don't know a whole lot about yet. They said they really didn't start seeing this—or being able to identify it, anyway—until the last five years or so, and this effects maybe one in seven hundred thousand."

"You're a mutant then, like the X-Men or something."

"Thanks for listening," she said, rising from the hood, but Brian pulled her gently back down.

"All I'm saying is there are those guys who could bleed to death from a paper cut—"

"Hemophiliacs."

"You're like the anti-hemophiliac. How are you going to bleed to death if your blood clots so much more quickly than everyone else's? And anyway, can't they give you some sort of drug to keep you from clotting? I know when my grandma broke both of her hips and she had to be in bed for like two years, they gave her some sort of blood thinner."

"I get to start my daily Coumadin ritual at thirty, and then I have to worry about the exact opposite happening."

"The whole hemophilia thing?"

"Yeah, but better yet, even if someday they make it so that I can carry a child without it killing either her or me, then I get to pass this on to her."

"Hell of a birthday gift, but who's to say she'd even get it anyway?"

"It's a dominant gene. All it takes is one expressive parent and it's a done deal."

"So who has it, your mom or your dad—?"

Shannen cut him off with a look.

"Sorry. Sometimes I forget."

"Car accident. Shit happens, or so they tell me."

"But your aunt and uncle treat you like any of their other kids."

"I know. I guess I'm lucky in that regard, but it's things like this that make me think about my parents a lot."

Brian suddenly straightened up and nearly knocked Shannen from the hood in his hurry to his feet. He looked back at her with an ear-to-ear grin, mischievous eyes alight.

"I can't believe I forgot," he said, thumping his hand on his forehead. "It's the whole reason I brought you out here tonight."

"I already told you we're not going to—"

"You just sit tight, I'll be right back."

Shannen shook her head dejectedly. She thought that for a second there she just might have gotten through to him.

"Don't move!" he shouted to her, popping the trunk with a rusty-sounding metallic whine.

Shannen stared up into the pristine sky. A low layer of fluffy blue clouds sat a world away on the eastern horizon, but there wasn't a single mar in the sky overhead. The stars twinkled like gemstones just out of her reach, lining the black velvet night.

There was a flash overhead, a comet caught by the tail by her peripheral vision. Closing her eyes, she sighed and made a wish.

"Shoot!" Brian shouted, slamming the trunk shut. "It's already starting!"

"What?" Shannen asked, slowly reopening her eyes as her boyfriend raced around from the back of the car, but by the time she loosed her wish like a butterfly to the sky and opened her eyes, she knew exactly what he was talking about.

It was as if the sky itself had opened wide. Meteors slashed in long arcs across the sky, one after another after another. It was the Chicken Little prophecy, the stars themselves appearing to just drop right from the heavens, burning a glowing orange-yellow as the atmosphere ate them alive.

"I heard on the radio that this is supposed to be the biggest meteor shower in something like a hundred years. At its peak, they said you should be able to see as many as a couple hundred in the sky at any one time. We're passing through the tail of Valman's comet or something like that."

"Valstad's comet. I remember hearing about it now, too."

"So move that cute little butt, girl, and help me spread out this blanket before we miss the show."

Grinning, Shannen hopped from the hood and grabbed hold of half of the blanket. The two of them spread the red and black blanket across the buffalo grass to the left of the car, and lie down, sharp blades of wild grass poking right through the blanket and into their backs.

"Headlights," Brian blurted, hopping up and racing back to the car. He leaned through the open window and shoved the switch, darkening the meadow. Four quick strides and he was sliding onto the blanket beside Shannen.

"It's beautiful," she said, awed, watching the streaks of light brighten the sky from every possible angle. With the conical green tips of the trees framing her vision that now seemed infinite, she suddenly felt so small and insignificant.

"I'm sorry about earlier," Brian said, sliding his arm beneath her neck, her head merging right into his shoulder.

"Me too," she whispered.

It was fantastic; streams of light ripping the blackness, leaving tracers in their vision as the only testament to their fiery existence. They filled the sky, disappearing as quickly as they appeared, frantic fireflies in the final seconds of life trying desperately to reproduce before burning out.

Yellow brightened to orange and then finally to a pale red, the streaks growing not just longer, but larger.

"They look so close," Shannen whispered, her brow lowering contemplatively.

The sky crackled with thunder, a growling sound like an avalanche tearing down a mountain. A meteorite knifed from the sky, growing larger and larger so quickly that Shannen thought she could make out the piece of rock and the tail of flame that trailed it. Whistling through the air like mortar fire, it dipped beneath the treetops before an explosion made the ground tremble beneath them.

"Did it hit the ground?" she gasped.

"I...I don't know."

He slipped his arm from beneath her and slowly climbed to his feet, rising to his tiptoes to try to get a better glimpse of the reddish glow over the pines at the far side of the lake.

"Do you smell fire?" Shannen asked, drawing in a deep breath. "I think I smell fire."

Brian was already walking toward the lake, slowly, stumbling through the darkness in a daze.

"Where are you going?"

"I'll be right back, I just want to see..."

"I don't like this, Brian."

"It'll just take a second."

"I don't think you should go."

"Relax, Shan. I'll be right back."

Her stomach flopped over, and her head began to throb. Something wasn't right. It was in the air all around her, tangible, like a mist that crawled across her skin and entered her body through her rapid breathing.

"Don't go!" she called to Brian who was now nearly to the shore of the lake.

"...right back..." his voice drifted from the night.

"Brian!" she screamed, her heartbeat accelerating madly, panic seizing hold of her form, curling her hands to fists, her trembling legs to walking stilts. She couldn't breathe fast enough to accommodate her oxygen needs, though in her own ears it sounded like she was panting already.

With one final look to the sky, the fireworks blazing wildly, she stumbled down the darkened path toward the lake.

III

"*So if you're just sitting there on the couch…GET THE HELL UP! It's like World War III out there, kids! The skies over Baghdad or something. I don't care if you're sleeping or if you're in your tighty-whities, man, drag your ass outside and take a look at this before it's over. A meteor shower like this comes once in a lifetime!*" the deejay hollered through the boombox balanced precariously atop the corner of the wooden shelf above his head.

"Little busy right now," Jason said, pulling his right eye from the microscope long enough to rub the crust of sleep from the corner. "But thanks for thinking of me."

He pulled his travel mug of coffee from the edge of the desk and took a large swig of the ice-cold brew, grimacing as he swallowed it back.

"*…like a friggin' free laser show up there! And I tell you what: there ain't nothing that goes better with lasers than Metallica. So all you boys and girls crank up the stereo and look up at the sky as those meteors come falling faster. Obey your master: me, the one and only Trick Turner. Master of Puppets, Mother Hubbards!*"

Blinking back his weary eyelids, Jason allowed them to close for a dreamy moment, just long enough to lubricate his dry retinas beneath his contacts.

The whole room rose and fell rhythmically, though it was only an illusion created by the aquariums that lined every available wall of the room. Wavering blue and yellow lines swirled on the pale white ceiling, marring every inch of visible wall between tanks. Filter systems and sumps whirred and groaned over the hum of protein skimmers and air pumps. The smell of brine was thick. Salt crystals crept from beneath every lid, climbing down electrical cords and etching the walls like ice. Every visible spectrum of light illuminated the room from the sodium halides and blue-tinted actinic bulbs that drew enough electricity that he could have afforded an apartment three times the size of this one. The sacrifices one must make for his passion. Try bringing a woman to an apartment where all of the furniture's been replaced by fish tanks. Good luck bedding her down on a futon mattress in the middle of the floor, surrounded by, as one of his few fleeting girlfriends had called it, "the manifestation of his dementia."

There were few people who could come close to comprehending what he was doing here. So he had thrown away that expensive medical school education... big deal! Not every grown man needs the respect and love of his parents, though a call at Christmas, if nothing else, might be kind of nice. It was one thing growing up to say that he was going to be a doctor, another thing entirely to actually be one. Perhaps had he asked himself the important questions early on he might have averted this colossal shipwreck that was his life, or then again, maybe not.

There were people who were meant to be doctors. He remembered them from med school. These were the people who secretly stenciled the name "God" into the labels of their lab coats and probably had the same identification in their underwear. But to be a good doctor, one had to be able to hold power over death, to be able to look the Reaper in the eye while pissing on his leg. What person would possibly want a doctor who didn't think himself God?

He had opened Pandora's box and learned all of her secrets, but what was life without mystery? All of the accumulated knowledge of centuries of physicians flowed through his fingers with magical ease. He could remove a bullet from a lung with no more difficulty than pumping a frat boy's stomach, close up a dozen stab wounds in the time it would take for a twelve-year old girl's pregnancy test to come back positive. And that was the problem. There was no more sanctity for life. With all of the advances in technology and endless options in treatment, every patient had a false sense of security that whatever they may do to themselves, there'll be a doctor who can save them. They were mechanics at a demolition derby. If these people had any respect for the enormity of the gift they'd been bestowed at birth, then maybe they'd think twice before smashing a beer bottle and taking it to another man's throat, or before climbing behind the wheel, drunk out of their gourds.

That had been the final straw.

It had been the second year of his residency, that crucial final year before the amazing world of private practice opened right up to him, bringing with it all of the monetary and societal perks most ordinary people would have gladly traded a lung and kidney for. That was five years ago now, but as fresh in his mind as a blunt trauma from a hammer. The snow had fallen early that October, slipping in over the Rockies before its customary Halloween debut. The storm hadn't been all that impressive: patches of ice on the roads, a dusting on all of the lawns and rooftops of those fortunate enough to be at home, but it was that critical first snow that weeded out all of the idiots from the roads. It had been precisely 10:46 p.m., a time to this day he couldn't keep from marking on the clock every single night. He had been frantically chugging bitter, syrupy coffee, though his hands already shook like an Al Jolson performance. Just shy of thirteen hours into a sixteen-hour shift. Already what every patient dreams of—an emergency doctor with the tremors, handicapped by sleep deprivation, eyes held open by toothpicks, and about as affable as a hibernating bear roused by a gentle goading from a cattle prod—he had been stolen from his caffeine fix by the pounding of footsteps, the squeaking wheel of a gurney, and the human clamor of restrained panic.

Car accident. Two fatally wounded at the scene. Two more, one critical, one more probably already debating whether or not to succumb to the beckoning of "the light", saturating the gurneys that squealed down the freshly waxed hallway. It was easy enough to believe them accidents having stripped God of His stigma. There was no predestination, no fate in the emergency room: only the hapless to treat and street as though churning them out through some mechanical assembly line.

Dr. Jason Milhouse found himself in Trauma Two. Little girl. Red hair. Green eyes. Her mother, screaming her name from Trauma One, identified her as Amanda. Blood streaked her hair from the open laceration through which he could clearly see her fractured skull beneath the curling flap of scalp. Neck still bracketed, lips painted a shimmering crimson, her entire body was limp. Her vitals were nonexistent, her pulse thin and thready.

Amanda's budding life expired at nine minutes till eleven. She had been so small...so small.

He had pulled his mask from his face and his cap from his head, bringing it to his chest with the same reverence as had they been about to play the national anthem. Throwing the swinging door wide, he had walked directly to the table where Amanda's mother was having her legs stitched up where the broken and sharpened edges of her shattered femurs had torn right through the skin and muscle. He didn't have to say a word. She could see it in his eyes, though he averted them quickly after she began shrieking and shaking her head violently back and forth, tears racing from her eyes and down her cheeks. By all rights, his own should have been welling, but by now he had seen this same scenario played out so many times that he was an emotionally devoid shell. No longer capable of summoning sorrow or grief, he was left with the gnawing rat of depression and hair-trigger rage.

He had heard this woman, whose name had been as inconsequential as her shoe size, screaming from down the hallway well after he had turned his back to her and slunk from the room. An hour prior she had been a happily married mother of two celebrating her husband's promotion with the entire family by taking them to the premiere of some new movie. Now she was widowed and childless. God, how lucky was she to have survived that wreck? Lord knows who might have ended up clearing out her husband's clothes from the closet with his lingering scent still fresh on everything from the bed to the bathroom. It's every mother's dream to curl up in their child's bed, holding the pillow tightly to their chest, knowing that every dream she had dared to conjure for the future was decomposing in cedar boxes.

There was a good reason Jason had never attempted to learn her name. Chances were he would have recognized it in the obituaries when she pulled that same crumpled car into the garage and closed the door, lolling off to sleep in the carbon monoxide haze with the ghosts of her family surrounding her. And who could have blamed her? There just came a point when acquiescence became an expectation. This was no high school girl whose boyfriend had dumped her or rebellious kid whose parents were just too darn mean. This was a woman whose life had been stripped completely and painfully from her with all of the kindness of a blind dentist with a hammer and chisel and a dry tank of nitrous.

Darrel Hunsaker. Now that was a name he would remember. Darrel Hunsaker was the kind of guy George Wendt made lovable on "Cheers." The kind of guy who would just lower the brow of his hat and drink until it supported him on the bar. Darrel Hunsaker, for whom a license revocation meant just one fewer piece of paper to carry in his weathered leather wallet. Poor Darrel Hunsaker and his miserable life. The world was just out to get him from the start. No sir, he shouldn't have to take responsibility for dropping out of high school. Wasn't his fault he was boning beef at the slaughterhouse. He certainly shouldn't have to take any responsibility for having the phone shut off, or losing the insurance on the soon-to-be-repossessed pickup. That most definitely had nothing to do with the twenty-five bucks a night he spent on the foamy-tap, piss beer, though he didn't have Norm's swelling gut as he had abandoned food to make getting loaded more cost effective. Poor Darrel Hunsaker who lost his thumb to the blade he used to pull brisket from a cow's ass because he was too hung over to stand fully erect. Darrel Hunsaker who drank so much that he hadn't the reflexes to press the big wide pedal with his right foot that would have kept him from T-boning the Honda sedan that would one day serve as a gas chamber to a grieving widow and mother.

Jason met Darrel ten steps down the hallway while trying to block that same woman's anguished cries from his ears.

Darrel was helped from the ambulance in a wheel chair, pissing and moaning about how his "goddamned Jew insurance company" wasn't going to pay a stinking cent and he was going to get screwed out of his livelihood by the "greedy Jew" hospital.

The steering wheel had snapped a pair of ribs to either side. Miraculously, the idiot could have walked away from that accident with no more than a couple scratches from the imploding windshield had he been wearing his seat belt. That was one of the effects of alcohol. In addition to dulling the senses past the point of breaking, it also kept the driver from tensing in preparation of impact. He was as relaxed as if he had been asleep, protecting him from stiffening his arms and fracturing his radius and ulna, keeping him from nipping off the tip of his tongue between gritted teeth. Where was the justice in that?

When the paramedic had passed him off to Jason with a not-so-discrete sigh of relief, he had no idea that this was the man who had sent him the little girl, the red-haired, green-eyed Amanda whose blood still dotted his forearms and scrub bottoms. He had wheeled the still griping man behind a curtain, ears deafened to the bitter protests. It wasn't until a few of the words started to filter through his defenses that the picture slowly came into focus.

"Stupid bitch just pulled right out in front of me," he sniped.

He wore a red and blue flannel shirt beneath a leather bomber's jacket worn past the black and to the raw hide beneath. Pants browned with dirt, he still smelled of the slaughterhouse, though with the undertone of the beer-ripened vomit crusting in his chest hairs and the thick stubble on his chin. At least the collision had robbed him of his precious ale, if nothing else. His right front tooth was missing entirely, the rest of the visible teeth rotted down to brownish nubs. The old-logo Broncos hat, the blue decomposed to a dirty brown, was pulled down so far that it obscured the man's eyes.

"I'll bet they jacked up my truck, too! Who's going to end up paying for that, huh? Me, that's who!"

"We need to get you up on this table so I can get a better look at those ribs," Jason had said.

"And that damned fool woman driver—chicks just shouldn't be allowed to drive, I tell you—all of that blubbering and crying! God! My head still friggin' aches. Shouldn't have pulled out in front of me in that little Jap piece of shit. That's what they get all right. Giving their money to foreigners instead of buying a Ford that can take a hit and then just drive right off like nothing. Like those Japs need any more of our money, God's sake, damned nips own half of downtown already as it is."

Jason leaned forward to help the man from the chair.

"What the hell you trying to do?" Darrel shouted. "Just patch me up so I can go. I don't need you feeling me up in the process."

"I need to help you onto the examining table...sir."

Jason leaned in again, carefully easing his hands beneath the man's armpits. Sure, he could have waited for an orderly to do it for him, but the way they had those poor guys so understaffed and running all over the hospital, it could have taken half an hour...half an hour of listening to Mr. Drunkandinsane blathering on and on in his blistering tirade. And that certainly wasn't going to work.

He could feel the warmth of Darrel's putrid breath on his cheek, crawling with the taste of vile stomach acid on his vomit-riddled, slimy white tongue.

"And then—get this—those stupid Jews made me wait for the second ambulance so they could take that screaming wench and her little Pollyanna-pigtails brat to the hospital first. You believe that? They pull out in front of me and they get treated like friggin' queens. Me, I'm sitting there with these broken ribs and shit—probably dying you know—and the idiot ambulance guy has the nerve to give me the stink-eye and tell me I can call a cab for all he cares."

That was when the switch tripped in Jason's brain. The timing would have been about right if Darrel had waited for a second ambulatory deployment. The screaming wench and her little Pollyanna-pigtails brat. Amanda, who had died on his table with her gray matter squeezed out of her head like cheese from a tube and her lungs filled with blood, and her poor mother for whom the next two weeks would be more overwhelmingly cruel than life had any right to subject her to. And here was Darrel Hunsaker with nothing more than a pair of broken ribs, playing the indignant victim. There was no remorse, nor would there be any to come with the dawn and the onset of sobriety. No guilt, no sorrow, no penance. Maybe he'd serve a couple of years for manslaughter, surely the cops were wrapping up their depositions at the scene and would be here to collect him in short measure. Maybe he'd just get sixty days. Either way, Darrel Hunsaker would be right back out there on the streets, loaded to the gills. Maybe next time God would get it right and it would be Darrel they scraped up off the asphalt, but more likely—and justified by his experience—it wouldn't be Darrel at all, but someone else's mother or father or wife or child.

But even in retrospect, Jason could no longer criticize Darrel for his absence of conscience, for his sickening lack of remorse, as he felt neither of those himself for what he did next.

"The little girl died," Jason said through tightened lips, still gripping the man beneath the armpits in preparation of the lift.

"Good luck getting my truck fixed now," was all Darrel had said.

Jason's hands slowly crept down the man's ribcage.

"We move to the table on three, ready?"

"Can I get some Vicodin then?"

"One."

His hands shook with rage, with fear, easing slowly downward.

"Two."

Jason yanked the man upward a second before the drunken Darrel would have offered the assistance with his legs, squeezing his hands as hard and tightly as he possibly could.

Darrel's screams still lingered in Jason's ears to this day, though even after half a decade they were anything but haunting, rather, they were almost comforting, as though in that one twisted moment, fate had turned a blind eye and let him have that one. The jaggedly snapped ribs perforated the man's diaphragm and stomach, requiring surgery, which led to a nasty two-week bout with a septic infection. All the same, Darrel was eventually able to walk out of the hospital under his own power the same morning a neighbor would notice the idling fumes seeping from beneath a closed garage. Jason never followed up on the resolution, as whatever sentence the judge doled out would have fallen far short of his expectations. Whether he received months or years, Jason could only imagine the things the other prisoners would be doing to Darrel Hunsaker, and that allowed him to sleep at night.

Jason walked into the administrator's office at the end of his shift and tendered his resignation without a second thought. There had been a malpractice suit, but the hospital's elite fleet of lawyers had fended that one off without even breaking a sweat, settling on a number so low that they joked they could have probably paid with gift certificates.

The first couple of years had been difficult as he tried to figure out just where he wanted to go with his life. He took a job at a blood bank as an overqualified and underpaid aide, doing nothing more complex than drawing blood and passing out orange juice and cookies. But up front in the waiting room they had a fifty-five gallon aquarium that had been donated and maintained by a little local pet store at the other end of the strip mall called "Tropical Dreams." His first impression was that the thing was just a stinky tank with rocks crammed into it.

There was one large yellow Tang that circled close to the surface, but otherwise most of the other fish whiled away the hours in hiding. This mound of rock was growing all sorts of red and green and purple algae, with tiny hermit crabs crawling all over it like spiders. There were snails sucking on the glass that were large enough to qualify as escargot, their shells stained with the same mottled colors of algae. But it wasn't until one afternoon when a snowstorm had basically closed them down without notice that he sat there in the little waiting area and actually spent what turned out to be close to five straight hours inspecting the contents.

It was amazing. It wasn't just a fish tank like the one he had when he was seven with the guppies swimming in circles with their colorful tail-fins just flagging in the water until they spat out a couple dozen fry to cannibalize. This was an entire world unto itself. But it wasn't just the fish he found intoxicating. Sure, their vibrant colors were mesmerizing, but it was the coral that opened his eyes to the passion that now consumed him. In this little tank there was nothing more than a red tree sponge, a couple of small polyp stony corals, an acropora and a montipora, and a mushroom coral, but they were downright mind-blowing. Until that point, he had thought of the corals that made up these reefs he saw in pictures and movies as hard, crusted rocks of no significance. They were far more than that, however. These were wonderfully bizarre-shaped creations molded not by the current, but by the polyps that lived within them. If he looked really closely he could see these small organisms, like miniature worms with an array of little hairs around their mouths like feathers, peeking out of hardly visible holes in the coral. They filtered nutrients and invisible species of plankton from the water with those feathers that ringed their tiny mouths, growing throughout their life cycles until, when they died, their exoskeletons added to the mass of the coral, increasing its size so that a new generation of polyps could live in this solid-looking, colorful rock that was, in all reality, a maze of almost microscopic catacombs. And this mushroom coral? It was actually two different species of symbiotic polyps, one capable of photosynthesis that drew nutrition from the saltwater, passing it on to another entirely that formed the actual mushroom that moored it to the rock and moved on its stem with the current to position itself for prime nourishment. One could not exist without the other. He was astounded by both how delicate these creatures were, and yet how eternal at the same time. Their physical structures could grow indefinitely, with each of the hundreds and thousands of different polyps adding their lives to the colonial being.

He bought his first aquarium the following day, his second within a month. By the end of the year he had close to a dozen. Now, three years later, he had lost count. He developed his own coral food with freeze-dried plankton that made them grow at an astounding rate. And he used his medical training to excise individual polyps and studied them night and day. There was even one particular polyp from green tree coral he could make multiply with nothing more than a drop of a solution of calcium and strontium infused saltwater exposed to direct sunlight for a couple of days. He not only grew these corals, but learned everything he possibly could: from the positive effects of trace elements in seawater, to the detrimental effects and LD50 of contaminants like ammonia, phosphates and carbon monoxide.

He set up his own retail website and auctioned off live coral fragments on eBay. So he only made about eight hundred bucks a week. It was a fraction of what he would have made in private practice, but it was more than enough to sustain the hobby that had become his life. Best of all, life was good. After all, how many people could actually say that they were doing what they loved?

Jason leaned back in his chair, the vertebrae in his back popping as he raised his arms to the ceiling and let loose a tremendous yawn. He slouched forward into the microscope, his eye no more than touching the ring, when a sound like an explosion shook the entire apartment building, ramming the lens into his socket.

"What the hell?" he spat, jerking his head back and rubbing his eye.

Static buzzed from the radio, suddenly and inexplicably driven from the air, and then droned into silence. The tropical blue glow from the ring of tanks behind him flickered, and then suddenly turned to darkness. The hum of equipment he had grown so accustomed to that he no longer even noticed it, was replaced by a silence that itself was far more deafening than the whirring of pumps and humming of UV sterilizers. He didn't even sleep in absolute darkness as the lights on the tanks were equipped with a timer that turned off the blinding sodium halide glare and brought to life a deep blue light to simulate moonlight on the ocean floor.

He sat there for a moment, waiting for the lights to come back on, listening for the gurgle of air through water from the silenced pumps.

Nothing.

There was a clamor from outside, muffled voices and the groaning of footsteps on the communal balcony. The wobbly iron rail squeaked on its rusting bolts.

Jason rose from the chair, knocking it backward onto the floor and slowly made his way across the main room, arms extended so as not to walk blindly into one of the tanks and knock it from its stand. Feet shuffling, he eased to the front door and threw back the latch. The crisp night air raced in through the opening door, and he stepped out onto the second floor balcony. His neighbors had made their way from their apartments as well and were now leaning against the iron rail overlooking the courtyard, their eyes focused far onto the distant horizon.

Mrs. Shelton from 206 to the left was out there in rollers beneath some sort of plastic cap. Her pink terrycloth bathrobe looked like a tent over her monstrous figure. Toes like plump cocktail weenies, with the nails painted cherry red, hung over the sole of her furry pink slippers. Her husband cowered behind her, his hairy gut hanging out from beneath his yellow, stained undershirt and over the top of his light blue boxers. The long hair on the top of his head, generally combed over the liver-spotted, bald scalp, stood straight up in the wind. But it was his hairy, bare feet that were the most disturbing, with yellow nails so long they were beginning to curl under; claws clacking on the balcony like Mr. Johnson's retriever he led down the walkway for the daily five thirty a.m. walks. Both wore matching expressions: eyes wide, brows lowered, mouths hanging slack.

"What's going on?" Jason asked, though no one even acknowledged that he had spoken.

Emil Carvasso from 204 to the right, who insisted upon being called Mr. C, had pulled his navy blue parka on over his bare chest. Purple patterned pajama pants flared in the rising wind. His mouth dripped into an O beneath his tremendous gray mustache, hair standing erect like a bird's nest.

Jason watched the man's Adam's apple rise and then slowly fall back into place, and then followed his stare through the branches of the towering maple trees, to where all of the others were apparently looking as well. The entire sky was alight with shooting stars stabbing through the black tapestry, meteorites blasting bright yellow explosions in the sky. But it wasn't the astronomical display that was the point of focus—even more magnificent than the outrageous Trick Turner had described it over the airwaves—but rather further down in the sky, closer to the horizon. His eyes settled upon what had summoned them all to the balcony.

Jason wrapped his trembling hands around the iron rail...and gasped.

IV

"Thanks again for staying late," Nancy said, dropping her soft leather briefcase, overflowing with ungraded papers, onto the chair. "These conferences always seem to run late."

"Not an issue, big sis," Cindy said through a yawn, pulling her socked feet down from the arm of the couch and wriggling them into the tennis shoes on the floor. She grabbed the remote from next to her on the cushion and pushed the power button, killing the syndicated episode of *Friends*. "He's been asleep for a couple of hours."

"How quickly did he wear down?"

"He's a fighter, Nan. He'll pull through."

"Headaches? Leg aches?"

"Not that he would have complained about."

"Sometimes I wish he would so I could try to do something for him."

Cindy walked across the living room and gently wrapped her arms around her sister, giving her a solid squeeze. Nancy shuddered against her, suddenly sniffing back the tears she had allowed to slip past her defenses.

"You don't have to be strong all the time. Sometimes it's all right to lean on someone else and let them be strong for you," Cindy said, stroking her sister's long, raven black hair. Her own hair was a shade lighter, and pulled back into a ponytail. She was a good four inches taller than Nancy, though built more like a rail rather than curved at the hips and bosom like her lucky sister. Nancy wore a smart gray skirt suit, and all she needed was a pair of dark-rimmed glasses to give her that whole "naughty school-marm" fantasy look with those two and a half-inch heels. She could only imagine how long it took a class of ninth grade boys to finally rise from their seats after the bell. Cindy, on the other hand, wore an oversized white sweatshirt and black sweatpants.

The only thing the two shared was their eyes: a pale, almost clear blue like the eternally frozen core of an iceberg.

"I have no right to lean on you any more than I already have."

"That's what sisters are for, right? And besides, you know I love hanging out with that nephew of mine."

"I'm sure you must have a lot of studying to do."

"You'd think so, wouldn't you? But nope, all I've got left now is a couple of classes, and then I am *sooo* done."

"My little sister the accountant. Mom and Dad would have been proud."

"No, they would have said 'Accountant? What, not smart enough for law school?'"

Nancy sniggered, covering her mouth and nose to keep the thinned snot from blasting out. "That's good." Sniffing, "That was Dad to a T."

Cindy gave her sister another squeeze and released her.

"Anyone call?" Nancy asked, wiping the smudged mascara from beneath her eyes.

"You mean did *he* call?"

"Anyone. Did anyone call?"

"Only telemarketers. I'm not sure, but I think you're going to start getting The Post. Sorry." Cindy paused. "I thought you guys were talking again."

"So did I."

"Does he even ask about Tim?"

"Not directly."

"Surely he could have grown up a little in a year and a half."

"I think he's trying."

Cindy shook her head and scoffed, crossing the room to the coffee table and grabbing her purse and jacket.

"He was scared. Can you blame him?" Nancy asked.

"For abandoning his wife and son? Yeah."

"It's easy to stand back and judge, Cin. Do you know what it's like to watch him slowly dying a little more every day?"

"Yeah, Nan...I do."

Cindy stormed back across the living room and to the front door. "Get some sleep, huh? You look like microwaved death." With a wink, she opened the front door and stepped out onto the porch. "Conferences again tomorrow?"

"Parents who'd rather I raised their children than they? Oh yeah, looking forward to it."

"Same bat-time, same bat-channel, then?"

"You all right doing it again?"

"Without a doubt."

Nancy leaned against the front door and watched her sister descend from the porch and onto the sidewalk that divided the browned lawn.

"Thanks, Cin," Nancy whispered.

She had just started to close the door when Cindy looked up into the night sky and quickly called back to her.

"Nancy! Come here!"

"What?" she asked, stepping out onto the porch and wrapping her arms around her chest. The night breeze knifed through her thin blouse.

"C'mere!"

Nancy clacked across the cement porch to the steps, right beneath the edge of the awning. Her sister was standing on the walk with her head craned up to the sky. Amber flashes highlighted her face.

"What is it?"

"Look up, would you?"

Nancy descended the pair of cement steps and looked up into the sky. Shooting stars raced across the night from every possible angle like fireballs playing connect the dots with the stars. Eyes sparkling, faces aglow, both looked drop-jawed into the wondrous night.

"You know he'd love to see this, Nan," Cindy said without taking her eyes from above.

"It would be irresponsible of us to—"

"Let him miss this?"

"Yank him out of bed and drag him outside. It's kind of chilly and the wind's starting to blow…"

"Come on, Nancy. You know he loves this kind of thing, and when was the last time you saw a meteor shower this…this crazy?"

"He does always put together that puzzle with all of the constellations…"

"And he has that telescope in his bedroom window."

"To watch all of the 'normal' kids play."

"I've seen him tilt it up. Come on. He's always cooped up in that house. Either that or at the hospital. Just this once, Nan. Just for a minute. Nothing'll go wrong, I promise."

Nancy lowered her eyes and looked to her sister, still mesmerized by the flaring streaks crossing the sky. She didn't know what she would possibly do without her little sister. Without Cindy she would probably already have pulled out all of her hair and quit her job to hole up in that little bedroom with her sick son until the bank came and took the house.

Finally lowering her stare, Cindy's eyes caught her sister's. She looked so exhausted, so worn, so…old.

Nancy simply nodded and dropped her eyes to her feet.

"Well then, come on!" Cindy exclaimed, beaming. She grabbed Nancy by the elbow and rushed her up the stairs and across the porch. They passed straight through the living room and bent right with the hallway, passing the bathroom and the closed door to Nancy's "office," really no more than a computer buried beneath a pile of manila folders and notebook paper, and to the end. To the left was the master, where Cindy could count on the bed her sister never used—as she generally fell asleep in the recliner beside her son's bed—to be unmade and the floor littered with clothes. To the right was Tim's room, the door standing wide with the flashing sky staining the carpet from the drawn blinds at the back of the room.

They crept silently within. It was a strange dichotomy of decoration. The wall to the left held a little net hammock brimming with stuffed animals from his old favorite Freddy the frog, which, when he was younger, he dutifully toted everywhere in the crook of his left arm, dragging his tattered blue blankie behind him in his right, to a variety of bears and dogs. The wall to the right was covered with posters of Spider-man and the X-Men, Michael Vick and Joe Sakic. It was his attempt to grow up away from the influence of other kids and from the confines of this bedroom that was now nearly his entire world. At the back of the room, the bed was pressed up beneath the window, the tan recliner in the corner beneath a heaped patchwork quilt.

He looked so small: no more than a wrinkle beneath that enormous Avalanche comforter. There was a rotation of three, a SpongeBob Squarepants and Finding Nemo besides, as the radiation treatments more often than not made his stomach go Vesuvius without even the slightest warning.

The thin breeze ruffled the bottom of the plain blue curtains to either side of the cracked window, shimmering in the reflected glory of the blazing sky.

Cindy released Nancy's arm and followed her around the side of the bed to the head, watching her lean over and gently stroke Tim's powdery, pale forehead. Atop his bald pate was nothing more than a hardly visible layer of white fuzz, and the half dozen moles they might never have known existed were it not for the Leukemia. His skin was almost transparent, kind of milky, yet the green veins beneath stood eerily out. Slowly, he opened his eyes from deep in the bruised-looking sockets, his lashes tearing through the gooey knots of sleep. He blinked a few times from beneath his thinned brows that looked haphazardly plucked, wetting the rising red streaks that tried to overtake the whites.

"You're home," he whispered, stretching a thin smile.

"Yeah, honey," Nancy said, leaning over and giving him a kiss on the cheek. "I'm home."

His face was swollen and round, his cheeks plumped like a chipmunk hoarding acorns before the coming of a snowstorm.

"What's going on outside?" he asked, noting the flashes of light covering the comforter atop him.

"You want to come see?" Cindy asked with a crooked smirk.

Tim looked to his mother and raised the question with what should have been brows.

"Come on, kiddo," she said. "Are you up for it?"

"Yeah," he said, pulling his arms from beneath the blankets and rubbing his eyes. His fingers were thin and bony, yet swollen at the knuckles, the skin hanging loosely from his arms like an old man's.

Nancy gently pulled the blankets down, trying not to show the horror in her face that she felt every time she removed him from the bed. His legs were thin and knobby, yet his stomach was distended like one of those Ethiopian children in the Sally Struthers commercials. It even stretched the oversized t-shirt that used to be hers. Now she let him wear it to bed as a pajama top, making him look even more minuscule and feeble. The navy blue pajama pants that would have matched the top were it not suddenly so constrictive, were cuffed at the ankles above his jaggedly bony, jaundiced feet.

"What is it?" he asked as his mother slid her arms beneath his shoulders and knees and heaved him from the bed with a grunt. His head lolled onto her shoulder and she positioned his legs around her waist, cradling him to her chest. "I can get Aunt Cindy to tell me if you won't. I can get her to do anything."

He smirked at Cindy, who pointed a finger at him in mock anger.

"It's a surprise," Nancy said. "But you can thank your aunt for talking me into waking you up."

Tim smiled at Cindy, garnering a wink in return.

"Better hurry or we'll miss it," Cindy said.

Nancy carried Tim out into the hallway and toward the living room. Each and every time she performed this same routine to take him to doctor's appointments and what not, she had no choice but to wonder if it would be the last, noting each time how he seemed that much lighter and more listless in her grasp. Passing through the living room, Tim batted his eyes uncontrollably, trying to adjust to the sudden influx of light assaulting his corneas. She eased him sideways through the front door into the cooling breeze of the night, and carefully across the porch and down the stairs onto the lawn.

"Wow," he gasped, his faint blue eyes straining to look upward while his chin still rested limply on his mother's shoulder. "Where's Chicken Little when you need him?"

Nancy laughed and hugged him tightly to her chest.

"They're all meteors," Cindy said. "You see, when they hit the Earth's atmosphere—"

"They burn up. I know. And those that make it through and actually hit the ground are then called meteorites. It takes just the right tra...trajec...trajectory to make it through the atmosphere, like trying to land a shuttle. It needs to be exactly the right angle or there'll be nothing left."

"I'll never doubt you again, professor."

"My dad told me about them." Nancy and Cindy shared an uneasy glance. "He said that generally they're small pieces of rock broken off from comets and then trapped in their tail. And since our planet has higher gravity it can steal them away."

"You're far more enlightened than I. Any more knowledge to impart?"

"I read somewhere that one hit down in New Mexico, I think, and left a crater the size of a football field. I think New Mexico's a straight shot from outer space since that's where all of the aliens go."

Nancy laughed. "And what do you know about aliens?"

"There's some sort of underground place where they keep the ones they catch, like in *Independence Day*, but I don't really think they're just running around everywhere like *Men In Black*."

"I figured the way you were talking you must have known something that I didn't," Nancy said, sliding her hand beneath his shirt and rubbing his bare back. Goosebumps rose along the far too obvious knobs of his spine.

"Just what that other little boy tells me."

"What little boy?"

"The one who talks to me at night."

"What are you talking abo—"

"He says it's very important that I don't die yet, that *I'm* very important."

Nancy was helpless but to look down at her son, her insides a tangle of emotion. She didn't know who this little boy could possibly be or if he was nothing more than a figment of her son's feverish imagination. Maybe Tim was going stir crazy living the life of exile in that bedroom. Regardless, it was the first time that she had ever heard him speak of his own mortality, and that was the kind of thing that could make a mother's heart stop in her chest.

"Of course you're very important," Nancy said, noting the odd reddish glow reflecting from atop Tim's head. "And you're a fighter, big guy. You'll kick this cancer."

Cindy could see the tears brimming in her sister's eyes, which she had seen so many countless times over the last couple of years. It was both terrifically sad and beautiful at the same time, the love and awe and adoration she had for this one dwindling, fading, shooting star.

"Yeah," was all Tim could add, yawning; his flaccid form growing even more so. His noodle neck softened and his head rolled gently to the side onto Nancy's shoulder where she could feel the warmth of his breath.

There was a faint whistling sound in the distance—high-pitched, shrill.

"What is that?" Cindy asked, turning to the right and toward the eastern sky, stained a pale yellow from the glow of the city lights.

The noise grew louder and louder until Nancy had to raise her voice to answer over it.

"What does the tornado siren sound like?"

"I think it's a deeper tone."

The red glow intensified quickly, making the leaves on all of the ancient elms and maples look as though they had caught fire and were towering over the street, burning.

"Get in the house!" Nancy shouted over the now deafening sound. "Get in the house!"

A ball of fire knifed through the sky directly overhead, thundering past with the sound trembling behind it like the passing of a fighter jet. The whole sky crackled and screamed in its wake.

Nancy raced across the lawn, leaping the two steps and crossed the porch in a single stride. Hammering the front door with her shoulder and ramming it right into the wall, she reached the end of the living room and slid onto the carpet.

"Did you see that?" Cindy asked, kneeling beside her sister.

"Meteorite," Tim whispered, the rumbling sound now growing distant.

"It looked like it was going to land right on the house!"

There was a loud explosion from outside and the ground shook.

"That really hit the ground, didn't it?" Cindy asked, surprised. She rose from her haunches and crept toward the front door.

The lights flickered once as if in warning, and then extinguished entirely.

"They'll come back on," Nancy reassured Tim.

"It's always darkest before the dawn," Tim whispered into her ear. "That's what the little boy told me. It's always darkest before the dawn."

Nancy eased out from beneath the doorway and into the center of the living room, watching Cindy carefully while she slowly stepped out onto the porch, her darkened form a shadowy silhouette against the night.

Cindy leaned around the frame and looked down the street toward the mountains. The "razorbacks"—so called because they looked like the bristled back of a hunched warthog—were the jagged black foothills just before the Rocky Mountains shot straight up behind. A cloud of what looked like smoke rose above them, swelling and curling like the thick gray smog from a post-Industrial Revolution textile mill.

"It hit in the foothills," Cindy called back over her shoulder.

"How far away?"

"I can't tell. Looks like somewhere just south of Red Rocks maybe."

"Whew," Nancy said, as much a display of true relief as a comical expression for Tim's benefit. "How 'bout we try to find some candles and we get you back into bed, mister?"

She had no more than taken a few cautious strides toward the kitchen—careful not to bang her shins into the coffee tables or the ottoman in front of the chair—when Cindy's haunting voice raised the hackles up the backs of her arms.

"Nan," Cindy whispered, stepping quickly back into the house. She was shaking her head furiously from side to side in disbelief, still retreating, yet unable to take her eyes from whatever it was that she was seeing. "Get back under that door frame."

"What's going—?"

"Nancy!" Cindy snapped, whirling quickly and then running toward her. "Get down!"

Cindy tackled Nancy and Tim to the floor right where they were, falling atop them on the pale gray carpet and throwing her hands over her own head.

From outside came a loud whooshing sound, a wind thundering toward them, grumbling and howling like a tornado.

"What's happening?" Nancy screamed, but her words were swallowed by the continuous roll of thunder that made the floor shudder beneath them and the glass rattle in the panes.

All of the windows imploded at once, though even the sound of a dozen panes of glass shattering in unison was drowned out by the roar of the wind. Shards of broken glass fired across the floor, covering couches and chairs and embedding themselves into the plaster in the walls. They hit Cindy in the back like buckshot, tearing right through her sweatshirt and pants, lancing into her flesh.

She snapped her head back and screamed up into the ceiling.

Fresh blood poured from the dozens of puncture wounds from the tops of her thighs clear up to her shoulders, sapping into the thick cotton, while the room filled with a haze of smoke.

V

"Come on out, William. You've got to see this!" Brad called in through the sliding glass door from the balcony.

The house that he had designed and overseen the construction of himself was built right into the hillside, surrounded on all sides by a thick mess of deep green pines mottled only by the golden shimmer of the rustling aspen leaves. The entire back of the house was tempered glass, from the roof that slanted to either side right down to the walkout basement. Standing on tall stilts, the deck wrapped all the way around the back of the house, becoming the porch out front at the end of the circular gravel drive. There was a small oval of grass beneath with a swingset and a thin path winding down the slope through the maze of trunks and to the small stream from which he and William had pulled many a cutthroat.

Brad had taken William's Radio Shack telescope out onto the pine deck, mounted it onto its little aluminum tripod and pointed it to the east into the sky over the vast expanse of twinkling lights that was the sprawling metropolis of Denver. The entire sky was filled with yellow slants of light.

"You've got to see this, son!" Brad called again, finally taking his eye from the lens and walking back toward the doorway.

Craning his head around the frame, he could see William, exactly where he had been all afternoon and evening since they returned home from the psychiatrist's office. The chair and loveseat made an L in the center of the open living room. In front of the couch was a heavy oak coffee table he and Jennifer had found in a little roadside antique store in the middle of nowhere, just south of the Maine State Line. It predated the Revolutionary war, but had taken only an afternoon of some serious planning and a new coat of veneer to make it look brand new. The craftsmanship was exquisite, hand-carved with enough tensile strength to support a Sherman tank. As for usage, however, it served the more classical role of a footrest for Brad's socked feet while he watched the tube, rather than for what it had originally been intended. Right now, it was home to a rather obstinate child who was missing one spectacular display of lights.

Sighing, Brad crossed the tiled foyer into the living room, his slippers whirring on the thick pile of the carpet like corduroy rubbed between thighs. He passed the couch and squatted next to the coffee table with a groan, and leaned onto his right side so he could see beneath.

"You're missing a heck of a show," he said, pulling the remote from atop the table over his head and directing it toward the fifty-three inch monster in dire need of volume control. He set it back with a clatter and looked to his son. "Decided to stop coloring I see."

William was sitting beneath the table, knees pulled to his chest and wrapped in a pair of scrawny arms, his chin pinned down against his chest as he was just getting far too big to be using the coffee table as his haven. Brad reached beneath and placed a hand atop the boy's arm. His skin was cold, clammy, damp with a layer of sweat that brought the hackles on his flesh to full alert. And he was shivering, no... shaking. He was trembling there beneath that table with his eyes as wide as those of an owl.

"Are you all right?" Brad asked, his brow furrowing. William flinched at his touch, shying further back beneath the coffee table. "You're not getting sick, are you?"

William just shook his head, loosing a line of slobber that had rolled past his writhing lips and clung from his chin.

"What's wrong then?"

William looked straight through him with those frightened, twitching eyes.

Brad nodded to himself. He felt so completely and utterly helpless at times like these. He wished to God that William would just give him a little sign that everything was all right there inside of his head where it seemed he liked to hide even more than beneath the coffee table. The requisite sketchpad and crayons were there beside him as always. With a smile and a glance to verify approval, Brad turned the pad so that it faced him and looked at the drawing. His face soured while he studied what appeared to be a mushroom cloud rising over the mountains.

"What's this?" he asked, consciously controlling his tone to make it sound like heightened curiosity rather than concern.

But William still just sat there, trembling and drooling.

Brad turned to the prior page where there was a wax drawing of a tall building with what looked like a radio tower atop it. The top was obscured by clouds, but the blue lettering was easily decipherable.

"Oh, I see. This is the Qwest building downtown."

He turned the page again.

"Are these...flowers?" he asked, studying the page where there was a drawing of a man—of that much he was certain—but it looked like there were little yellow flowers growing out of his face and arms around his clothing.

"Not...flowers," William shuddered. "Them."

The ridge of his brow lowered, the pressure squirting a pair of tears from the corners of his eyes to roll down his blotchy red cheeks.

Brad sighed. Sometimes his emotions overwhelmed him. He loved the boy more than anything else in the world, and that was why it just gutted him when there wasn't a damned thing he could do to help. William should be out on the balcony staring up into the sky and wishing he could be an astronaut, not cringing beneath the coffee table with bubbling saliva clinging to his quivering chin.

All of the shrinks—and there had been plenty—had warned that the coffee table was his metaphorical shell, and that removing it from atop him when he was cowering beneath could be detrimental to his psyche. But Brad's parental instincts told him that what his son really needed right now was the love of his father, and the table just wasn't tall enough to accommodate.

Slowly, he brought his head out from beneath and lifted the table, bringing it down on its side.

William shrieked and immediately threw his hands atop his head.

Brad crawled in closer and wrapped his arms around the trembling child and brought him to his chest. Crying and wailing, William threw his arms around his father and squeezed as hard as he possibly could.

"It's all right, son," Brad said, sniffing back a tear of frustration-relief-exasperation. "We're going to get through this. You and me. We're going to be all right."

"They're coming," William whispered.

"Who's coming?"

"Tonight."

"Who's coming tonight?"

William just shivered and merged even further into his father's embrace, his wet cheeks leeching right into Brad's shirt. The two sat there on the floor in front of the muted television with the black sky flashing behind them for a long, silent moment.

"I love you," Brad whispered. "You know that, right?"

He could feel William nodding against his chest.

"Never forget that. Whatever life may hold...I'll always be here for you."

William sniffed and gave another squeeze before letting his hug subside.

"You sure you don't want to look through the telescope?"

William nodded.

"All right, then. I think it's long past time we got you into bed, partner. I know your mother would have kicked my butt if she knew I had you up this late."

Still holding his son to his chest, Brad groaned and struggled to his feet. He had no more than turned toward the hallway when his shadow lengthened on the floor in front of him and the carpet took on a pinkish hue. The floor began to vibrate and it sounded as though a helicopter was about to set down on their roof. Slowly he turned, his mouth falling slack in awe.

The entire sky was red; the tinted glass was imbued with the color of a rose. Louder and louder the rumbling grew until it shook the entire house on its foundation. The telescope perched out on the rail wriggled its way free and toppled over the edge before the beam that had once supported it freed itself from the nails and broke loose. Black treetops bowed and swayed violently at the will of the wind. A pattern of pine needles were ripped from their moorings and assaulted the glass.

"What in the world..." Brad mused, no longer able to hear his own voice over the constant thunder. Even William's screams couldn't penetrate the roar, though his flailing form and pounding fists certainly toyed with Brad's balance while he eased his way back toward the wall of glass that was the back of the house.

Reaching the sliding glass door, he could feel the deck shaking, shuddering, trying to tear from the house and tumble down the hillside with the rocks that bounded down the slope, hammering trunks with a sappy thump before tumbling pall-mall into the forest. The glass shivered in its framework, casting glinting reflections throughout the room. Even the distant city lights faded to a wan glow beneath the red sky.

He caught just the tail end of fire; the blinding flare of light streaking through the right side of his peripheral vision before the impact jarred him from his feet. He collapsed to his knees before the sound of the explosion boomed in his ears.

All he could do was force his wobbly legs to stand, and watch the enormous cloud of dust rise to the south like a mushroom over the mountains. It grew and swelled straight up into the sky in defiance of the heavens, and then began to expand.

The mass of gray dust swirled and plumed and churned, rising upward and then rolling back toward the ground before advancing up the hillside. For a moment it appeared as though it was stationary, the bottom curls of smoke twirling back under the cap of the mushroom, but then with a speed and ferocity the likes of which Brad had never in his life witnessed, the cloud quickly began to expand. It raced outward like a giant tsunami in all directions: a wall of gray smoke and debris tearing through everything in its path.

Brad turned and raced toward the front of the house, his mind rehashing the trees ripped right from the ground and tossed upward before the mighty wrath of the explosion. Breathless, panicked, he turned quickly to the right and plopped onto the stairs, sliding halfway down to the tune of the entire back of his house shattering. Shards of glass flew by at the top of the staircase, some even tinkling down the stairs to land beside them.

He wrapped his arms around William's head and did his best to shield him before the cloud of dust tore into the house, filling every inch of airspace, roaring like a turbine engine directed at their ears. Pebbles and rocks and dirt hammered the walls, tearing through the plaster and embedding themselves in the drywall. The stairs moved beneath them, knocking Brad up against the wall. He coughed into the impenetrable dust, and the entire world went gray.

VI

Night on the Sixteenth Street Mall was a fantasy stolen from reality: a non-stop parade of the beautiful people, the young, and the upwardly mobile. With the exclusive clubs and fantastically expensive restaurants, this closed off section of roadway in downtown Denver was a veritable who's who of the under thirty-five crowd. Surgically sculpted cleavage was the order of the night, blooming out from designer dresses that had never known a hanger on a rack. Men with plucked brows and gelled hair, straight off the cover of *GQ*, clambered down from their three-quarter million penthouse studios to flash their money and roguish good looks in hopes of conquering one of the Barbie doll bleach-blondes like they already had those first few rungs of the corporate ladder. Here you'll find the wasted, wanton youth; the mayor's and governor's kids, sons and daughters of money gifted through living trusts, and those who would never know a day on the job. For them, this was their living, hopping from club to club, making sure not that they had the time of their lives dancing and cavorting, but that they were seen doing so.
For this fleeting moment in life, this was the Serengeti Plain of yuppie conquest, where champagne-drunk women were savaged like wounded gazelle.

This was where he came to play.

Ronny Brewster was anything but a member of the nouveau riche caste of debonair hunks flashing their cosmetically whitened smiles and deep brown tans from the beaches of the Caribbean. The closest he actually came to conversing with any of these snobs was when one turned him down for a second mortgage on his crumbling, turn-of-the-century bungalow or in court where his soon-to-be ex-wife's lawyer was hell bent on slowly bleeding him dry like a stuck pig.

Life wasn't fair. Sure. Statement of fact. But from time to time it did throw him a bone.

"Ronny," a voice crackled into his ear. He placed his hand over his right ear to drive the earpiece further down the canal and listened closely.

Standing to the side of the front door of Club Euphoria in a black suit so tight it felt as though he could rip it with a single flex of his monstrous biceps, with that little curled white cord hanging from his ear, he felt like a secret service agent. The tendons popped out on the back of his thick neck, his wide jaw gnashing his teeth. His eyes narrowed beneath his dense brow, stretching taut the forehead that was hardly distinguishable from the cleanly shaven scalp. The goatee that encircled his mouth was as thick as a lumberjack's, matching the arms and legs that could have passed for tree trunks. Pulsating lights from the open doorway stretched his long and shifting shadow out across the tiled courtyard and toward the fountain, firing squirts of water high into the air, imbued with color from the red and blue lights directed up from beneath them. Dozens of sharply attired men and women milled about the fountain, pausing only long enough to determine which club they should hop off to next.

Overhead, the sky itself reflected the pomp that surrounded him: streaks of light tearing through the darkness like a fireworks display.

"Code twelve," the voice said.

With a nod of understanding, the corners of his lips creeping up and into a smile, Ronny turned from his post and passed through the doorway.

Techno-dance music assaulted him in a wave, the pulsing base thumping hard against his chest. He passed the coat check window without a sideways glance and strode directly down the stairs and to the packed dance floor. Scanning past the hoards of people, bumping and grinding like naked pagans beneath the light of the full moon, he searched for the source of his beckoning. There were fifteen different codes running the gamut from escorting beautiful drunken women from the pursuer who couldn't understand the meaning of the word "no," to controlling the scene and helping to evacuate the patrons in an orderly fashion in case of a fire. But it was code twelve that he lived for. Code twelve, that magical call that forced him to bite his cheeks to keep from grinning like a madman.

There.

On the far side of the floor, his eyes latched onto the reason for his summoning. Granted, there were a good dozen bouncers all around the club, but none of them were half as imposing as he. This was what he lived for. The only thing that turned his crank was adrenaline, which he could now feel rising from his tingling toes all the way up his spine. Fingers fidgeting at his sides, fighting the urge to prematurely curl them into fists, he knifed through the sweating masses, eyes fixed stolidly on the area surrounding table thirty-eight, where some pretentious suit appeared to be giving one of the waitresses about all she could handle.

Light refracted from the overload of gel in the man's hair, whatever material his custom suit was crafted from shimmering almost like sunlight from a trout's scales. He had one hand on the waitress' hip, his thumb looped beneath the strap of her apron, holding her close to him despite her hands pressed against his chest in protest. All three of his buddies, crammed back into the booth with their red noses and imported beers, cheered him on.

"Is there a problem?" Ronny asked, his voice so deep and booming it sounded like a boulder cracking free from the face of a mountainous slope and tumbling down the hillside.

He could see the relief in the waitress' wide blue eyes when she looked to him, finally managing to push herself out of the man's grasp.

"No," she said, straightening her tiny black apron beneath a lacy top so revealing it could have passed for lingerie. She cast a quick glance to the man whose hands had reluctantly found their way into his own pockets. "Is there?"

"Like the lady said," the man said, his tone dripping with contempt, but his eyes unable to meet Ronny's. He looked back to his friends and sniggered, drunkenly wobbling there as though fighting some unseen wind.

Ronny looked to the waitress, her long blonde hair framing her face in the current Rachel-do, and raised the question with his eyebrows.

She simply nodded once and hesitantly looked back to the table.

Ronny was just about to turn his back and walk away, dejected, when from the corner of his eye he caught the man reach out quickly, like a striking cobra, and grab the waitress' butt and squeeze.

Before she could raise a hand to defend herself, Ronny was upon the man. With two hands the size of racquets, Ronny seized the far smaller man by the shoulders and cleaved him from the ground, bringing their faces together.

"Time to go," he snarled into the man's face, hoping upon hope that there was a large stain now running down the legs of that fancy suit.

"Do you know who my dad is?" the man shouted, his voice cracking.

"Tell your friends to gather their belong—"

"You won't even be able to get a job at McDonald's when he's through with you!"

"We can do this one of two ways—"

"I'll sue you and this club for every last cent!" he shrieked.

"—the easy way, which I would recommend—"

"Put me down you steroid junkie!"

"—or the hard way, which is what I'm hoping for."

"Darren!" one of the others at the table shouted, but then looked back into his lap when Ronny turned toward him.

"What we're going to do now," Ronny said calmly, though his lips were peeled back from clenched teeth, "is slowly walk across the dance floor and through the front doors, where I would be happy to hail you a cab...sir."

"You're making the worst mistake of your life here, chump."

"Yes, I know. Daddy, suing, no McDonald's for me."

"Don't you dare talk down to me!"

"Walk with me before this turns into a scene," Ronny said, already noting the slowing of the dancers on the floor, their eyes finding their way to where he was only now planting the man back down on his feet. He brushed the wrinkles from that shiny jacket and threw his arm over the man's shoulders like they had known each other all of their lives. He gently coaxed the man to walking and eased him onto the floor, glancing casually back over his shoulder to ensure that this fellow's compatriots were falling in tow.

The dancers parted curiously in front of them, sparing only a single questioning thought before mashing right back into place. Ascending the stairs, the cool breeze from outside gently caressed their sweating faces on the way to the open door.

"You take care," Ronny said, shoving the man through the doorway and allowing his friends to pass before barring the entrance back into the club with his enormous form, crossing his arms over his chest.

The man stormed out into the middle of the courtyard, his black leather loafers splashing the puddles formed by the water driven from the fountain by the rising wind that whistled furiously between the tall buildings. Throwing his hands into the air, he appeared to be having some sort of heated argument with the heavens, before lowering his palms to the top of his head and running his fingers through his sticky hair.

"Just let it go, Darren," his friend said, sidling up to his buddy and placing a consolatory hand atop his shoulder.

Darren shrugged out from beneath it and whirled, already raising his first finger to waggle it in illustration of the red-faced point he was preparing to make.

"I wouldn't pull that finger out unless you're prepared to use it," Ronny said, the left corner of his mouth creeping into a smirk.

"You think you're *sooo* smart, don't you, Mungo?" Darren barked, wagging that finger with callous disregard to the serious beating he was unknowingly preparing to be dealt. "Maybe you think that here, in the middle of the night, you're superior to me with that…that…steroid-induced Hulk thing you've got going on, but come daylight, I'll bet I could make you cry like a little girl."

"Come on, man," one of his friends interrupted. "Let's just get out of here, okay?"

"No," Darren snapped, driving his Armani-suited friend backward with that lone, pointed finger. "We're not going anywhere until this jerk understands what a colossal mistake he's made!"

He strode right back up to Ronny, his lower lip shoved forward but quivering with rage and fear all the while. Nostrils flaring, the blood pooling in his face, his entire head began jerking quickly from side to side with the furor of his emotions.

"Look at my face, asshole!" he shouted, spittle spraying violently past his lips.

Ronny merely unclenched a fist and raised it to his cheek, dabbing at dampness on his skin with the back of his hand. He lowered it slowly and inspected it beneath the suddenly much lighter sky.

"When you lose this crummy job, I want you to see my face. When the bank forecloses on whatever hovel it is you dwell in…I want you to see my face. And when the police show up at your door in the morning and lock you up with the other steroid-head sodomites and you're taking it three ways from Sunday…I WANT YOU TO SEE MY FACE!"

Those final words tore through the last of his restraint and he screamed them at the top of his lungs in a voice that came out as shrill as a harpy, though none so much as heard. His face stained auburn from the fiery sky, eyes peeled insanely wide, he was quite possibly the only person out there in the courtyard whose vision hadn't found its way skyward to the source of the deafening roar that trailed the rapidly fading glow.

Ronny smiled and slowly lowered his eyes from the sky, the tremendous rumbling still doddering in the concrete beneath his feet. He reached casually out with both hands and tightened his fingers into the fabric of the man's jacket, and with one clean motion, raised him from his feet and into the air.

"Guys like me," he shouted over the drone of what he assumed to be a jet, still maintaining that pleasant façade that must at one point have endeared him to the in-laws, "don't get fucked. You understand, daddy's boy? We do the fucking!"

His eyes narrowed and his lips rolled back from maniacally bared teeth, contorting that grin into something more closely resembling the snarl of a starving jackal preparing to tear into the festering, abandoned carcass of a zebra.

The ground dropped beneath him, nearly jarring the man— terrified to the point that he had frozen solid, eyes pinched shut in anticipation of the blow that would next scatter his teeth across the tile—from his grasp. Regaining control of his equilibrium, Ronny took a step forward, craning his neck so as to see the flashing sky over the tremendous skyscrapers, that from this vantage appeared to stretch infinitely upward.

Eyebrows raised, he studied first the small patch of visible sky overhead, shooting stars lancing through the tapestry of the night, and then the faces of those around him, all of whom had stopped what they were doing to ask the same unspoken question with their uncertain, fearful eyes.

A roaring sound, like the torment of the forceful wind before the wrath of a tornado, rose from nowhere with such volume that it rattled the night itself, turning the streaks of light above to squiggles. Paper and trash were ripped from everywhere around and blasted mercilessly through the open corridor. Women's hair snapped across their faces, dresses ripped nearly waist high. Several people were cleaved from their feet and toppled to the ground, while others moored themselves to anything within reach from light poles and railings, to the statuesque carved shapes of the junipers. The pigeons that had bedded down for the night on the windowsills and roofs high above took to panicked flight from the trembling buildings only to be swallowed by the wind and hammered back against the construct and dropped hundreds of feet to the concrete with a sickening slap. Feathers freed themselves from their lifeless, shattered forms, torn right from the down by the wicked wind, only to have the pathetic carcasses bound after them down the sidewalk like sloppy tumbleweeds.

Ronny looked to the man he still held above the earth, his tie blowing horizontally with such force that it snapped like a whip, even the massive amounts of gel unable to withstand the tempestuous bluster. Darren's feet clacked together, and were it not for Ronny's iron grip, the jacket would probably be sliding along the pavement into the heap of trash and debris the wind pinned to the side of an enormous planting box filled with flowers now devoid of their formerly breathtaking petals.

The lights flickered once, the neon blazing as if with a power surge, snapping, pulsing, the light creeping across the ground from the open doorway behind him strobing, and then all at once extinguished.

He could barely make out the shapes of the masses now filling the courtyard, having filed out of the darkened clubs and trendy eateries to stare up into the firecracker sky. An arm shot out in front of his face, pointing skyward. Slowly, he turned, following the direction of the raised arm.

Screams filled the night; so loud that he could even hear them over the turbine growl that seemed to be coming from all around him now. It rattled his bones and shook his lungs as he tried to inhale, finally forcing him to lower Darren to the ground, though his fists still curled tightly into the fabric of the man's jacket.

He could see the source of all those screams, the pointing fingers, and felt his heart drop into his stomach.

At the far end of the mall, tearing through downtown, was a churning wall of smoke and dust with a ceiling that looked to be well into the stratosphere. It swallowed the Qwest building whole, the brilliant blue sign atop it that could be seen from thirty miles in all directions vanished in a fraction of a heartbeat.

Cars were lifted from the ground and tossed before the mighty wind, slamming into storefronts and buildings and skittering across the ground on their hoods. Bodies were thrown into the air, bouncing from walls and hammering the walk. Pebbles and sharp debris pelted Ronny like a storm of locusts, drawing blood from his exposed hands and face. The man in his grasp was ripped from his hands like a kite and catapulted into the air, nearly taking Ronny with him, but instead, knocking him backward onto the ground where he slid a good ten feet before slamming his head into a bench. His eyes lolled upward with the colored blossoms expanding in his vision. He had but time to draw one final, dust-riddled breath before the wall of dust hit him like a truck, crumpling him beneath the bench like a tuna forced into a sardine can, pinning his face against the ground, his head between his knees.

The steel bolts that held the bench to the cement snapped like dry reeds, the wind wrenching the bench into the air and launching it into the impregnable dust like a cruise missile. Ronny's lifeless form followed, arms flailing jointlessly like a rag doll, head flopping to the side on his broken neck. He disappeared into the explosive cloud with the rest of the bodies like autumn leaves.

2 | The Dust Settles

I

"Brian!" Shannen screamed through the thick cloud of dust that surrounded her like a fog, retching out a pair of guttural coughs through her dry, ripped throat.

She dripped of lake-water from head to toe, stinking like a trout coated in a sloppy mossy sheen. Her stringy hair, thick with rapidly browning mud, hung like dreadlocks over her shoulders, knotting and tangling. Her bangs sapped to her forehead, sticking to her eyebrows, framing her haunting, black-stained eyes like those of a raccoon from her smeared and running mascara. Tears dragged that charcoal-looking mess down her cheeks, pocked with swelling drops of blood, dissolving into the layer of muck-water that attracted the fine particles of ashen debris to her face like a magnet. Her wet sweater clung to her, heavy, cumbersome, the material already fraying and pulling apart around the small rips in the fabric. Small rivulets of running water formed amazingly beneath her jeans, streaming under the far too tight denim, soaking into her socks and filling her shoes. With every step her soles sloshed with a noise resembling flatus, the dirt from the unseen path forming a thick crust of mud beneath them like platforms. Shivering violently, each and every little hair follicle prickled like the quills of a cactus, she stumbled forward, the uneven ground invisible though it lie no more than five and a half feet south.

"Brian!" she screamed again, the final syllable trailing into a shrill scream. Her raw throat felt as though it split right down the larynx. She wheezed through the cloud, fanning her hand before her face to try to free up a solitary breath of clear air in attempt to ease her already tremendously burning lungs.

She couldn't see anything through the churning cloud of dust. The thick tree trunks that filled the entire area only vaguely announced their presence as a mirage-like shade a moment before she clumsily stumbled face-first into them. Formerly eternal trunks lie sideways across her path. Some leaned at haphazard angles, the needle-stripped branches propping them from the earth, while still others had been snapped right down the center, a lone tree-trunk monument to the upper half, wherever it might now be. She hadn't the slightest clue where she was, and hoped that by simply walking a straight line in the direction she had initially headed, she would eventually run into Brian. Though the way the explosive expanse of the cloud had knocked her from her feet and catapulted her into the air, there was no way of knowing whether he was even still al—

No! She couldn't think that...couldn't bear to allow that seed to take root in the back of her brain.

"Brian!" she rasped, immediately consumed by a coughing fury that stripped the last of the mucous from her trachea.

She had barely rounded the shore of the lake to the far side, still dreamily looking up into the star-streaked sky, when the first hint of the enormous cloud of dust swelled high up over the pointed tips of the pines ahead of her. Stopping, her heels pressing the shed shells of freshwater clams deeper into the mud with the stones, the entire bank littered with the black and white, chalky remains of the droppings of the geese who had taken to quick flight from their nests in the tall cattails at the first thunderous sound of the falling star, she was helpless but to watch it develop. That cloud of dust rose like a tower, swelling overhead until it nearly washed out the entire sky. It roared with the ancient voice of the pained earth god, churning and curling, until all at once, it drew the air toward it, forcing her to stumble forward, fallen needles flying into the air from the detritus, and then exploded outward.

There was no time to move. The gray cloud of dust blasted toward her like a great tsunami, tearing through the pines that fell like toothpicks before its might. Needles and bark hammered her as though fired from a shotgun, stabbing straight into her face and arms and chest, immediately summoning swelling globules of blood to the surface. She had no more than opened her mouth to scream, her arms only now rising to protect her face, when the cloud itself slammed into her.

It felt like a gigantic fist pounding right into her, knocking the wind from her suddenly compressed chest. She buckled forward, arms flailing at her sides, and then was tossed violently backward. Her mouth filled with a clogging wad of dust. Head snapping backward, unable to see anything but the congested cloud firing shredded bark and dirt past her face, she slammed into the lake and was driven all the way to the bottom, large, rounded stones driving up and into her ribs. Every last iota of her strength was consumed fighting the urge to open her mouth to tug for air. Everything was black. She couldn't even see the faint glimmer of moonlight overhead on the choppy waves that made that small lake look more like the break of an ocean on jagged rocks. The water urged her under; pulling her further and further out toward the middle, dragging her across the bottom, thick with slimy moss that grew upward from the muck in tree-like strands of phlegm. Large branches and chunks from trees that could have served as firewood sunk down toward the bottom, dropping toward her like mines laid from an Navy-PT.

The thought of one of those large wooden limbs pinning her to the bottom stirred the panic within. She kicked and clawed and propelled herself upward, the pressure in her chest growing so great that her stomach started to convulse, her gag reflex expelling what little air remained in her chest past her pursed lips. Even upon breaking the surface, the waves making her rise and fall, she couldn't inhale through the thick cloud that still pelted her with sand like she was caught in the middle of a dust devil. She forced herself to swim, not even semi-aware of just how far she had been cast out into the water. Appendages burning from oxygen deprivation, head throbbing, her pulse thumping so quickly it sounded like bongos in her ears, she swam. Waves slapped over her head, firing spouts of water straight up her nostrils and forcing her to close her eyes. Eternity passed before she reached the shore, and even then she had absolutely no way of knowing exactly which side of the lake she was on. All she could do was curl into fetal position there in the mud, and cough out the spittle-ridden water, the taste like swimming through sewage, and try to suck the little bit of air from the dust into her burning lungs.

Her thoughts were jumbled, discombobulated. There was only one thought that penetrated the fear and panic and chaos, the darkness and the frigid cold that caused her to shake as violently as a dog tossing water from its coat.

Brian.

"Brian!" she screamed again, her voice cracking and weak.

Shannen had to wrap her arms around her chest to try to control the heat loss. Her toes and fingers, surely as red a lobsters, no longer throbbed at the mercy of the pins and needles, but instead now felt fiery hot, like blazing coals embedded in her shoes. Stumbling forward, each time she slammed a foot or shin into one of the crumbled, fallen trunks, a bolt of pain flared straight up her legs and into her hips.

"Brian!" she screamed again through what felt like the last tattered strands of her windpipe, and then dropped her head and allowed the sobs to have their way. Shoulders shuddering, back bouncing, she hid her face in her hands and succumbed to the torment.

"...nen..." an almost spectral voice drifted in from the darkness. It was so small that it could easily have been a wisp of the wind, trailing the thundering advance of the cloud that now stormed down the foothills across the Front Range.

Slowly, she dropped her hands from her face, the dust immediately mixing with the fresh tears, and looked up into the nothingness of the gray.

"Shannen!" her name materialized from the void.

"Brian!" she screamed, lunging to her feet and stumbling into a trembling jog. "Brian!"

Branches snared at her sweater and tore through her cheeks, snagging tangles of hair, but for the moment she was oblivious. She just hurdled forward as fast as she could force herself to go, scurrying over the sappy, splintered remnants of the age-old trees that looked to have come under mortar fire.

"Brian!"

"Shannen!" he called back from somewhere that sounded close enough that she could have reached right out and touched him.

"Brian?" she called, stopping and twirling in a circle, staring frantically through the dense fog of dust that was only now beginning to settle on her shoulders like ash.

"Shan," he said, and her heart leapt at the warmth of his hand finding her own.

"Oh, Brian," she moaned and threw her arms around him, pulling herself right against his chest.

"Did you see that?" he asked, holding her with shaking, unsteady arms.

"I couldn't find you," she cried, her hands kneading the tattered edges of his shredded letter jacket. Even the shirt beneath had been ripped away from the bare, bleeding skin beneath. She squeezed him just to make sure that he was real.

"Careful!" he snapped, wincing. "I think I might have broken a rib or something."

"I'm just glad you're alive!"

"Me, too. For a minute there I thought, maybe...Are you okay?"

"Now that I've found you?" she whispered, the tears and dampness from her face soaking into the shoulder of his ruined jacket. "Yeah."

They stood there, embracing in the fog, barely even able to see each other for a long moment. Shannen didn't want to let go. Ever. All she wanted to do was to let him hold her in his arms until everything became all right again.

"Shan," he said, prying her from his chest and moving her back a step. "You've got to see this!"

"What?"

"Where it hit!"

"We'd better get you to a hospital."

"We'll go in a minute. Let me just show this to you first. It's amazing!"

"Brian—"

"Come on, Shan! This is a once in a lifetime opportunity. You absolutely will not believe this!"

Before she could raise voice to another futile protest, he yanked her by the hand and dragged her forward.

"It's just up here!"

"Bri—"

"Just let me show you and then I promise…we are so out of here."

She nodded, though mainly for her own benefit as she could barely make out his outline through the quickly settling dust a stride ahead of her. There wasn't even the hint of a star overhead, nor did the nearly full moon penetrate the dust above their heads. Startled and injured birds—though she couldn't determine what species merely by their voices—one by one called out over the wind, shrieking in wounded agony from the ground where they had been slapped from their nests in the treetops or driven down right from the air. Countless destroyed branches, leaves, and needles crunched beneath their tread, making it sound as though they were walking on a mat of cereal.

"Can you see it?" Brian asked, the excitement bounding from his voice.

"I can't see anything."

"Right over there," he said, pulling her in front of him and stretching his arm over her shoulder so she could follow the line of sight straight down his forearm and past his extended finger.

"What is it?"

"It hit the ground, Shan!"

"Let's get out of he—"

"Watch your step," he interrupted, guiding her forward with his arm now around her shoulder. "The ground drops off pretty quickly right here."

"Brian!" she chastened, and then shrieked when they walked right over the lip of a giant, smoldering chasm, forcing them nearly to run to maintain their balance on the crusted and hardened earth. There was no way of telling the size of the hole as the far side was still obscured by dust. But by the rate they were running and the length of the slope, she could tell that it was enormous.

She could see it out there, a good hundreds yards ahead if the size wasn't deceptive, fading in and out of the winds that still blew sheets of dust between them. An orange glow, like a branding iron cooling over an extinguished flame, rested at the bottom of the crater. Heat emanated in waves, drying her skin to cracking with each advancing step. It was smothering in her chest, as if they were standing on the edge of a forest fire. Both were forced to shield their eyes with their hands to keep them from baking into the skulls that were beginning to throb from the heat.

"I can't go any further," Shannen said, panting and forcing her feet to come to a skidding halt. The ground beneath her smoked, the impossible torridity melting up through the rubber soles of her shoes and scalding her feet. She hopped from one foot to the other like she was barefoot on a sun-blanched, sandy beach.

"God," Brian said, shifting his weight uncomfortably. "Can you see it?"

What she had erroneously assumed to be the smoldering meteorite that had slammed into the earth was in reality nothing more than a hole leading even further into the ground. Orange light glowed upward in streams like sunlight into a dark room, the dust hovering in the bright glare.

"Look at the size of that tunnel!" he exclaimed, his face washed in the same orange glow. His eyes were wide with excitement, and Shannen could only now see the cuts that covered his face like he had been sprinting through bramble. A line of blood, which looked black in the oddly fluorescent glare, trickled down his forehead from a significant gash along his hairline. He shook his head from side to side in disbelief, his mouth working its way slack. "You could drive a truck down that thing!"

"You need a doctor," she said gently, reaching toward his forehead, but he cringed before she even laid a finger atop it.

"Imagine if we could get a piece of that thing. We could sell it on eBay for a freaking fortune."

"Brian..."

"Wait here if you want...but I've got to go a little further."

"It's not safe," she said, but he was already skidding down the slope and away from her.

"Brian!"

"I'll just be a minute!"

Shannen stomped her feet in a huff, immediately regretting it. Her feet exploded with sharp pain. Wincing, she trapped the rising shriek of agony in her mouth, finally biting her lip to force it to subside.

"Idiot!" she grumbled beneath her breath and turned back to look toward where they had come from. The crest of the crater was so far up the hill now that it was invisible behind the cloak of dust.

A hissing sound rose above the wind: not the sound of a serpent rising to strike its defenseless prey, but more like the sound of gas escaping through a cracked pipe. But she paid it no mind, instead deciding she was going to walk right back up to the lip of the chasm and wait for her pigheaded boyfriend away from the scalding heat. She would hear the sound for the rest of her life, every morning upon waking, and waiting for her in the silence of solitude.

"Shan!" Brian screamed, his voice trilling. The high-pitched squeal drove the goosebumps right up her spine.

She turned quickly, her legs immediately sprinting down the slope.

Smoke funneled from that hole, stained that same orange, firing straight up into the sky like a tornado. The overwhelming stench of rotten eggs accosted her with such convulsive repulsion that she slapped a hand over her mouth and nose so quickly that it hurt. But neither the blasting smoke nor the smell mattered, for all she could focus on was Brian, down on his knees ahead of her with his head hanging to the ground.

"Brian!" she screamed, sliding down the coarsely blasted slope until she skidded onto her rear end right next to him.

His shoulders heaved violently and his back arched over and over like a frightened cat.

"Are you all righ—?" she started, but was cut off as his head quickly snapped forward and he fired a stream of vomit across his hands and the dirt.

She recoiled, but leaned back in, placing her hand on his forehead. The skin felt as though it was burning, preparing to blister.

"We've got to get you to a doctor!" she shouted, slipping her hands beneath his armpits and trying with all of her might to bring him to his feet, but only managing to lift his rear end a few inches.

"I don't..." he sputtered through a gurgling mouthful of vomit, "...feel so good."

He launched another stream of wet chunks from his open mouth, strands of pukish saliva dangling from his lips before snapping free.

"Come on, Bri. You've got to help me! I can't get you out of here on my own!"

Pressure filled her chest and she could feel her airway starting to constrict.

He burbled up one final mouthful of rancid bile, spraying it all over his legs, before choking it back with a sickening *gak*.

"Come on!" Shannen screamed, digging in with her heels and trying to drag him uphill.

"*Gurk! Grek!*" Brian sputtered, yanking his arms away from her to grapple with his throat.

Losing her balance, Shannen slipped down the gravel, crawling through his sloppy mess that she couldn't even begin to smell over the all-consuming scent of eggs.

"Help!" she screamed back over her shoulder, and then looked into her boyfriend's face. "Bri—"

His eyes were popping right out of their sockets, awash beneath a shimmering layer of crimson. The bloody slashes across his cheeks were widening right before her very eyes and spilling red rivulets over his chin and onto the collar of his shirt. Curled fingers clawed at his throat, peeling back the skin like the rind of an orange to expose the draining juices beneath.

"My God," she gasped, immediately wrapping her arms around his chest and straining to force him to rise.

"Shan—" he blurted, slopping a mouthful of blood onto the top of her head. It drained warmly over her scalp, sliding down her forehead and into her brows, tickling her ears and slithering down her neck.

"It's going to be all right," she whimpered to him, her heart beating so fast it caused her words to tremble. "I'll get you out of here, Brian! Don't worry. You're going to be all right."

The muscles in her back and legs protested verily, the tendons threatening to snap, but she goaded him upward, despite the searing pain and the cramping in her chest that felt as though someone had slipped a hand through her ribcage and was squeezing her lungs.

"You're going to make it. You'll see! We'll get you to a doctor and then everything will be fine."

Shannen dragged Brian over the crusted lip of the crater, losing her balance and tackling him to the smoldering turf.

The last of the stilled air trapped in his chest slipped past his lips with a groan, her weight atop him evacuating the contents of his bowels into his pants with a slurp.

"Brian?" she moaned, shuffling quickly off of him and placing her ear right over his mouth. No breath sounds filtered into her ear canal. No warm respiration tousled the fine hairs.

She rose to all fours and looked into his face.

An even coating of black blood covered the entirety of his features, running freely back through his sideburns and puddling in his ears. His own fingers had carved thick lacerations into his neck, gouging so deep as to clip the jugular, which spurted like a pinprick in a hose from the right side of his Adam's apple.

"Brian?" she whimpered, reaching out with a trembling hand to place her first two fingers on his carotid.

Nothing.

"Brian!" she screamed into his face, that pumping fountain of warmth spraying her jaw and forcing her to quickly bat her eyelids. She grabbed him by either side of the face and raised his head from the ground, searching what remained of his eyes for some sign of life: a spark, a glimmer, even a wink to let her know that this had all been some kind of fiendish prank.

A yellow squiggle, what looked like some sort of worm, wriggled through the sheen of blood, flagellating across his bare eyeball.

"No!" she screamed, dropping his head to the ground in shock.

She jammed her finger right into his eye to try to scrape that worm off of him with her fingernail, but it quickly propelled itself right into the corner of his eye and disappeared beneath the fold of skin.

"Come on, Brian! Get up! You have to get up!"

But he just lie there, still, his fingers frozen in the claws that had rent his own neck wide.

"I love you! You have to help me! Damn it! Get up!"

She tugged at his hands but only succeeded in bringing his back from the charred, wild grasses before depositing him right back into place with a thump.

"Come on!" she whined, plopping down onto the ground in front of him, her head dropping to her chest. "Come on…"

Sniffing, lips writhing, she forced herself to rise again. Walking almost sleepily behind Brian, she leaned over and grabbed his wrists, and began the arduous task of dragging him back to the car.

II

"Up and at'em, all you lazy bastards. It's like a friggin' free laser show up there! And I tell you what: there ain't nothing that goes better with lasers than Metallica. So all you boys and girls crank up the stereo and look up at the sky as those meteors come falling faster. Obey your master, me: the one and only Trick Turner. Master of Puppets, Mother Hubbards!" he said, and then flipped the toggle that cued the tune and silenced his mike.

Trick Turner, born Richard Martin Turner, rolled the chair

backward, rested his head atop the high leather back, and stared up into the ceiling. The small, irregularly spaced holes in the sound-damping ceiling tiles faded in and out like when he tried to stare at the freckles on the tip of his nose when he was a kid. Back then, while zoned out, the world nothing more than a nondescript rift of euphoria, he fancied himself able to reach deep into the magnificent and awed annals of time and glean from it the hidden secrets of life.

The freckles were gone now, but the way those little dots on the ceiling drifted in and out of focus, the music vanishing from his perception, he found himself once more swimming in vertigo. There were no mystical lessons to be learned this time, no delusional logic to try to decipher, but he was given the answer to the most important question of all. It wasn't until this very moment, this one unprecedented glimpse into the cosmic tapestry of life, that he finally understood.

This wasn't what he wanted for his life any more.

As a teenager, Rock n' Roll had been life. Jamming on the guitar all night, partying with his buddies, chasing girls, drinking, drugging, and playing the soundtrack to his life as high as the damned stereo would let him. Everything had been about having a good time, taking life on his own terms. But it just wasn't that way anymore. Here he was… about to roll over the ol' odometer to thirty, and still pretending he was still the same eighteen year old punk who convinced a half dozen girls he was a close personal friend of Jon Bon Jovi's and that he was charged with the cumbersome burden of helping to cast a budding starlet for his next video. Truth be told…he now lived in a one-bedroom apartment with a guitar and an iguana.

All of his old buddies were married off in the suburbs, raising kids and planting gardens, working in offices with computers and responsibility. None of them even tried to keep in touch anymore. Why would they? There no longer was any shared ground between them, nothing to talk about but the old days, which most of them had long since filed away in some hidden cabinet where their wives couldn't find them. At first he had mocked them all ("Shackled to the system," he had joked), but it wasn't until the ceiling dots all aligned and opened his feelings up that he realized in that moment of universal understanding that he wanted what they had. More than anything, he wanted what they had.

Rock n' Roll wasn't the same anymore.

All of the bands he had grown up on had faded into obscurity, their message dragged along with them. There had been a day when guys took up the guitar to get chicks and party, to live like a rock star. Man, bands like Kiss and Poison, Guns n' Roses and Skid Row, they had it made. They lived it hard and fast, sparing no expense and leaving no blonde unturned. It was decadence at its finest, pure poetry in art. But all of that disappeared one fall day when a whining little heroine junkie released a song about the scent of his girlfriend's pits with their now defunct deodorant. Melancholy became the order of the day. Depression was en vogue. You were nobody if you weren't on lithium, and if you washed your hair or didn't threaten to kill yourself at least three times a day in your personal journal, they took away your flannel. Rock n' Roll turned into Piss n' Moan. But even that was better than it was today.

Corporate rock reigned supreme. Every song was identical to the next: same three chords, just change the arrangement. There was a formula for making money, and damned if those record execs weren't going to reach right down your throat to take it. There was the debut album and the sequel, though the sound had already grown tired and there would be no third. He hadn't heard a guitar solo on a new release since...God, probably since '93. And even the bands that had endured through those self-deprecating "grunge years," no longer worshipped the spirit of the beast, but rather became addicted to the making of money.

Here again, a single day from turning thirty (two hours and the change, anyway), and bickering with a self-righteous station manager over a raise from thirty-three grand a year to thirty-five after close to a decade of service. They hadn't even had to pay him a penny for that first year as an intern. Home was where the ants lived under the sink and the ring around the toilet was the only one any girlfriend of his would get even remotely close to, and even that sometimes scared them to panicked flight. There was nothing but cheap beer in the fridge, and, believe it or not, his mother had actually been right in her assertion that Cheetos couldn't be considered a staple food. The most gratifying conversations he now held were with his iguana, which he had never even bothered to name.

The time had come.

Batting his eyes back into focus, he sat upright in the chair and laced his fingers in the center of his lap. He stared straight ahead into the soundproof glass mirror which allowed them to see in from the outside, but prevented the on-air talent from becoming distracted by the Looky Loo's. Gray hairs spotted his heavy stubble, and he could even see crow's feet forming beside his once sparkling hazel eyes. His long brown hair was tucked behind his ears, hanging every bit as flaccidly as it had as a greasy teenager. He was a grown man sitting alone in a room, still wearing a tour shirt he bought when he was fifteen years old, despite the fraying neck from which chest hairs now stuck out of like weeds. But seeing himself now…actually seeing himself, he couldn't help but smile. And laugh.

Hell, they were probably watching him from the other side of the glass paying off whoever won the bet as to when he would snap. But it didn't matter now. It didn't matter at all. His future wasn't in this aquarium. It was somewhere else, somewhere out there, just waiting for him to find it. There was a classic Mustang out there in the parking lot with an old cassette deck and a mess of tapes scattered across the floorboard just waiting for him to come out and take the reigns.

Yes, sir. Tonight would be the last night on the air for the mighty Trick Turner. And he was going to go out in style.

He leaned forward and flipped on his microphone, interrupting the last twenty seconds of the song, but he didn't care.

"Listen up all you ugly mugs out there," he said, grabbing hold of the microphone to really belt out his swan song. "This is the state of the music address, so you all better pay attention. I wanna talk to you now about money. After all, that's what music's about, right? Moneymoneymoneymuuuhh-nay! This is big business. We're talking tobacco-type moulah here."

He cast a glance back over his shoulder to his producer in the adjacent booth. Jerry Morgan, who wouldn't have known a good time if it gnawed on his ankle, sat there, bemused as ever, checking his stocks in the newspaper with his wingtips on the console. He was the kind of guy who wore a tie to work and actually looked forward to the opportunity to line up next to the bosses at the urinal to try to sell himself as management in that thirty second window. But thank heavens for small favors. Tonight, the office snitch was about as oblivious to what Trick was about to do as to the fact that he would be passed over for the next promotion by the morning girl, whose sole qualifications generally were poised to—oops!—fall right out of her top.

"Time to trump the Metallica cause. I say bravo to them in their war against Napster! They've earned every penny of the thirty-some-million each must have in their bank accounts. After paying seventy-five bucks a seat for their last show a couple of months ago, I can understand how they must be feeling the recession, as well. Heaven forbid some teenager download a song and not forward them their thirty pieces of silver. What we need to do is make it so that these kids have absolutely no access to the music unless they personally hand the boys in black a wad of cash. Take the songs off the radio! How easy would it be to just press record on a tape deck? Pull the videos, or produce them with record-lock technology or something. Only tour.

It's even better than selling a twelve dollar disc that they only get a percentage of, right?

"And why stop there? I think authors should be picketing libraries. Why should they be forced to let countless thousands of people read their material without compensation, huh? They should print the books in the old green and red 3-D, that way, you can't even read them without buying the special glasses directly from the author for thirty-five bucks that are made of sugar and dissolve after three hours in the open air. I tell you, guys like Picasso and Monet should be standing in front of their paintings in museums with curtains covering their works, and only yank them back for a few seconds when the patron's credit card clears the bank.

"And athletes? I don't even know how they can play for the chicken scratch the clubs feed them these days. If I were a wide receiver, I'd refuse to catch the ball unless the quarterback rubber-banded a stack of bills to it in the huddle. Pucks should be made of solid gold, and the goalie gets to keep what he saves, but the shooters can take what they make. And basketball players should be paid, not just per basket or dunk, but per tattoo.

"So this is it for me, kiddies. It's the end of the line for your old pal Trick, my farewell to thee. But you know I couldn't disappear up the chimney without leaving a gift. So here goes...I want each and every one of you, no matter where you are or what you're doing, to scurry off and grab your tape recorders. Throw in a blank cassette and push record now. Ready? 'Cause what I'm going to do right now is play the whole new Metallica disc uninterrupted, but we're going to do it the legal way, so what I want each of you to do is get thirty nickels and put them in the mail to Metallica. Not twenty-nine, not thirty-one. It's only a dollar fifty plus postage for those of you who're thinking you're going to need a second after-school job to pay for it. Now make me that promise, and wish me luck.

"Good ni—" The lights snapped off in the booth, along with them the power, then immediately resumed with a whir. "Looks like they're going to start to smoke me out here in a minute," he chuckled, looking again to his old buddy Jerry reading the paper with his finger, still oblivious to his last tango. "Good night to all of you out there who keep the torch burning. Don't you dare let that flame burn out while I'm gone."

The lights extinguished again, the darkness lingering only long enough for the emergency generator to kick in. No more had the red light above the metal box on the wall lighted, then the whole building began to shake.

Trick turned to Jerry, who by now had set his paper aside and was looking back with the same puzzled expression.

Trick pressed the button on the console that connected him to the control booth.

"What was that?"

Jerry just shrugged and slowly rose to his feet, chewing nervously on his lower lip.

Trick followed suit, making sure to start the disc he had promised his fans, and walked to the door that connected the two booths. He opened it and stepped inside.

"You felt that didn't you?"

"Yeah," Jerry said. "How could I not? The whole floor seemed to drop right out from under me."

"Couldn't have been an earthquake. Not here in Denver."

"I've heard of them having small ones up in the mountains."

"But not down here."

"You don't suppose someone crashed a plane into the building, do you?"

"Yeah, Jer. I'm sure the Qwest building ranks really high on the terrorist agenda, right between Starbuck's and Sal's Laundromat."

"Then what do you think it was, genius?"

"I don't know, but I'd guess the odds of us figuring it out in this room are pretty slim."

Trick threw open the door leading back into the hallway and recoiled at the cloud of dust that exploded into the room.

"Christ!" he gasped, tugging his shirt over his mouth and nose and holding it there with his hand. "What the hell?"

He eased out into the hallway with Jerry at his heels, guided down the long passage by the red glow of the emergency lights bracketed to the walls. The thick cloud that clogged the artery made each of those lights look like a glowing ball of crimson gas that penetrated the dust no better than an eighteenth-century streetlamp in a London fog. Eyes watering, coughing dryly into his hand, he crept down the hallway, passing one unseen door after another until he thought for sure he must have made it into the lobby.

Jerry's hand pressed against the small of Trick's back, goading him forward. What sounded like thunder rolled outside, following the breeze through the opened windows.

"Hey!" Trick shouted, trying to fan the dust from in front of his face with his free hand. "Anybody there?"

There was no answer from the cloudy room, the dust now swirling at the whim of the wind.

"What happened here?" Jerry mumbled, his voice muted by whatever he had chosen to cover his face with.

"Come on, Tina!" he shouted again. "I know you're in here somewhere, polishing those nails of yours."

"We should get out of here."

"Really? Ya think?"

"Fine then, smartass!" Jerry barked. "You're on your own!"

Trick felt the pressure from the hand disappear on his back, but never saw Jerry pass through the choking dust.

He continued forward, his next step bringing with it the sound of shattered glass crunching beneath his tread. Slowly, he knelt and brushed the ground with his fingertips, immediately jerking his hands back. A droplet of blood swelled to the surface on his index finger.

"Damn!" he snapped, pressing the wildly painful tip into the palm of his hand.

Another couple of steps further and he could feel the unabated wind blasting into is face. Unfurling his left hand, he reached forward and found the edges of the windowpane, shattered glass rimming the seal, and nearly threw himself backward. The walls of the lobby were essentially nothing but glass from floor to ceiling, and he could easily have taken another pair of steps forward and walked right out of the building and fallen sixteen stories to the street below. But that glass was supposed to be shatterproof, wasn't it? How many times had they thrown a shoulder into those windows in jest, played butt-ball against them over the night shift?

"Tina!" he shouted again, whirling to find the front desk. Since he was standing by the windows, then that would make the desk directly behind him on the other side of the pane of etched glass that separated the waiting area from the main office. Walking a straight line, holding his shirt between his teeth and feeling with both arms in front of him so he didn't walk straight through that pane of glass, he stepped over one of the potted palms that lie on the floor and nearly tripped. There was so much glass beneath his feet that he felt as though he was walking on a crunching carpet of dead insects, just waiting for a sharp shard to lance through his Chuck Taylor's and sting him.

His hand drove right into some sort of warm sloppy mess a split-second before his hips rammed into the back of a chair.

"Tina?"

Sticky hair tangled around his fingers, peeling right loose with it when he quickly brought it back to his chest and wiped it up and down his shirt in disgust.

"Tina?" he asked one last time in a feeble little voice, but he already knew the answer.

He reached out again, lower this time, following the rise of the chair, over the upholstered backrest, and to the body seated within. Tracing the line of the back, he rode it up over the strap of a bra beneath the silky-feeling dress, and to the exposed skin above. Warm fluids greeted his probing fingertips, followed quickly by their origin. Several large chunks of glass protruded from her neck and shoulders, which was surely the reason that the back of her head had been carved to a squishy mess.

"God!" he gasped, jerking backward and tripping over that same damned potted palm, only this time, losing his balance entirely and landing squarely on his rear.

He screamed as the glass made short work of his jeans and stabbed into his cheeks, knifing right through the palms he had thrown behind him to try to catch himself.

"Jerry," he called, his voice tremulous and reticent with the tears that squirted from the corners of his eyes.

Eyes pinched tightly, teeth grinding; he brought his trembling hands into his lap. He couldn't seem to breathe, each shallow attempt bringing him to the verge of hyperventilation. Shaking so furiously with the pain that he could barely make his fingers function, he gingerly pried the glass from first his left palm, and then his right, dropping the bloody shrapnel one by one to the ground.

"Jerry!" he screamed again, his voice faltering to a shrill wail.

The only response was a throng of retching from somewhere across the room, a gut-wrenching, violently convulsive heaving sound.

"God," Jerry's voice sputtered from somewhere in the cloud. "Help me."

Cringing in pain, pressing his bleeding palms together in front of him to keep from planting them back on the ground for leverage, Trick eased to his feet and limped forward. He brushed at the glass embedded in his posterior with those palsied hands, knocking free whatever he could despite his own whining protests.

"Where are you?" he called, nipping a chunk from his lip in an attempt to bite back the agony.

The only response was more coughing trailing off into a gurgling sound like air bubbles rising to the surface in the water cooler.

"Jerry?"

Shuffling forward, hands wrapped in his shirt to try to slow the bleeding, Trick felt the air in his lungs growing heavy, like the oxygen was mutating to mercury and settling at the bottom of those thin sacs, trying to tear free through the bottom.

"*Kack!*" Jerry choked from just beneath him.

Quickly, Trick lowered himself to his haunches and reached toward the source of the sound. Jerry's face drifted in from the dust briefly before slipping right back out of sight, but that was all that Trick needed to see. Jerry's face was coated with a black mess of blood made viscous by dust, his mouth agape, lips peeled awfully back from his teeth. His tongue hung from his mouth as he desperately tried to clear his own airway to attempt to choke down a single swallow of air. The veins and tendons on his neck stood out like electrical cables beneath a painter's tarp, and he was tearing at them with his own fingernails, summoning fresh blood to the surface in flowing rivers.

"Somebody help!" Trick screamed, lunging forward to try to peel the man's hands from his neck before he decapitated himself.

"Somebody!"

III

The gray cloud rose over the tops of the elms like a giant thunderhead, drawing with it the screaming wind. His bangs slammed at his forehead, scratching it like straw. Mrs. Shelton screamed from his left, a roaring sound like a jet engine swallowing her cries.

Jason's fingers were wrapped so tightly around the rail that he couldn't wrench them free any more than he could force his eyes to tear themselves from the cloud that bore down on them like a child's heel preparing to stamp a handful of ants. Trees were ripped from the ground by their roots and tossed before the thundering cloud, a macabre showcase of the devastation and fury of nature's wrath. He screamed somewhere in his mind, sand and pebbles blasting his face with such ferocity that he was forced to close his eyes and mouth.

"Get inside!" Emil Carvasso shouted from his right, tugging on Jason's arm. His bathrobe blowing behind him like a cape, he pried Jason's fingers from the rail.

The roar of thunder grew so loud that the balcony started to rumble beneath their feet. Fractured chips of concrete freed themselves from the bolts that secured the railing, setting it to wobbling before sending the whole long iron works clattering to the sparse, yellowed grass of the courtyard below.

Jason turned; heavy with the weight of Carvasso's hand tightly gripping his arm. He focused on his own doorway, mere feet in front of him, suddenly well aware of the cracks forming along the seal where the patio met the building, and the unstable shaking of the cement under his feet.

The two had no more than reached the doorway when the cloud slammed into them from behind, throwing them inside hard enough to clear the living room. Jason never heard the shattering glass over the howl of the wind. Instinct closed his eyes in preparation for impact, forcing him to hold his breath.

His shoulder slammed into the doorway that separated the living room from the kitchen, his momentum sending him sprawling across the linoleum and beneath the kitchen table, knocking one of the legs off and toppling it to the floor behind him. With a display of sparks and lights before his closed eyes, his head bounced off of the back wall before coming to rest with a thud on the floor.

The wind tore through the apartment, smashing through the kitchen window and scattering it across the patchy lawn behind. It sounded like a wind tunnel, swooshing and wailing through the small apartment like a malevolent banshee, dragging everything on the counters from papers and utensils to the toaster and the microwave to the floor, where they swirled in shattered bits, trapped in an unseen tornado.

The taste of copper drained from Jason's sinuses into his mouth, coating his tongue. Blood trickled in parallel lines from his nostrils, darkening with the immediately congealing dirt.

Water flowed in along the floor, the rapidly expanding saline pool sapping right into his clothing and stinging the abrasions on his face. He could only imagine his fish flopping around atop the substrate, gasping for air in that jaggedly shattered glass rectangle, the coral polyps poking their feather-ringed mouths out of their holes one final time before jerking right back into their cactus-shaped catacombs to die in the open air.

His head felt as though someone had driven an ax right down the center, and for the life of him he couldn't force his eyes to focus, instead, dreamily drifting in and out of the haze in their own dilated fugue. He forced himself to all fours, his shoulder exploding with a sharp pain that nearly dropped him right back onto his face in the half-inch of saltwater draining from the vinyl into the apartment below via the heat duct built into the floor. Hair slapped to his face, dragging stinging water into his eyes and rinsing the mud and blood over his lips where he gummily tried to clear them before just dragging his mouth across the back of his arm.

He tried to stand, rising up above the top of the table before the wind smacked him up against the rear wall of the kitchen and dropped him right back onto the floor with a splash. Shaking his head to rattle the cobwebs that seemed to be knitting their way right down into the convolutions in his brain, Jason again forced himself to his feet, this time prepared for the buffeting of the wind. Clinging to the top of the table, he eased his way around it and out from being directly in front of the doorway, the wind dying down the closer he got to the stove. Dirt pinged around in the aluminum ductwork, falling down through the grate from the oven hood and forming a small pile between the four coiled burners. The drawers beneath the counter had rattled themselves open a good couple of inches. He yanked them back one by one, listening to the clattering sound of the contents, gingerly running his hands through silverware, through stacks of expired coupons and catalogs from every marine supply house known to man, until finally he found what he was looking for.

Grasping it firmly in his left hand, even the negligible weight of the thing more than his right shoulder could bear, he flipped the switch forward and a dim glow hovered before him in the swirling dust like a firefly. Jason brought the lens to his face, shining the flashlight into his eyes to make sure that the bulb was indeed working and that it was just that incapable of penetrating the cloud that had settled there in his apartment. He lowered it back to the floor, vague hints of reflected light rising back up to him from the brine. With a nervous sigh, he licked the crusting dust from his lips and apologized to the tatter of flesh hanging from his cheek with his tongue, finally coaxing his legs to motion and slapping across the puddled floor to the entryway.

Flashing the light from side to side, the beam able to peel back just a few feet of the fog before dissipating into a whitish glow of nothingness, he slowly stepped from the linoleum to the carpet, the wet pile splashing beneath his already waterlogged shoes. Glinting shards of light lined the wall to the left, like the glistening teeth of a rabid wolf, water still slowly sliding between them and dripping to the floor. Tank after tank, he followed them right down the wall, praying that even one had made it, repulsed by the sickening crunch of the hard corals he had worked so hard to propagate disintegrating beneath his heel, the squash of the tangs he had bred and raised from fry popping under his weight.

He whirled in disgust, walking back past the doorway to the kitchen, toward the other side of the living room, where the tanks, he hoped, might have fared better.

The wind, though it had tapered substantially, still knocked the doorknob back and forth against the wall behind, blowing the curtains inward with flagging, snapping sounds from the disintegrated front window, dragging the hovering dust inward to meld with the water.

He had to focus on the diffuse ray of light to keep from stumbling right into one of the broken tanks and disemboweling himself, as they were all right about waist level. Shuffling forward, sliding his feet through the piles of broken glass and organic detritus rather than setting them atop it to allow a stray shard to slice right through the sole of his foot, he passed the first tank with a disheartened shake of his head. He knew full well that those hundreds of miniature fragments he had been raising (all small polyp stony corals, with a dozen different color variations of Staghorn Acroporas and finger leathers from turquoise to pink and peach), half-inch frags clipped right from his very own display pieces and then cultured to close to four inches tall, were all dead the moment they met with the air.

"Damn it!" Jason griped, shaking his head just a little too hard and having to grab it as a wave of pain rose up from his neck and over the top of his skull.

Just his luck, each of those corals would have pulled in close to sixty bucks each by themselves, not to mention that they were his first generation of enhanced polyps capable of not only photosynthesizing in low light, but able to withstand normally toxic ammonia and nitrite levels. He had engineered them himself by promoting the growth and replication of but a few exceptional individual polyps, and re-colonized the whole coral with them. They were disease resistant, viable in a wider range of pH and salinity than any wild coral, and capable of growing at close to four times the rate of their ocean bound brethren. This was his work, his life, his dream; the catacomb chambers of those little stalagmites already filling with oxygen and beginning to disintegrate from the inside out.

Jason brushed the tears from his eyes with his left forearm, sniffing back the dejection and disgust, and started forward again, only to slam right into something fleshy and forgiving. It made a groaning sound: that same unforgettable, repulsive gas escaping from a corpse sound he had heard so many times during his hospital tenure, standing over the gurney with that helpless feeling of being unable to save his patient. Slowly, it slipped from the tank to the tune of tearing terrycloth, and sloughed to the floor.

Placing a hand atop the fully saturated bathrobe and following it over the slope of the shoulder to the front of the neck to test the strength of the pulse in the carotid, his probing fingertips found their way right inside of the warm laceration that opened his neck wide like the mouth of a Muppet. His middle finger traced the rim of the cleanly opened trachea, filled with a foaming mess of salty bubbles, and his heart dropped from his chest into his stomach with that same acidic splash he remembered all too well.

There was no point in screaming or sprinting to the phone to call for help. Not only had his windpipe been slashed, forcing him to drink the water from the rapidly draining tank right into his lungs, but also both matching arteries had been irreparably severed.

"Thank you," he whispered, clenching his features against the swell of tears and emotion, and placed the flashlight in the standing water long enough to drag his palms down the man's jaggedly cut forehead to close his wide eyes. "Thank you for saving my life."

And with that, he rose to his feet and made his way along the breeze, following it straight through the living room and out onto the front balcony.

To the right, the cement had snapped free, dropping eight feet to the walkway below, exposing long, rusted rebar that bowed downward from the crumbling edge. The whole balcony grumbled beneath his weight, leaning a couple inches further from the building. He flashed the light across the now slanting cement. Sand and dirt still clattered against the brick face of the building at the will of the dying wind, but far slower now, petering to nothing more substantive that the faint patter of drizzle.

As for the fish, the coral…there was nothing he could do for them now. But the others…those who had been lining the railing when he had, in retrospect, foolishly walked out through his front door to see what had caused the explosion and the trembling floor… them he could potentially help. He had been a doctor after all, right?

"Hello?" he called, his voice echoing in the hollow courtyard.

His arcing light ticked back and forth across the floor, guiding his feet.

"Does anyone need medical attention?" he shouted, but there was nothing but the silence beneath the fading wind to answer.

The entire area reeked as though someone had knocked over a dumpster filled to capacity with eggs that no children had found on Easter, now close to three months prior. Foul aromas rising from those rusting, vile, bacteria breeding metal constructs was nothing unusual, as there was an almost constant stench emanating from it like some hobo had crawled in there to die. But this smell was extraordinarily intense, bringing back memories of the multitudes of chemistry labs he had endured from high school all the way through med school. Burning metallic sulfur. That was it. Not eggs, but a chemical reaction.

The light flashed across something that reflected back and he stopped dead in his tracks.

It was glossy and red, a crescent glimmer that he recognized as easily as he could identify that plump little toe it was attached to. He guided the light up from the foot and over the invisible ankle, and up the stubbley leg to the dimpling, adipose swell of the knee. A fuzzy pink robe crossed her thigh, the matching sash flopping across her exposed stomach. There was a single furry slipper peeking out from beneath her rear.

"Mrs. Shelton?" Jason asked. "Can you hear me?"

There was no response at all as he eased around her side and followed her arm to her wrist, her hand already tightening with rigor mortis about her throat. He felt the pulse for insurance, knowing full well by the tight tendons in her wrist and the force it had taken to make the humerus roll in the socket, she had already expired. Her skin was still warm, but there wasn't even the faintest hint of anything flowing through her veins.

Dropping the arm back to her chest, he caught a glimpse of her fingers. They were covered in blood, trailing down around the wrist he had just been holding.

"What the—?" he started, raising the flashlight up her neck and to her face, and then quickly had to turn and clap his hand over his mouth.

Her entire neck had been scratched to hell like she had been caught in some sort of mortal struggle with a mountain lion. Now he had seen just about everything during his tenure as a physician, things that would make even the most seasoned attending physician make a quick dash down the hallway to the bathroom. But this...this was like nothing he had ever seen.

Mrs. Shelton, whose name he only knew because she had taped it to their little black mail slot with one of those label guns, had ripped her own cheeks from the corners of her mouth all the way back to just beneath her ears. Tatters of curling flesh like pork rinds bled sloppily down onto her exposed teeth, her jaw forced impossibly wide. She must have somehow popped the whole mandible out of joint, swelling tongue hanging lazily from it like a dog claimed mid-pant. Her eyes were bathed in crimson, opened so wide that it looked as though the eyeballs were merely sitting atop the sockets like red golf balls on tees.

It took but another flash from the light in his hand to see Mr. Shelton crumpled against the building in his doorway, yellowed t-shirt soaked in the blood that poured directly down from the folds in the man's neck. His pallor was unmistakable, even beneath the veil of his own fluids, and his bowels had already evacuated themselves through his light blue boxers and squished through the hole around his engorged thigh.

Jason walked quickly toward the staircase, passing a pair of closed doors, and crept carefully down the wobbling iron stairs that appeared capable of pulling down what remained of the balcony.

He looked out to the street where he couldn't see the head or taillights of a single car passing on the deserted street. No one called for help. There wasn't a single cough from someone trying to force the masses of dust from their lungs—like he doubled over quickly to do—or crying to be freed from beneath fallen rubble. Not a single barking dog ripped the night in panicked fright.

Only the droning of car alarms wailed in the distance.

His face crumpled into a knot of concern.

"No sirens," he mused, working his way to the middle of the courtyard to flash the light across the fronts of the apartments. "Where are all the sirens?"

There should have been cop cars racing down just about every street, ambulances deployed en masse, fire trucks screaming off into the night.

But there was nothing.

"Hello?" Jason railed at the top of his lungs, his voice reflecting back from the brick structure.

Just the car alarms, unnervingly blaring in dissonant odds to one another.

"Is anybody there?" he screamed, abandoning the courtyard and running past the building to the street.

He stumbled through the weed-tangled grass and to the sidewalk, his footsteps clapping like gunfire. Standing there beneath the ancient elms, the skeletal arms robbed of the leaves that now filled the gutters well past capacity and blew down the center of the street, broken limbs littering the front lawns like a bone yard, trunks standing in broken, headstone-like reverence to their former majesty—standing there, Jason shouted with all of his might until his throat parched and prepared to crack.

"Hello!"

The crumbling, leaf-covered sidewalks were desolate to either side. He could discern but the faint halo of a solar-charged streetlamp, illuminating the disturbing outline of the car beneath it, standing on its side. Water sprayed from a smashed hydrant, the geyser spewing up into the air to thicken with dust and clog in the grates that couldn't accommodate the masses of organic material clogging them, forcing the water to stream out into the middle of the road.

"Hello!"

No curious onlookers funneled out onto the porches of those old houses across the street, the glass from the shattered windows sparkling on the lawn like fool's gold.

"Is anybody there!" he screamed, his voice faltering to a falsetto.

There was a body lying face down on the cement stairs leading up to the porch of one of the turn of the century houses. Still. Unmoving.

"Anybody!" he screamed again, his throat raw and caked with dust, stumbling out into the middle of the street, and collapsing to his knees. His arms flopped palm up on the wet asphalt, his chin dropping to his chest.

"Somebody," he whispered, tears pouring from his eyes and dripping from the tip of his nose.

"Help me…"

IV

Cindy craned her neck back and screamed with every ounce of her humanity, the dust blasting through her hair. The chandelier on the ceiling above the dining room table just before her swung upward with such force that it shattered against the ceiling into crystal shards, the light bulbs exploding into a fine mist of glass to be embedded in the wall beyond. Lamps were tossed from the end tables and smashed into ceramic bits before the tables themselves were ripped from the carpet and bashed against the drywall. Leaves followed the dust through the shattered panes, swirling about the center of the living room, trapped in an updraft.

Nancy groaned beneath Cindy, finally able to recapture the breath that had been knocked from her chest, but unable to inhale anything more substantive than a gritty mouthful of dust and crunchy dirt. She clung tightly to Tim against her, holding him so fiercely that he cried from the pressure on his back more than the fright.

"Mommy!"

She could barely make out Tim's frantic cries beneath the roar of the turbine engine that had apparently backed right up to the front of their house and blasted its ferocious wrath toward them, his cries only merging with Cindy's agonized wails.

"Are you all right?" Nancy tried to call over the clamor. The drawing of every single breath felt like she was trying to fill her lungs through one of those little red straws they used to stir coffee at work. Her back was a torturous crumple; her cranium swelling with a wave of pain from bouncing her head so roughly from the carpet. It was all she could do to maneuver her right hand into Tim's armpit to ensure that she could still feel his pulse.

He was shaking so violently, tears sapping onto the side of her face and running into her ear, his warm breath rapidly heating the nook of her neck. But it was Cindy's screams that positively mortified her, filled with such tremendous urgency and pain, her shrill cries trilling through a mouthful of whatever warm fluid snapped free from where it dangled from her chin and slopped down onto Nancy and Tim.

"Somebody!" Nancy screamed. "Help!"

But if no one had heard Cindy's fantastically pained screams, there was no way they could have heard Nancy in that voice so soft she could barely even hear it herself.

"Hold on, kiddo," she whispered into Tim's ear, more for her own benefit than his.

Holding him to her, she rolled her shoulders to the right, pivoting at the hip just enough to free their torsos from beneath Cindy, who collapsed immediately to the carpet where they had been, making the removal of their legs relatively simple.

"Stay right here!" Nancy barked through the constant thunder, pressing Tim into a sitting position in the doorway leading to the kitchen. "I'll be right back! I promise!"

He just nodded, his thumb finding its way into his mouth. A small laceration brought a couple of swelling droplets of blood to the surface of the wound along the side of his head just behind the temple, but outside of that he appeared none the worse for wear.

Forcing herself to tear her eyes from her son, she crawled quickly over to Cindy, who just looked up at her with tear-drenched, pinched eyes, her lips curled downward to connect her by strands of saliva to the floor. Her face was bright red, save for the streaks of black where the dust clogged the tears like mascara draining over her cheekbones. The formerly white sweatshirt was muted gray, with black splotches like sand dollars widening in overlapping polka dotted patterns. Powdered with a fine layer of dust, and standing anywhere from an inch to close to six inches from the tattered cotton blend, were a good dozen sharpened shards of glass, running from her upper buttocks all the way up to her shoulders. In that frightened moment, Nancy could only think of Tim's little dinosaur encyclopedia and his very favorite, the Stegosaurus.

"Cindy!" Nancy leaned over and shouted directly into her sister's ear canal. "Can you hear me?"

Cindy just nodded, dragging her face up and down along the carpet, staining the cream color with a slop of mud and bloodied fluid.

"I'm going to get the First Aid kit! You just hang tight, and I'll be right back to help you! All right?"

She hesitated to wait for a response, lunging to her feet at the first sign of another nod. With the thickened cloud of dust she could barely see further ahead than her fingertips, waving in front of her to keep her from running straight into a wall. And to make matters even more difficult, the furious wind had rearranged the furniture. The coffee table lie on its back against the couch with all four legs standing straight up in the air like a dog knocked by traffic to the side of the road. The loveseat had been turned ninety degrees so that it was now in the center of the room where there had formerly been a walkway around the coffee table. The entire entertainment center at the back of the room lie face down on the floor, the plastic casings of the VCR and surround sound system pounded into oblivion amidst the wooden shrapnel of the center itself.

The hallway toward the bedrooms appeared as nothing more than a vague darkness to the left in her vision.

The toilet hummed, having been lifted an eighth of an inch from its seal and allowing a puddle of water to creep out along the linoleum from beneath. So long as she followed that sound she would be able to find the door to the bathroom, and from there, the medicine cabinet above the sink.

Feeling along the wall, her fingers caught the trim to the door and she hurried inside. Everything in the formerly sparkling white room was coated with a layer of settling dust, from the opaque glass sliding doors of the tub to the white and gray, marble-mimic Formica of the sink. The mirrored medicine cabinet had been torn from the wall and scattered across the floor where both of their toothbrushes sat in the expanding toilet water. She knelt, flattening her palm against the floor and splashing it back and forth to try to find what she was looking for. There! A white box against the wall, barely peeking out from beneath the heap of white hand towels that had fallen from their rings on the wall.

Snatching it up, she raced right out through the door and across the living room.

Her mind alternated with images of her son, so small and feeble there in that doorway, propped like an old Raggedy Ann doll in the abandoned room of a girl gone off to college, with that line of blood along the side of his head, and her sister, glass protruding from her back like spikes.

"Tim!" she shouted, plopping down right next to Cindy on the floor.

He looked dreamily to her from the doorway, and slowly rolled over to all fours and crawled toward her.

Unsnapping the white plastic case, she dumped the contents onto the floor in front of her and grabbed the small packets of disinfectant wipes. Ripping open the package, she immediately used the first to wipe the congealing line of blood from the side of his head.

"Are you hurt anywhere else?" she asked, the roar of the wind dying down to the point that she could now communicate over it in little more than a shout.

He shook his head, wincing at the sting of the dampness on his head.

She tore open a packet of gauze and taped the way too large square above his ear.

"Is he...okay?" Cindy moaned through gritted teeth.

"I think so, but we need to get you taken care of now," Nancy said. She cringed and reached forward to take hold of the first piece of glass. "Are you ready?"

Cindy just pinched her eyes and balled her fists in response.

With a good yank, Nancy freed the glass from her sister's back and tossed it across the room to her right. She repeated the motion; one after the other after the other until Cindy positively shook with the pain. Each piece of the sloppy glass she cast aside had a good quarter-inch of blood along the sharpened lower edge, dripping fresh fluid with each extraction.

Finally able to release the breath she had been holding in her chest, Nancy threw the last piece to her right and leaned down next to her sister's ear.

"Talk to me, Cin. I want to hear your voice."

"Ouch," she whispered, eliciting a taut, nervous laugh from Nancy.

"Very concise."

The wind tapered to a cool breeze blowing through the front of the house, dragging the swirling dust to the back wall where it began to settle on the couch.

"I need to get your shirt off, so I'm going to have to drag it over your head. I'll try to do it as quickly as I possibly can," Nancy said, shifting Tim to the side from where he had curled up right against her hip. She twisted her fingers into the bottom of the sweatshirt. "Ready?"

Cindy's head bobbed gently against the carpet.

Carefully, Nancy peeled the shirt up toward Cindy's shoulder blades, jerking it at times from beneath her stomach and chest. There was so much blood on her back; a sticky layer clinging to the fabric like she was tugging the furry pelt from the carcass of a deer. As gently as she could, Nancy goaded her sister's arms upward and eased the shirt over her head, throwing it behind her with a slap where it smacked the wall.

"This is going to sting," Nancy said, wincing herself, tearing open the packages of several of the antibacterial wipes.

She pulled one out, expanding it to fit her palm. The wounds were serious, drawing blood to the surface like sap seeping though the knot of a pine.

"Timmy?" she whispered, making her voice as calm and level as she could manage. "Do you feel up to doing mommy a favor?"

He looked up to her with his wide eyes, batting out the dusty particles that immediately clung to the surface.

"Can you go into the kitchen and grab the phone?" she said, placing the wipe down on Cindy's back and gently wiping clean a patch of the drying blood to expose the penetration of the wound. Cindy's whole body trembled and she started to cry.

Tim slowly rose beside her, unable to take his eyes from his aunt's back.

"Pick it up and dial 911, all right?" She leaned forward so that her eyes could grab his attention. "Tell them to send an ambulance to our house."

He slowly nodded, still watching the blood quickly rise back to the surface as his mother cleared away patch after patch of the dark fluid, but managed to start his feet moving. A half a step at a time, he backed away, finally able to wrench his gaze from the carnage and dash into the kitchen.

"Stay with me, Cin," Nancy said, taping a stretch of gauze atop one of the sufficiently cleaned punctures before the dust could thicken into the blood.

"Not… going anywhere," Cindy forced through gnashed teeth.

"No dial tone!" Tim shouted from the kitchen, his voice high-pitched and panicked. He couldn't even see his mother through the dust.

"Hang it up and try it again."

Nancy cleared another patch and secured the gauze to it, already beginning to show signs of the fluid leeching through.

"Nothing!" Tim shouted.

"Make sure it's plugged into the wall."

Nancy gingerly unsnapped Cindy's white bra to ensure that there were no hidden wounds beneath and continued down her back.

"It's plugged in, mom! What do you want me to do?"

"Come back over here by me. My purse should still be right over there on the couch…I hope. Can you grab it and bring it to me please?"

He darted past her in his little pajamas faster than she had seen him move since before the cancer. Maybe it was just the adrenaline and he was going to end up paying dearly for it later, but for just that one moment it was wonderful to see him able to move—and with such fluidity—all by himself.

"How are you holding up?" Nancy asked for no other reason than to make sure Cindy was still conscious. Her breathing had slowed and her shoulders no longer heaved, but rather rhythmically and shallowly rose and fell. She couldn't even hear her sister's muffled cries rising from the carpet.

A shaking thumb rose slowly from Cindy's clenched fist.

Good enough.

"Did you find it?" Nancy called to Tim, who appeared before her out of the gray cloud that hung there in the living room.

"Yeah," he panted, dropping the purse beside her and plopping down on the carpet. His head wobbled slightly on his rubber neck and he appeared to be having a difficult time wheezing through the dust to catch his breath, eventually leaning against her and dropping his head into her lap.

Nancy spared a hand for just a moment to stroke his fuzzy head.

"Got one more favor in you, kiddo?"

"Mm-hmm," he moaned sleepily.

"Reach into my purse and grab my cell phone. All you have to do is push 911 and then press the send button with the picture of the little green phone."

Without even raising his head, he grabbed the purse by the handles and knocked it to the floor, spilling out stray tubes of lipstick and the hard candies. His tiny hand slipped inside, rummaging around for a moment before coming back out with the phone.

Nancy heard the buttons beep as he dialed the numbers, finally clearing away the now dry blood from the last wound she could see.

"It isn't even ringing."

"What?"

"No sound at all."

"Did you press the button with the green phone?"

"Uh-huh."

She strapped the last piece of gauze to Cindy's back and grabbed the phone from her son.

"It isn't working, mom," Tim said, but she was already dialing the number for herself.

"Come on…" Nancy said, her lower lip slipping between her teeth.

Silence.

She quickly pressed the red button to end the call and dialed it again.

"Pleasepleaseplease," she whispered, pressing the send button and bringing it to her ear.

Again...nothing.

"Shit," she said with an apologetic look to Tim. "Pass me my purse."

He did so with what appeared to be the last of his energy, slowing like a winding-down tin soldier, barely able to drag it close enough for her to grab.

She yanked it over his head and into her lap, shoving her hand inside and fumbling around until she found her keys. Leaving the purse on its side with it contents littering the floor, she brought Tim to her chest, cradling his back while his neck simply rolled onto her shoulder.

"We've got to get Aunt Cindy to the hospital," she said, speaking as clearly and calmly into Tim's ear as she could manage, hoping that she had hidden the sheer, all-consuming panic that held sway over her from her son. She headed right for the open front door, following her memories and the intensifying feel of the wind more than her eyes. "I'm going to buckle you in first, and then I'm going to come back for your aunt. You're going to need to be a big boy for me and wait in the car while I go back in to get her, all right?"

Tim nodded, dragging his crusty nose up and down along the side of her neck.

"That's my trooper," she said, hitting the front porch and easing her way forward so as not to tumble down the stairs and flatten them both on the walk.

She slid her feet along the concrete, now littered with countless broken tree limbs and more leaves than she had ever seen on the ground, even during the fall. The dust had thinned out here to the consistency of the kind of thick fog that rolled in off of a warm-water quagmire on a frigid winter's morning. Her shoulders were already coated with it.

She curled her nose at the stench, pursing her lips to keep from dragging the foul inhalations in along her tongue, quickening the pace to keep the vile aroma from stimulating Tim's all-too-sensitive nausea reflex.

Thrusting the key into the lock on the driver's side door, Nancy immediately reached around the frame and pulled the plug on the back door of the old green Saturn Wagon. She readjusted Tim's weight and hurried to the front passenger door, yanking it open and leaning inside to place her son gently onto the seat, grabbing the seat belt and pulling it quickly across his chest and buckling it beside the console. Heading around the back of the car, she opened the back door and left it standing wide, hurriedly dashing back up the steps, her heels clacking like maracas, and into the house.

Breath heavy and heaving like she had been running a marathon rather than making the same jaunt she did every morning to gather the newspaper, dirt crusting in a ring around her lips and nostrils and eyelashes, she stumbled through the furniture obstacles and crouched beside her sister.

"I'm going to need your help, Cin," she said, noting how she could now clearly hear her voice over the conspicuous lack of thunder. A car horn blared in the distance and it sounded like someone's alarm system had been triggered, but otherwise the wind had died down to almost a peacefully calm whistle. "I'm not strong enough to get you to your feet by myself."

"Sissy," Cindy whispered, and slowly struggled to pull her arms down, her hands beneath her chest to push herself up.

Nancy reached beneath Cindy's left arm, latching onto it like those old plastic monkeys in a barrel, and groaned, dragging her sister upward. She threw her left arm across Cindy's chest to try to drag her toward the door.

"I can't feel my feet," Cindy whispered, able to bend at the knees, but her toes dragged uselessly along the carpet.

"We just need the blood to drain down your legs."

"What in God's name is that smell?"

"I didn't want to say anything because I thought it was you," Nancy smirked, nearly biting off a chunk of the inside of her lip returning her teeth to grated against the strain.

"Me? How in the world could you possibly think...? That was a joke, wasn't it?" Cindy sputtered a laugh, tucking in her elbows while they passed through the front door. "I almost didn't recognize it... uhn, coming out of your mouth."

Nancy's back felt like a smoldering fire was creeping up from her lumbar and rising to crackling flame in her shoulders. It took all of her strength to drag Cindy through the tangle of debris strewn across the lawn and to the car.

"Duck," Nancy grunted through the strain, and plopped down on the back seat, slowly sliding backward to draw her sister in atop her.

Cindy moaned, doing her best to keep from screaming and allowing the pain to take complete hold of her faculties. Each of those wounds felt as though the glass was still lodged in there beneath the tissue, jammed into the muscles, and tearing ever wider with the exertion. The tape tugged at the fine hairs on her back, tearing at the scabs forming in the mesh of the gauze. And even through the pain that ground her teeth like lockjaw, tightening every muscle into a constrictive knot, she couldn't help but wish she had taken the time to put on a shirt before letting her sister guide her to the car.

Nancy reached up and behind, unlocking the door, her hands fumbling along the armrest before finally finding the handle and pulling. The door disengaged with a click and Nancy shoved it backward, carefully sliding from beneath her sister and depositing her rear end on the driveway. She pulled out her legs and staggered to her feet, closing the door behind her and running around to the driver's side, bending Cindy's legs at the knees to make sure that she wouldn't smash them in her hurry to close the door.

Jerking the keys from where they still hung from the lock in the driver's side door, she plopped in and shoved them into the ignition, turning them quickly and pinning the gas pedal to the floor. The engine roared to life and she slammed her door shut, immediately tugging the shift from park into reverse. Tires squealing, scorching the cement with thick black rubber streaks, she launched the car backward from the driveway and jammed the brakes, the tires skipping and skidding on the layer of dirt that coated the street beneath the blowing leaves.

"You okay back there?" Nancy called over her shoulder, flipping on the headlights and throwing the car into drive.

"Mm-hmm," Cindy responded, wincing through the pain that stabbed into her like so many fresh daggers.

Gravel shot from beneath the tires before they finally caught and fired the car forward with a lurch. Dust clogged the headlights to the point that Nancy could see no more than twenty or thirty feet ahead when the wind wasn't nice enough to rise and clear them a momentary path through the fog. The windshield wipers flapped back and forth, dragging piles of dust like snow into their wake, though still leaving a streaked, thin sheen across Nancy's vision. She placed her hand atop the windshield washer button, and nearly fired those twin sprays of blue fluid, but caught herself just in time before she turned her windshield to mud.

She could barely see the houses to either side of the residential street, especially considering that there wasn't a single light on through any of the windows, and there wasn't a pane of glass in any of them to reflect their headlights. Occasionally a scattering of what remained of the windows would shimmer like pixie dust atop a lawn before fading back into the darkness.

The roof had fallen in on the tri-level on the corner, exposing the bedroom above the garage and depositing the basketball backboard onto the driveway atop the smashed car parked beneath. An elm tree a good twenty feel taller than the two-story behind it had somehow been uprooted and deposited directly atop the house, splitting it in two right down to the top of the front door. Cars parked to the side of the street sat there like in some forlorn alley, windows smashed in, the rapid explosion of dust tearing slashes through their paint jobs, often times even toppling them over onto their sides.

There were taillights ahead: a lone pair of slanted red eyes staring at her through the thinning dust.

"That's the first car we've seen since we left," Tim whispered.

"Yeah," Nancy agreed having not even given it a thought.

They slowed, preparing to take the final right turn that would lead them from their sleepy little suburban neighborhood and to the busy streets that would take them further into town and to the hospital. The car wasn't moving, but it wasn't until they were upon it that they were able to discern why. The front tires had popped up over the curb, the undercarriage wedging it against the concrete rise. Thin fingers of black smoke were ripped from beneath the partially opened hood and dragged downwind.

"Don't look!" she shouted to Tim, but by then it was too late. They were already beside the car to their right, from his vantage making it just barely out of his reach should he have rolled down the window and attempted to pet it as he went by.

His head turned to follow when they passed, at first the entire scene not making that much sense. The driver initially looked as though she was trying to fish something out from the floorboards that may have been jarred loose by the impact with the curb, but she wasn't moving at all. Her form was slumped over the wheel with her arms lying limply to her sides. The dashboards flashed with the reflection of hundreds of small balls of glass from where the windshield had exploded. Long blonde hairs flowed from the hole in the glass like an octopus trying to climb out, matted flat against the sleek black hood of the Mitsubishi sedan.

Tim gasped and recoiled into the seat, straightening his head so that he could realign his eyes with the headlights at the sight of the woman's face. Her eyes were fixed wide, matching her gaping mouth, her skin marbleized with crimson streaks. What was left of the bridge of her nose looked more like a squashed cooked tomato, her swelling tongue lagging over her lower row of teeth like a moray eel peeking out from a hole in a reef.

"Was she...?" Tim whispered, nervously tangling his fingers in his lap.

Nancy merely nodded, turning past the sign that read "Autumn Heights: Covenants Controlled" on a big wooden placard and flipped on her signal, flashing like an expanding blossom in the dust, and prepared to turn out onto Wadsworth Parkway.

She stopped the car.

"What's going on here?" she asked, brow settling down upon her eyes.

Sitting there with the turn signal flashing and clicking monotonously, she stared ahead at the mess of cars that littered the street in front of her. An old, rust-red Ford four-by had slammed into the back of a Buick, riding right up onto the trunk and parking there. The driver of the pick-up, sat still in his seat, head back, looking up to the ceiling past the brim of his hat, the passenger leaning against the side window with her face pressed flat against it. The headlights pointed over the roof of the Buick. And while she couldn't see the driver of the smaller car, the passenger door stood wide, its occupant lying face down on the asphalt with the dust swirling through his hair, arms sprawled across the road.

And there were more cars…everywhere, clogging the road to the point that she couldn't turn out onto it. Red taillights glowed and headlights reflected back from the fenders they had rammed into. It was as though she had turned right out of the Rockwell vision of suburbia in hell and into a still life of a demolition derby. Smoke trails twirled and swelled above the mess of cars before being ripped down the street on the wind. Shattered glass and plastic littered the road, sliding along the blacktop far more slowly than the layer of leaves that tumbled atop it. The strip mall across the street was all but invisible in the darkness beyond the dust; even the 7-Eleven, alight twenty-four hours with those thousand watt halogens over the four pumps in front of it was just a memory in the blackness.

"What's wrong?" Cindy asked, trying to raise her head from the upholstery, but able to do little more than lift her cheek a half an inch from the seat with the lightning bolts of pain ripping through her flesh.

"I…" Nancy started, slipping the gear into park. "I don't know."

Unable to steal her eyes from the mangle of traffic before her, she lowered her left hand to the door and tugged the handle. The dome light came on and she had to paw at her eyes before she could swing her feet out onto the street.

"I'll be right back," she called back through the door she left standing wide, and walked out in front of the car and into the headlights.

This was insane. She could see the people in the cars; some of them no more than black shadows hunched over the seats, but none of them were moving. Not one. A car horn blared in the otherwise surreal silence from the weight of the stilled driver atop it.

Slowly, she walked forward, her heels clacking like a faucet dripping in the still of the night. Burning oil, smoke, and dust accosted her senses, filling her sinuses like foam expanding and lodging itself within. The scent of leaking gas mingled with the puddle of vomit that the passenger of the Buick had passed out right in the middle of, his hair already thick like a bird's nest with the clutter of leaves.

To the left, past the smoking skeleton of the raised Ford, she could see nothing but a long line of red taillights leading down the arrow straight road as far as she could see. Still... unmoving despite their crooked and askew alignment. Heart dropping in her chest, her stomach suddenly and sickeningly queasy, she looked to the right, only to see the same parallel lines of red taillights heading straight toward the absolute blackness where the bright skyline of downtown should have been. No residual glow painted the undersides of the clouds from the expanding squalor of the metropolis, and not even the fluorescent blue of the Qwest sign atop the tallest building downtown beckoned to her.

Before she even knew she had willed her legs to motion, she was running down the side of the street with her heels clattering like ball-peen hammers striking the pavement. Her head lowered as she passed each car, looking through the windows to the unmoving silhouettes within. Tears streamed down her cheeks and her breaths were starting to become shallow, choppy.

"Help!" she screamed, her feet finally slapping to a halt beside an Expedition where she could see through the side window the outline of a pair of child seats in the back, the rounding of the small heads of the lifeless bodies strapped in place.

"God?" she whined beneath the tremulous rising of the sobs that would soon no longer be denied. Looking right up into the heavens, she couldn't pry the light of a single star from the churning cloud of darkness above, not a sparse glimmer from the heavens.

Head down so as not to see through the windshields of the stalled cars, their engines still running despite the smoke that wafted out from beneath the crumpled hoods, so as not to see the expressions on the faces of the men and women and children that had died so suddenly... She made her way to the double yellow lines in the center of the road and slowly spun in a circle.

Not a single car moved.

"Can anybody hear me?" she screamed, buckling her neck back and raging up into the sky.

No answer but the drone of the car horn.

"Anybody!" she wailed, clambering up atop the hood of a white Lexus and standing on her toes to see if she could see any sign of life in the distance.

The pairs of red lights stretched until they vanished against the horizon line in both directions, though that was the only light she could see at all. The rest of the city from the face of the mountains to the west, to the termination of the flat land to the east, was completely absorbed by the darkness.

She plopped down onto the hood of the car, and looked around for a moment, unable to stop shaking her head in disbelief.

Slowly, Nancy slid from the warm hood of the car and found her feet, swaying on trembling legs...and started the long walk back to her car.

V

"Are you all right?" Brad shouted right into William's face, madly wiping the mud from the boy's tear-stained cheeks back to his ears and hairline. Grasping him by the sides of his face, he pulled him forward through the cloud of dust until their noses touched and he could see right into William's eyes. "Talk to me! Are you all right?"

William sniffed back the thin lines of mucous growing brown and viscous, trailing from his dirt-rimmed, crusty nose to the edges of his parched lips. His eyes shimmered with a layer of tears, eyelids frantically batting to keep the layer of dust from settling atop them and congealing inside of his head. He nodded slowly and wrapped his arms around his father's neck, merging into his lap.

Brad choked back a sob of relief, pinching the tears from the corner of his own eyes, and embraced his son against his chest with everything he had.

"I was so scared for you," he whispered, running his trembling hands up and down William's back. "I don't know what I would do if I lost you."

He rocked back and forth, there on the stairs, listening to the roar of thunder petering in the distance, trying to soothe William's frantic breathing he could feel both with his hands and in the warm spurts of breath against his cheek.

"Time to go," William said in a voice so small that had his mouth not been right against Brad's ear he might never have heard it.

"Time to go where?"

"Got a long walk ahead of us, Dad. Better get started."

Brad peeled William from his chest so that he could look into the boy's eyes. They were wide and round and ringed with matted dust like a chipmunk's, but even through the fear that forced the eyes to shiver in their sockets, he could see the seriousness lurking behind.

"I think maybe a better idea would be to get you off to bed so I can figure out how we're going to get this house fixed up again. So why don't we head off to your room and find some pajamas—"

"There isn't much time," William said, climbing from his father's lap and taking the much larger hand with his own small, cold fingers. "They'll be coming soon, and we need to be well on our way when they do."

"Who'll be coming?" Brad asked, completely perplexed by the entire direction of the conversation, yet still pushing himself to his feet to allow the child to lead him. It was such a rare thing for William to invest this much effort into talking, and the last thing in the world he wanted to do was to discourage it, regardless of how remarkably bizarre and paranoid he sounded.

"Do you smell that?" was William's only response.

Brad curled his nose from the stench that crept through the broken glass like a physical entity, filling the air and lingering in his sinuses, dripping down the back of his throat.

"Yeah," Brad said, his chest tightening. It felt as though his trachea was shrinking, trying to close the rush of vile air off from his lungs. "Rotten eggs."

"That means they'll be coming."

"I'd hate to see the chickens who laid those eggs, if that's who you're referring to."

William stopped at the top of the stairs and looked back to his father, their eyes on the same level with Brad trailing by a couple of stairs. He gave Brad a placating smile and then turned to head down the hallway.

"Oh-kay," Brad muttered under his breath.

William led him through the cloud of dust that hovered in the living room, glass grinding into the carpet beneath their feet. Brad coughed up a dirt-laden wad of phlegm from his chest, his lips unable to hold it back. It lurched past and flopped to the ground.

"So where are we going?" he asked, trying to keep his voice as light as possible, though his mind was turning fits about how he was even going to begin to fix the house. As he had designed and overseen the construction of this place, it was like a child to him, and he couldn't bear to see it in this deplorable state of ruin.

"We need to get the others before…" William said, pausing at the doorway to his room.

"Before what?"

"Before it rains."

He walked through the doorway and into his room, leading Brad straight toward the bunk beds at the back. The windows to either side had shattered inward, the wind blowing right into their faces, trying to force the dust through the open door.

William released his father's hand and dropped to all fours in front of the bed. Carefully, he flattened himself and slipped his entire right arm and his head beneath the bed, feet kicking in the air until he found what he was looking for.

"What are you doing, William?" Brad asked, dropping to his haunches to try to peer beneath the quilt that hung from the side of the bed, into the darkness beneath where William grunted in apparent struggle with some large object.

Without answering, William shimmied backward until he was out from beneath the bed, and yanked his Harry Potter backpack out. It was stuffed to overflowing, with clothes hanging out from between where the zippers had been unable to close. He stood, shoving his arms through the straps and hiking it up onto his back, bending slightly forward to brace the weight.

"What is all of that?" Brad asked.

"Clothes," William said as if the answer had been completely obvious. He lifted his pillow from the bed and shook it. A flashlight fell out and bounced on the mattress. Grabbing it in his right hand, he flipped the switch and pointed it at his father with a contented grin.

"You're, um..." Brad said, unable to find the words, "...certainly well-prepared."

William brushed past him and through the doorway into the hall, leaving Brad to just follow him, scratching his head. The light stained the dust a pale brownish-yellow in conical arcs, flashing glimpses of the framed pictures lining the walls, though none of the images were discernible beneath the layer of dust. The frame of the doorway to the master bedroom appeared in the light, surrounding a rectangle of darkness, the circular pattern of light slowly coming into focus on the back wall of the room above the bed.

William coughed from the dust, a deep, retching bark like croup, triggering a matching reflex from his father.

He pointed the light first atop the bed, and then to the floor beneath it, highlighting the frilly skirt that his mother had picked out, and feminine though it was, his father had been unable to part with.

"Yours is under there," William said, holding the light steady.

"Mine?" Brad asked, staring at the ruffling folds in the pink floral fabric.

"It's too heavy for me to pull out. I could barely get it under there."

Brad looked to William, who gave him this impatient "Well, what are you waiting for?" expression.

Stepping to the side of the bed, Brad lowered himself to the floor and reached beneath the skirt, raising it with his shoulder in hopes of being able to see whatever was beneath. Knocking his slippers aside, he stretched his arm until his fingers grazed something, the fingernails making a sound against the fabric like a quickly drawn zipper. He solidified his grasp on a cold, metal pole, tightening his fingers around it and tugging at it until he was able to back out from beneath the bed.

The flashlight showed him a black strap and two parallel black belts connecting a pair of metal posts. Leaning back, he tugged at one of the belts, finally pulling the entire works out from beneath the bed.

"My old hiking backpack?" Brad mused, pulling the drawstring to loosen the flap at the top. He folded it back and stuck his hand inside, grabbing hold of the collar of a shirt and tugging it out.

"Please don't pull it all out."

"I thought I lost this," Brad said, holding up a thick blue sweater. "You told me you hadn't seen it."

"Don't be mad."

"That was a year ago! And here are my jeans and long underwear. My old coat. My stocking cap! William..." but when he turned he could see the hurt in William's face as though he had just slapped the boy after being presented with a gift. "You've certainly been a busy little beaver, haven't you?"

The boy's expression softened, allowing his prideful chest to swell just a little.

"We've gotta go," he said, taking one of the shoulder straps from the harness and presenting it to his father.

"I don't think...no, William. What we need to do is get you to bed. It's already..." he started, turning his head to look to the clock out of habit, though if it were still even atop the nightstand, it was bathed in darkness, "well, past your bedtime for sure."

"Dad—"

"This will all look different in the light of day. I'll call Carl and get him out here to take care of the windows, and Terry has that cleaning crew—"

"Dad?"

"We could probably even have it all done by mid-afternoon. Maybe just for tonight we could sleep in the car. I doubt any dust could get in there with the windows rolled up tight. And the garage is on the front of the house, and there aren't any windows in the—"

"Dad!" William shouted, immediately causing Brad to lose his train of thought and turn to face him. "If we stay here we'll die!"

"Son…"

"If we stay here, we will die. That much I know."

"What kind of father would take his son from his home in the middle of the night with nothing more than a backpack and a flash—"

"The kind of father who wants to see his child live."

"Will it make you feel better if we loaded up in the car—"

"The car's useless."

"—and drove around a bit to show you that everything's all right?"

"Nothing's all right. That's why we need to move quickly."

"We're not going anywhere."

"We need to go now. That's what they're telling me, Dad. We're running out of time."

"Who's telling you?"

"The voices."

"Maybe we'd better take you to a doctor instead. You liked that Dr. Grunwald, didn't you?"

"I need you to believe me!" William shouted, tears streaming down his face, impatiently stamping his feet.

"I do believe you, William," Brad said, voicing the words for his son's benefit, though inside he worried that he was going to have to have his only son committed somewhere for observation and evaluation. "It's just that—"

"Fine!" William barked, firing spittle and snot. He brought the light from the lens to his own face, directing it right into his eyes, the retinas contracting quickly.

Brad gasped, recoiling from his son so quickly that he fell backward onto the floor. The shock stole his breath; his heart rising so quickly in his chest that all he could hear was the throbbing of his racing pulse in his temples.

At first he had thought it to be nothing more than the halogen reflecting from the dampness of the tears surrounding William's eyes, illuminating the rims inside of the lashes like the setting sun over a clear, pristine mountain lake. That is…until they moved.

It was impossible to tell just how many of them there were. Those…things ringing his son's eyes…they were just…just…

"It's the air," William said, easing slowly toward his father and then kneeling before him. "Something's changing in the air, making them come out of hiding."

Brad just stared at them, still highlighted by the beam from the boy's flashlight pointed straight up into his eyes. They were like miniature flowers, each one no more than a quarter of an inch tall. Orange and yellow, they stood from beneath his lashes, but rather than petals, they were ringed with miniature filaments like wispy feathers, each forming a small concave bowl like the floating seeds to be blown from a dandelion.

"That's the only reason I can focus well enough to speak clearly, Dad. They're being quiet, not talking and talking like they always do, but listening...listening for the others to awaken."

Swallowing the lump lodged in his throat, Brad reached up and took his son by the hands, pulling him forward into his lap. William leaned his head against his father's chest, listening to his heart beating so fast it sounded like a playing card in the spokes of a bike.

"We'll get them out of there," Brad said. "Don't worry, son. I'll get them out of there."

"You can't, Dad."

"I'll just get some tweezers and—"

"They're a part of me...always have been. They say they found me through my mother's umbilical cord, otherwise they would have died."

Brad opened his mouth to speak, but nothing came out. He just sat there, stroking his son's dusty hair with his hand.

"Do you believe me, Daddy?"

"I don't know what to believe."

William sat there a moment longer before rising from his father's lap and turning to face him, their eyes no more than a few inches apart.

"Do you love me?"

"Of course I do, William. You shouldn't even have to ask—"

"Then put your backpack on and leave with me right now."

"We need to get you to a hospital."

"They're the ones who told me that the meteorite was going to hit. They could hear the others way out there in space. They don't talk like you and I, but use something like ESP. I don't hear their voices, but rather they're translated through that voice inside of my head that I use to think, like it's my own brain that's talking to me, but I know its them. Sometimes they even show me pictures, but I don't think they do it on purpose. I'm not even sure that they know I can hear them. I don't think they'd tell me the things they do if they thought I could understand."

"What do they tell you?" Brad whispered, reaching gently for the corner of William's eye, but those little feathers folded right up and quickly disappeared beneath the lower lid.

"Just that the others are coming, but I see images sometimes...like the tallest building downtown, the one with the big blue sign, which is why I know we need to go there. They show me other things, too. They're like dreams, if I don't try really hard to remember them, they'll just go away, which is why I try to draw them as soon as they show me before I forget."

"What's going on here?"

"Do you remember what happened to the dinosaurs?"

"I've heard many different theories..."

"They're all dead, Dad. Extinct. And unless you can figure out how to believe me, that's what's going to happen to all of us, too."

"You know I love you more than anything else in the world..."

"But you don't believe me."

"I'm trying."

William crouched and tugged the crumpled clothes from under his father's rump, cramming them back into the pack, and then pulled the drawstring tight.

"I'll make you a deal," William said, grabbing the heavy backpack by the strap and dragging it toward his father. "Come with me now. We'll walk straight toward town. The hospital's right at the bottom of the mountain. If by the time we get there you still don't believe me, then you can take me in. But if you do...then you have to trust me."

"Okay," Brad said, slowly easing to his feet and taking the strap for the pack and slinging it over his shoulder. "But only if you let me drive. That way we're at the hospital in under twenty minutes if you're wrong."

"You're wasting your time."

"That's the deal. Take it or leave it. Either way, you and I are getting in that car right now."

"What are we waiting for, then?" William asked, grabbing hold of his father's hand. Brad could feel the feathery tips of something in his son's hand tickle his own palm before slipping back into the pores from which they had arisen. His mind was a convoluted tangle of jumbled thoughts as they walked through the settling cloud of dust and toward the garage.

He was through the door and pressing the button against the trim, standing there waiting for the garage door to rise up against the ceiling, staring blankly at the faint glimmer from the hood of the car in the darkness.

"Dad?" William asked curiously.

Brad just looked at him, his face a good ten years older there in the darkness.

"I don't think it's going to open. There's no power."

Brad looked at his finger holding the unlit button, and then dropped it to his side and walked to the center of the garage, feeling the air before him until he ran into the release cord to disengage the overhead door from the track. Heading to the end of the garage, he reached down and grabbed hold of the lowest bar, cringing at the feel of the spider webs on his hands, and raised it upward with a grunt.

The passenger door was already slamming shut by the time he turned around, the shocks of the forest green Grand Cherokee squeaking slightly under William's shifting weight.

He tracked the mental checklist. Insurance card? Check. Credit card to pay deductible? Check. After all this time he had convinced himself that he was doing what was in his son's best interests, but he had been wrong. No matter how much love and stability he had provided, no matter how much time and effort he had afforded, in the end, it hadn't been enough. He was going to have to put William in the hands of someone who could do a better job of helping him. Brad had failed. Now he had to do the one thing he feared in life more than anything else in the world. Now he had to drive his son down to the hospital, knowing full well that it would be only he who made the return journey.

3 | It's Always Darkest...

I

Headlights pierced the dust hanging like a fog over the long crosscut gravel drive winding down the hillside. Ageless pines loomed over the dark road from either side, black, formless sentries still holding their guard despite their severed limbs lying in heaps atop their shed needles that littered the road. The going was slow, too slow for Brad, especially since he was forced to hammer the brakes, filling the air with gravel launched from beneath their locked tires, to keep from slamming into one of the massive boulders that had come to rest in the middle of the drive. Reflectors flashed from gated driveways leading up into the solitary acreages of heavily forested hillside where the frighteningly rich had come to hide from the prying eyes that would love nothing more than to see their mansions slide down the slope and into oblivion. Corners came too quickly, veering so tightly that it was all Brad could do to make sure the car stayed on the road he could hardly even see by now. It was like driving through a blizzard, though in the snow at least the powder reflected the headlights back up toward them, giving them some idea of exactly where the ground was, while now it concealed itself beneath the ever thickening dust, settling upon it from the cloud that sat right atop them.

"Stop right here!" William shouted suddenly, tossing his backpack from his lap to the floorboard.

Brad pinned the brake to the floor.

"What is it?" Brad gasped.

William had the door open and his feet hanging out before the car had even grumbled to a skidding halt.

"Are you all right?" Brad shouted after William as he bolted from the car and dashed to the shoulder. He threw his own door wide and scampered around the hood, dragging his hand through the thick mat of dirt that coated it. "William!"

"Just a minute!" William's voice called back through the haze and the darkness that stood between them like a physical entity. It had been the flash from a single orange reflector, the only one that had managed to stay attached to the aluminum gate when the boulder had cracked free from the formation up the hillside and hammered it like a speeding truck. It was the one from the vision, the one thing he would never share with his father.

Down the hill he could barely make out the roof-line of the Abernathy estate, a tall gable perched above the front door, a rounded arch separated from the rooftop meant to frame the red of the setting sun on vernal equinox. But it was the gate itself that he had stopped for.

The whole works had buckled inward with the impact of the stone, tearing the upper rail in two. One half bowed inward, wedging the now stilled rock between it and the other half, which protruded directly outward like a crude, jagged sword. He grabbed that extraordinarily sharp piece of metal and, digging in with his heels, pulled it toward him with all of his might, listening to it groan only meekly.

"What are you doing?" Brad asked, jogging to a halt beside William.

"Help me pull this just a couple more inches."

"Why in the world—?"

"Just please, Dad," William begged, pleading with his eyes. "This is really important."

"Whatever it takes to get back in that car," Brad grumbled, jerking on the metal, though it pinched into his palms so ferociously that he feared the skin would open right up. He managed to bend it outward just a couple of inches before the metal refused to budge any further. "That's as far as it will bend. Okay?"

William closed his eyes; the irises rolling jerkily beneath the eyelids like the boy had dropped off into REM's like a narcoleptic.

"Yes, Daddy," he whispered, crocodile tears swelling from the outer corners of his eyes before slipping free to roll through the dust on his cheeks. "At least now it will be quick…"

"At least what will be quick?" Brad stammered, throwing his hands up to his sides in exasperation. But William was already climbing back into the car, wiping his tears with the back of his sleeve.

Without a word, Brad clambered into the driver's seat and headed back down the winding road. *At least what will be quick?* he wanted to ask, but there was really no point. William's answers seemed to be for different questions, or somehow encrypted like he was supposed to crack the riddle with his secret decoder ring. The only thing he could think to say was, "Think we can make it to the hospital without having to stop again. You nearly gave me a heart attack! And for what? So you could play with the broken gate!"

"This way you, I mean…this way it won't be unbearable. It'll be fast."

Brad turned to William, taking his eyes from the road entirely so he could study the expression on his son's face. And though he could see little more than the glint of tears on the boy's cheeks, hear him sniffing back the thin mucous that tried to muck its way through the layer of dirt, he could see an air of confidence around him. Like somehow this whole disaster had cracked him right out of that quasi-autistic shell, leaving in its place a normal-looking boy on his way to pitch against the worst team in the league. Were it not for the unusual, no, almost insane way that he spoke, Brad would have believed the dust that had gutted his house to be the cure. Hell, he'd have chopped the damned thing to toothpicks himself if it would have afforded him the key to unlock his son from that iron maiden he'd been holed up in since birth.

"Brakes," William said plainly.

"What?" Brad started, wondering how that played into the conversation. When he finally looked forward, he had time enough to stamp the brake pedal and look for a gap in the trees. His headlights reflected back at him from the side of a car sitting perpendicular to the road directly in front of him, stalled right there on the side of I-70, the highway that would have led them right down into Denver. Jerking the wheel to the right, he crashed through a stand of scrub oak, the sharpened branches screaming as they tore through the paint on the side of the Cherokee and ground into the metal. The right tire bounced into the air from a snaggled trunk, the rubber from the tire thumping against the undercarriage on its journey beneath the car. The exposed rim dug into the dirt, gripping tightly enough to swing the rear of the car a hundred and eighty degrees, where it came to rest with the most transient little bump against the already splintered trunk of a bare pine.

"You okay?" Brad asked, glancing to William, though he was unable to un-knot his clenched fists from the steering wheel. His knuckles stood brightly out from the darker color of his fingers and the back of his hands, his arms locked straight like metal posts.

"I told you the car wouldn't do us any good," William said through a smirk and threw his shoulder against the door to pry the bowed metal open.

"Was that an 'I told you so?'" Brad pondered aloud. William already had his backpack secured to either side of his neck and was heading off through the headlights toward the road. "Your mother's stock in trade."

He climbed out himself, legs shaking, palms sweating, and looked back to the tangle of thistle they had torn from the roadside, most of which still poked out from beneath the tailgate.

"Don't forget your backpack!" William called from the very edge of the choked lights, no more than an illusory silhouette fading in and out of the dust.

"You wait for me!" Brad shouted, hurriedly leaning past the driver's seat and unlocking the rear door. He yanked it open and pulled out the pack, trying to slam the door with a hip, though it only screeched and buckled, refusing to crumple back into place. He raced after his son before he lost track of him altogether.

Twigs and needles snapped beneath his rapid tread, the whole of the earth spongy and Nerf-like with detritus.

"William!" he shouted, leaving the glow of the headlights behind and stumbling while the ground dropped beneath him, sloping quickly in carved gullies down through the patches of wild grasses and hardened dirt to the shoulder of the road.

"Right here," William said, standing beside a long black sedan that angled across the gravel shoulder. The taillights formed a red glare, the headlights smashed against the hillside. The motor still hissed and spat scalding fluids that skipped like hot grease from the engine block. William stood beside the passenger door, hands framing either side of his face, pressed firmly against the tinted window.

He jerked back quickly as though caught in some illicit act, turning to face his father at the first sound of his approaching footsteps.

"What happened here?" Brad gasped, noting first the car William had just been staring into, and the handful of other scattered red lights, eerily spotting the otherwise deserted highway. He hurried to the passenger door and jerked it open, half-expecting to find someone in desperate need of assistance.

"Don't!" William shouted, but by then it was too late. Brad was already ducking into the door, preparing to scoot across the seat toward the driver when he suddenly stopped.

His heart ceased beating...the world spun around him like he had crawled through the mouth of a tilting vortex, rather than the passenger door of a Sable. Slowly, ever so slowly, he eased forward. His hand trembling like an aspen branch against a violent wind, he placed his first two fingers against the side of the driver's neck.

She was dead.

He scrambled backward; unable to steer his gaze from her mouth, stretched inhumanly wide with her tongue rigidly fixed between her agape teeth. Her neck bowed absurdly backward, her head resting atop the headrest with her long black hair trailing down behind. Fixed eyes studying the upholstered roof, her hands still clung tightly to the steering wheel. Static blared from the radio, crackling maniacally from the dashboard, from which smoke poured through the vents like a gas chamber. The engine sputtered, and then finally coughed to a grinding stop, though her foot was still pegged atop the pedal.

"Get back!" he shouted to William, scooting past the edge of the seat and depositing himself squarely on his butt.

"I already saw."

"Jesus...Jesus, she's dead."

"They're all dead," William said matter-of-factly, gesturing to the other stalled cars littering the roadway. "All but a few, anyway."

"You knew this?"

William just nodded gently.

"How the hell did you know this was going to happen?"

"Because they told me," William said, taking his father by the hand and goading him politely to walking. "The others...regular people, their bodies can't breathe the air like we can, and definitely not like *they* can."

"So everyone else is...is..."

"Dead."

"Christ," Brad said, running his free hand through his tangled hair as he always did when he reached his threshold of frustration.

They passed an old, primer-gray TransAm. The passenger's head had smashed through the window, impaling the back of it on the jagged shards. Already congealing blood coated the door beneath the tangle of long blonde hair, running all the way down to the runners and dripping into a black puddle on the asphalt. The driver's face was crumpled around the steering wheel, balls of glass filling his dark hair from the impact with the rear of the F-150 in front of it, knocking the windshield directly inward. The Ford's rear gate sat atop the hood of the TransAm, the toolbox in the bed having opened, scattering the rusted contents all across the chipped plastic liner. Smoke twirled between the two at the point of impact, alternately pluming upward, and then being ripped downhill by the gusting wind.

The passenger door had popped open with the collision, releasing the empty beer cans from the floorboards that clanged and pinged over the gravel on the shoulder. The driver lie face down on the seat, his hooked fingers having torn right through the upholstery and into the yellow foam padding beneath. He had been furiously trying to claw his way out of the car, despite the seat belt that was wrapped so tightly around his waist that it had drawn a layer of blood from his gut to soak into his pit-stained, white "#3 Forever" t-shirt. The stench of vomit poured out the door even faster then the gasoline that dripped from the crumpled gas tank.

"We'd better walk faster," William said, urging his father from the opened door that curled his nose. "We've got a long way to go before dawn."

II

Nancy blew out the flame on the match and dropped the smoldering little wooden stick onto the plate in the center on the coffee table she had righted in the middle of the family room. A dozen candles burned from various points in the room, vaguely flickering in reflection from the mirror behind the dining room table beneath a veil of dust. None of those little candles, that now converted the scent of the room to something of a cross between a spice rack and a flower garden, were more than a couple of inches tall, intended more for decoration than their more functional use. Wax streamed down the sides of those little colored stumps faster than it had any right to, the wicks already disappearing beneath the rapidly hollowing craters of clear liquid that pooled under the short flames.

They only needed to last until dawn.

Then there would at least be sunlight, whether the power came back on or not.

She plopped down on the couch and sighed, staring up into the ceiling. Tim was bundled securely in his bed. The strain of the night had drained him of all but consciousness, though that too succumbed readily after a moment in the silent darkness. She had pulled the emergency tank of oxygen from the hall closet, tucking the matching prongs into his nostrils and looping the thin plastic hosing over his ears. For God knows how long, she had sat there, scrutinizing his breathing, watching his chest rise and fall so subtly that it did little more than wrinkle the thick comforter. And thank heaven for batteries, making it possible for her to slyly insert the probe of the thermometer into his ear far too frequently to monitor his slight fever. It was all she could do to drag herself from his bedside to check on Cindy, who was across the hall in Nancy's bed, lying face down on the mattress atop the covers for fear of even the minute weight of the blankets irritating the wounds.

Nancy had checked Cindy's vitals as she had grown so accustomed to doing with her son. And while her breath sounds had still been worrisomely shallow, her pulse was strong and regular, though her skin felt cool to the touch. So long as no fresh blood seeped from those gashes, or threatened to overflow from beneath the gauze, it looked as though she just might be all right. Granted, it would have been far more comforting had they been able to get her to the hospital, but—

No, she didn't want to think about that, didn't want to risk remembering the looks on the faces of the dead, packed bumper to bumper, up and down the road. Daylight would help her sort out the whole thing. So long as she just kept herself busy, going from one bedroom to the next, ensuring that what remained of her family—her sole purpose for existence—still lived, then she would get through the night.

Lord only knew how long the power had been out, or when this had actually begun. Time lost meaning in the absolution of darkness, slowing down to a fetal crawl. Hours could well have stretched across days for as long as it felt. She just needed to keep busy...keep moving...keep—

"Mommy," Tim's meek voice echoed from down the hallway.

She sprinted down the black corridor, slamming her knee against the trim of his door without so much as a peep to acknowledge the pain. Her heart crept up into her throat as it always did when he called her in the night, each time half-expecting to find him gurgling through his own vomit. She couldn't think, couldn't breathe, fear seizing hold of her body like a marionette.

"What is it?" she panted, dashing to the side of his bed and immediately wiping her hand across his mouth to make sure that it wasn't frothing with thick fluid.

"We've got to pack now," Tim whispered, tugging, somewhat surprised, at the cords in his nose that hadn't been there when he had passed out.

"Are we taking a vacation in your dream?" she asked, forging a wan smile.

"No," he said, confused by her response. "We need to pack as many warm clothes as we can fit into our bags. They're going to be here any time."

"Who's going to be here?"

"That other little boy. The one who talks to me when I'm asleep."

"It's just a dream, honey. If you close your eyes right away, then you can probably slip right back into it."

"No, Mom, you don't understand! We have to leave when they get here, and we're not even packed yet."

"We're not going anywhere else tonight, sweetheart. But tomorrow we'll get you and your aunt to the doctor so he can make sure that you're both going to be all right."

"No!" Tim barked, yanking the tubes from his nose and struggling against the comforter to prop himself shakily on his elbows. He grunted with the exertion, baring his teeth and dragging his legs from beneath the comforter to dangle them over the side of the bed. "There isn't much time!"

Nancy climbed quickly over the bed and caught his legs, trying to force those bony appendages back beneath the covers, but Tim fought against her, the tendons in his calves jutting out from the loose skin like those connecting chicken meat to a drumstick.

"Please, Timmy!" Nancy begged, crying. "You need to rest."

There was a knock on the front door.

Nancy froze in place, craning her ear to the origin of the sound as though it might have been a figment of her imagination. If she heard it again, though...

Another knock.

"Stay right here!" Nancy whispered sharply, slowly lowering Tim's legs and easing stealthily across the carpet. She was only a few feet through the doorway and into the hall when she heard the knocking again, louder this time.

"No one's here," a muffled voice said from beyond the front door.

"Try it again," another said.

Nancy slunk from the hallway and into the living room, pausing long enough to grab the broken leg from one of the corner tables and hold it up to her ear like a baseball bat.

"Who's there?" she called, her voice trembling nearly as much as the wood she brandished above her shoulder.

"Um," the voice started. And then in a whisper, "What am I supposed to say?"

"Tell her who you are," the other said, this time easily discernible as the voice of a child.

"Sorry to bother you this late, ma'am. My name is Brad Morris. I think maybe...maybe you should hear what I have to say."

"I've got a bat!" Nancy shrieked, her voice cracking.

"Tell her I need to talk to Tim," the child said.

"Ma'am, my son...William. He says he needs to talk to Tim."

"Go away!"

"Have you been outside yet tonight?" Brad called through the door.

Nancy waited in silence, taking a small step toward the door and silently sliding the chain lock into place.

"How do I say this? Everyone else…everyone else is dead."

Nancy slid the deadbolt back with a twist of the knob, and opened the door inward as far as the chain would allow. She peeked out with one eye, her nose creased along the center by the edge of the door. With her makeshift bat held just high enough that she was certain they would be able to see it wagging over her shoulder, she looked the pair up and down.

The man was wearing a short-sleeved Polo shirt that looked as though he had spent the day wrestling hogs in a sty. His pants were creased and muddied, his right knee poking through a tear in the khaki fabric. Tennis shoes coated in mud, leaves caught in the laces, he could have been any derelict freshly crawled out from the drainage ditches downtown where they made their homes beneath the bridges.

The boy looked little better, with his hair wildly standing up atop his head, his face coated with a tan powdering of dust. His clothes were the same ragamuffin style, like he had been living off of berries in the mountains for the last couple of weeks.

Both wore backpacks that appeared far too large to carry, forcing them to hunch over to brace the weight.

"What do you want?" Nancy asked sharply, wary of any potential advance from the man she feared might try to force his way through the door.

The man looked to the boy, raising a silent question with his shoulders, receiving a nod in return.

"This is going to sound crazy…and believe me I know. But my son here…well, he knows things."

Nancy held her ground at the door.

"Please…we're not going to hurt you."

"Would you say so if you were?"

"I guess not," Brad acknowledged with a shrug. "But we're not going to. I'm an architect, and probably about as non-confrontational as anyone you'll ever meet. We live up in Clear Creek Canyon, and though you probably can't tell from the way we look now, I'm reasonably successful. And were it not for my son, I'd probably still be hunkered down in my house with all of the broken windows and settling dust like you. Part of me still wishes I were, but we've seen some things…things you probably wouldn't even believe."

"Like what?"

"Well, we had to walk this entire way, straight down the highway, since there were stalled cars all over the road that would have made it impossible to drive. The people in each and every one of those cars—all of them—were dead, just sitting there in the darkness with their engines still running until they ran out of gas."

"I saw that, too," Nancy whispered. "What happened?"

"I'm not really clear on exactly what transpired, but here it is as I understand it..." Brad started, sighing as he removed the backpack from his shoulder and set it on the porch. He rolled his neck, working out the kinks. "When that meteorite hit, the force of the impact caused the outward explosion that drove the huge wall of dust away from the point of impact, breaking what appears to be pretty much every window in town. But I think that, in and of itself, wasn't what...you know, killed everyone.

"Now this is the part where I get a little hazy on the details, but from what my son theorizes, there was some sort of change in the atmosphere that followed that everyone else couldn't seem to be able to breathe. I can remember smelling something that reminded me an awful lot of rotten eggs—"

"Me, too," Nancy interrupted.

"And I don't know much—well, anything for that matter—about chemical reactions, but I do know that sulfur, like that white, chalky powder left over after those cow ponds dry up, tends to smell that way."

"So say this atmospheric change was responsible for all of the death, then answer me this: why are we still alive?"

"I wish I knew."

"Are they here?" Tim asked from the hallway, feebly dragging his old Batman backpack into the room by the straps.

"Get back in bed, honey," Nancy said, hurrying to him, but Tim sidestepped her in the darkness and skulked up to the partially opened door.

"Hi," he said, his little pale face peering out, eyes alight from deep in those dark sockets. "Nice to finally meet you."

Brad recoiled from the boy who looked like a zombie: almost the living version of those he had seen hunched over the steering wheels of their cars on the way into town.

"Nice to finally meet *you*," William said excitedly, walking right to the crack in the door and extending his hand. A bone-thin, knobby wrist followed skeletal fingers through the gap to shake William's hand. "You look like you feel better."

"A little. I'm always tired, though, but I think I'm ready to go."

"You're not going anywhere!" Nancy snapped, blinking in surprise.

"That's my mom," Tim whispered. "She's overprotective."

"And for good reason," Nancy said, having overheard the entire transaction.

"Why don't you come out onto the porch so we can talk?" Brad asked, taking a step back from the door. "I promise we won't make a rush for the door or anything like that."

"I'm not sure—"

"Come on, Nan," Cindy said, leaning against the wall in the hallway. "They've got me kind of curious now."

"You shouldn't be up."

"I feel fine, just a little sore is all."

"You two are going to be the death of me, you know that?"

"But you love us anyway."

"Doesn't mean I won't strangle you myself."

"So if I'm wrong about this guy, maybe he'll save you the trouble."

Nancy cast her a sharp look she could feel icily knifing into her, even in the darkness.

"It's called a sense of humor, sis," Cindy said, limping into the room. "Yikes. Might want to look into investing in one of those."

"Yeah. Really funny. You're a real comedienne."

"Thank you, Denver. Good night!" Cindy said, hobbling over to the entryway where she closed the door and slid back the chain latch, opening the door all the way. "Hello middle of the night strangers, I'm Cindy. The little guy here is my nephew, Tim, which I guess you already know, and the less-than-gracious hostess glaring angrily from behind me would be my sister Nancy."

"I'm Brad, and this is my son, William," he said, bringing the boy in front of him and resting his hands nervously on William's shoulders.

"So tell me, Brad and William, what brings you here tonight?"

"We want you to come with us," William said.

"Where are you going?"

"My son seems to think we all need to go to the Qwest building downtown," Brad interjected.

"And why is that?" she asked. Cindy had every intention of dropping to her haunches like a catcher in front of the boy, but the spikes of pain stabbing into her back made it so that she could do little more than bend just enough at the hips to place her palms on her thighs to look the boy in the eyes.

"That's where the others are going to be."

"Who are these mysterious others?" Cindy asked with a wink toward the boy's father.

"I don't know yet," William said, his serious tone a direct contrast to that from which the questions were posed.

"How many people are going to be there?"

"I don't know that for sure either."

"So what you're saying is that we all need to walk downtown to meet up with a certain number of people whom you really don't know."

William nodded.

"All right then," Cindy said, clapping her hands. "Sounds good to me."

"Have you lost your mind?" Nancy barked.

"Can we, Mom?" Tim pleaded.

"You're sick," she said to Tim, and then to her sister, "and you're injured. Neither of you are going anywhere."

"Aren't you going to ask how we found you?" William asked in a small, nervous voice.

Nancy withdrew the finger she was wagging at her sister, and turned to face the small, dirty boy standing there on the porch with the dust being dragged earthward behind him like drizzle.

"How is it that of all the houses we passed we decided to stop at yours? And how do I know your son's name?"

"Okay, elaborate," Nancy said, pressing her palm against the back of the door to close it in a hurry, planning exactly how she was going to immediately flick the deadbolt back into place. And then what? All of the windows were now shards of glass covering the carpet. How difficult would it be for them to crawl through those wood-framed, rectangular holes and do whatever it was they intended to do regardless?

"I don't remember exactly how old I was, but this was like four or five years ago, anyway. My dad took me to Chuck E. Cheese's for my birthday, and since they don't have one of those up in the mountains by us, we had to come down here. I was playing in the ball pit, you know, that big tub of red and green and blue balls with the netting surrounding it. There were only a couple of us in there at first, which was fine, but then all of a sudden there were like twenty kids in there, some of them way too old to be playing in the ball pit. They had to be like thirteen or something. So I started to feel really uncomfortable, I think I was even crying, and I tried to get to the door so I could climb out of that thing when someone shoved me from behind. I fell forward and smacked right into some other kid. We knocked heads square on, well, noses anyway. Mine bled—"

"And so did Tim's," Nancy cut in.

"Yeah," William said. "So did Tim's."

"So you would be the guy who felt so bad about our kids colliding that you gave us all of those tickets you had won so Tim would be able to get one of the big stuffed animals on the wall," Nancy said, looking to Brad.

"I'd nearly forgotten all about that," Brad said. "Believe me, I still feel terrible about the whole thing."

"Don't. It was because of that day that the nosebleeds started. And if I hadn't taken him to the doctor to check on them, then they might never have tested his blood in time to find the elevated red blood count to diagnose the leukemia in time."

"That was you?" Tim asked. "I didn't recognize you. All I really remember was seeing stars and then I had blood all over my shirt."

"And I don't know for sure, but this is what I think happened. Some of my blood must have mixed with yours. Maybe you sniffed it back into your nose, or maybe some of it got past your lips and into your mouth, but I think that maybe a couple of these...things, that live inside of me might have gotten into you."

"What things?" Nancy asked, taking Tim by the shoulders and dragging him back from the doorway.

"Should I show her, Dad?" Tim asked.

Brad shook his head quickly from side to side, looking from the corner of his eye to Nancy in hopes that she hadn't seen his response, only to find her puzzled stare fixed stolidly upon him.

"Show me what?" she asked.

"It might be a little soon for that," Brad said.

"God help me, I'll close the door right now!"

"Okay!" Brad said, nodding to his son.

William leaned over and pulled the flashlight out of his backpack where he had stashed it, having grown tired of carrying its weight in his hand. He flipped the switch and then brought the light to his face.

"What am I supposed to be looking at?" Nancy asked, but slowly the answer became clear. At first, it appeared as though his eyes were ringed with the golden crust of little balls of sleep, his nostrils encircled with crust, but then it started to move. The hardly noticeable balls of what she had mistakenly thought to be sleep, slowly opened like flowers to the first rays of the sun rising over the plains. The same thing happened in his nose, with those little flower-like things—the entire blossom no more than a quarter of an inch wide—blooming around his nostrils with brilliant yellow and orange like spontaneously generated fire preparing to blast from his nose like a dragon.

"Please don't close the door," Brad said calmly, reading the primary thought blazing at the front of Nancy's mind as clearly as had there been a neon sign mounted on her forehead. He gently lowered his son's arm, forcing the light from his face and to the ground. "Believe me, I wasn't anything close to prepared when he showed me either. But it does go a long way toward believing what he's saying."

"That's how I found Tim," William said, his voice urgent. "You see, I think when we ran into each other, a couple of these things got passed from my blood to his. It wasn't until a few months later that the ones inside of me started to communicate with those inside of him. It's like they have ESP or something. All of their minds are connected together like some sort of single colony brain."

"There's nothing like that in Tim," Nancy snapped defiantly, causing Cindy to rest a reassuring hand on her sister's shoulder. "And even if there were, the doctors would have found them in any of the countless tests they've performed on him over the last couple of years."

"They hide. That's what they do, and it wasn't until recently that I even started to be able to see them outside of my body, though I've had them my entire life. Somehow they knew this was coming, and were just waiting for the right time to emerge. You see, I think what happens is they can be passed along as spores or something, and Tim got some of the dormant spores. It just took a couple months to incubate them and turn them into these things…"

"There's no way that my son has any of those things, so I think it would be best if you were to leave now."

"Please," William said. "Just check him. Now that the air is how they like it, I think you'll be able to see them."

"Please leave," Nancy said, the calmness in her words betraying the explosion lurking beneath.

"But you'll see—"

"I think we'd better go," Brad said, grabbing William's backpack and passing it to him.

"But if they don't come with us, they're going to die."

"We can't force them to," Brad said, looking back to Nancy and then quickly away from the reddened anger in her face.

Nancy slammed the door, the sound echoing like gunfire down the empty street. She turned to Tim and Cindy behind her, who were both probably every bit as startled as the two on the porch.

"That was less than hospitable," Cindy said. She held one of the candles in a short candlestick in her left hand, sitting on the coffee table with Tim coaxed up onto her lap. "Besides, I think there's something you might want to see."

"If it's anything other than both of your backsides walking back down the hallway to bed, you can save it for another time."

"The kid was right, Nan," Cindy said, looking up to her sister. "You should see this."

Nancy quickly hurried to her sister's side, immediately inspecting Tim's face where the candlelight flickered and danced along his cheek.

She looked first to the corner of his eye, hoping upon hope not to see what she had seen growing from beneath the other boy's lids. There was nothing on his eyeballs; nothing tucked into the small corners where the tear ducts were hidden. Her eyes followed the line of his nose down to his nostrils where the only thing she saw was the subtly reddened rims from the plugs for the oxygen line. No frightening growths there either.

"Time for both of you to go to bed," Nancy said, standing fully erect and turning in disgust at the thought of allowing herself to buy into the whole story even long enough to check Tim's face. "We'll forget all about this by tomorrow and we'll get both of you in to the doctor first thing."

"In his ear, Nancy," Cindy said levelly. "Look in his ear."

Nancy turned slowly and studied the serious expression on her sister's face. She didn't want to look, but found her legs moving toward them again regardless. Placing her left palm on the coffee table for balance, she leaned forward and looked into Tim's darkened ear canal, the shifting light alternately illuminating it like a swinging lantern in a mine shaft.

A small orange blossom, feathery petals extended, peeked out from deep within, slowly folding up those feathers and slipping back into the darkness, only to be replaced by another, which appeared like a worm peeking out of a hole in the ground, and then unfurled its petals.

Extending her pinkie and the long, well-manicured nail, she eased it into his ear and carefully scraped around in hopes of exhuming that parasite like she occasionally had to do the waxy build-up. She pulled her finger out, unable to feel anything but the thin layer of wax that wedged itself at the base of the nail against her skin. Holding it to the candlelight, she inspected it, but there was nothing but the wax.

"Why were all of those cars stalled out on the road, Nancy?"

"Accident."

"Why didn't we stick around to help?"

"You were bleeding and Tim...he should have been at home in his bed."

"They were all dead, weren't they?"

"If you don't rest—both of you—you can't get better."

"Weren't they, Nan?"

Nancy dropped her eyes to her lap where her fingers were nervously picking the packed wax from her nail.

"None of those cars are going to be moving in the morning. And if we can't get out of the neighborhood, then we can't get to the doctor, either. So unless you have a better idea, then I think we might want to consider what those guys were saying."

"He needs to be in bed," Nancy cried, the tears she had kept at bay finally spurting from her eyes. "We can't take him out there."

"Mommy," Tim said, reaching out and lovingly placing his right hand on her cheek, drawing her eyes to meet his own. "We need to do this."

"I won't risk your life by taking you out there in the middle of the night as sick as you are. What kind of mother would that make me?"

"And I won't risk yours by allowing you to stay here. What kind of son would that make me?"

Their eyes latched for a moment. Tim gave her a warm smile.

"I know how this is going to play out," he whispered. "And I'm not afraid."

"Tim…"

"But if we stay here, Mom, all of us—you and Aunt Cindy included—none of us will make it. Could you live with that?"

"It's my job to take care of you, to make sure that nothing ever happens to you."

"We need to go, Mom," he whispered, wrapping both arms around her neck and hugging her. She could feel the warmth of his breath on her ear. "Please."

Nancy looked to Cindy, whose tears drew tracks down her own cheeks as well.

Cindy reached out and stroked her sister's silky hair, tilting her head to the side, lips trembling, and nodded, swallowing back the lump in her throat.

"You know I love you more than anything," Nancy whispered, trying to keep the sound of her frightened tears from her voice.

"I've never doubted it for a second," Tim said, kissing her on the cheek and releasing her from the hug.

Still feeling the ghost of his arms around her neck, she wished she had never allowed the embrace to end, that she had simply knelt there on the living room floor, hugging her only child, the light of her life, for all eternity. Rising from the floor, she hurried to the front door, sniffing back the tears in hopes of finding a voice from the heart that felt as though it were being ripped to tattered shreds.

"Wait!" she called, throwing the door wide.

The boy and his father were standing there on the walkway in the middle of the front yard, only this time the man held the handle to a red child's wagon.

"He, um…" Brad said, fumbling for the words. "…he thought you might change your mind, so we just went next door and got this wagon. I don't think they're going to have much use for it anymore."

"Promise me that you will help me to look out for my child like he was your own," Nancy said, watching the man's eyes intently when he answered, trying to glean the truth from his soul as well as his words.

"You have my word," Brad said, nodding slowly.

"If any harm comes to him…"

"None will. Not so long as I have a say in the matter."

"And you…" she said, turning to William, her lower lip puckered to fight the sorrow that threatened to turn to uncontrolled sobs. "You did this to him." William looked to his shoes, uneasy beneath the weight of her glare. "Your father says that you know things. So tell me this…Promise me this! Promise me that my son will be all right!"

William forced his eyes from the ground and looked past her through the doorway to where he could only vaguely see Tim in the darkness, sitting on his aunt's lap. The outline of the boy's head nodded, the verbal okay resonating in his head as though Tim was speaking directly into his ear.

"I promise," William said, though he was unable to look her in the eyes. He just took his father's hand, and tried to keep the pathetic smile he had managed to forge on his face from faltering.

III

Shannen's ears were deafened to her own choked sobs and wails. Her cheeks thickened with mud where the tears sucked up the dust. The fluids that drained from her nose and slopped from her mouth thickened similarly, clinging in sloppy clumps to her chin. Knotted and twisted with dust, her hair hung limply in front of her eyes and down her back in crusted locks. She had even become numb to the screaming pain in her back and shoulders from the terrible exertion of having to drag Brian by his arms through the darkened maze of pine trees. His jacket and pants were torn from having to jerk his limp form free from the branches and detritus that snagged his clothing. There was no choice but to acquiesce to the panic and fear, allowing it to consume her mind so as not to notice just how increasingly cold and clammy his hands were becoming in her own sweaty grasp.

She had given up on screaming for help. There was nothing left of her raw throat to carry the words from her brain that repeated them over and over and over in all-consuming terror.

Backing through the bramble, not even able to see where she was going but hoping she had pointed her rear end in the right direction, she dragged him, unable to take her eyes from his face. His mouth was still fixed awkwardly into the scream that had died on his lips; his eyes rolled up beneath the lids, the lower crescent of those formerly beautiful blue eyes staring up at her in cold stillness. The blood that had formerly pumped out of his rent neck was now congealed to a dark brown mass; the claws he had used to draw it curled and frigid like forked spades in her grasp.

The rancid stench of rotten eggs had faded, or perhaps she had merely adapted to it. Craning her ears, she listened for the distraught call of the ducks from the pond to guide her from the woods, but there was no sound but the faint wind and the trampling of snapping twigs and brown needles underfoot.

The trees began to recede to either side, opening the clogged path.

She didn't even notice she had exited the forest until she could see the edge of it beyond Brian's pointed toes. The lake was surely hidden somewhere beneath the cloud of dust from which only the jaggedly snapped tops of the trees that had managed to stay rooted peered like old wooden tombstones from a low lying fog. Quickly looking from one side to the next, dry eyes searching through the raining dust, she located the car.

Shannen moaned, dragging Brian toward the car until his rigid, hooked fingers pried their way loose from her grasp and dropped to the ground. She looked apologetically down to him, glancing quickly back over her shoulder to the car, and then back to Brian.

"I'll be right back," she whispered hoarsely, and turned and ran toward the car.

The entire roof of the old Mustang was flattened, the supports that framed the windows crumpled. Glass littered the entire area from the smashed windows. The formerly pristine hood was patterned with all sorts of scratches and gouges, exposing the dull gray metal beneath the chipping paint. A thin line of smoke twisted out from beneath the partially popped hood.

Grabbing the handle of the door, Shannen nearly fell backward onto the wild grass when she yanked, but the door remained stuck. Leaning forward, she jerked the handle again, tugging and tugging until it finally swung outward with a metallic screech and a groan of buckling steel.

She ducked her head and climbed in, oblivious to the balls of glass that prodded mercilessly into her posterior, poking holes in the vinyl seats. She couldn't even sit fully erect as the ceiling had been lowered too far. The explosion had thrown the car into the air, rolling it onto its roof before somehow, miraculously, depositing it back onto the tires that now bowed outward.

The keys were still in the ignition where he had left them. She grabbed the knob for the headlights, but it was already pulled out into the "on" position, pumping amps through the shattered bulbs and snapped filaments.

The radio buzzed with static, though she tuned it out as white noise along with her own ceaseless cries.

Turning the key, she stamped the gas pedal. The engine roared and then stuttered before regaining its strength, belching black smoke from under the hood, the breeze carrying it right through the absent front windshield. She took her foot from the pedal, listening to the motor grumble and buck, the entire car shaking, making sure that it would stay on while she ran back to grab Brian.

Hopping back out, she raced to where she had left her boyfriend and quickly grabbed his hands. Both shoulder sockets made a snapping sound when she drew his arms upward. His hair dragged through the sharp buffalo grass, his stiff neck having frozen in the impossibly unnatural position in which she had left it crumpled.

"Just a little more," she croaked. "You'll be all right."

Leaning him against the open car door, she walked back around and straddled his waist, bending down and grabbing his jacket to either side of his chest. Screaming with the fresh rockets of agony, she pulled him up and wrapped her arms around him, swaying before finally steadying the two of them in what from afar would have looked like an embrace.

Stumbling around the door, unable to more than shuffle her feet, she dragged him toward the driver's seat, falling atop him as she tried to duck his head to keep from slamming it into the frame. She scurried quickly over him, scooting onto her knees in the passenger seat and struggling to pull him up inside. The waist of his jeans snagged on the stick shift, causing the car to threaten to lurch like a bronco from the gate, but she managed to drag him across and onto her lap. Swinging his legs around, she planted his feet on the floorboard, forcing his knees to bend though they had no intention. It sounded like pencils snapping, but she ignored it, straightening his torso and propping his head atop the headrest. She climbed back into the driver's seat and slammed the door. She could feel the air still coming in from around the ill-fitting seal, but a shove with her elbow confirmed that it had at least latched.

Shannen reached up with her left hand and grabbed the seat belt, crossing it over her chest and buckling it by the console. She looked to

Brian, his neck cocked toward the ceiling, unblinking eyes staring right up into the warped roof.

"Sorry," she sobbed, leaning across him to reach the passenger's seat belt and brought it across his chest, buckling it next to her own.

She pressed the clutch and wiggled the stick, wrenching it to the left and then slamming it forward into first.

The Mustang lurched, spewing another thick black cloud, and rolled uneasily forward. It took all of her strength to crank the wheel to the right, driving over the uneven grasses, to finally turn around and settle into the eroded ruts of the road. She could distinguish little more than the grass median between the two dirt tracks, trying her best to keep it centered down the middle of the hood. It bounced from rock to rock, hopping like a rabbit down the all but invisible road.

Tremendous branches ripped from their moorings appeared as if from nowhere right in front of the hood, leaving her no time to even think of stomping for the brake before scraping right underneath the car, scattering the few remaining ponderosa needles across the hood. Large grains of glass skittered across the dashboard with each turn, some sliding down the holes and into the heater vents, others falling into her lap and littering the floorboard around her feet.

"Hold on," she said, pressing on the gas.

The speedometer crept past fifteen miles an hour, reaching for twenty before coming to rest behind a thick crack in the plastic shield, obscuring it from sight. The engine growled and started to rattle the entire car, but she was unable to slam the stick down into second no matter how hard she fought with it. She eased off just enough to cease the shuddering of the Mustang, bringing the little white needle back into view to the left of the crack.

Dust raced through the window, striking her face and eyes like pellets fired from an air gun, but she had to keep her focus on the road. Any time now, the trees would fall back from the right side of the road, where the shoulder would drop off hundreds of feet into the lush woods. Often they would even pull over on that wide, sandy shoulder, up against the guard rail and stare out at the city lights that stretched off clear to the far horizon where they met with the twinkling stars like the reflection of the night sky on a tranquil pond.

Though tonight she would have gladly traded a kidney for just a hint of the city, a single luminescent star burning from the vast parking lot of a shopping mall, the stacks of lighted floors from the distant high-rises of downtown. But she could no more than glance through the dusty gap where the passenger window had once been, for each time she turned to look, she could see that same, tortured expression fixed on Brian's face. And it wasn't changing.

Brian was dead. That was easy enough to see.

He hadn't even tried to take a breath in forever, and no matter how cool he might have been trying to play it, surely even he would have been repulsed by the feces that crusted his blistering flesh to his boxers. She just simply couldn't allow it. For if she permitted that painfully obvious revelation to slip past her defenses for even a moment, she would completely lose control of her faculties and wind up curled into fetal position on the side of the road, rocking back and forth and sobbing uncontrollably.

"You'll be all right, Brian. You'll see. We'll get you to a doctor and he'll be able to fix you right up," she said, forcing herself to talk to him to keep the silence from solidifying the finality of his fate in her mind. "What's that, Bri? Turn up the radio you say? Whatever you want, hon."

She reached forward and cranked the static up, pressing the black buttons that twitched the red needle from preset to preset, finding nothing but static on every station before finally bringing it back to the station he would have wanted the most.

"Sounds like every station is playing the same song."

Finally the trees faded to the right, and she was lucky to catch a glimpse of the guardrail before driving straight into it and sending the car rocketing over the edge of the cliff. The brakes snagged the road, screaming on the asphalt before sliding sideways onto the shoulder, firing pebbles in their wake.

This was the lookout all right. She had been here many times. But nothing was as it should have been.

There was no carpet of light stretching from as far as she could see to her left, all the way across to her right. No towers of pocked yellow clumped into the small area that was downtown. There were no long lines of light from the runways at the airport, no blinding glare from the ring of lights encircling Coors Field. There was nothing but blackness lurking beneath a foggy mass of dust, as though she were instead standing on some distant Scottish moor and staring out across the cold waters of the Atlantic. The nothingness stretched infinitely outward, failing even to form a horizon.

Pulling the handle, she shoved at the door several times before it finally popped open and she crept out onto the shoulder. Her aching legs couldn't even lift her feet from the ground, dragging them rather through the dirt, adding just that much more dust to the cloud that sat atop her and elicited a violent throng of coughing. She watched the unimaginable stretch of darkness, waiting for even a single light to flash on, to see spinning cherries or hear the call of a police siren, but there was nothing.

Nothing.

Bumping into the guardrail, she forced her legs to lift her feet over the thick aluminum rail one at a time, ultimately propping her rear end on it. Her head shook of its own accord, side to side, her brow lowering not just in disbelief, but in argument with her eyes that just had to be deceiving her.

"*...hear me?*" the radio crackled from behind her. "*Anyone out there...ear me?*"

She turned to face the car. It had been so long since she had heard any sound other than her own arguably psychotic voice that she wondered at first if it was real or if her ears were in cahoots with her eyes.

"*...out there?*" The voice emerged from the static, fading in and out. "*Can anybody hear me?*"

"I hear you," Shannen whispered, staring down into the darkness where somewhere there was a man leaning over a microphone who sounded every bit as isolated and desperate as she. "Please...please, keep talking."

"*...anybody—*"

IV

"—hear me?" Trick shouted into the microphone.

The emergency light buzzed from the metal box on the wall, staining the thin haze in the room a pale red. Dust settled atop the console, a thin layer lining both the inside and outside of the soundproof glass.

He checked all of the incoming lines, but, like every other phone on the floor from the reception desk to the private offices to either side of the hallway, there was no dial tone.

"If anyone out there can hear me, I want you to come down here to the station. It's hard to miss. It's the tallest building in the entire state, and it's right smack dab in the middle of downtown. God, what is it? Thirteen fifteen twelfth avenue? Something like that. Just follow the big blue neon Qwest sign...never mind. Not like there's any power to it now anyway."

There was no way of knowing how long the backup generator would run. That was part of the appeal of positioning the radio station where they had. It shared the same power grid with three major private hospitals, and damned if anyone would allow that area to potentially lose the life supporting power for more than a few minutes. The greatest test to the backup power, or so far as he could remember anyway, lasted only about ten minutes, and that had felt like an eternity at the time. How long had it been now? Could it possibly have been as long as an hour? Two?

After watching Jerry die right before his very eyes, Trick had run down to the floor beneath, bursting through the office door of whatever brokerage he had ridden past on the elevator every afternoon without bothering to learn the name. There was no one there but a single maintenance man, who couldn't hear Trick's cries for help since he was collapsed on the ground next to his push-cart of cleaning supplies, already brittle with rigor mortis. The floor beneath, a level dominated by a maze of cubicles with computers and swiveling chairs, with pictures of strangers framed on every desktop, had been completely abandoned.

Realizing the futility of searching for assistance in professional offices in the middle of the night on a Friday, he bounded down the stairs, watching the numbers on the doors, rounding each reddened landing beneath the emergency lights. His pounding footsteps echoed from the hollow confines, stretching clear up to the roof before coming right back down to the very bottom of the well. By the time he hit the main floor and threw himself through the door, hammering the release bar with his hip, he was so completely out of breath that he had to double over there in that mirrored hallway, surrounded by nothing but stilled elevators, sucking whatever oxygen he could from the dust, dryly spitting the grime from his gummy tongue.

Potted palms were strewn across the walkway, leaving a trail of dirt from shattered ceramic pots all the way across the floor to their exposed clusters of roots. Balls of glass covered the floor like marbles, and the dust had been so thick that he had been forced to constantly rub his watering eyes with his fists.

The security men who worked the front desk at night—watching the monitors from every floor with all of the interest of a televised checkers match—still sat at the desk. Trick had raced up to them, leaning right over the front counter, and shouted directly into their faces. One man was slumped forward, his face planted on his clipboard amidst a widening pool of blood, his cap punctured with small holes like bullet fire. Another leaned backward in his swiveling chair, hands draped limply to his sides, his tongue swollen so large in his mouth as to keep his teeth from closing back together. He had torn the collar from his shirt, exposing a blued and scraped neck, distended from what looked like an orange lodged in his throat. A third man lie on his back on the floor behind the desk next to his capsized chair, still clinging tightly to the revolver he had used to end his suffering with a spattering of gray matter across the floor and up the wall behind. Yellowish chunks, rife with dark hair and fragments of cranium, had hardened in the draining lines of blood across the list of businesses and the floors they inhabited.

It had all been so overwhelming that he had walked all the way across the lobby and through the revolving doors, when he could have simply passed through where one of the windows had formerly been.

Even at that time of night there should have been activity down there on the street, obnoxiously loud party guys and gals stumbling by, arm in arm, a handful of kids milling about a shared brown-bagged forty, hurriedly trying to spray paint their tags onto one of the benches or marble facades. Generally a good half dozen taxis lined the street in front of the building, waiting either for a call to transport one of the undoubtedly rich and wasted clubbers home, or for a cop to run them all off from the yellow-curbed fire zone.

"Hello!" he had screamed at the top of his lungs, standing there in front of the building with his head buckled back to the sky. But there had been no reply.

Still walking, his shaking legs moving for no other reason than the fear of standing still, he made his way out into the middle of the courtyard. No one stood around the small fountain, now nothing more than small spigots jutting up from the ground, surrounded by the shredded remnants of the junipers that had been uprooted from the triangle-shaped marble planters. There wasn't even a single person sitting on one of the benches...

He probably could have walked right by and never noticed them, so long as he hadn't looked down. Perhaps the wind had stirred in such a way as to expose them from the rapidly falling dust, now accumulating on the ground like snowfall, his feet leaving tracks. There, crumpled beneath the bench like sardines crammed into a pill bottle, were a good three or four distinct bodies. Arms and legs hung out from beneath it like an octopus trying to reach under the seal of a door. Twisted and inhumanly bent, appendages were defined by the jagged bones protruding from the skin. The only possible means of distinguishing one from the next was by the color of the torn sleeves, and even then there was no clear way of telling just how many bodies were folded and jammed into that small space.

He recoiled from the sight, from the rising stench, turning to the street only to see even more bodies, pinned up against the high curb, wedged into the rectangular gaps above the drainage gates like casually discarded refuse. Debris bounced merrily down the middle of the vacant street, finally coming to rest at the end of the block on the side of the building where all of the cabs had wound up, tossed from the road by the rage of the wind and meshed into a tangle of metal up against the light rail car, pinning it against its little station.

He tried not to count the bodies, tried not to notice the carcasses drifting in and out of the dust at the periphery of his vision, just lying there face down on the ground with their clothes flagging uselessly in the wind. There had to be twelve, no, fifteen human lives that had ended right there in the courtyard in front of the radio station, and at least six more inside. That was more than twenty dead people, and, outside of himself, he had yet to come across another living entity.

"There," Trick said, fitting the mobile microphone to his head. It looked like an old set of "cans," the kind of earphones one might have expected to see someone wearing while roller skating back in the late seventies with their Daisy Dukes and socks yanked up over their kneecaps. A microphone curled around in front of his face, topped by a foam damping piece to keep him from sounding like he was spitting all over the mike. "I am no longer tied to this desk, and, assuming that there's anyone out there who can hear me, I'll continue to broadcast until we use up the last of our juice.

"I'm not counting on the city fixing the power anytime soon. Maybe none of you have been able to get outside tonight—as quite possibly you're lying dead in your room—but it looks like you missed one hell of a corpse storm. There are bodies all over the courtyard right out in front of the building, and everyone stupid enough to have been in here burning the midnight oil, save for moi, of course, is threatening to turn to compost. Even the brain trust of security guards in the lobby are probably losing a hand of cards for their souls in the afterlife as we speak."

Trick slipped his arms into the backpack that contained the power supply for the remote unit, shouldered it, and plugged it into the transmitter clipped to his hip. With a sigh, he left the control room and found his way back out into the hall.

His stomach cramped with nausea, and his head was pounding like there was a woodpecker inside of his skull trying to chip its way out of its calcified prison. The thought of joining the others out on the sidewalk with their insides already liquefying, just lying there in wait for the scavengers to come tear their meat from the bones so their fluids could nutrify the soil...

"So maybe I'm not the world's foremost expert on megadeath, that's the mass extinction event outside, not the band, for those of you who may have just become confused. My education came from a bunch of underpaid, under-interested teachers who would probably rather have taken their own lives than suffer through another never-ending day, had they been smart enough to figure out those confounding child-proof caps, anyway. Hell, I don't think my shop teacher could have passed Prison Mechanics 101 and made a shiv. But I did watch the news. It was the only way my parents would allow the television to stay on during dinner, and believe you me, they needed it on as much as I did. The only thing worse than the quote unquote food that crawled up on our TV trays to die, was the conversation that surrounded it."

He walked through the station, stopping by the front desk and looking down at Tina's body. She had been a real looker all right: legs that went all the way up from the floor into that short skirt that was hardly thick enough to qualify as a belt, and a smile that could melt you the moment you walked through the door. But now he could hardly bear to look at her. Her throat was black and bruised, and her entire body was starting to swell, not just like taking on air, but lumpy knots of pooling fluids standing out against her now translucent skin through which he could see her webwork of thin green veins. Taking her by the hands, the tissue connecting the skin to the bones and muscle already loosening to the point that it felt as though he were about to pull her flesh off like gloves, he dragged her across the room, through the shattered glass and litter of papers, toward the open side of the building. The wind blasted in with enough force that it threatened to capsize him from his feet, so he sat down, scooting along the carpet to the edge of the floor, dragging Tina along with him.

"There are a lot of things I learned from the news. I remember when we invaded Granada. I still haven't got the slightest clue where that is—or where the Falklands are for that matter—but we certainly made short work of those poor bastards, didn't we? Might as well have been invading Coney Island for all of the resistance we met. And how could any of us forget the assassination attempt on Ronald Reagan. Anyone remember the name of the man who took the bullet for him? No. No one. But I'll sure bet all you kids out there know the name of the loony toon that pulled the trigger, eh?

"But otherwise, there's little else on the nightly news to leave an impression. These trained monkeys behind the desk have to hype the most trivial stories to make them sound like they're all life and death struggles. 'Tonight at nine o'clock, we'll hear from a woman who nearly lost her life in a harrowing battle with a cowlick. We'll have her inspirational story along with an important consumer warning for those of you considering baiting mouse traps with your genitalia.'

"I found high school sports about as intriguing as the amateur lawn-mowing championships, and local events and politics positively tedious. Who cares whether or not the mayor made it to his five year-old daughter's ballet recital while working diligently to write a quarter of a percent gas tax hike to pay for additional greens-keepers at his private golf course? But there was occasionally that one good story that made you think. I remember this one blurb about an outbreak of malaria or scabies or some other third world disease in Africa, I think. All I remember was there were huts in a jungle. It could have been California with the inflated price of property for all I know, but what I do remember, stayed with me all this time. These people, these fly-riddled corpses, who succumbed to the disease, had to be burned instead of buried to keep the disease from spreading, to keep the mosquitoes from drawing their blood and spreading it to the others. They had these bodies stacked as high as a fraternity-sponsored beach bonfire, and just kept piling them in until the smoke turned black."

Trick looked one last time to Tina, brushing her scattered bangs from in front of her bright blue eyes, half-lodged beneath her pink and swollen lids, and then pushed her body out the window. He hoped the wind didn't drag it back in through the broken windows on the lower levels, so it would fall down to the courtyard with the others.

He arose and crossed the room to where Jerry was still propped up against the wall. Grabbing him by the collar of his shirt, he dragged him back over to the absent wall.

With a sigh, Trick sat back down and pulled Jerry over next to him, the man's stiff left arm hanging out the window like a Rolex-gilded flagpole.

"I don't think I understood exactly why they had to roast all of those people like that at the time. It seemed so primitive and barbaric. 'Damn it, Pete. Mom's dead, too. Better throw her out on the barbecue with Aunt Sue.' But I think I get it now.

"I wish I knew why all of these people died, but more than that, I wish I knew why I didn't. Maybe this was some sort of terrorist germ warfare-type thing. I don't know. But I watched my producer tear out his own throat trying to breathe. Not one of those things that's very easy to forget, mind you. The last thing I want to do is to have to go through that myself. I'd rather hop right out this window here in front of me and take my chances with the sidewalk, than to have to endure the kind of agony he went through.

"So that leads me back to the point of my story. It's like the plague in Merry Old England out there, minus the black cloaked man wandering the streets, clanging his bell and shouting to bring out your dead. Though I guess in proposing what I'm about to, I'm taking on that role myself. Now this may sound inhuman, but versus the alternative, I don't see much of a choice. If whatever killed these people is contagious, then we have no choice but to attempt to destroy this virus or whatever it is, before it can destroy us. So right now—and

I hope his mother isn't listening—I'm going to shove my producer out the window and down to the street with all of the other bodies. Boo and hiss all you want, but the prospect of carrying these bodies down a couple dozen stairs and risking contracting whatever it is that gutted them, sounds only slightly better than defiling them in a romantically necrophiliac-kind of way.

"God speed, Jerry. Say hello to Wile E. Coyote for me, would ya?" Trick said, crawling down to Jerry's feet and pushing on his shoes. His rigid form slid relatively easily over the lip of the window, teetering, wobbling, and then plunged off into the darkness.

Trick rose to his feet, emotionally exhausted, or perhaps stoically numbed, and headed through the front doors of the station and out into the hall.

"If there's anyone at all out there—anyoneanyoneanyone—come on down to the station. It'll be the tall building with the bonfire in front of it," he said, coughing with the exertion of opening the phenomenally heavy door to the stairs. "We'll make it a party. BYOB. Bring your own bodies. But then again, we should probably have more than enough to go around here."

He thundered down the stairs, his shirt sticky with sweat, legs aching from his second jaunt down the hundreds of stairs, which was more exercise than he'd experienced in all the years combined since high school.

His voice echoed loudly in the stairwell, reverberating in the cans in his ears like he was shouting down into a chasm.

"Okay, here's the deal. All kidding aside...I'm scared to death here. I don't even know how long it's been since I've come across another living soul. So if there is anyone out there who can hear the sound of my voice, come down here to the station. Please. I'll rummage up all of the free t-shirts and CD's you want, just please drag your ass down here and prove to me that I'm not stuck in the middle of some sort of *Twilight Zone* episode."

His voice faltered and he had to bite his lip to keep the childish cries welling in his chest from overtaking his restraint. Tears blossomed from his eyes and drained down his cheeks.

"Here's where I would generally cut to a tune," he said, rounding level after level, continually funneling downward toward the bottom. "But since that's currently not an option, I have no choice but to announce to you that effective immediately, our new format will be talk, talk, and more talk. But low and behold, it's all going to be commercial free. See, there's a silver lining in every smothering dust cloud."

The soles of his feet throbbed from slapping down on those

cement stairs in his old, black Chuck Taylor's, that by now had worn clear through what little cushioning had been provided, his feet protected by nothing more than a thin flap of rubber.

"Now should there actually be someone of any significance—no offense to you my dedicated listeners—out there jerkin' the gurken to the sound of my voice...how's about a little help here? I'm talking to all of you military types and law enforcement officials. I'm thinking quarantine, though with my absolute lack of military training and initiative, I could be wrong. Heck, why not napalm the entire area? I'd appreciate an air lift out of this hell first, but I'd be the last person on this earth to blame you right now for just nuking the entire godforsaken city."

Trick pounded down the last flight of stairs, leaning up against the wall by the door only long enough to catch his breath. He pitied whatever audience there might actually be out there, listening to him wheezing like an old man, coughing up gobs of phlegm. Apparently that came with age. Happy thirtieth birthday, Richard Turner, yours is the gift of life.

He pried the door to the lobby open and stepped into the elevator corridor, nearly jumping at the sight of his own reflection from the mirror with a false hope so strong he nearly lunged across the walkway and slammed face-first into the mirror in an attempt to hug his reflection.

"I suppose it's a little too late to worry about finding some latex gloves by now, huh?" he muttered, walking around the security desk and slipping his hands beneath the armpits of the closest security guard. Wrenching him from his chair, sending it clattering to the floor, he dragged the man through the dust and glass, and through the front of the building. "Now to see if our little gravity experiment work—"

Trick had to turn quickly from the sight, dropping the security guard to the ground and slapping his hand over his mouth and nose in a futile attempt to hold back the vomit that sprayed right through his fingers and ran down his shirt.

"Christ Almighty," he coughed, spitting out the vile remnants.

Jerry and Tina—though he could hardly bear to think of them in those terms any more—had landed within a few feet of one another, both of them splattering like watermelons. They had drifted a good dozen feet from the face of the building, landing right in the middle of the ring of nozzles surrounding the fountain.

"Here'd be a unique twist for a Gallagher show," he said, forcing himself to chuckle, though the ghastly laugh sounded more like the precursor to insanity in his own ears. He picked the guard up again and hurried backward, dropping him right in the middle of the repulsive mess with a sloppy splash, and ran several steps away to keep from having to look at or breathe or smell any part of that gruesome display.

"Now I'm going to let all you wannabe radio announcers out there in on a little trick of the trade. Want to know how to get that unique radio voice, you know, the one that sounds so deep and husky? They'll probably kick me out of the union for revealing the man behind the curtain, but here it is...smoke. The more you smoke, the better you sound."

He walked back into the building, fishing his lighter and a smoke from the boxed pack of Kool menthols jammed into the pocket of his jeans. Behind the counter he went, lighting the smoke and puffing desperately.

"They don't let you do this on the air any more. Won't even let you do it in the building. Want to know why every radio station now goes to those thirty and forty-five minute sets of straight music? It's so the deejay can smoke. Come by the building any time, day or night, and you'll see the talent out back by that little ashtray dragging them down like their lives depended on it."

Dropping to all fours, he crawled beneath the desk, careful not to so much as look at the man with the pistol lying an arm's length away. He talked with the cigarette dangling from the corner of his mouth, wincing at the smoke riding into his eyes.

"Most of us were born with these normal voices. No character, no unseen charisma. We have to work long and hard on loosening these vocal chords and making it so that our lungs have the air capacity of one of those little balloons some surgeon will eventually use to scrape out the insides of our clogged arteries. Orson Wells, man did that guy have the voice of legend! And Wolfman Jack? I'd be surprised if he didn't smoke the entire town of Raleigh in an afternoon.

"That's why you don't hear too many old guys doing this job. They're all dead. Either that or their jobs were usurped by some other young kid with the Marlboro voice who'd work for pennies on the dollar. I tell you, after the indentured servitude they call an internship, he'd be happy to be making enough to buy a value meal instead of fishing it out of the dumpster after close. Believe me, I was there once."

His knuckle jarred the object of his search, knocking it onto its side to the tune of the clatter of glass. It was there just as he knew it would be. The way those guys looked up at him when he walked through the doors at night, like he'd caught them watching Tina cross and uncross her legs through the monitor, he knew they were up to something. That, coupled with the ever-present TicTac dispenser, sealed the deal.

Grabbing hold of the long neck of the bottle, he backed from beneath the desk and staggered to his feet, heading right back out to the middle of the courtyard.

"Ohhh-kay..." he said, standing before the heap of bodies, studying the black label of the fifth of Jack Daniels, marking the line of fluid no more than a few swigs from the top. He unscrewed the cap, letting it drop to the concrete and roll off. He looked at the bottle again, studying it for any sign of visible virulent growth, shrugged and tossed back a gullet full. Cocking his head, he breathed the gust of fire, and then shook the contents of the bottle out over the tangle of bodies.

"So I assume since no one has come here to stop me from doing what I said I was going to do, then either I'm doing the right thing, or there's no one left out there to care. Either way, I'm almost beginning to wish I'd stopped at 7-Eleven on the way in and picked up a big bag of marshmallows."

He held the lighter out in his hand, suddenly aware of the awesome power contained within, and knelt next to the man he had just dropped atop the others. Striking the flint with his thumb, he cupped the rising flame behind his free hand, and lowered it to the security guard's sleeve, saturated and reeking of Jack. Flickering and dancing, threatening to extinguish itself, he held the flame against the cloth, wondering for a second if this was actually going to work. Already searching his mind for any possible containers filled with flammable fluids in the office, he had to throw himself backward onto his rear end at the sight of the bright blue flame that raced outward across the bodies.

"Need another log for the fire," he said, tucking the lighter back into his pocket and heading through the front of the building. "Got a long night ahead of me, folks, and by the time I'm through, I'm guessing the FCC is going to need to add a few new words to their list of 'you can't say that's.'"

Crouching behind the desk, he inhaled one last time and let the spongy butt drop from his mouth. He took the guard—now growing branches in Dante's seventh circle—by the ankles and slid him out into the lobby. Glancing over his shoulder, he could see the rising flames, sputtering tufts of black smoke. Maybe it was he who was traversing the path through hell, trapped in the undiscovered eighth circle where all bad radio personalities go. All he needed was Kasey Kasem counting down the corpses.

"Dear God," he gasped, finally bearing the gravity of the situation squarely on his shoulders, watching the thick smoke parting even the formerly impregnable dust. "Have mercy—"

V

"*—on us."*

Jason planted his face in his hands, those last six words reverberating not just in his head, but in his very soul.

He had been walking when he heard the voice coming from the stereo of one of the many cars sitting dead in the middle of the street. The driver of that old Celica was crumpled over the wheel with his forehead on the dash, blood draining from his eyes right down his face and onto the steering column. Pinned between a van and a Suburban, the front and rear smashed nearly all the way into the cabin, the last trails of smoke had died with the engine hours prior. Only the radio drifted from the shattered window, the abominable horror of the situation purveyed through the poor bastard whose words had forced Jason to sit down on the curb and listen in appalled reverence.

Lord only knew where he was by now. He had simply set out walking in no direction in particular, determined to just keep going until he finally came across someone else, anyone else. The further north he got, the more stalled cars filled with festering corpses he came across. Dead animals, cats and dogs mainly, littered the sidewalks and lawns; some still attached to the leashes they had been using to lead the sweatsuit-clad walker behind them, others at the far reaches of the ropes that tethered them to the stakes in the yard. Birds lay on the ground around the trees they had formerly resided within like shed pinecones. Squirrels dotted the dust-coated grass of the parks.

He had never realized just how much noise there actually was on even the stillest of nights, until it was gone. There was no distant rumbling of a train or the wail of its horn. No helicopters knifed across the starless sky. Chirping birds, cats dashing through the hedges, dogs barking protectively from back yards: all were conspicuously absent.

When he had heard that voice coming from inside of that car, he had nearly turned cartwheels in his rush toward it, thinking, however erroneously, that it was the man within who was talking to him. He had recoiled quickly at the sight, of course, but the sound of that voice, coming from another living person, no matter where he might be, at least gave him hope. For a while he had thought himself to be the only survivor, and there was no more terrifying feeling in the world. After little more than fifteen minutes of walking, he was already entertaining the notion of prying some old matron's hand from her poodle's leash and hanging himself from one of the streetlights. After an hour he was more than ready to wrap his mouth around the exhaust pipe of one of the idling cars.

But now he had a goal.

Luck be his lady, or maybe it was the hand of fate that guided that first step to the north, toward the center of town. Either way, he was headed in the right direction and very anxious to meet this Trick Turner whom he had heard so many times on the radio and never once given a second thought to.

Climbing from the curb, his legs strode forward with renewed energy. He didn't even look into every car window that he passed as he had thus far, watching each of the deceased for the slightest sign of movement, before moving on to the next. His eyes rose to the horizon, prying at the cloud of dust for the first sign of the towers that would signal downtown. He found himself jogging, his arms churning at his sides. He raced through one intersection after the next. There was no time to pause to search for the street signs that had been ripped down by the wind, still attached to the wires that had once held them aloft with the traffic lights, leaving only the tall metal poles as monuments to their former existence.

Jason marked his passage by the changing of the architecture. Large Victorians faded away, as did the deep green yards in front of them, the overgrown tree roots tearing up the sidewalk. The houses grew smaller, shrinking to bungalows, along with the lots, now no more than weed-infested brown patches in front of cement porches crumbling to powder. Wood showed through from under withering, peeling paint. Children's toys: tricycles, wagons, plastic basketball hoops, were left untended in the yards, giving rise to concern for the children who, God willing, were still neatly tucked into their beds, never even aroused from their dreams on the way to the afterlife.

Gigantic deciduous trees, elms and maples nearly as old as the dying houses themselves stood either barren of foliage, all but the most sturdy of branches stolen from them, or were fallen across the road, crumpling the unfortunate cars beneath. But it wasn't until he came across the first storefront, some sort of general store slash market with the name hand-painted in Spanish above the doorway, the window smashed in despite the bars that still shielded the insides, that he knew he was getting close.

Abandoned warehouses, the windows boarded up with graffiti-smattered plywood, rusted out cars decomposing behind the barbed wire topped chain-link fences, passed to the left, the gaps between exposing small cul-de-sacs lined with houses that looked like they should have been condemned. A river gently burbled from beyond.

Panting, he grabbed at his side and slowed to a walk, sucking hard for oxygen. All he wanted to do was just get to that station, to another human being. Nothing else mattered. Even his Hippocratic instinct, stimulated by each passing car, though it was readily apparent that there was no helping the occupants, had faded to memory.

It was all about survival now. And the chances of that grew exponentially greater with the addition of another.

He forced himself to run again, his legs burning from oxygen deprivation, his lungs violently expelling the massive amounts of dust that filled his alveolar sacs. Squalor metamorphosed into urban renewal, with apartments reminiscent of the kind of seedy motels that made Hitchcock an icon, into towering structures with penthouse suites costing more than he ever would have been able to afford, even as a doctor. Parking structures rose from beneath the ground, the gates permanently lowered to eternally bar all access while the attendant in the miniature booth took the time to allow his flesh to waste from his bones.

Shattered storefronts, nearly half of them either Chinese restaurants or coffeehouses, lined both sides of the street now. Their signs still promised them to be open, though he was sure the food was no longer warm, but the patrons who had run screaming from the establishments only to drop dead on the sidewalks were in no position to complain. Most appeared to have clawed apart their faces, eventually falling into a now dry puddle of their own blood, while a few blessed individuals were lucky enough to have been struck by passing motorists and either dragged beneath the cars or pinned between them in the ultimate gridlock.

It was like snapshots from a foreign war. Everything was in shambles. Brick and mortar piled on the sidewalks where it had fallen in chunks from the buildings. Glass from all of the shattered windows formed a carpet beneath the faceless dead, with dust curling like smoke from their stilled forms. Immobile cars, their ultimate fate betrayed only by the faint glow of the few headlights and taillights that hadn't been shattered upon impact. Everything was various shades of brown and gray, from the sky to the buildings to the corpses that lie before them. It was as though he had stepped right out of the twenty-first century and into 1940's Poland behind the cresting tide of Nazi aggression.

There was no sprinting now. Not with all of the people that had curiously wandered out from the storefronts, and piled atop each other in their panic to rush back into the doors leading up to their apartments above. There were bodies atop bodies, human stacks of decomposing pancakes.

And the smell...it was beginning to intensify. First, the gasses had been trapped within the bodies with little chance of escape, swelling and swelling and swelling until they were able to distend the abdomens. The contents were then forced out of the intestines through the anus, to slowly belch out through the open mouths around the near seal formed by the engorged and bloated tongues. Cellular rot even began to seep through the microscopic pores in the skin, forming a thin waxy layer of putrescence, thickening with dust, sapping the clothing into it like a second skin. Sure, there had been many they had been unable to save in the ER. The morticians had no choice but to cut them open as quickly as they possibly could, removing all of their internal organs before dissolution to liquid form, soaking through their blackening skin. There had been occasions where one of his patients, while waiting a little too long for the overburdened autopsy staff, had begun the process there on a gurney, draped beneath a bloodstained sheet. The first time he had been infuriated that no one had seen to his patient, throwing the sheet back in rage, only to hurriedly replace it as the aroma accosted his unprepared senses and rushed the bitter coffee that had been his life sustenance in syrupy gushes from his stomach.

But that was just one.

This was that same smell intensified to the power of infinity. He imagined it to be the smell of a slaughterhouse on the cutting room floor, the drain clogged with various innards, backing up and growing warmer. Even that wasn't repulsive enough, though. The smell now was a sentient aromatic entity that arose from the ground on tendrils before snapping free and slithering up his nostrils to linger in his sinuses and die, dripping vile excrement down the passage to his nose and onto his tongue. He had thought Trick's rush to burn the bodies to be a tad excessive, but it wasn't until this moment that he truly realized just how right the man had been.

Each of these corpses was a breeding ground for bacteria and viral infection, the white blood cells no longer able to fend off their pathogenic advances. Were it indeed some sort of biological agent or infection that had dropped all these people in their tracks, they would be replicating beyond comprehension right this very moment, their population rising into astronomically large numbers. It was imperative that they destroy these bodies before they release a wrath of pestilence of Biblical proportion. It was overwhelming. There were far more bodies than they could ever hope to round up in a lifetime. One man's fire was nowhere near enough, like trying to face down a swarm of locusts with but the sun and a magnifying glass. They would have to burn the entire town to the ground, scourge it from the face of the earth. And what if it was like this in Colorado Springs as well? Pueblo? Fort Collins? Surely some sort of National Guard fortifications would have been flown in by now to set up camps for the wounded and provide shelter and food for whatever survivors there might be. No, this extended further than the mile high city. And what about Kansas City or Salt Lake? Hell, in the time he had been walking they could have mobilized the entire Red Cross Army and flown them in from California by helicopter. Even foreign allies would have had more than enough time to streak a pair of fighter jets from halfway around the world to fill the skies overhead.

Just what in the name of God had actually happened?

He had to force it from his mind, force his feet to step over the masses with detached indifference. Walking out into the street, using the less cluttered shoulder to weave through the parked cars, he kept his eyes to the sky, watching the skyscrapers rise higher and higher above him. He couldn't look to the ground or he would begin to speculate as to the lives of the rotting minions, to the pain they must have endured in the process of succumbing to the disease or whatever. As the victims had bled out through their eyes and clawed at their own throats, it was obviously a very powerful pathogen that affected both the central nervous system and the respiratory system. It was how he imagined an astronaut might look were he to shed his helmet and take a good deep breath out there in space.

Maybe that was it. He had nearly forgotten about it until now, but he suddenly remembered the smell that had trailed the thunderous cloud of dust. Sulfur. It had smelled like sulfur. Burning sulfur in combination with oxygen could easily transform common carbon dioxide into the toxic sulfur dioxide by replacing the carbon atom and bonding with the two free oxygen molecules. That would definitely produce a similar effect to what he saw in the gruesomely tortured bodies. He had learned a little bit about it in medical school during the Gulf War when the Iraqis were torching their own oil wells. It took specially trained men in full HAZMAT gear days at a time to extinguish the fires, as the fumes were so potently toxic.

What if a meteorite, still ablaze from its descent through the atmosphere, had slammed far enough into the crust of the earth to meet with an unknown reserve of shale oil? The sudden exposure to the intense heat, coupled with the enormity of that layer under the ground could potentially have led to such a reaction. It was unlikely, but remotely plausible. For the meteorite to have remained burning long enough to incur such an unlikely chemical reaction, it would have needed considerable exposure to oxygen, even while underground, especially since it displaced so much air outward with the force of impact. It would have basically had to have landed squarely in the middle of a network of catacombs or...

"Mines," Jason said aloud, closing his eyes.

The entire front range of the Rocky Mountains was nothing more than one big mine. Prospectors had first riddled the foothills with tunnels to harvest gold from the rocky veins. Next coal and uranium had been excavated from within. Finally quarries gouged the red rocks from the ground to ship all around the country to trim yards.

He was grasping at straws and he knew it, looking for any possible alternative to what appeared to have been a biological contaminant. It could have been anything! The meteorite could have slammed right atop a hidden silo, detonating the nuclear warhead lying dormant within. They were only an hour's drive from NORAD after all.

A funnel of black smoke appeared over the top of the five-story brick apartment building to his right, the front of an enormously tall building coming into focus through the dust beyond. His heart skipped in his chest and he felt an elation like never before in his life. He ran, sprinting around the end of the apartment building and then to the right past a pile of smashed cars.

There! At the limits of his vision, he could see the orange and gold flames fluttering spastically, belching bursts of black smoke so wide that it appeared to fill the entire courtyard. He dashed across the street, kicking through the tumbling leaves and newspaper pages ripped from their stacks at the stands, running wildly up to the front of the building before slowing.

Glass ground to sand beneath his feet while he walked the final stretch of sidewalk and to the edge of the courtyard, staring around the side of the building to the shadow slowly dragging another body through the thick dust.

"...and I think by now I've passed that point of an acceptable level of talking to one's self and qualify now for a pair of fuzzy bedroom slippers. Next thing you know, you'll see good ol' Trick Turner wandering through City Park pushing a shopping cart filled with paper bags and carpet scraps, mumbling in answer to the prodding questions of the voices in his head."

Jason hesitated as though staring at a mirage. Slowly, he walked forward, his eyes fixed on Trick's back while he labored, shoulders arched, pulling some large man by the heels through the standing mess of dust and glass.

"But I suppose since I've already crossed that line of accepted human behavior and traipsed into the realm of the deviant, probably no harm in reciting some tasteless jokes, eh?"

Jason walked toward Trick from behind, listening to the wonderful sound of the man's voice in his ears. It was almost angelic, like the voice of God Himself speaking directly to Jason.

"So this guy's got this wooden eye, right? And there's this hair-lip. No wait. How does it start again—?"

Trick looked quickly back over his shoulder, his features first tightening, and then quickly widening in joy. He dropped the stiff legs from his hands to the ground. The right shoe popped off, exposing a swollen sock that by no rights should have been able to squeeze into the far smaller shoe.

"Ladies and gentlemen," he said, walking right up to Jason and wiping his right hand on his jeans. He extended it to Jason, who gladly took it and shook it with a smile on his face. "I'd like to introduce you to my new very best friend in the whole wide world. This is..."

He bent the microphone from his mouth and toward Jason.

"Jason Milhouse."

"Jason Milhouse," Trick said, unable to stop shaking the dirty man's hand. He looked like he had crawled through the entire length of the sewer to get there, but Trick wouldn't have cared if he'd shown up with all sorts of weeping open sores and a wart like a horn on his forehead. He was just ecstatic to be in the company of another living, breathing human being. "Come on over to the fire. I've saved you a seat and everything. Can I offer you a corpse? I have a wide variety."

"No thanks," Jason said, smirking. He couldn't control his elation. "Two's my limit."

"You and I are going to get along just fine, Jason Milhouse," Trick said, throwing his arm over Jason's shoulder and leading him toward the fire. "Just fine indeed."

VI

Nancy pulled the wagon down the middle of the street, straddling the double yellow line with the squeaking, rusted white-walled tires. Tim was sound asleep, curled up on his side in fetal position, wrapped like a human burrito in the blanket from his bed. Cindy walked a couple of paces behind, moaning occasionally from the pain in her back, but always managing to forge a smile when Nancy looked back.

None of them spoke, merely walking along in silence. Conversation would lead to observation, and the last thing that any of them wanted to do was talk about all of the bodies inside of the cars they passed to either side. It was easier to listen to the sound of their own footsteps, to the uneven creaking of the wagon wheels, contented with the presence of the others.

Nancy had changed from her skirt suit into jeans and a plain white t-shirt, favoring a pair of Nikes to the high heels. She had packed a sweater and a jacket for both she and her sister at Tim's insistence, deciding it better to simply give in and saddle up with a backpack than to argue with him. It felt like she was toting a sack of bricks however, her shoulder blades positively aching from the strain of the weight atop them and having to pull that wagon along behind her.

The whole thing just seemed so insanely stupid to her. By all rights they should still be sitting there in their own house, sleeping in their own beds and waiting for the morning to come. Were it not for their new companions, whom she was growing to resent and loathe a little more with each passing step, they most certainly still would be. Sure, the man seemed nice enough, as did his son, though he was almost frighteningly creepy, but the fact remained that they had stolen her out of her small, but cozy little world and dragged her out into the night, using her son against her as a bargaining token. She'd show them, though. As soon as they reached St. Michael's North Hospital, she'd abandon them and take her family in to see a doctor as she planned to from the start. Let them walk the rest of the way to downtown and dance naked atop the Qwest building for all she cared.

She could see the hospital down there, rising back up on the other side of the steep slope. There was but a faint, dim red glow emanating through the windows like smoldering embers. No lights flashed from the helicopter pad atop it, that large squared landing sitting strangely vacant. Flashing lights sparkled red and blue, alighting the entire emergency bay and the overhang above the entrance.

At the bottom of the hill, a river ran beneath a cement bridge, feeding the thick greenery that grew from its bank, halfway up the slope to either side where it had been chopped back to make room for the houses and businesses. To the right, a cemetery reached as far as they could see into the dust through wrought iron gates. The wind had stolen the flowers from the graves they had once adorned, trapping them against the base of the fence. Thousands of brightly colored petals slid gently across the road beneath the undercarriages of the stalled cars, forming a floral path like out of a dream before them. Tombs topped with statues of heralding angles and winged cherubs were framed against the sky, their golden placards facing the street dulled by the dust. Granite headstones poked from the ground, some of them wrenched right out of the dirt and deposited on their faces, while still others had just broken right down the middle, leaving the jagged remnants to mark the dead. It was almost surreal to be staring past the dead and into what should have been their final resting spot, the hallowed ground meant to preserve their souls, rather than the exhaust filled cabs.

With each step, her hopes sunk just a little. There was no activity up there. Not a single car circled the parking lot trying to get out onto the jam-packed street. No nurses raced from the front doors to the ambulance, or waited on the roof for the delivery from the Flight for Life crew. It just sat there like any of the other houses on the hill: still, vacant-looking.

"Do you want me to pull the wagon for a while?" Brad offered, carrying William against his chest. He stumbled. William's weight, added to his own and those of the two backpacks, was apparently his threshold. They had yet to rest for fear of giving themselves time to more carefully study the contents of the cars around them, knowing that once they even paused it would be just that much harder to force their legs to carry them forward again. But they were going to have to take a break soon before they all just passed out right there in the middle of the road.

"I'm all right," Nancy said, though every muscle in her body positively ached. The arches of her feet felt like they had collapsed, cultivating calluses the size of golf balls. "I think we'd all better rest here shortly, though."

"I'm with you on that one," Brad said. "My legs are starting to feel like noodles."

"Why don't we stop up there at the hospital?" Nancy gambled, looking up from beneath her sweating, dust-matted brow for the man's response.

"Sounds like a plan—"

"No!" William shouted, raising his lolling head from his father's shoulder.

"Why not?" Brad asked, craning his neck back so that he could see his son's face. "If by some chance someone like a doctor or a nurse lived through this, then I think it's definitely in our best interests to have Tim and Cindy looked at. Or if not, then I still think we should at least load ourselves up on medical supplies, don't you?"

"I agree," Nancy said, surprised.

"No!" William argued vehemently. "We can get everything we need from the ambulance, but please don't go inside!"

"Why not?" Cindy asked from the rear of the group.

"I don't...don't want to tell you," William said, squirming in his father's grasp until Brad finally lowered him to the ground and took him by the hand.

They walked in silence for a moment, waiting for William to change his mind.

"Whoa!" Brad spat, hopping back.

"What?" Nancy asked, immediately stopping the wagon and glancing quickly over her shoulder to check on Tim.

"The river," Brad said.

So many large branches and debris raced along the surface of the water that it had dragged them beneath the bridge, lodging them between the cement supports like some sort of great beaver dam, forcing the river to find another route. Frigid water spilled around the guardrails, rising up and over the road, running through the wooden posts. The entire bridge was submerged, though without light from the sky to reflect from the surface, it remained as black as the asphalt.

He could tell by looking at the tires of the cars stalled out in the middle of the bridge that it was about mid-hubcap deep, but with the current, the footing promised to be treacherous.

"Everyone ready to get wet?" Brad asked. He looked back and smiled. "Should've thought to bring the raft."

Lifting William again from the ground, he held him to his chest and started forward, the water rising over the soles of his shoes and immediately soaking through the material. It was so cold that it felt like icicles stabbing into his feet, dragging fallen leaves and needles up over his ankles. With the movement of the river, he felt like he was moving sideways. The water climbed past his ankles, soaking into his pants, easing upward until it was nearly to the middle of his shins. The pull of the water was irresistible. He staggered to his left, fighting back to center himself on the road and pushed on. Slowly, the freezing water lowered back from his shins to his ankles, and then all the way back to the bottom of his feet.

He stepped from the water, feet sloshing on the asphalt, socks squishing within his shoes, and set William on the ground.

"You wait for me here," Brad said sternly to William. "I'm just going to help them get across and I'll be right back, okay?"

William nodded, and Brad waded back into the stream.

"We're going to have to carry the wagon," he called to Nancy. "Maybe it's high enough that the river won't get inside, but I'd hate to take the chance of it toppling." He envisioned the boy, wrapped tightly in that blanket, unable to raise his head from the rapidly racing water to scream for help. "What do you think?"

"I'll just carry him if you wouldn't mind pulling the wagon."

"You sure you want to wake him up?"

"Yeah," Nancy said, looking down at her far too pale son. "It'll give me an excuse to make sure that he's—"

Alive? Brad thought, staring at the child's face that was so white it looked like a sickly full moon.

"—doing all right."

"He looks to be holding up pretty well," Brad said, trying to at least appear sincere. He really didn't relish the prospect of helping a hysterically grieving mother to bury her son.

"Timmy's a trooper," she said, returning his pseudo-optimistic, weary smile.

Brad splashed out of the water, his feet squeaking and squirming on the rubber insoles.

"Ready?" he asked, looking from Nancy to Cindy.

"Need help?" Cindy offered, watching her sister strain to lift Tim from the wagon and juggle him against her chest.

Nancy just shook her head, biting the inside of her lip from the sudden strain that raced up the muscles in her back. The edge of the blanket unfurled, hanging all the way down to the ground. Brad walked over and grabbed it, bringing it back up over the boy and tucking it back in against Nancy's chest to hold it in place.

"Sorry," he said, hoping he hadn't manhandled anything he hadn't meant to.

Nancy smiled meekly back at him and took the first step into the water, wincing at the suddenly frigid water on her toes.

Brad knelt and took the handle of the wagon, rising to his feet in preparation of dragging it through the river.

"Don't mind her," Cindy said, sidling up to him. Several strands of bangs had loosened from her ponytail and now flapped across her face. "She doesn't mean anything by it."

"I can imagine how difficult it must be having a child that sick. I don't know what I would do in her situation. I'd probably be pretty jaded, too."

"She'll be better if she can get Tim in to a doctor. It's the reassurance from a medical professional that she needs. To her, it's like they're speaking in the voice of God, or something. But whatever works, right?"

"Yeah," Brad said, offering his free elbow to Cindy, who took it with a smile and slowly scooted toward the water.

Brad's toes were already pruned and halfway frozen to the bone, but Cindy had been completely unprepared, the cold sending spikes of pain right up her legs and into her back where it felt like her puncture wounds had turned to firecrackers and were exploding right through her skin. She gritted her teeth against it, choking back the whine that arose from her chest.

"Are you okay?" Brad asked, leaning closer to her face, having noticed her eyes were squeezed shut and her teeth were bared from her curled lips.

"Fine," she said through the grimace, trying to make her voice sound flippant, but succeeding only in making a noise that sounded like a dog squealing about a cactus needle in its paw.

"If you want to climb into the wagon, I'll bet I could pull you across."

"I'll make it," she said, the pain subsiding enough for her to offer him a consolatory wink. "Thanks, though."

They watched Nancy ahead of them, swaying from side to side to steady her balance against the current. The edge of the blanket that Brad had tucked back in had already fallen back out, the tip floating on the surface of the water which leeched right up it into the fabric. The water rose clear up to her knees, making her look like she was thrashing about in it.

"Wait up a second if you need help," Brad shouted to be heard over the gurgle of the river. "We're right behind you."

Nancy didn't answer. All of her concentration was focused securely on maintaining her balance there in the water. Maybe she should have taken the help when it had been offered, but right now it seemed more imperative to just get herself and her son out of the rising water. She shuffled on, sliding her feet along the invisible asphalt, making sure she could feel anything in her path before she tripped on it and fell atop her son into the water. In his condition she could easily drown him in the fraction of the time it would take to climb back up from on top of him. Even if all she did was get him wet, how long would he last out there in the night without another significant source of heat to dry his body?

The wagon began to float, the water pressing it upward from beneath. Brad had to fight against it to maintain his balance and keep from being pried from his feet.

With tremendous relief he watched Nancy rise from the water, the surface slowly draining down to her ankles so she could slosh forward, kicking arcs of water out onto the dry pavement where William was wait—

"Where's William?" Brad shouted, lurching forward and nearly knocking Cindy into the water. "He was...I left him right there!"

Cindy let go of his arm, allowing him to charge forward unimpeded, jerking the wagon so hard that the wheels bounced from the road. He raced right past Nancy, dropping the handle of the wagon next to her. It rolled slightly backward, the rear wheels dipping back into the water.

"William!" he screamed, racing up the hill, craning his neck to be able to see over the crumpled cars that had slammed together, piling atop one another, unable to stop on their way down the slope. "William! Answer me right now!"

The muscles in his legs throbbed mercilessly, yet he ran faster than he had ever run in his entire life. He could barely breathe, barely think. Panic had swooped in with such speed that it had seized hold of him like an eagle knifing from the sky. His eyes flashed from side to side, peering into every shadow and every opening in the woods to either side of the road so quickly that by the time his mind was able to rationalize what he was seeing, he was already looking at something else.

"William!"

He was a hundred yards up the hill; his crumpled lungs incapable of filtering enough oxygen from the dust, but determination drove him on.

"Where are you? Answer me!"

"Dad," he heard a voice cry faintly from off to his left.

"William!" He cleared the buckled hood of an Escort in a single sliding leap, landing on the other side and stumbling in the direction of the sound before regaining his balance and sprinting once more.

The hospital towered over him, perched on the hillside like a shadowed, sentient guardian. With the fading pink light filling the windows, they looked like a hundred eyes staring down at him, watching him, waiting for him to get just a little closer. All of the bark and landscaping gravel that surrounded the trunks of the trees planted atop the railroad ties that held the dirt in place beside the road had been dragged down across it by the wind. The whirling red and blue lights from an ambulance glowed from atop that same hill, though there was no droning siren to accompany it.

Rather than wind around the road and up into the parking lot, he leapt right up the face of the railroad ties, scrambling across the now exposed dirt and raced straight through the nearly packed parking lot toward the main entrance.

"William!" he screamed again, his voice cracking.

"Over here!" William called back, his silhouetted form appearing in front of the lights, hand waving above his head.

Heaving with relief, tears wetting his face, Brad ran the last twenty feet and stumbled to a halt in front of William, dropping to his knees and pulling his son tightly to his chest. He immediately pushed William to arm's length and brushed the hair from his face.

"Are you hurt?" he choked, inspecting his son with his hands and eyes.

"I'm fine, Dad."

"I told you to wait right there, son! Right there! Do you have any idea how badly you scared me?"

"Sorry, Dad. I just thought it might be a good idea to start getting the stuff we needed. We don't have much time to waste."

Brad sat there on the ground, conflicted with the urges to both hold his son as tightly as he possibly could, and to throttle him by the throat for running off like that.

William eased from his father's grasp and headed back toward the emergency room entrance. The ambulance lie on its side, bent around the support column for the overhang covering the half circle in front of the glass doors. Those lights just rotated endlessly in circles, the color drifting off into the haze. Its left rear door was open, having dropped flat against the ground. In front of it was a pair of silver canisters that looked like scuba tanks, and a large white, plastic box with nothing more than a little red plus sign on the side.

Walking past the tanks, William ducked through the doorway and into the ambulance. He grunted, straining against the weight of something, before his rear end poked out of the darkness and he dragged out the object of his search. It was another canister like the first two. There was a little blue handle atop it, like the knob of the faucet in their back yard, ringed on three sides with a metal collar. A wide blue label was pasted to the front of it, identifying it as oxygen, with all sorts of warnings and fine print beneath.

"What's all that for?" Brad asked, finally able to find the strength to stand and wobble forward.

"Just things we're going to need."

"First aid kit," Brad said, staring down at the white plastic case. "Three tanks of oxygen. What in the world can we possibly do with three tanks of air?"

"Will you help me with this?" William called, slipping back into the darkness of the cab.

"Help you with what?" Brad asked, lowering his head to duck beneath the one closed door.

"This," he said from the darkness, patting what sounded like a mattress.

"Oh God," Brad gasped, nearly throwing himself to the ground to get his head out of the confines of the ambulance before he vomited.

"Breathe through your mouth," William said impatiently.

"I...uh, oh God, son. I can't go back in there." He heaved, rolling over the contents of his stomach but producing nothing more than a sliver of saliva that slapped from his chin to the ground. "Just leave it alone and come out, William."

"I need your help, Dad! I can't get this out of here by myself!" William poked his head out of the cab and stared across the parking lot where he could now see the top of Cindy's head bobbing up the drive toward the parking lot. "We have to get this out of here before they get up here! Please, Dad! Please help me!"

"And then you'll stay out of there?"

"Whatever you want!"

"Promise?"

"Please! They're almost here!"

Brad drew a deep breath, trapped it behind his pursed lips and plunged right under the closed right door of the ambulance. It wasn't working. Whether he could smell those bodies rotting in there in the still air or not, he still knew that they were there. He could taste the decomposition on his tongue, lingering in his sinuses and draining down his throat, feel their slippage on his skin, crawling all over him like ants. Reaching forward, he flailed his hands around, eyes closed so as not to see the bodies he knew had to be close enough that he could have been sitting right atop them. William took his hand and lowered it a few inches, wrapping his fingers around a cold metal pole.

That was good enough for Brad, whatever it was that he had in his hand, it was what his son was hemorrhaging for. He leaned backward, bracing his heels on the seal of the flattened door, and threw his weight behind it. There was a loud metallic screech, the sound of dragging a rake across the hood of a car. The staling air in his chest crept out from between his lips from the exertion.

He jerked again, this time freeing the metal pole from whatever it had snagged on, propelling himself backward onto the concrete with that thing landing squarely on his chest. Pawing at it, trying to shove it from atop him, he smacked a small black wheel that just spun in a half dozen circles before settling back into place. Mercifully fresh air—and by now that term was relative as it was clogged with so much dust that it was more like a slow burial—filled his chest and he was able to calm himself enough to crawl out from beneath the metal construct.

A white mattress sat atop the metal frame he had been prying at, black straps dangling over the sides, one of the buckles clattering against the rise of a pole from one of the wheels. It was a gurney. There was a stain in the middle of the white sheet that covered it, a Rorschach mosaic of blood that was the spitting image of a skull and crossbones.

"Thanks," William said, discretely tugging the sheet free from where it was hooked under the mattress, wadding it up and tossing it back into the ambulance.

"What do we need this for?" Brad asked, almost afraid to hear the answer.

"Tim needs to stretch out. It's not good for him to be curled up so tightly in that wagon, and besides, we need the wagon to transport all this other stuff unless you think you can carry it by yourself."

Brad just looked at William. In the course of a single night he had gone from an almost autistic child incapable of speech to a young adult testing the taste of sarcasm on his tongue. There had been so many occasions where Brad had knelt by the boy where he crouched beneath the coffee table, just looking at him, wondering what he was thinking, wondering if the patterns his mind generated were even of the wave-length to produce thought as he knew it. He imagined his son in a warm, cozy dark place like the moments just prior to drifting off to sleep. A wonderful world where there was no fear, no worry, no stress, none of the bad things that plagued the so-called normal mind, just translating the images in his mind into Crayola color. And here he was now, conversing with his son as though all of that had been a dream. At one point, William had needed him more than anything else in the world for the basic element of survival, but in the span of a handful of hours, now only needed him to help with the heavy stuff.

"Sorry," William said, feeling the twang of guilt from the look on his father's face. He wrapped his arm around his father's stomach and gave him a big, genuine hug. "I didn't mean to hurt your feelings—"

"I'm fine," Brad said, reveling in the hug and returning his around the boy's shoulders.

"I just need you to remember one thing."

"Hmm," Brad said.

"I can see what's going to happen...not just what's going to happen in the next five minutes or whatever, to that I'm as blind as you. But I can see what's going to happen if we don't keep moving."

"What, William? Let me in."

"Sorry," William said, giving his father a parting squeeze and backing out of the embrace.

"William..."

"What happened?" Nancy called from the second row of parked cars over. "Is he all right?"

"Fine," Brad yelled back. "He was just finding supplies."

He turned and looked back at William who stared ashen faced at the front doors of the hospital.

"So you know why we need these oxygen tanks, but you're not going to tell me."

Brad could only see his son's back, but he could tell the boy had nodded.

"You can tell me anything," Brad said. "I love you. I won't ever judge a single word that comes out of your mouth."

William still stared straight ahead, the hackles prickling up his shoulders and spiking from his neck.

"Will you tell me when you're ready?" Brad asked, slowly walking over to William's side and placing his arm around his son's shoulder.

William nodded again, trying to hide his face from Brad, though he could obviously tell that the boy was crying.

"What's wrong?" Brad asked, his face knotting with concern while his hands felt the goosebumps all over William's flesh.

"We can't go in there, Dad. Promise me you won't let her go in there." His voice dripped off into a sob and he looked up at Brad with the same frightened eyes of the child Brad had grown so accustomed to seeing. His face was lined with muddy tears and his lips quivered.

"I'll do my best, William."

"Please," William whispered. "The bad woman's in there."

"That's a whole lot of oxygen," Cindy said from directly behind them.

Both whirled. William hurriedly brushed off the tears and sniffed back the clear fluid that drained from his nose.

"I'm going to see if I can find a doctor," Nancy said, walking determinedly right past them and toward the front doors.

"I think if there were one he would have helped the people in the ambulance by now," Brad said, trying to position himself between her and the automatic doors. He looked nervously to William.

"Not if there were already so many people that needed to be helped inside."

"Please," Brad said, jogging around her and stopping in her path. "I don't think it's a good idea."

"You'll have to pardon me, but I really don't care what you think. There's no way you can stop me from going in there."

"Don't go in!" William called after them.

Nancy stopped and turned to look at him, startled by the curious level of fear in the boy's face.

"I don't care what kind of paranoid delusions you two share," she whispered, turning to Brad. "Personally, I think it's just terrible what you've done to that child, but worse, I think that trying to stop me from taking my son in to see a doctor is downright evil."

She pushed her way right through him, leaving him standing there, helpless but to watch her go.

Nancy dragged the wagon right up to the front doors and carefully lifted Tim out, cradling him against her chest. She stood right in the middle of the sensor pad, waiting for the door to slowly open. Without so much as a glance back over her shoulder, she walked right into the pale red glow.

"Wait!" Brad shouted, racing after her. He could hear William's little feet padding quickly along the ground behind him, echoing off the face of the building.

He hit the door running, shouldering the glass door, and nearly barreled into Nancy from behind. His footsteps smacked to a thudding halt, disturbing the almost surreal sound within.

There wasn't a single voice to be heard in what should have been a chaotic emergency room. Static buzzed from the CB radio behind the admission's desk. From all around he could hear a single tone amplified in stereo. It was a sound he had heard before, a sound he would never be able to scratch from the record in his mind. That one monotonous tone that signaled that his life had suddenly ended. It was the same tone he had heard from the monitor at his wife's bedside, the long, droning electrical sound of the expiration of her life. The doctor couldn't possibly have turned it off soon enough, but not before engraving that tone into his eardrums as though driven straight through the timpanic membrane by a sharpened pencil.

And now that sound came from everywhere, bouncing off of the walls and resonating with a physical quality that he could feel vibrating in his sternum. It was as if every monitor connected to every patient blared the same deadly tune in harmony, and there had been no one left to shut them off.

Nancy had stopped right there in the middle of the lobby, her mouth and nose buried in Tim's blanket to keep from inhaling another whiff of the stench.

The admit nurse leaned forward against the pane of Plexiglas that separated her from the incoming patients. Her forehead smashed against the pane, blood had congealed to a black hardness over her eyes that looked like patches, a puddle of that same dark fluid curling the papers before her on the desk. To the right, chairs were lined in rows to face the television set bracketed up on the wall, the picture nothing more than a black and white jumble of static. Dozens of people were either slumped over in their chairs or sprawled out on the floor in a mess of shattered glass. A woman in a shawl still sat erect with her lifeless baby in her grasp, her head simply lolled over with her chin resting on the infant's fuzzy head as though her last act in this lifetime had been to give the child a parting kiss.

Dirt and leaves covered the floor, having both blown in through the shattered window and toppled from the planters that lie on their sides in the middle of the walkway.

"Is anybody here?" Nancy shouted.

"Let's just get out of here," Brad said, sliding his hand atop her shoulder and trying to subtly turn her around.

"Hello!" she shouted again. "Is there a doctor here?"

Brad looked back through the doorway.

William was standing on the sensor pad to the door, causing it to bounce back and forth against the wall. It fought to close before receiving the impulse to open right back up. He was shaking his head from side to side and appeared to be looking right through Brad.

"Hello!" Nancy screamed again, her voice trilling into a sharp scream.

"There's no one here," Brad said, guiding her more urgently this time. "We should just get out of—"

"Help me!" a weak voice called from somewhere off in the belly of the hospital.

"Oh my God!" Nancy blurted, turning quickly to Brad. "There's someone else in here!"

Brad looked back to William, who was now visibly trembling. Cindy walked into view from behind him and draped her arm over William's shoulder. He jumped at her touch. Chest rising and falling heavily, he shook his head faster and faster.

"Someone else is in here!" Brad called back to his son in hopes of justifying what he was about to do next.

"Please, Daddy, no," William whispered, but it was too late. Brad had already turned and was heading for the gray doors leading back into the actual emergency room.

"Help!" the voice called again, barely audible over the piercing hum.

Brad yanked on the handle to the door, but it wouldn't budge as it was controlled by a magnetic release button from behind the admit desk. He dashed across the lobby and heaved one of the chairs from the ground, pointing the four heavy legs ahead of him, and slammed it into the Plexiglas, knocking the nurse backward and to the floor, her chair sliding across the floor behind her. The glass cracked and trembled, splintering out diagonally. One more pounding from the chair and the glass shattered, sending large triangles skittering across the floor around the handful of corpses lying behind, out of view.

"Don't let him go in there!" William screamed, whirling to grab Cindy by the shirt. He begged her with his eyes, panicking, on the verge of hyperventilating, and then turned again, staring through the open doorway, unable to draw even a single breath.

Brad brushed the glass aside and hopped up onto the counter, quickly dropping behind it and disappearing into the crimson glow. The formerly locked doors opened almost immediately and Nancy rushed through, clinging so tightly to Tim that her knuckles had turned a transparent white.

"Daddy!" William shouted, swallowing the lump in his throat and taking the first trembling step forward. He looked up to the frame of the door as though it were lined with teeth, about to swallow him whole. Closing his eyes, he planted first his right foot and then the left, testing the water, before darting through after him. "Don't go up there!"

"We should help whoever's in there," Cindy said, following him through the doorway.

"You don't understand! I tried to keep it from happening! I can't control it now! Don't you see? Because of that lady up there, my Dad is going to die!" he screamed back into her face, and then raced toward the desk and hopped up on top of it.

The door closed slowly behind them, the teeth fitting firmly into place and the lips sealing tightly.

It was now too late.

4 | Arise

I

Shannen stumbled forward, toes dragging on the sandy sidewalk, and fell forward onto the branch-riddled lawn. She couldn't control her sobbing any more than she could consciously draw a breath. Hyperventilating, her back bucked with the throes of each wail, tears covering her entire face. Her stomach grumbled; tightening, threatening to relieve her of its acidic contents.

She couldn't believe she had left Brian, left him right there in the passenger seat of the Mustang with the door wide open, but there was no way of driving that smoldering wreck any further. Highway 85 had been crammed with cars, making it impossible to turn out from that gravel-laden side road. And none of them were going to be moving any time soon. Only a few cars even still partially illuminated the impossibly dark night with their fading head and tail lights, and coupled with what she was hearing on the radio, it didn't sound as though the rest of the city was any better off. She had tried though, slamming the already buckled hood of the Mustang into the traffic, driving the stalled vehicles back and up against the far lane, but was unable to clear enough room to even attempt to drive down the shoulder. That collision had been enough to kill the already sputtering engine, the oil having drained out along the dirt road.

She had left him there. She had left Brian all alone in that car, half-out on the highway in a tangle with a Taurus and a Camry. It was all she could do to sit him back up in the seat, his body now so brittle that she feared it would snap. Leaving the door wide, in case…in case what? In case he decided to get up and try to catch up with her?

As soon as she reached a phone—any phone—she'd be able to call for help. That was the idea anyway, even though she could tell from the man on the radio that there was no help to be found out there. But it was the premise of that plan that allowed her to leave him. The true fact of the matter was that in the rational half of her brain, the silent portion that stood back in whispered awe, reserving judgment and opinion until everything started to make some sort of coherent sense, had at least spoken up enough to kick her in the rear. Brian was dead, and the chances of him awakening from that state of slow decomposition were simply non-existent. As were her own chances of survival if she were to stay by his side until he turned to nothing more than a skeleton of blanched bones sitting in a puddle of his own liquefied flesh. She needed to find her way to the other survivors, and at least she knew of one.

Since she had survived, who was to say that her family hadn't? So she had started walking, focusing her mind on her aunt and uncle, her cousins, who were really more like a brother and sister, rather than on the love of her short life she had left in that car on the road with all of the other faceless dead.

She had left him. Dear Lord, she had left him there. Alone.

"I'm so sorry," she moaned, jarring loose a wave of teardrops.

Crawling forward, stirring settled dust from the long blades of browning grass, Shannen pushed herself to her feet and staggered on. She had no idea how long it had taken her to traverse the highway to finally descend into her own neighborhood. There had been a Conoco, the first thing she had found on the way into town, where she had frantically raced past the silent cars at the pumps, their drivers lying face down in a pool of gasoline, and right to the payphone next to the entrance. There had been no dial tone, no matter how many times she tapped the button on the hook, no matter how many times she slammed the receiver down or how much she screamed. It had been the same at the darkened KwikWay and the Diamond Shamrock. Even the cell phone she had managed to tremblingly extract from the breast pocket of the bloated and rigid clerk's blue and white striped shirt had been little more than a useless piece of plastic, serving only as a means of venting her frustration by screaming and spiking it against the wall. After that, she couldn't remember a single car she had passed, or even turning by the fire station to enter her neighborhood.

Houses passed to either side, houses she knew and recognized from making this same walk back from the bus stop all through junior high, from passing every time she went to the store or school or the mall. There should have been something of a comforting feel to them, a familiarity and the promise of the comfort of home, but instead of projecting warmth and intimacy, they appeared as lifeless as any of the faces she had passed. Shattered windows leered out over closed garages, exposing not the life and love from within, but the flat darkness that now lurked in their void, having permanently extinguished the light. They were like large skulls lining the road, watching her with distracted indifference as though she was no more than a fly circling their already cleaned carcasses.

Shingles littered the lawns, exposing the bare black felt beneath. Potters, wooden and ceramic alike, had been blown from porches, milk-boxes smashed against the front doors, tearing through the screen. The fallen leaves from the barren trees covered the street like an already browning carpet. Mailboxes lie crumpled on the sidewalks nowhere near the splintered stump that had once held them aloft.

This wasn't the Locust Street she had grown up on. It couldn't be.

Locust was dead now. There was no lingering residue of life. For the first time since she had brought that little mutt home from the pound, Mrs. Timmerman's fluffy red and black Rottweiler/Chow mix, Barney, was silent. Even Mr. Griffith's television, which blared through every open window to announce the nightly failing if his hearing aid at a volume akin to a sonic boom, sat quietly somewhere in the blackness through those shattered windows. And just up ahead was her own house...

Shannen ran past the last three houses, hardly able to keep her balance. Stumbling, lurching: the sound of her footsteps thundering back at her from the closed garage doors was like Quasimodo with that galloping limp. Her heart rising, breaths coming with Uzi-fire rapidity, she cut across the lawns, dodging a patchily needled blue spruce, rounding a young clump of aspens, and finally throwing herself through a boxwood hedge. Falling to her hands to maintain her balance, she propelled herself toward the front door, racing up the half-dozen cement steps and to the landing. She turned the handle and threw the door inward.

"Aunt Jessica!" she screamed, slamming the handle of the front door into the closet door behind with a crack like a hatchet chop. "Where are you?"

It was impossibly dark, a deeper shade of pitch than during her middle of the night raids on the refrigerator. Dust settled like sand falling from an hourglass in front of the shattered bay window, the remnants crackling and crunching under her weight, grinding down into the now brown-stained carpet. The couch in the living room had been knocked onto its back, the chair to the left standing askew against the grandfather clock it had toppled over a Norfolk pine in the pot her aunt had made, and against the bookshelf. Half of the books were already on the floor, the wind coming through the absent window riffling through the pages as though by the unseen hand of a ghost.

"Uncle John!" she screamed. "Emma! Hunter!"

She paused, cocking her head to listen for any sound whatsoever.

Maybe they weren't there. Maybe after the dust began to settle, they had realized that she wasn't there and set out to find her. Yeah, they were probably out cruising the streets right now looking for her. That stoked the smoldering kindling of hope, and her spirits began to rise. Sure, it was Friday night after all. Well, Saturday morning to be more accurate. Emma had dance class and Hunter surely had one of his countless baseball games. Like every Friday night this summer, they probably didn't even get home from all of their running around until close to eight, and Aunt Jess never had dinner on the table before nine.

They had all probably even been awake when that meteorite had smashed into the ground and after huddling beneath the dining room table with their plates clattering over their heads, the shattered glass from the windows cascading across their half-consumed dinners, they had set out to find her. That was how it must have happened. If she stayed here long enough, they'd eventually come back here to check and see if she had made it back here on her own.

It was actually going to be all right.

Shannen breathed a tremendous sigh of relief that she could feel rise from the tips of her toes and through her fantastically exhausted flesh, though as it exited her mouth it sounded more like she was crying.

She was home.

Sniffing back the flood of mucus that came with the tears of relief, Shannen made her way through the living room on legs that were finally ready to give out. The archway passed overhead with the portrait-sized, framed photo of all of them on Shannen's first Christmas with her new family, the family that had opened their doors, as well as their hearts, to her, without asking for anything in return. She had been so lucky, so blessed to have this wonderful new family while by all rights her world could just as easily have come to an end, a family who right now was driving around—

"Driving around?" she whispered, her brow knotting.

She entered the kitchen, shaking her head, and pulled the cordless phone from the wall bracket. Pressing the "Talk" button, she waited for the sound of the dial tone that would never come. She fingered the same button again, to turn it off, but the little red power indicator light wasn't even on. The button didn't even make a beeping sound when she pushed it. She traced the matching cords from the bottom of the cradle, straight down the wall and to the outlet beneath. The cords were intact, as was the large, square black plug that brought power from the socket, and the thin gray cord that was plugged firmly into its jack.

"Probably set out on foot," she said, trying to chase the now rising sense of doubt.

There was a growl from her stomach; the cramping innards rising on an acidic plume. With a grimace, she cradled both arms over it.

"Aunt Jess?"

She turned around, smelling not just the overpowering scent of her aunt's pepper-rubbed filet of sole, but something else rising from beneath it...something pungent, something growing in the stagnant air like mildew from beneath a pool towel left on the tile in the bathroom. Before her eyes had even begun to adjust to the darkness through the doorway and into the dining room, her olfactory senses began to separate the smells, defining that gut-churning layer beneath to be similar, if not identical, to the aroma she had left behind in the Mustang.

"Please, God," she whispered, the tears springing from her paling face anew. "No..."

The floor creaked beneath her advance, moving toward the dining room on wobbling legs that wanted nothing more than to deposit her right there on the Spanish tiled floor. Her feet swept silently, slowly, and try as she might, she couldn't delay their progress.

The blackened table took form from the darkness.

"No!" she screamed, shaking her head.

She whirled from the living room and threw herself to the floor, mashing her face against the tile and pounding her fists against the floor. Wailing, wrought in a throng of uncontrollable blubbering, she rolled over onto her back and shrieked up to the heavens.

"Why?" she wailed, stamping her feet and kicking the cupboards, causing a clanking of pots and pans knocked from their perches within. "Are you up there? Can you hear me? Let it be a dream! Let me wake up! Please, Lord! Make it stop!"

And with that, her heart slowed. She blinked through the tears to the ceiling, staring at the idle ceiling fan; the edges of the blades so thickly rimmed with dust that it looked like fungus.

Shannen had reached her limit, and her body had simply shut down. Her arms and legs grew warm, the rise and fall of her chest slowing to a pace that could have been mistaken for deep sleep. Red and gold splotches blossomed in her vision, wandering lazily in arcs across the ceiling. The tears had already begun to steam dry on her heated face, and she began to blink rhythmically like she was going to drift off into unconsciousness.

"I need to go now," she whispered, the words penetrating her own ears in the silence before she even considered where the thought that had formed them had originated.

Go where? Where in the world could she possibly go?

The guy on the radio had been alive.

Alive.

She dreamily rolled over and found her way to her feet, pulse drumming hard and melancholy in her temples. Face whitening to a stoic, emotionless pallor, she crossed through the kitchen, past the living room and up the stairs to the second floor. Weightless, yet simultaneously encumbered by the tug of gravity threatening to crumple her depressed form like a can, she stopped in front of the first door to the left. Hunter's bedroom. Staring inside, blinking, feeling the cool wind against her face from the broken window sticking her long hair to he cheeks, she floated inside as though sleepwalking and to the foot of the bed. Fist curling unconsciously into the Colorado Rockies comforter, she dragged it from the bed and behind her on the carpet, passing through the doorway and into the hall. Without pause, she went through the opposite doorway and into the room that she and Emma shared, similarly pulling the matching, but inversely colored printed covers from atop their twin beds.

Shannen tucked the bundle into the crook of her left arm, the mess of blankets trailing behind her like the train from a veil. She made her way further down the hall to the end, brushing open the partially closed door and into the master bedroom. With glass and leaves crumpling under foot from the now permanently opened sliding glass door that led out to the balcony, she walked up to the bed and closed her fist around a handful of the fluffy, peach colored comforter with the purple designs. Turning, she headed back toward the hallway with it slithering off on the bed and following her toward the stairs.

Each loud thump from her feet on the hollow staircase, echoing from the storage area underneath, sounded like the lone beat of a drum to mark the rising of the sun over a battlefield strewn with fallen soldiers.

With a jerk, she pulled the blankets from around the final rail of the banister and walked across the living room, oblivious to the disintegrated glass-topped coffee table that snagged at the covers and the lifeless body of Emma's tabby, Leonardo, curled permanently in his favored spot on the wing-backed chair. Releasing the comforters to the floor, she first grabbed the one from Hunter's bed and walked around to the back of the table, gracefully draping it over his slumped form, his face fixed between his hands in the middle of the plate of half-eaten fish and dried blood. Unblinking, she made the return trip for the next, her own blue and red comforter her aunt had bought for her the day she moved in to match Emma's and make her feel as though she belonged, and carried it to the foot of the table. Spreading it by the corners, she let it flutter down over the high back of the chair, settling down on the body of the woman who had taken on the job of being her mother without ever treating her as anything but. She had toppled sideways, the arms of the chair pinned against the underside of the freshly polished oak table, holding her from the ground like she had merely leaned over to grab her dropped fork.

She repeated the process for Emma, lowering herself beneath the table and spreading it across her, planting a kiss atop her cloaked forehead.

"You were my sister in every sense of the word," Shannen whispered. "And my very best friend…"

She crawled out and grabbed the final comforter, the king sized downy quilt she had enjoyed curling up inside immediately after her aunt unloaded it from the dryer, and carried it to the head of the table. Her Uncle John had toppled backward from the table, landing squarely on his back, still seated in the chair. His hands were frozen around his neck, his feet hanging in the air. She looked deep into his opened eyes, crusted beneath a sheen of clumping blood, and laid the comforter atop him.

Shannen walked over to her vacant seat at the table, pulled out the chair and sat down, lacing her fingers between the silverware that had been set out for her just in case she had made it back in time for dinner. She stewed in the silence, listening instead to the cherished memories of laughter and fighting and joy playing through her mind like the flickering reel of an eight-millimeter projector.

A faint smile crossed her lips; her eyes gently dripping closed. They were sitting all around her, living, breathing, not covered with their ornate death shrouds. Hunter was complaining about an outfielder who cheated him out of a home run by using the chain link fence to propel himself upward. Uncle John agreed through a mouthful of spicy fish that caused him to swallow a cough, promising to file a complaint with the league to the sniggering of Aunt Jess at the far end of the table, who had seen as well as he that the ball had been caught a good ten feet from the fence. She took a sip of her nightly glass of red wine, caring more about her antioxidant level than having mismatched the drink with the meal, and gave a quick wink to Emma and Shannen, who giggled back and forth through fork-loads of salad about their usual conversation piece: boys.

"Thank you," Shannen whispered, her lower lash pooling with the swelling tide of tears. "Thank you for bringing me into your home and making me a part of your family."

She rose, scooting the chair carefully back beneath the table and crossed through the kitchen to the stairs leading down and into the family room. At the far end was the door to the garage, which she passed through into the absolute darkness. Without even bothering to flip the switch she knew by now would never work, she coaxed herself to the center of the garage, raising her hands above her head to feel for the release cord to the garage door. She tugged it until she heard the metallic snap, and then raised the garage door from the floor. On the far side of her uncle's black Pathfinder, leaning against the wall, was Hunter's obnoxiously loud motorized scooter. Backing it out onto the driveway, she unscrewed the gas cap and filled it with the red and yellow metal can just inside the door.

Capping the tank, she primed it several times and then took hold of the cord, yanking it until the motor kicked on and it burped a small tuft of black smoke.

Shannen climbed atop it and squeezed the handle to give it some gas. It squealed like a rice-grinder, the sound enough to tear the fabric of the silent night, and turned it away from her house for the last time. She gave it one final, longing glance back over her shoulder, and sped back down the sidewalk toward the highway.

II

"Where are you?" Brad yelled, running down the straight hallway. The highly polished white floor reflected the emergency lights mounted every twenty feet or so, staining the entire aura of the room an awkward pink, like the desolation on Mars.

Curtains fluttered to each side of the hallway, some drawn tight, only the bottoms riffling when he raced past, others, however, stood wide. A doctor in a bloodied white lab coat had managed to claw his way from one of them out into the hall, only to serve as a short hurdle to Brad who hadn't the time to stop to survey the dead.

"Say something!" he shouted, pausing to listen, to peel the potential response from the drone of life-support monitors. Nancy's shoes squeaked from the high luster of the floor. He held up a hand to her, placing his opposite index finger over his pursed lips.

She stopped, holding Tim against her chest and looking curiously to Brad, who just stood there, chewing lightly on his lower lip, focusing.

"Can anybody hear me?" a faint voice called from the distant end of the hallway.

Brad had turned and was sprinting down the pink corridor before the voice had even finished the sentence. The hallway ended at the foot of a staircase, leading upward and around to the floor above. To the left, the polished steel elevator doors reflected his haggard image back at him. He raced right past them and up the stairs, clearing them two at a time, his footsteps sounding like a battering ram trying to knock the entire building from its perch on the hillside and down into the river. Grabbing the railing, he swung himself around the midway landing, hurling himself upward and to the second floor.

He stopped at the start of the hallway, holding his breath to keep from panting like an old dog in the sun, trying to focus all of his energy into his ears. The droll whine of the machinery had faded to a muffled hum. It was almost like the sound of a bee buzzing somewhere, out of sight, down one of the hallways, the first of which led straight ahead as far as he could see, another branching off to the right and terminating beneath a reddish circle of light.

Glass facades, sliding doorways, as though walking through any one of them would take him out onto a deck and into the dusty night, lined either side of the hallway. Vertical blinds shielded the rooms beyond from sight: pale yellow slats that didn't close all the way, but allowed but the most fleeting glimpse into the room like the spinning wheel of a nickelodeon picture show. Within each room he slowly passed—carefully placing his feet so as not to make a sound that might cover the cries for help—was but a single bed, the walls behind the raised heads stacked with glowing machinery. Thin tubes protruded from each, cascading down into the lifeless bodies now no more than lumps in the sheets.

A sign labeled "Intensive Care Unit" was mounted to the ceiling above the nurse's station ahead in bold black letters. There was a dry erase board pegged to one of the support pillars, divided into long rectangles, each of which had a name and a dozen combinations of letters that discretely clued the assigned nurses in to their charge.

In front of the desk, a nurse, clad in pink scrub pants with a baby blue top, was crumpled behind her toppled cart of spilled medications, small glass vials shattered to small shards in a mess of pills and needles. Her laminated identification badge was stuck face down in a small pool of her own blood, her shoulder length brown hair crusted in thin black dreads.

Papers were scattered all over the desk from the manila folders they had once inhabited, the nurse formerly perusing them lying on the floor amidst the small gray keys from the broken keyboard she had dragged from the desk in her attempt to steady herself. A splash of blood had dried on the filing cabinet behind her where she had smacked her face, jarring loose the pair of teeth that lie on the crimson-stained tiles.

"Hello!" Brad called down the hallway, his voice echoing hollowly.

"Help me!" the voice screamed from directly ahead.

Brad immediately burst into a sprint, flying down the hallway with those sliding glass doors passing to either side like mile-markers beside a speeding car.

Another desk approached, this one labeled "Burn Unit." The light board behind it was still on, illuminating the black and white x-ray film of a thoracic cavity, easily identified by the faint outlines of the ribs and organs within. A nurse, still wearing the green paper covers to her shoes, tied over her ankles, and the matching hair net, was sprawled out across the floor, her latex-gloved hands framing a crusted puddle of blood-streaked vomit.

"Help!" the voice screamed again.

"Keep talking!" Brad yelled, slowing to a walk, peering through the thin gaps in the slats for any sign of movement. He could hear footsteps in the hall behind him, but forced them from his mind, concentrating to triangulate the sound of the pained-sounding pleas.

"228! Please God! I'm in room 228!"

Brad raised his eyes to the numbered placards above the doors, immediately veering his attention to the left and the even numbers. Jogging, eyes fixed on the black numbers identifying the room he needed, he jogged forward, grabbing hold of the handle on the door and sliding it back. The door was far lighter than he had anticipated, the force of his exertion slamming it backward and nearly knocking it from its track.

The high-pitched beep of the life support monitor wailed at him immediately from within the room, the glass having nearly muted its penetration into the hallway.

"Get me out of here!" the woman screamed.

She was inside of what looked like a plastic cage. That eerie red light shimmered from the see-through curtains that hung around all four sides of the bed. Overhead, a fan that looked like an oversized oven hood whirred, circulating the fresh oxygen inside of that clear tent.

A pair of bare feet hung out from behind the curtains at the foot of the bed. The flesh looked like it had been cooked, the left foot split right down the top like a frankfurter, the exposed edges black and weeping yellowish fluid.

Save for the small light above the head of the bed and the flashing lights from the monitors, the room was awash in shadow. He could barely see the television mounted on a pivoting arm to the wall and the bureau beside it; the door leading to the bathroom a mouth of darkness. His own shadow lined the floor in the pink light that crossed the tile from the open door behind, riding up and over the lifeless body of a doctor in a white lab coat, her fingers coated in the fluids she had carved from her slashed neck.

There was a large woman crouching atop the bed, sitting like a catcher awaiting a pitch. Her short black hair stood from her head like a ruffled nest of spikes, wild gray eyes peering out over the green mask that covered her mouth and nose. Arms wrapped around her huffing chest, gloved hands tucked into her armpits, she was shaking like she had just climbed out of a frozen lake. Pale blue scrub pants hid her thick legs; her yellow and pink floral patterned top barely able to contain her enormous stomach and bosom.

"I watched her die!" she shrieked, irises vibrating back and forth in her barely restrained panic. "Blood...blood just pouring out of her eyes and neck. Jesus Christ! She just...just tore her own throat out."

"That's an oxygen tent, right?" Brad asked, fingering the long plastic curtains attached to both the ceiling and the floor.

"Y-yeah. I climb-climbed in here when I started to...started to feel sick," she said, her sagging chin jiggling as she spoke.

"Is that your patient?" Brad asked, nodding to the pair of burnt feet.

"I couldn't sit in here with him! He-he was...he was..."

"It's all right—"

"Get her out of there!" Nancy shouted from the doorway.

"Wait!" Brad snapped, whirling to face her. "If I'm right and the only reason she survived was because she was in that oxygen tent, then we need to be extraordinarily careful."

"I'll stay here if you want to try to find an oxygen tank or something. It's not like we can move that entire tent, and we certainly can't leave her here either."

Brad turned to the nurse.

"Where can I get a portable tank?"

"There's a whole rack full of them in the supply closet behind the ICU station. And you'll need a mask, too!"

"Be right back," Brad said, racing past Nancy and back into the hall.

She eased closer to the plastic curtain, studying the frantic woman who reminded her of a caged lion, waiting to pounce on the unsuspecting zookeeper.

"What's your name?" Nancy asked, her voice meek. She stared into those wild, panicked gray eyes.

"Karen," she said, panting. "Karen Fletcher. Registered nurse."

"Nice to meet you, Karen," Nancy said, trying to calm the woman by lowering her voice and using the most soothing tone she could muster. "I'm Nancy, and this is my son, Tim."

"Keep him away from me!" she screamed, hopping up on the bed and nearly driving her head into the grate above. "He's sick too! Just like the rest of them! Don't let him near me! Don't let him near me!"

Nancy recoiled, stumbling backward and flinching when she crunched down on the dead doctor's hand.

"He's sick," she said, heart thumping mercilessly, "but not like the others. He has leukemia. We came here looking for help."

Karen eyed Nancy, trying to read her mind through her fearful expression, finally allowing her gaze to trail down to the still sleeping child in Nancy's arms. Her lips moved as she went down some mental checklist, verifying what she saw versus what she would expect to find from a latter stage radiation patient. Her only experience with radiation was where it pertained to burns, and had never actually even strolled through the oncology wing in the three and a half years that she had worked there in the hospital, but his symptoms appeared consistent with her expectations.

"No help here," Karen said. "I've been...screaming for hours. Hours. No one came. They're all dead, aren't they? All dead?"

Nancy nodded solemnly, unable to drag her eyes from the other woman's. The way she looked: skittish, nervous...sent the hackles up her spine.

The large woman leapt from the bed and to the floor, pressing the entire front of her body against the plastic sheet, her eyelids peeled back so far that it looked as though those streaked eyeballs could have simply rolled out.

"Get me out of here!" she screamed, a small expanse of steam forming from her breath against the curtain. She raised her fists above her head and began pounding them on the giving plastic.

Nancy scurried backward into the doorway, watching in heart-pounding terror.

"They're all dead!" the woman screamed again. "Don't leave me in here to die with them! Get me out! Get me out!"

Nancy unconsciously shook her head, stumbling even further in retreat.

"Don't just stand there! Get back in here, you bitch! Get in here and help me!"

The woman hammered the plastic over and over with those meaty fists, beating and beating and beating, head jerking back and forth, cheeks flapping, until she elicited a faint ripping sound from the curtain. She stopped all at once, eyes rising to the top of the curtain where they lingered for a moment before she finally took a long step back and leaned against the bed. Dragging her eyes back down, her reddened face now noticeably paled; she looked directly at Nancy.

"I'm sorry," she whispered in a voice so meek Nancy could barely hear it. "I didn't mean to yell at you. I'm just so scared...

so…scared…"

"It's all right," Nancy said, though she still couldn't bring herself to walk back into the room. All she could see was that woman's blazing eyes while she tried to tear right through the one thing that was potentially keeping her alive.

"What was all the screaming?" Cindy asked, placing a hand on her sister's shoulder before quickly removing it when Nancy flinched as if she had placed a branding iron on her bare skin. "Are you okay?"

Nancy nodded, but couldn't wrench her eyes from the woman in the curtain, who just sat there, staring right through her.

William sidled silently past both, walking tentatively through the doorway and into the room.

Karen cocked her head to the side and, unblinking, watched him approach like an eagle eyeing a mouse from its perch.

"What's your name?" she asked, sliding forward from the bed and to the plastic divider, pressing her palms and face flat against the surface.

"William."

"That was my father's name, too," she said, her mask tightening over a widening smile.

He looked to the feet behind the bed from the corner of his eye, his stomach gurgling at the repugnant sight of the seared and blistered flesh.

How had the man who should have been inside of the tent ended up outside of it? He could see it in his mind as though it were happening right before him at that very instant. There was the woman, inside of the tent with the man atop the bed, gently changing his pus-saturated bandages, and administering pain medication through his recently changed IV bag. She looked up in time to see the doctor, who had just come in on rounds, drop her clipboard and collapse to the floor, looking up through eyes hazy with a sheet of blood. Watching that woman tear out her own trachea trying to breathe, Karen had simply stood there, frozen, either unwilling or unable to take action. She had stared down at the doctor's body, the pool of blood widening until it looked like a drain backing up under her white coat that soaked it up like a paper towel, listening to the hardly conscious, severely burned man, come alive with fear. Finally, wearing a bewildered mask of contemplation, she lowered her stare to the man in the bed, watching him flail around as best he could to try to get out of there. She had reached toward him, placing a hand to either side of his bandaged chest in his armpits, using her size and leverage to raise him from the bed. Drawing a deep breath, she had pulled him against her chest with one arm while he screamed to high heaven from the pain from his exposed nerve endings. With her free hand, she unzipped the curtain and shoved the man quickly through it. He dropped to the floor in a heap, screaming and in more pain than he had ever imagined, while Karen zipped the tent back up and released her stale breath, climbing atop the bed to position herself right beneath the oxygen vent in case she had allowed anything to enter.

She had sat up there on that bed, breathing the pure air and watching the already tortured man wriggle and writhe around on the floor until his exasperated reserve of fluids drained from his cooked flesh.

Karen lowered her right hand and extended her first finger, curling it over and over toward her to summon William closer. He shuffled in hesitant advance, his breathing growing increasingly rapid and shallow.

"You killed that man," William said.

"There wasn't enough air for both of us," she whispered barely loud enough to be heard over the humming fan above. "He kept screaming. Screaming. He wouldn't stop. He was using up all of the oxygen with his panic."

William stood his ground, studying her, trying to learn everything he possibly could about this woman in hopes of potentially stopping the inevitable.

"Why are you looking at me like that?"

He watched the way her neck jiggled before she spoke, the way her eyes narrowed with thought, the way her shoulders first moved before giving rise to her meaty arms.

"Quit looking at me. Stop," she said, raising her eyes to make sure that the others, still hovering in the doorway, hadn't heard. "You think you can judge me? You! A kid? You have no right."

Her left foot tapped with the swelling of rage, those little green booties flopping like she was trying to squash a frog.

"It was him or me. This tent doesn't produce enough oxygen for two. Its only purpose is to keep infection from settling into the open wounds since he burned his skin off. And besides, he wouldn't have survived long anyway, not with those burns. It was only a matter of time before we sent him down to the morgue anyway.

"I did the guy a favor."

William took another step closer, bringing his face to within an inch of the plastic, the tip of his nose within a sparse few of hers.

"Trust me," he said, fixing his line of sight directly into her pupils. "You would have preferred the death you forced on that man to the one you have coming."

Her nose crinkled and her eyes slanted. Placing both hands on the curtain, she pressed it forward until her hands were against his thin chest.

"Oxygen!" Brad called, bursting into the room and stepping over the doctor.

Karen jerked her hands back and shoved them into the hip pockets on her scrub top.

"Thank heavens," she said, finishing her glare at William before widening her eyes in delight. "Please...Please bring it to me."

Brad walked around the foot of the bed, careful not to step on the man who looked like he had been turned inside out, and bent to take hold of the zipper.

"Ready?" he asked.

"Zip it up really quickly. Set the tank inside and then close it as fast as you can. I'm going to be right here under the oxygen."

She climbed up on the bed and ducked her head back, pressing her masked mouth right up to the grate in the ceiling. Balancing herself, she lowered her right hand and gave Brad a pudgy thumbs-up.

He nodded, taking a deep breath before drawing that zipper up so fast he nearly left his feet, knocking the tank inward and then pulling the zipper down in one clean motion. Karen sat up there a minute longer, abusing the air, and then filled her lungs and hopped down. She tucked the tank under her arm like a football and climbed right back up onto the bed, holding it beneath the purified breeze to blow off whatever particles may have clung to it like she was following protocol in a clean room.

Slowly, she lowered it to the bed, heaving out her spent air and replacing it with as much of the new as she could hold. Cheeks puffing out like she was hoarding acorns for a long winter, she knelt atop the now tangled blanket. Beads of sweat formed on her forehead like the precipitation of water on a glass of lemonade. Her hands shook when she reached for the plastic mask, cupped to fit over the entire lower half of her face with a little metal clamp to hold it on her nose. Looking nervously across the room to the others, head twitching, she ripped off her paper mask and replaced it with the plastic one, securing it with the strap around the back of her head and pinching the clamp over the bridge of her nose. Chest visibly heaving, she reached a shaking hand for the valve atop the canister, and cranked it a good three or four times to the left.

At first she didn't breathe, fighting against the propelled air assaulting her pinched lips. She shook her head in silent argument, her throat bobbing up and down like a robin trying to regurgitate a meal for her chirping hatchlings, before finally curling her hands to fists and sucking in a long breath.

Her eyes widened and her stomach contracted, bringing with it a barrage of heaves, flopping back and forth like she was possessed. Beet red, she jerked to a halt, tears streaming down her cheeks, and climbed down from the bed.

"Are you sure you want to do this?" Brad asked, refusing to give up his control of the zipper before she was certain.

"I need to get out!" she shrieked, the plastic over her mouth fogging over.

"That oxygen tank won't last forever. You're taking your chance—"

"Let me out!"

Brad nodded solemnly and took a step back. Karen dropped to all fours and tugged and tugged at the zipper until it rode up the track. She crawled out, holding the gray tank to her chest, looking wildly from one to the next, before her eyes settled on the doorway and she bolted toward it, nearly bowling right through Nancy and Tim in the process.

"We need to go now," William said, drawing his father's attention. Brad still stared through the doorway where the woman had just departed with such haste, puzzled.

"I think maybe you're right," he said, taking his son by the hand and leading him across the room, growing so accustomed to the bodies scattered everywhere now that it was instinctive, like evading the sharp-topped toys that littered the floor in a child's bedroom.

William walked right past Nancy and Cindy into the hall, giving Tim a wan smile as he had awakened just enough to slit his eyes.

"How 'bout you?" Brad asked, stopping by Nancy. "Are you ready to go?"

Firming her lips, she averted her eyes and just nodded.

"It'll all work out," Cindy whispered into Nancy's ear. She gave her sister a reassuring squeeze around the hip and followed William down the hallway, while Brad stayed with Nancy, falling further behind the others who were nearly to the end of the long corridor and preparing to descend the stairs.

"I could carry him for a while," Brad said. "I'm sure you could probably use a rest."

"I'm fine."

"I didn't mean to offend you."

"No," she said, the corners of her lips working upward into a weary smile. "You didn't. I'm used to this by now. I've been doing this for as long as I can remember. It's just one of those parent-type things. I'm sure you must know what I mean. You can't waste a single second when it comes to your children, because you never know how many are left."

"Yeah," Brad sighed. "I've only now started being able to sleep through the night without checking on William a dozen times, just in time for him to be a teenager...and then I'll have to start right back up."

A genuine smile graced her lips.

"You should do that more often," he said, starting down the first stair.

"What?"

"Smile."

Nancy leaned against the rail and began the descent, muscles she didn't even know she had complaining from her legs.

"I'd like to see you try in this situation," she said, her smile now vanished.

Brad ran his hand across Tim's damp head, noting how far it appeared that the boy's eyes had sunken into his sockets, and bounded downstairs to make sure he could see William.

Nancy made her cramping legs hurry as well so as not to be left too far behind.

"William!" Brad called, barely able to see his son who was already nearly to the entrance of the emergency room.

William stopped and turned around, nearly bumping into Cindy's stomach.

"Did you see where that woman went?"

"No," William called back, glancing over his shoulder through the broken glass at the admit desk to where the front window had been and the night awaited. He didn't know exactly how much time they had left, but they needed to be to their destination by dawn. That, he knew for a fact. All was lost if they didn't arrive before the first light... and the coming storm.

"That's probably for the best," Nancy said quietly.

"Why?" Brad asked.

"Did you see her eyes? There was something...something about them."

"Would we be better off leaving her? What would that make us?"

"I think maybe we might have. And I'm pretty sure your little boy knows it, too."

"He dragged me out of the house in the middle of the night, made me walk for miles to find you—"

"But he didn't want us to come in here."

"You were the one who insisted."

"Maybe I was wrong."

Brad blinked at her, unable to comprehend how in one moment

the woman would have been willing to tear the entire building apart brick by brick to find a doctor, and now that they had produced the next best thing, she couldn't wait to abandon her.

"Don't ask me how I know," Nancy said, walking past the dumbfounded Brad. "I'm not even sure I know myself. But the further we get from that woman, the better off we're going to be."

"That's crazy. We can't just ditch her."

"I think we can if we get out of here before we bump into her again."

"It wouldn't be right."

"Right versus survival? My instincts have been honed over the past few years. I can awaken from a sound sleep—while only getting two hours a night, mind you—in time to grab a tissue to stop his bleeding nose the moment before it even starts. I can tell he's going to swoon and get him to a couch before he feels dizzy. As irrational and insane as that may sound, they're all I've got, and they've served me well. And right now, they're telling me that we need to get the hell out of here and leave that woman here before we find out what's behind those eyes."

"What if we had left you?" Brad asked, lowering his voice.

"Look into my eyes," Nancy whispered. "Do you see anything to fear?"

Brad's looked into her face. His eyes narrowed and then expanded back to normal.

"No."

"You're a parent. Do you trust your instincts?"

"For the most part."

"If I'm wrong, what's the worst that could happen?"

"We damn that woman to her death."

"And what if I'm right? I don't feel like burying my child tonight, do you?"

"No," Brad said, shaking the forming image from his head. "No."

"Then we go on without her," Nancy leaned over and whispered into his ear as they reached the admit desk. "Agreed?"

Brad nodded without looking to her, and wrapped his arm around William's head, hugging it to his hip. He ruffled the boy's hair before opening the door into the lobby, holding it for Cindy to walk through, and then Nancy.

He was just about to walk through when William tugged on his shirt.

"Daddy!" William whispered sharply.

"What?"

"Please don't let that woman come with us."

Brad looked down at his son, at the shimmering of tears that glistened a pale red on the surface of his eyes, at the urgency in his face.

"Okay," he said, bending over to kiss William on the forehead.

He guided William through the lobby and out through the cracked, but intact automatic door, walking right into Cindy's back. She nearly screamed at the pain.

"Sorry," Brad said, hurriedly taking a step back. "I didn't mean to—"

And then he saw what had caused them to stop right where they were, looking over their shoulders and into the middle of the circle drive beneath the collapsing overhang.

"What took you so long?" Karen asked, smiling widely with a full mouth of teeth behind that plastic shield. She was sitting atop the oxygen tanks, already lying flat inside of the wagon. "I missed the company. And I tell you, I thought talking to those paramedics was tedious before...whew, try talking to them now."

She nodded to the open door to the back of the ambulance.

"So..." she said, clapping her hands. "Where are we going?"

III

Jason grunted and heaved another body atop the pile, billowing a cloud of the thick, black smoke into the air. Charcoal ashes gusted upward, bringing with it the mouthwatering, yet somehow revolting smell of roasted meat. Wiping the blackened sweat from his forehead with the back of his arm, he slunk over to the bench where Trick was leaning back, legs stretched out in front of him, lazily dragging from a cigarette while he stared up into the cloud of dust that still lingered over them. He patted the slatted bench next to him.

The whole works rattled when Jason plopped down, exhausted.

"You smell that?" Trick asked. He was still wearing the headset, though he had given up actively talking into it. Hours had passed since he first strapped it on, and only Jason had, as of yet, responded. His body was tired, his voice worn thin, but more than that, he was just emotionally spent.

"I'm trying not to," Jason sighed. "All it would take is a bottle of barbecue sauce and I'd be over there sacrificing what little of my humanity remains."

"No, not that," Trick said, still watching the sky. "Rain. It smells like rain."

Jason leaned back, rolling his cramped neck over the top of the bench beside Trick's.

"I wouldn't have noticed if you hadn't mentioned it."

"Ozone, my friend. The most beautiful scent in the entire world. There's nothing I love more than sitting out on the porch, listening to the rain drumming on the road and funneling from the gutters and inhaling that intoxicating aroma."

"Poetic. Too bad there are so many holes in the ozone layer now. Not too long now and there'll be nothing left of it."

"While I'd enjoy being tan as a native—and the chicks would dig it for sure—I don't think I could live my life without every now and again smelling it."

"Right now I'd trade my entire olfactory sense for a greasy burger and a chocolate shake."

"Throw in a thick slice of French Silk pie and I'd be there with you."

"Don't even start in with the pie."

Neither wanted to continue that line of conversation. It was painful to even contemplate the rumbling in their stomachs. Sure, there was a vending machine inside from which they could pull a bag of chips or a candy bar, and soon both would have to, but it just wasn't the same thing at all.

"You can't even see the rain-clouds through the dust," Trick said.

"The accepted theory as to the demise of the dinosaurs speculates that it was a meteorite that led to their extinction. When it hit, it threw enough dust into the sky that it got trapped in the atmosphere and nearly entirely blocked out the sun, causing the first great ice age."

"You think that could be what's happening here?"

"I can't possibly imagine it would be."

"We're stacking a lot of dinosaurs on that pyre over there, man."

"We're just wasting our time, you know that? We could spend our entire lives pulling corpses out of houses and still not get them all. There are what, three, four million people in the metro Denver area? We'd have to do a hundred a day for the next hundred years, and by then whatever potential infection they might be carrying would have slipped right through the carpet with the rest of their flesh."

"Cheery thought, but you're going to have to change your attitude if you expect me to help you re-colonize the human race. Granted, I like a little dirty talk, but damn."

Jason snorted a laugh, pausing to look to Trick, and then let it all out, laughing like a madman. Trick smirked and drew the last drag from his smoke, launching it in the general direction of the fire. He couldn't help but chuckle when he looked to Jason, his entire body blackened from the smoke and ash except for his eyes and lips. Surely, he had to look the same. Two Al Jolson rejects sitting there on a bench in the middle of downtown...laughing, while human beings roasted on an open fire.

Where was Norman Rockwell with his pallet and easel for this moment of Americana?

"We're going to have to come up with a better plan," Jason said, sighing loudly while he expelled the last of his laughter.

"Like what?"

"Well...maybe first we should test the bodies to see if we can positively identify the cause of death. If it's viral, then we'd better get cracking on some sort of antidote or treatment. Bacterial...and we're already on borrowed time. But if it's something else, like...I don't know, like a chemical reaction or something, then we would need to figure out why it affected everyone else differently than it did us."

"What kind of chemical reaction could it possibly be? My only relevant experience in that area is mixing gas and booze, lighting it and tossing it into vacant lots when I was a kid."

"After it first happened, I thought I smelled sulfur."

"Lucky you. All I could smell was rotten eggs."

"That's the smell! Now if we both smelled it, then maybe there is something to that theory."

"You some sort of scientist or something?"

"Once upon a time."

"Good enough for me," Trick said, pulling another cigarette from the pack and lighting it. "Continue with said theory, professor."

"I'm anything but an expert, but when I was in school I remember learning about how the Iraqis were burning their oil wells to keep our soldiers from being able to take control of them. So we had to send in these specially trained army guys in all sorts of protective gear, and it would literally take weeks to put out these fires. From what I understand, under the ground in these wells were reserves of hydrogen sulfate, which is an extremely lethal type of sulfuric acid. When they extinguished the fires, the molecules gathered an extra oxygen molecule, converting to sulfur dioxide, which attacks the respiratory system like nobody's business, eating right through the lungs and trachea."

Trick sat up.

"I watched my producer tear out his own throat trying to breathe."

"Right!" Jason said, growing animated, talking enthusiastically with his hands. "I'll be the first to admit that I don't know jack about the geography of this place, but I do know that they used to pull a ton of coal and uranium out of the foothills around here. It could be possible that beneath the shale reserves, there could be high-pressure vents capable of producing hydrogen sulfate, similar to an oil well. If that meteorite hit with the right trajectory and enough force to drive it deep enough into the ground, it could have penetrated a sizable vent. And the heat from burning through the atmosphere could have ignited the already highly flammable gas."

"And the explosion of dust could have put it right back out."

"Blowing with it an astoundingly lethal cloud of sulfur dioxide."

"Sounds reasonable. You buying into it?"

"It's all I've got."

"So what now?"

"I guess that leaves us with what's left. How is it that we survived, and yet everyone else didn't?"

"I'm going to go with smoking good looks, but that only covers me. We're going to need a different explanation for your ugly mug. Any ideas?"

"Were you exposed directly?"

"I'm guessing so. You?"

"I'm pretty confident...yeah."

"Do you have any health problems that you're aware of? Any respiratory or circulatory diagnoses of any sort?"

"Nope."

"Me either."

"Now let's say we run some tests or whatever it is you're thinking. Say you prove that it was this egg-fart gas that did everyone in, what then? Best you can determine is why we didn't die. That doesn't help any of the others, and we're still just as alive and alone. What's the point?"

"The point is that if we lived, then surely others did as well. If it's something in our genetic make-up that allowed us to survive, then we need to isolate it before we could even hope to bring any future generations into the world."

"I already told you, my brother. I like you well enough and all, but—"

Trick stopped, his brow furrowing. Cocking his ear skyward, he bit his lip and tried to concentrate, looking to Jason, who appeared to have heard it as well.

"Thunder," Jason said.

"Yeah, but something underneath it, too, like a bass track... nothing really obvious, but you can tell it's there all the same."

"If it rains, our fire's going to go out."

"Shhh!" Trick snapped, placing his finger over his lips.

There was a distant buzzing sound that was barely audible beneath the grumbling sky, high-pitched, like static humming through high voltage wires, the sound of a bee only inches from his ear.

He rose from the bench, walking slowly toward the street, tilting his head from side to side to hear it drifting in and out on the wind.

Jason followed, isolating the sound from the coming storm, but it sounded like nothing more impressive than telephone wires strung in the dust over his head.

Trick closed his eyes and smiled.

"What?" Jason asked, catching up and noticing the bizarre expression.

"It took me a minute, but I'd know that sound anywhere. Damn kids waking me up all hours of the day. I never thought in my life I'd ever actually be glad to hear that sound."

"I don't get it."

"Listen," Trick said, swaying. He raised his hands and conducted the sound like it was symphonic. "I once devoted a whole show to the abolition of those stupid things. 'How lazy are kids getting these days that they have to strap a motor to a skateboard to make it go?' I said. 'And how pathetically uncoordinated must one need to be to mount handles to it to keep from falling?'"

Jason shrugged.

"A go-ped, m'man. One of those god-awful loud pieces of crap that all of the kids are riding these days."

"There's someone else out there?"

"And if by some stroke of fate it's a chick, then you and I won't have that messy debate over who has to wear the wig."

Trick positively beamed, offering his hand to Jason with a smile stretching from ear to ear.

"Congratulations," he said, shaking Jason's hand and nodding like a contented pigeon. "Throw another shrimp on the barbie, 'cause we're about to have company."

Pulling his hand back, he jumped into the air and pumped his fists to the heavens, heading immediately to the center of the deserted street to wait anxiously. The sound grew louder, buzzing like a blender, echoing from all of the tall buildings and funneling right down the street toward them.

A shadowed form raced around the corner, slowing only long enough to skirt the jumbled metal wreckage of taxis, weaving through the broken glass, and then right down the dashed white lines in the center of the lanes. Long hair flagged behind the shadow; contour coming into focus, clearly defining the rider as impressively female.

"Hey!" Trick shouted, waving his arms over his head like he was coaxing a taxiing airplane into the gate.

The rider hopped off of the go-ped before it even came to a halt, letting it clatter to the ground and slide sideways with the motor sputtering.

"I'm so glad you're here!" she said, tears crackling in her voice. She raced right up to Trick and threw her arms around him, hugging him like they had known each other all of their lives.

"Where else would we be?" Trick asked, smirking.

"I thought..." she said, sniffing. Tears glistened in her eyes. "I thought for sure you'd be gone with as long as it took me to get here. I had to stop for gas four times. And everyone else is dead, and I didn't even pay for the gas. I just rode off."

"It doesn't sound like anyone's going to complain, kid. But if it makes you feel better, I'll spring for it if anyone does. We're just ecstatic that you could make it."

"We?" she queried, prying herself from Trick's embrace and looking curiously around the desolate street.

Jason just gave a little wave when she turned in his direction.

"That's Jason," Trick said. "And I'm sure since you heard my broadcast, that surely means that I need no introduction."

"You're Trick Turner. My boyfriend listens to your show because he says you're the only deejay who'll play the songs he likes."

"Sounds like a hell of a smart guy." He looked to the go-ped and tested his ears for the sound of another, but was greeted with only silence. "He won't be joining us, though...will he?"

Shannen's lips curled inward and she tried in vain to keep the replenished tears from spurting in engorged droplets from the corners of her eyes. She tried to vocalize the words, but if she were to so much as open her mouth, it would all come flooding out. She looked up into the man's face, shook her head to the contrary, and then looked right down to the ground.

"What's your name, sweetheart?" Trick asked, gently laying his arm over her shoulder and guiding her back toward the courtyard.

"Sh-Shannen," she sputtered, the clear discharge from her nose dotting Trick's shirt, though he didn't seem to notice.

"Well, Shannen...I don't know much about affairs of the heart—just ask my ex-wife if you can find her—but I do know that nothing takes the edge off quite like raiding a vending machine. You game?"

Shannen forced a smile, and thanked him with a nod.

"Don't worry, kiddo. I know this is all a lot to try to take in all at once, but you should be really proud of yourself for finding your way down here." He looked to Jason for help with reassurance, but Jason was staring at the girl like he was either trying to tailor an outfit for her by sizing her with his eyes alone, or thinking of doing things that, even under the circumstances, were probably still illegal by the looks of her.

"Never mind my friend here, he's been worried about the perpetuation of our species. Don't take it personally. He seems harmless enough."

"Jason," he said shaking her hand as a mere formality, oblivious to anything Trick had said. He was too busy trying to physically assess her for any sign of altered health. "Do you have any health concerns or recent diagnoses?"

Shannen looked to Trick, leaning closer into his side.

"We're working on a theory," Trick whispered into her ear. "It's all right. I was just joshing with you a second ago. Bad joke I guess."

"Yes," she sniffled, watching Jason's face light up. Even Trick tensed somewhat at the answer, slowing momentarily before resuming the walk over the curb and into the courtyard.

"What?" Jason said, biting his enthusiastic tongue for fear of shouting at her in his excitement.

"The doctor says I have something called a Prothrombin II mutation. Factor V Leiden—"

"A clotting disorder?" Jason mused. His face tightened into an unattractive knot of concentration akin to the look of being crippled with constipation. "I'm not familiar with that one."

"They only recently started diagnosing it. Only one in seven hundred thousand gets it."

Jason's lower lip crept into his mouth and he bit down repeatedly on it.

"It means my blood can form clots at any given time in my veins without exposure to air."

"Irregular shaped platelets?"

"I don't know."

"Increased blood pressure?"

"No."

"Do they propose that it's inherent?"

"How so?"

"Genetic. Is it genetic in origin?"

"Yeah. They say my children will automatically get it, if technology even advances far enough in the future for me to be able to have children."

"Are you on any medications? What precautions did they recommend?"

"Aspirin regimen for now. Coumadin or heparin by the time I'm thirty. I can't use the pill or—"

"Your ovum may clot in the fallopian tubes."

She nodded.

"Increased risk of hemorrhaging, clotting in the extremities—"

"I had to have one surgically removed from my leg."
"How old are you?"
"Seventeen."
"And you had a venal thrombosis?"
"Arterial."
"No way. There's no physical way a clot could have formed in your artery. That's the kind of thing that happens to bed-ridden eighty year-olds, not kids your age."
"But it did."
"Um," Trick said, lifting his arm from around Shannen as they reached the bench. It was like listening to a couple of Mexicans ahead of him in the line at the grocery store. He only caught a few words here and there, which only confused him even more. "Why don't I go get something to eat while you continue…talking?"
He walked toward the building, scratching his head.
"Did they check your pulse oxygen level?"
"I think so?"
"Was it normal?"
"I can only assume."
"The blood draw. Did they take it from your arm?"
"Yeah. I have to have blood drawn every couple of months or so. They take like eight vials."
"I wish I knew the oxygen concentrations in your alveolar blood," he mused, rubbing his chin. He sat there silently contemplative.
"I think for my blood to be able to clot so easily that it must have a higher level of oxygen in it."
"That's a reasonable theory, but there's no real way of testing for it now. I wouldn't even know where to begin. Phlebotomy wasn't my strong suit."
"You're a doctor then?"
Jason smiled thinly and wiped the foul taste of charcoal from his spread lips.
"One in seven hundred thousand, you say?"
"That's what the doctors told me."
"There are only three of us. Odds would dictate that there are at least…" He paused, eyes rolling up and to the left. "Well, at least a couple more of us in the metro area alone."
"I've got a plethora of culinary delicacies," Trick called, crunching over the scattered glass. "See? Check me out. I can talk all edjumicated, too."
"'I have'," Jason said, smiling coyly. "'I have a plethora of culinary delicacies,' if you want to be technical about it."
"No, my good friend. What you have is a whole lot of nothing. I,

on the other hand…I've got an armful of the kind of goodies that God would have grown Himself had he the genius of my personal idols, Mr. Frito and Mr. Lays."

He dumped a pile of bagged chips, candy and cookies between them on the bench, recalling a red bag of Doritos and tearing it open so quickly a couple dropped out onto the ground.

"I didn't figure anyone would mind if I just smashed in the case and grabbed as much as I could carry," he said through a crunching bite. "I'm now a victim of the whole mob mentality thing. I'm like, a real looter now. I suppose I should probably say something politically correct now. Free Rodney King! Beat Reginald Denny! Free snacks for all!"

Jason ripped the wrapper from a Ding Dong and shoved half of one into his mouth, the cream filling covering his upper lip right up to the tip of his nose.

"I fink cheese duck ease," he mumbled through the engorged bite.

"Like my sainted father always said from his pulpit at the head of the table: get the dick out'cher mouth when you talk."

Jason sniggered, licking his lips. His Adam's apple rose, and it took all of his effort to force that huge mound of chocolate down his gullet.

"I think," he said, preparing to inhale the remaining half. "I think she's the key."

He flinched when a large droplet of cold water splashed in the center of his thigh, soaking right through the denim and against his skin. Craning his neck back, he looked up into the churning layer of dust in time to have another slap him on the cheek.

"Rain," Shannen said, holding out her palm. A drop landed on her forearm.

"Wash away the old to begin anew, the earth's cleansing ritual," Jason said, smearing away the blackened mess on his face with the dozens of droplets that pocked the muck.

Trick nodded and walked around to the front of the bench, giving Shannen a subtle shove with his hip to scoot down and make enough room for his rear end.

Under normal circumstances, all would surely have run back into the lobby, seeking the sanctuary from the rain in the warmth of the indoors. But now…all three sat on the bench, sucking matted chocolate and cheesy crumbs from their dirty fingers, allowing their bodies to be cleansed by the blessedly pristine, cool water.

Little did they know that it would be the last peaceful moment that any of them would experience for a long time to come.

IV

"My feet are killing me!" Karen screamed, her voice echoing back at her from the buildings growing increasingly taller with each passing block. She had to readjust the oxygen mask over her first, bulbous chin. "Can't we take a break? I don't think I can walk any further."

"Make her stop," William growled under his breath.

"If only," Cindy said with a wink.

"I'll bet I've got stress fractures in both tibias! I don't suppose any of you brought a pair of walking casts, huh?"

Brad winced. He fancied himself a patient man. After all, he had raised a child with an unknown psychological malady by himself for more than a decade. But even he was close to the point of slapping her upside the head with a two-by-four and carrying her the rest of the way himself if it meant she would shut up for just one single moment. She had begun complaining before they had even reached the end of the hospital drive, and that had been easily a couple of miles ago.

"Can't someone else drag this stupid wagon for a while? Why do I have to be the one to do all of the work, for crying out loud?"

Nancy looked back at her over her shoulder with a frown of disdain. With so many broken bricks littering the sidewalk from where they had been shaken loose from the buildings, and the cars haphazardly wrecked throughout the road, they had been forced to stop pushing the gurney on its wheels and carry it with Tim atop it. Brad, whom she was slowly actually beginning to somewhat respect, had walked the last half-dozen blocks backwards, though he struggled with the weight of his cargo and nearly lost his balance several times.

Tim stirred, as he had occasionally done every fifteen minutes or so.

Nancy looked down at him and forced a smile.

"How ya feeling, special guy?" she asked, trying to hide the strain in her shoulders and back that crumpled her features.

He coughed and dragged the back of his hand across his upper lip, streaking his wrist with a fine line of blood from his nose.

"Like a million bucks," he retched through his parched throat.

She stared at his nose, waiting for the swell of blood from his nostril that would be the prelude to the opening of the floodgates. Her maternal instincts screamed for her to stop right then and there and pinch the bridge of his nose in the white sheet they had used to cover him, forcing it to stop before it got going. They were getting close now, and the sooner they got there, the sooner she would be able to fawn all over him like she should be doing this very instant. If she stopped every time she felt the urge, however, they'd still be looking at the downtown skyline from the distance, rather than having to break their necks to look straight up. She'd watch it carefully, though. If so much as a single droplet rolled down his lip, she'd pounce on it like a tiger on a cube steak.

"That's my boy," she said, her lips wriggling to force the unnatural smile from her face, but she held them at bay. "Try to get back to sleep. We'll be there before you know it."

He cast her the same unbelievable expression, and closed his eyes.

"The kid has an itch on his nose and you all gather around like it's the end of the world or something, yet here I am, walking on two broken legs, dragging a couple hundred pounds of oxygen and no one cares."

"Ya think?" Cindy leaned over and whispered into William's ear. He clapped his hand over his mouth to keep from laughing.

"I heard that, beanpole!" Karen wailed. "I don't see you doing anything useful! Why don't you take a turn for God's sake? Don't give me that crap about your poor back! I'm a nurse! I see people worse off than you dragging themselves into the emergency room every day!"

"Will you stop complaining if I do?" Cindy snapped, turning to face the woman.

Karen's face was corpuscle red, right up to the tips of her ears, and there were huge sweat stains expanding from the pits of her scrubs all the way up to the v-cut neckline.

"I could always crack you upside the head with one of these tanks."

"You could always leave," William said, forcing his trembling chin to stay firm.

"You'd like that, wouldn't you?" Karen said, languidly closing the gap that had formed between them. One of the wagon wheels snagged and she grunted to jerk it free, the canisters clanging within. "I'll bet you'd like nothing more than for me to die out here all by myself."

Rather than fading as she slowed to a stop, her cheeks grew more intensely red with the furor, lips peeling back from gritted teeth.

"Feels like someone drove a bunch of nails right through my feet!"

"Hold up a sec," Brad said to Nancy, and then watched his son.

Karen rolled the wagon right up behind her heels and plopped down atop it, lifting her right foot up into her lap and pulling off the white shoe. Grimacing, she slipped her thumb beneath the cuff of her sock and peeled it down over her heel, pulling it all the way off and draping it over her calf. She kneaded the balls of her feet, wincing at even the slightest applied pressure.

"We're almost there," Brad said, rolling his shoulders and readjusting his grip on the handles of the converted stretcher. "We can all take a break as soon as we get there."

"I'm taking a break now!" Karen screamed. "Leave if you want. I don't care!"

"Is there anything we can do to help?" he asked, trying to maintain at least the façade of patience.

"Are you a doctor?"

"No."

"Then what could you possibly do to help? I suppose you could flip me a burger if that's what you do. That would be of some use," she said, suddenly jerking her head back, her face puckering as though she had just eaten something bitter. There was something in her chest, an enormous ball of phlegm maybe. She reared back and coughed, but produced nothing but the feeling that her convulsive reflexes were about to kick in if she didn't get it out quickly. She hacked and retched, wrenching up a wad of mucous that was nearly large enough to fill her mouth and dropped it right into her oxygen mask. Slimy and foul, it rested against her chin, but she couldn't bring herself to lift her life support even long enough to dump it out.

Brad looked away for fear of throwing up at the sight, instead choosing to stare in through the bars over the glass-less windows of a liquor store. It reeked to high heaven from all of the shattered bottles and the mass amounts of alcohol covering the floor, preserving the corpse lying in the aisle. The clerk, with his little green vest and bad toupee, which looked as though someone had begun scalping him from the hairline back and lost interest halfway through, could do nothing but watch from behind the counter, his eyes staring blankly from where his head rested on the cash register.

"Jesus," Karen groaned, hardly able to breathe. No matter how much pressure she applied, those knots were simply not going to work out of her feet. Leaning forward, she looked for what literally felt like nails driven through the soles of her feet, expecting to find blood dripping into an expanding puddle on the concrete, but saw nothing. She was just about to put her sock back on when she saw something under her big toe nail. At first she had thought it was blood, but the coloring wasn't quite right, rather than a deep red, close to black, it was a brighter red-orange, like the Indian Paintbrushes that dotted the field of weeds behind her townhouse. Gouging her fingernail beneath, she tried to scrape it out, but it disappeared under the nail. There was nothing there now, but she was left with the impression that it had looked like a fungus peering out from beneath the crescent of the nail, but she couldn't think of a single type of fungal infection that was a striking color like that.

"We've got to keep moving," William said, gnawing on a hangnail.

A single large droplet of water splashed onto the dust-covered sidewalk, immediately balling into a brown mass.

"Do you think you can walk again?" Brad asked, twisting his grip on the stretcher.

"Don't patronize me," Karen said, doubling over when she surprisingly coughed something else up again. Tears squeezed from her wet eyes. She tugged the sock back on and shoved her foot into the leather shoe, twisting at the ankle until it seated itself within.

Cindy eased closer, and with a sideways glance, lifted the handle of the wagon and waited for Karen to clamber off.

Wheezing, Karen heaved the oxygen tank, attached via the thin plastic tube to her mask, from atop the others and hugged it to her chest. She lumbered forward, feet slapping soundly on the pavement to the tune of her meek squealing. Her throat burned like the mucous membrane was being peeled off from her palate all the way down into her chest. Phlegmy strands filled her windpipe faster than she could swallow them back, making it harder and harder to inhale sufficient air, or exhale anything that didn't come up in a mouthful of clinging goo. The roof of her mouth was starting to feel fuzzy, like it was coated with a layer of moss.

The raindrops came with increased frequency, dotting the shoulders of their shirts and wetting their hair to their scalps. It felt glorious; finally beginning to wash away the caked sweat and dust, the scent of the dead that clung to them like a reptilian skin preparing to shed.

"How far now?" Nancy asked, nervously watching the droplets that rolled down either side of Tim's face from the continental divide of his nose. His eyeballs fluttered beneath his closed lids, his lips working around voiceless words.

"Not too much further," Brad said, noting the urgency in her voice and doing his best to hurry his pace though he rose and fell over crumbled piles of brick and mortar.

"There!" William shouted, pointing over the top of the old municipal court building to a funnel of black smoke pillaring into the belly of the lingering dust above.

Cindy ground her teeth at the pain in her back from dragging the wagon, the edges of the scabs working their way loose from the lacerated edges of flesh to allow fresh seepage to dampen the taped bandages. The rain provided momentary relief, but quickly turned to a stinging sensation.

The smoke drifted from behind tall buildings, making it difficult to pinpoint its precise location, but if William was right, and the Qwest building was the place that they needed to be, then that would be easy enough to find. It towered over them like a tree must have looked from an anthill, a black, squared spire rising into the night.

The rain came harder, summoning more and more droplets from the thundering sky. It patterned the ground all around them, slowly rising to form a trickling stream down the clogged gutter, widening to work around the tangles of branches and leaves and corpses to find its way to the burbling sewer grates.

William looked impatiently upward, and then to one of the numerous bodies that lined the sidewalk. If they weren't with the others by the time the rain caused…

The voices in his head, *their* voices, began chittering anew. Their silence broken, their words and images flowed by so quickly that he couldn't even keep up. They were excited, exultant, chaotic, but the one clear thought he could pluck from the machine-gun rapidity of their communications was that they were here.

They were here.

"Come on, Dad!" William said, holding his forehead and grimacing at the level of concentration it had taken to force that one simple combination of words through the yelling inside of his head.

He slapped at the raindrops on his arms, brushing the smaller particles of water onto the ground as quickly as he could, like he was swiping off ants or spiders crawling on his skin, which was what the once comforting raindrops were beginning to feel like.

"We have to get out of the rain," he blurted, running back to Cindy and taking her free hand to try to urge her along.

Karen was conspicuously quiet for the first time since they had left, head lolling down onto her chest, watching her shuffling feet sifting through the rubble. There was so much pain. So much pain! It was all she could do to just keep her legs moving, keep from collapsing right there in the sidewalk. Her insides felt as though they were liquefying, a stabbing pain bristling from within and poking through her skin like spikes. She belched a foul taste like rotten eggs, unknowingly draining a line of blood over her lower lip and onto her chin.

"Let's try putting the wheels down again," Nancy said, straining to force out the words. Her eyes narrowed to slits from the pain that resonated from her back. "It looks like the road ahead might be clear enough to wheel him for a while."

Brad nodded, ultimately thankful for the reprieve, and stepped down to the asphalt from the curb, rounding the smashed rear of an Isuzu Rodeo. The shattered plastic from the tail light covers crackled underfoot. Looking to Nancy, he slowly lowered his end of the stretcher, balancing it with her to keep it level, and then popped the latch beneath to extend the legs.

"Hurry!" William shouted, immediately driving the butts of his palms against his eyes. The voices were growing louder, and not just the voices of those he was accustomed to having inside of his head with him, but others…infinite voices bouncing back and forth from the insides of his skull like so many rubber balls fired from cannons.

"We're almost there," Brad said, his mouth dropping slightly askew while he looked at his son who was shaking his head like he was trying to clear the cobwebs from a concussion. He stepped around the side of the gurney and took the handle on the side, helping Nancy to propel it more quickly down the center of the road.

Cindy followed, rolling the wagon off of the curb, the tanks clanging like church bells. She cast a quick glance back to Karen, who was starting to sway like a drunk, her progress veering slightly to the left before being quickly over-corrected and taking her too far to the right.

William gritted his teeth and broke into a sprint, tearing right down the middle of the street that was now tilting to either side beneath his feet. The slap of his footsteps on the thin coating of water on the street echoed from all around, intensifying the feeling of the loss of equilibrium.

"William!" Brad shouted after him. He looked to Nancy, who gave him the nod of approval to his unvoiced question, and then dashed after his child who was now nearly to the end of the street where there was a tangle of smashed yellow cabs. "Wait up!"

He had to slow to maintain his balance, the sound of his feet smacking the pavement coming back at him like a hammer striking a railroad tie.

"William!" he called again, unable to run another step. His knees shook while he walked, barely able to support his weight. He could see his son's silhouetted form round the corner of the building to the right and onto the street beyond, but he couldn't stimulate himself to run another step. "You wait right there!"

He ran his hooked fingers through his matted hair, knotting in the tangles and having to tear through it to exit over the back of his skull.

With the last of his strength, he stumbled more quickly, undoubtedly looking as awkward as it felt. Heading around the side of the building where he had just seen his son pass, he found himself in the middle of a deserted street. An amber glow flickered from the side of a tall building, trails of smoke twirling in front of it, illuminating the entire courtyard between the two skyscrapers. William's small form bounded up over the curb and into the glow. Three others arose from nowhere, as if they had been lying in wait, towering over him.

"William!" he shouted, positively willing his legs to run. Fear chased the pain from his legs into numbness. Heartbeat trilling, his pulse throbbing in his ears, he sprinted through the heaving breaths, crossing that two-lane road in no time flat and hopping over the curb to snatch his son from his feet and bring him to his heaving chest.

He panted, chest rising and falling so quickly and violently that he couldn't even goad the words of relief past his parted lips, spraying spittle and strands of saliva down his chin with each exaggerated exhalation. Wrapping his hand around the back of his son's head and holding it tightly to his chest, he looked at the others. Their faces were swathed with blackness, the firelight framing the wild hair surrounding their heads, outlining their imposing looking forms like the sun shining from armor.

"Stay back!" he gasped, having to cough through the smoke that accosted his lungs and parched his throat.

"We're not going to hurt you," a feminine voice said, slowly easing forward and toward him. Brad rotated his body to distance William from her advance.

One of the others reached out and took her by the shoulder, stalling her encroachment.

"My name's Trick," the shadow said. "This here is Shannen, and to my right is Jason."

"Brad," he said nervously, scrutinizing them through narrowly focused eyes. His tightly wound body began to soften, but he still cradled William outside of their reach.

"And who's this?" Shannen asked, slipping out from under Trick's hand and taking a step forward. Brad turned William even further away, but she managed to get close enough to brush his bangs from his forehead and look into the boy's face.

"William," Brad whispered.

"Is he your son?"

Brad nodded.

Shannen smiled and leaned right into his face. "What do you say to a bag of chips?"

William raised his head and looked to his father, who gave him approval with a nod and cautiously replaced him on his feet.

"You surprised me," Brad said, watching William stroll back into the firelight holding the girl's hand. "I didn't see you at all back there in the shadows until you were standing right over my son."

"Natural reaction," Trick said. "I get that from chicks all the time."

Brad smiled and sighed.

"How far have you come?" Jason asked, offering his hand.

"Just up Clear Creek Canyon," Brad said, wiping his sweating palm on his thigh before reciprocating the gesture. "You?"

"I just live down past Washington Park by the university. Didn't take me all that long."

"So I suppose you heard me on the radio," Trick said, shaking Brad's hand as well.

"I don't listen to much. Sorry."

"I mean tonight."

Brad shrugged.

"If you didn't hear me on the radio, then how did you know that we would be here?"

"My son," Brad said. "He, um...he said that you'd be waiting."

Trick turned and stared at the boy perched on the bench, shoving handfuls of chips into his mouth like he hadn't eaten in weeks. He turned back to Brad with a curious expression of skepticism.

"Are you saying he's psychic?"

"You're here, aren't you?"

A squeaking sound interrupted the still night, drawing all eyes to the corner of the building at the end of the street in time to see Nancy wheel Tim around the corner with Cindy right behind, wagon in tow.

"How many of you are there?" Jason blurted through a widening smile.

"Six of us in all."

"Six!" Jason shared an elated shove in the shoulder with Trick.

"Great!" Trick said. "This guy here had me worried for a while that we were going to have to pull a rabbit out of our asses to repopulate the planet."

"Is it just the three of you then?" Brad asked, watching the girl take a hulking bite of what looked to be a Twinkie and offer the other half to William, who snatched it from her and plowed it past his teeth.

"Yeah," Jason said. "Shannen there's seventeen. Trick's the deejay that led us here, and I'm—"

"Let's back up," Trick interrupted. "Back to this kid of yours. How did he know to bring you here?"

"Same way he knew to lead me to the house where we found the others. He says he hears voices."

"Like a dog telling him to take a .44 with him on his nightly walks?"

"He's not crazy, if that's what you're implying," Brad snapped, taking exception. "Until, heck...this morning—it seems like a week ago now—we thought he was autistic because he never really talked."

"And now he's predicting the future?"

"I guess so."

"And who have we here?" Trick asked, smiling while he brushed his hair back into place with his hand.

Nancy stopped the gurney behind Brad and sidled up to him, slipping her hand between his arm and ribs, taking him by the elbow.

"You're Trick Turner!" Cindy said, allowing the wagon's handle to clatter to the ground. "You did a live broadcast from my school a while back!"

"Front Range?"

"Yeah." Cindy reached out and took Trick's hand, shaking it. "I don't know if you remember me. You bumped into me and spilled my coffee all over both of us."

"Accounting student. I remember by that book you were carrying. I thought you were just pure evil the way you scalded me and then didn't even offer to take care of me."

"I believe I was trying to take care of my own blistering wounds thanks to you."

"Oh, it wasn't that bad."

"I looked like a lobster from the neck down."

"Still do."

"What is that supposed to mean?"

"I don't know. Joke that fell flat. Just step over it and help yourself to some goodies over there, just try to refrain from stabbing me in the eye with a pretzel or something."

"I can't make any promises," she said with a wink.

Nancy rolled her eyes. "I need to get my son inside out of the rain, and I think we all could use a trip to the restroom."

"Right through the front of the building to your left," Trick said, offering her his hand as well. "Name's Trick."

"As in 'or treat'?"

"Precisely." Trick laughed. "Now's where you offer an introduction."

"I'm Nancy. This is Tim."

"What's wrong with him?"

"He has leukemia."

Jason walked over to the boy and lowered the blanket from his face, exposing the pale white, marbled cheeks and the red-ringed, puffy eyes.

"Stay back!" Nancy nearly shouted, relinquishing Brad's arm to slap at Jason's hand.

"Don't worry. It's all right. I used to be a doctor."

Nancy stared at the dirty man standing before her in cynical doubt.

"Where'd you go to medical school?"

"University of Colorado."

"Really? Here in town at the health science center? Tell me you're an oncologist and I'll hug you right now!"

"Emergency medicine, I'm afraid. Blood and guts mostly. But I'd be happy to take a look at him."

"Wonderful," Nancy sighed. "Let's just get him in out of the rain first, okay?"

She grabbed the gurney and rolled it forward until it hit the curb. Jason helped her lift it up and over.

"So he's receiving chemo treatments. What stage?" Jason asked, helping her wheel Tim toward the collapsed front of the building.

"I thought you said there were six of you," Trick said, drawing Brad's attention back from where it had followed Nancy.

"Yeah," Cindy said, returning with a crumpled bag of miniature doughnuts.

"What happened to Karen?" Brad asked.

"She was right behind us when we came around the building."

Brad walked into the middle of the street and scanned the shadows, looking for the woman, but there was no sign of movement, of any life whatsoever. He glanced back over his shoulder to make sure that William, who was now working on licking cream filling from his fingers while he braced his forehead with his right hand, was going to be all right.

"Karen?" Brad called, a small part of him hoping that she just might have decided to take her own course instead of joining them.

He walked curiously across the street and up onto the far sidewalk, rounding the side of the office building and staring back down the street from which they had come. At first, all he could see was darkness, his eyes having adjusted to the slight glow from the fire and making it difficult to slip back on the nocturnal glasses he had only minutes prior been accustomed to. After a moment of walking, stumbling over the lumpy crumbs of red bricks and stepping on a watch on someone's wrist, he was finally able to pry her form out of the shadow. She was sitting there in a big lump right in the middle of the curb, holding that tank of oxygen to her chest like a newborn cradling a blankie. Her head sagged down against her chest, the dark strands of hair lining her cranium like the rays from a black sun. Legs crumpled beneath her, she looked like she could have died walking, were it not for the slight rise and fall of her shoulders.

"Are you okay?" Brad asked, taking incrementally small steps forward. There was something about the way she kind of lolled her head around in response that made him nervous.

She let out a groan that sounded less like a contemplative measure of speech than gasses escaping involuntarily, a byproduct of cellular deterioration.

"I'm going to need your help," Brad said, reaching beneath her limp right arm and bracing his feet for the impending exertion. "I don't think I'll be able to lift you by myself."

"Why did you all leave me?" she whined.

"There are other people up there. We'll get you something to eat and drink as soon as you can help me by standing up."

"My legs ache really bad," she whined, raising her head just enough to show Brad her pale face. Tears dragged the mascara from her eyes in gray streaks down her cheeks, forming a ring around the seal of the oxygen mask, while within, the clear surface was thick was a bloody gelatinous mess of phlegm and mucous, so much that he couldn't even see her mouth or nose behind.

"I'll lift at your arm. You just push off with your legs."

"Feels like there's something under my skin, crawling through the flesh and tissue. Eating me…eating me alive."

Thunder boomed overhead, releasing the full ferocity of the storm. The raindrops doubled in size in the blink of an eye, now coming so hard and fast that his shirt was immediately saturated and sapped to his skin. Rivulets of the cold fluid drained through his hair and traced the contours of his face before trailing in a line from his chin. Those engorged droplets slapped the asphalt and cement so hard that he couldn't hear anything over them at all.

"Come on, Karen!" he shouted, batting his eyelids to keep the fluid from washing over the sensitive surface. "On three!"

She looked like she was melting with all of the rain, her clothes darkening by three shades, the whole composition of her body being dragged downward and into the cement.

"One!" he yelled, spitting out a mouthful of the dirty water that had rolled over his lips the moment he parted them.

"What's happening!" she gargled through a mouthful of viscous fluids. Curling her fingers to claws, she started scratching furiously at the opposite forearm, carving reddening parallel lines into the skin. "Get them off of me!"

"Two!"

"Get them off! Get them off of me!"

"Three!" Brad barked, jerking upward with everything he had left, only to find that her legs had already responded and she stood of her own volition. "This way!" He ducked his head and tugged the collar of his shirt up over the top of his head. Still holding Karen by the arm, he hurried back toward the others.

The rain drove with such velocity that it splashed back upward as though trying to make the return trip. It sounded like sledgehammers pounding on the denting roofs and hoods of the eternally stalled cars. Water already accumulated in the middle of the road, rising in the gutters to the tops of the sidewalks, and then right over. The clogged drains were of no use, simply allowing the water to rise and rise until, in a matter of just a couple of minutes, it was starting to move the bodies from the ground, washing them like beaver-chewed logs downstream.

Throwing his free arm across his forehead to shield his eyes just enough to try to see, he dragged the cumbersome woman through the middle of the street and toward the others. They were now hurriedly rounding up all of their drenched food and hustling through the front of the building and out of the rain. The shrinking flames from the fire raged against the rain, hissing and sizzling, but to no apparent avail. Swells of black smoke intensified and widened, churning upward and into the belly of the night, while the lapping flames expelling them were forced down against the human charcoal, waning and flagging until they were little more than glowing embers.

The flesh of Karen's arm was repulsive in his grasp, not only was it quivering with adipose wiggle at each pounding step, but the upper layers had the consistency of a balloon filled with clotted oatmeal. It felt like the flesh was rotting right away from the bone and readying itself to slough free.

"Almost there!" Brad shouted, as much for his own benefit as hers. "Just keep going!"

Leaping up onto the curb, splashing standing water clear up past his knees, he darted for the front door. Karen seemed to be gaining a little bit of strength, as he now no longer felt as though he were supporting and dragging her, but rather towing her along.

Passing through the shattered glass and into the building, Brad released Karen and took another couple of steps before collapsing to the ground. Chasing the water from his head and hair with his hand, he tugged his shirt back into place and let out a long sigh.

"I don't think I've ever been out in rain like that in my life," he said, smoothing the ribbons of fluid from his face and then wringing it from his shirt.

Karen walked right up to Trick on trembling legs, swaying slightly. She fixed her eyes on his; head rolling unimpeded from side to side on her flimsy neck. A gurgling growl worked its way from her stomach and through her mouth. She buckled back and forth, her cheeks puffing out, stomach contracting ferociously, and then doubled over to spray vomit through the seal around her mask. It fired arcs of foul smelling fluid in all directions.

"Whoa!" Trick gasped, jumping back. He looked to Cindy, who was, just like he, staring wide-eyed at the woman in shock.

"William!" Brad shouted, looking around and suddenly realizing that he had seen the boy walk into the building from the street, but hadn't once seen him since he had entered. He pushed himself to his feet, stumbling as his legs prepared to give out on him.

"He was right here a second ago," Shannen said, twirling in a circle. "William?"

Brad's heart rose into his throat, his panicking stare flirting from one shadow to the next, all around the bleak and glass-littered lobby, until finally, he saw William's small, thin silhouette standing off to the side just inside of the building.

"There you are," he said, trying to hide the fear in his voice.

He walked up to his son and wrapped his arm over William's shoulder, pulling him closer. A spray of water, more like a mist, drifted through the broken window, coating them like they were standing on a beach and watching the waves break on a jagged rock formation.

"It scared me when I couldn't find you," Brad said.

William just stared out into the night.

"That's my job, you know. Worrying? That's what dads do best."

"Time to go, now," William whispered, unable to steer his eyes in from the rain and to his father.

"We just got here, son. Maybe we'd better figure out what to do next before heading back out into that storm."

"There's...no time," he whispered in a voice so small that Brad could barely hear it over the drumming rain.

"William..."

The boy whirled around like a startled snake, rising up and grabbing hold of his father by the front of the shirt before he even had time to react.

"Right now!" he screamed. His eyes grew so wide with panic that Brad could see the miniature feather dusters peeking out from under his eyelids, netted in the lashes, like brightly colored, crusted balls of sleep. "If we stay here any longer, we're going to die! Can't you see that! We will all die here!"

All other conversation fell still in the lobby. Even Jason and Nancy, who had been off in their own little world deep into the waiting room checking on Tim, paused to look across the lobby.

"You're scaring me, William," Brad whispered, trying to pull the boy to his chest so that maybe he could calm him a little.

Karen had plopped down in the middle of her own vomit on the floor and begun jamming her pudgy fingers into her ears, scraping at what felt like spiders scuttling around in her auditory canals. She turned slowly to look at William, wincing at the pain caused by her fingernails, the stinging source of the small lines of blood that trickled over the lobes of her ears, dangling there like round ruby earrings.

"We're all going to die anyway," she said, huffing to draw air through the congealing mess in her mask. She looked up to Trick and Cindy, who towered helplessly over her, unable to do anything but watch her grotesque display. Her eyes widened to the point that both could feel her stare on them like pins poking into their flesh.

"Not if we leave now," William said, begging his father with his eyes, with a jerk on his shirt.

"Too late!" Karen screamed, followed by something of a high-pitched cackle. "They're already here!"

"Make her shut up," Trick said, backing blank-faced from the woman on the ground.

"We're all going to die!"

Trick turned away from her and walked quickly toward the door. He needed air, needed to get away from that woman. He couldn't breathe, couldn't focus, the room was spinning around him like he was halfway through a fifth. Focusing on the drone of the splashing rain, the darkness pulling to him like a magnet from the courtyard, he leaned against the frame from one of the imploded windows, trying to force the woman's cries from his head where they echoed hollowly like firecrackers in a closed room.

"All gonna die, all gonna die!" she muttered, rising to her feet and tucking the nearly drained tank under her right arm. "We are all going to die!"

"For the love of God!" Trick screamed, clapping his hands over his ears. "Someone shut her up!"

"Sit back down," Cindy said, trying to maintain the façade of calmness in her voice, though she visibly shook when she touched the woman and tried to coax her back to the ground.

"Can't you hear them all!" Karen screamed, swatting away Cindy's hands and whirling to face her. "They're everywhereeverywhere!"

"Dad, please!" William shouted. "We've gotta go!"

"Shut up!" Trick screamed, unable to take it any more. "Shut—"

Something moved outside.

"We're out of time!" William screamed, tears bursting from his eyes.

Trick peeled back the darkness, watching for the shape he had seen move only a moment prior, but everything was still now. Parabolic cups of rain patterned the standing water covering the courtyard.

"Everyone grab whatever you can carry!" William shouted,

releasing his father to run to the center of the lobby.

"They'll find you wherever you go!" Karen screeched, lunging to grab William by the arm. She pulled him to her and lowered her face to bring it within inches of his own. Wildly insane eyes locking on William's, she shook him as she screamed. "No matter where you run, no matter how far…they will find you!"

"Get away from him!" Brad shouted, jerking William from her grasp and picking him up from the ground. "You touch him again and I'll kill you myself!"

"Guys…" Trick whispered.

"Everyone needs to calm down!" Jason barked, rushing across the room to separate the combatants. "Panicking won't help anything! We need to calmly and rationally figure out what we're going to do—"

"Guys," Trick said, louder this time.

"We should just stay here," Nancy said from the far side of the room where she had positioned herself between Tim and the rising chaos. "We all need to rest awhile. Everything will look better after getting a good night's slee—"

"*Guys!*" Trick shouted at the top of his lungs.

They all stopped and looked toward him.

Trick's back was framed against the first hint of the rising sun, lightening the night by but a single shade of gray. He stood motionless, unable to withdraw his stare from the courtyard, though right now that was what he wanted more than anything in the world.

Hidden beyond the thick cloud of dust and tall buildings, what precious little sunlight filtered through shimmered on the raindrops only enough to define a spherical edge, like a glittering aura of pixie dust.

"There are people out there," Trick whispered, closing his eyes and then reopening them to verify that they weren't deceiving him.

There…just at the edge of sight in the courtyard, barely made visible against the blackness beyond, were a good dozen silhouettes. They stood perfectly still, unmoving, arms out to their sides like human crosses, ankles pressed together. If Trick hadn't called their attention to it, none might ever have noticed. Faces cocked back to the sky, palms to the heavens, they looked like statues collecting the rain.

"We have to go!" Tim screamed. "Now! Before they're all awake!"

Jason walked past Trick and out the door into the courtyard, brow lowered contemplatively. He could easily recognize that there was something wrong with the way they were all standing there, not betraying so much as a single breath, as though they were made of marble.

"Hello..." Jason said, startled by the quiver in his own voice.

He walked closer, watching the statuesque shape draw nearer and nearer until he was right beside it. Water puddled in the extended, cupped hand, similarly filling the eye sockets and draining down the cheeks.

"Are you all right?" he asked.

"Get away from it!" William screamed from behind.

"Not if he needs help," he answered barely loud enough to hear it in his own ears.

Jason reached tentatively out and placed his hand on the man's arm, and then quickly recoiled. Something had moved...more precisely, something had squirmed beneath his fingertips. Inching forward, unable to bring himself to place a hand back on that cold, clammy, squirming skin, he watched the side of the man's neck for a thumping sign of a pulse.

Mouth open, filling with rainwater, the man stared upward with wide eyes that didn't even blink when the drops landed directly on them. Were it not for the charcoal-varnished badge on the man's chest, Jason would never have recognized the security officer's uniform. The sleeves were burned back to the torso, itself nothing more than a wet, black mess of tattered remains that hissed and smoked with the barrage of water. His black leather shoes smoldered, visibly issuing thin twirls of smoke, sizzling with the pattern of the rain that leapt like droplets of boiling oil. Even his skin was cooked to a deep black, hardened, splitting like a marshmallow left too long over a campfire. Lips burned back to where they connected with the jaw, exposing his long grayed teeth and withered gums, ears crisped to pork rinds to either side of his head, his hair had fried right down to his blistering, peeled scalp that exposed patches of his carbon-scored skull.

"Jason," Trick said from the doorway, gnawing on his lip. "I think maybe you'd better come back..."

"Just a sec—" Jason started, but then stopped. "My God..."

The man's skin came alive right before Jason's eyes. Tiny blossoms bloomed from every pore on the man's bare black flesh, shooting through like fine, yellow hairs before opening right up into what looked like a circle of small, feathery petals, immediately masking his flesh in fluorescence as though hurriedly colored outside of the lines by a child. Those wispy extensions collected the rain, urging it toward the center of the blossom in fragmented bubbles, and then quickly closed back up and slipped beneath the skin, only to rise right back up and bloom again.

"Polyps," Jason whispered. They looked just like the small, ringed mouths that opened from the porous holes in the coral skeletons he had studied with such fascination.

The man's face quickly jerked at the sound, turning directly toward Jason with eyes covered with those little organisms like a coating of fungus.

Jason stumbled backward, unable to see anything but the man's fuzzy visage...and screamed.

V

Engorged raindrops hammered his face, loosening the skin from the already deteriorating connective tissue that held it in place against his skull. They pooled all around him, rising up past his opened mouth and nostrils, standing stagnant in his ear canals. His neck had turned a deep purple from the bruising surrounding his snapped spine, rotting into a swollen black with the cellular death. Whatever had once filled this physical shell, call it a soul, a life force, whatever, was now well on its way to its final destination, leaving behind the human refuse that was now Ronny Brewster.

Even if there had been anything left inside capable of feeling through the dead nerve endings, he never would have felt them pass through his semi-permeable skin, soaking up the water like a flesh sponge. Maybe his white blood cells would have been able to attack the microscopic spores expelled from the meteorite, tossed into the stratosphere with the dust, and then returned, packing the spherical droplets like bacteria in swamp water, before they could incubate, before they could hatch. But feeling them and stopping them would have been two separate things entirely. The atmosphere was now conducive to mass replication, even had he been able to survive the toxic levels of expunged gasses, they would have eaten him alive from the inside out. How long could any man, even one of such impressive physical prowess as Ronny, tolerate the sheer agony of those organisms hollowing out his marrow, carving tunnels through his compact bone, thickening his blood like slush, and packing in every pore like so many needles?

The deep freeze of space kept the spores from hatching for the millennia they were trapped like so many particles of dust in the comet's tail, the heat from its burning passage keeping their communal mind awake, though not alert. They cast out a net of consciousness, calling to others of their species in a dream that never seemed to end, until now. Their minds joined together in one voice, all reveled in the birthing joy of tearing through their membranous sacs, their formerly eternal prisons, and breathing their first breaths of life. Billions of tiny voices called out at once in unison, their collective consciousness wrapping around the same words, one mind linked to every other. With one solitary purpose, one life mission, they awakened to pursue their destiny.

They—this species so far removed from its origin as to have passed that knowledge from its collective consciousness—were the definition of a biological anomaly. A parasitic organism that didn't entirely consume its host. A symbiotic entity that killed. They simply occupied the body, using their own electrical charge to stimulate the brain, the muscles, the internal organs, borrowing the physical structure as nothing more than a gigantic Petri Dish in which to reproduce unchecked. Their own individual lives— if they could indeed be considered as much as they were part of a singular mind made of a minion of parts—lasted but a single season, which could be anywhere from a day to several months depending on the polyp. They hurriedly gave birth to but a single clone before dying, their external skeleton hardening and calcifying to add to the growing mass. Like the coral reef, which grows but a precious half-inch a year with the death of the countless polyps, their lives and deaths are devoted to the communal benefit of all. But unlike the coral, they require a host, a mass of porous tissue capable of the biological functions that they are not: thermoregulation, cellular respiration, motility, and digestion. While coral polyps share a mutually beneficial relationship with the zooxanthellae algae that provide them with photosynthetic nutrition processed from the sun, and reciprocate by feeding the algae with living matter like plankton or microscopic shrimp snatched from the water with their feathery fingers, these vastly superior, yet similar-looking polyps use the ultraviolet rays that filter through the atmosphere to generate photosynthetic, bio-available ATP's. They use these Adenosine Triphosphates, the basic unit of chemical energy equivalent to biological electricity, to convert the sulfur ions in the air to a type of salty mass similar to the remainder left in an evaporated cup of seawater. The byproducts of this process not only strengthen the exoskeleton, but serve as food to the photosynthetic cells that form around the mouth of the polyp at the base of the tentacle-like extensions as well. As they produce more ATP then they could ever hope to consume, they pass it through a thin membrane rooted into the muscles and bloodstream, expunging it through fibrous, dendrite-like filaments into the host to keep the decomposition at bay. This chemical triggers the agonist muscles to perform the primary biological functions necessary for the host to provide the living, breathing, physical means of transportation, accommodation…the very source of their existence.

They've done this before, this re-colonization process, countless times. The memories are scored into their shared minds, passed through infinite generations. Like a bird innately has the ability to fly, the urge to migrate, or a crocodile instinctively knows how to build a nest of mud and sticks to bury her eggs just deep enough to allow for a temperature of eighty-six degrees, this species knows infestation. By leeching through the skin and into the blood and tissue in the fluid their membranes are most permeable to, they can hatch and flagellate to every part of the body. Rooting into the internal structures, from the heart and kidneys to the brain itself, forcing these organs to obey their will through electrical stimulation, the same energy they use to communicate with each other, essentially bridging the gap between their will and the host's understanding. Granted, the host cells will not survive forever. No amount of forcing the lungs to breathe can glean enough oxygen from the dangerous air to perpetually stall cellular atrophy and death, only postpone it long enough to create an exoskeleton of their own chitinous, dead masses. By the time the host is no longer capable of sustaining itself on the minuscule amount of available oxygen molecules, these polyps, these symbiotes, would have made the necessary alterations to the physical structure to allow the host to function through the same means of photosynthesis that provide their sustenance. In the end, rather than merely occupying the host…they become the host.

Ronny's vacuous eyes stared blankly at the raindrops splashing on the water, slowly drawing contrast in shape and definition, the dead black that occupied his vision melting away. Squiggled polyps squirmed across the dry surface of those orbs, lancing sharpened tails through the tough surface and cornea, popping it like a balloon before embedding into the ocular nerve. Feathery appendages opened in its stead, microscopic white crystals forming on the hairy extensions, feeding electrical energy into Ronny's system. Were he still alive, Ronny would have experienced a different type of sight. He would have seen in much the same way as a spider, through hundreds of different inputs like eyes. But rather than each focusing on a picture like a moving photograph, they sensed everything, picking up the subtle vibrations from the objects around him, drawing images in retrospect by filling in the gaps of the darkness. There was no color, only varying shades of gray. No texture, only depth: like viewing the world through a night vision security camera.

His left hand twitched in his sight, his thumb brushing the downy, feathered rings that lined his nose, sending them darting back beneath the skin for sanctuary. Energy, electricity, surged through his brain, beckoning his body to comply with the unspoken orders. Pushing himself to all fours, the broken bones in his thighs poking right through the rent flesh and muscle, he forced himself to his feet. The nerves screamed of the crippling physical pain, but the parasites were deafened to it. Pain was of no consequence to the communal whole, nor was it any longer of concern to Ronny. The body now simply did as it was told, the polyps rising from the bloodstream to fill the gap in the torn skin like a bandage of spongy, gold and orange moss.

Both arms raised simultaneously to either side, parallel to the ground, catching the driving rain in his cupped hands, feeling the infinite spores slipping through the skin and into the bloodstream where they hatched and fortified the numbers, filling into an almost matching number of infinite pores and follicles. Rolling his head back, his snapped neck allowing the back of his head to drop against his shoulder blades, he opened his mouth, the patterns of rain drumming his upper, hard palate and through the cribriform plate toward his brain. They fell right into his nostrils, sped along their way by the pulsating feathers, moving them through peristalsis like cilia up into the mouth and straight down the gullet to spread throughout the entire body from the carotids and jugulars.

The more polyps that hatched, the stronger he became.

Their mass adhered to his vertebral discs, fusing his spine back together and slowly raising his head up from where it lolled loosely like a tetherball. His broken ribs reattached; the long gouge down his side where the wind had slammed him atop a lamppost before dragging him on, filled with the minions of feather-ringed mouths before closing the wound entirely. They covered his bald head like the down on a newborn baby's, coating every available millimeter of skin, poking through the fabric of his tattered clothing, absorbing it into their growing mass.

He could see them without looking, for he knew they were there. He could here them announcing their birth in his mind. All of them, one by one rising from the earth where they had lain in anticipation of decomposition, their mangled bodies whole, filling with the hatching spores raining from the dust-clogged sky. They were all around him, standing like crosses to mark their former gravesites.

Soon they would begin. Soon.

For now, they must build their strength, fortify their physical forms. As in the times past, there was much work to be done. This atmosphere won't last forever. It will need to be supplemented with more sulfur dioxide mined from the ground. Every world was different, as their collective memory could espouse. There were variables that needed to be eliminated as soon as they were identified.

Adverse changes in the weather, in the physicality of the location, even in the host's biology could all lead to a mutual death. The imploding planet that had spawned the meteor they trailed through space for eons had been one such example. They had inadvertently exposed the core of the planet through infinite generations of harvesting deeper and deeper into the ground, mining the gasses until it became so unstable that it basically collapsed in upon itself.

This planet had a different problem, as those that were already here would attest, though they were few, but merged their memories with the collective consciousness. There had been something else that had not only stalled their advance, but had eliminated them every bit as efficiently as the expulsion of the volatile gasses from the earth had their hosts. They were unclear in their memory as to exactly what it was and its origin, but they all shared an image of a vast expanse of white. And because of those memories, it would be different this time. They would learn from their mistakes. These new hosts were already vastly superior to those in their memory reserves, large reptilian beasts without the necessary physical attributes to allow them to dig, to colonize. These new and improved bodies would work much better. They were smaller and less awkward, capable of sustained activity.

This time there would be no mistakes.

This time they would fulfill their shared destiny.

Awaken, the communal voice announced simultaneously inside each and every being's head.

Ronny lowered his arms in unison with all off the others, slapping them to his sides in an eerie clap that echoed throughout the entire city. To his right was the gold and orange patterned, fuzzy face of the man, Darren, whom he had been preparing to pummel when it had all begun; though neither recognized the other as such. It was as if their lives had begun again anew, wiping clean whatever slate had formerly been tarnished. Now they simply were parts of the whole.

There was much work to be done.

Like the hierarchy of bees, each had a specific function within the community. Upon command, Darren would join the masses and head toward the point of impact to begin the process of forming the hive, begin the digging. Ronny, on the other hand...Ronny was special. His physical form possessed attributes that the majority of the others did not. He was capable of running farther, lifting more, and within the webwork of his brain was a specialized instinct that separated him from the pack. Ronny was a hunter. As he was in life, he would be in his rebirth.

The communal mind had something of particular importance in mind for Ronny. Assurance of their survival depended on the elimination of variables that could potentially put a wrinkle in their plans. There was one variable that they could all sense, one that they had never faced before in all of the times they had begun colonization. This time... this time there were survivors. It was of no consequence how they had survived; it was now merely a function of elimination. The few—those that had anxiously awaited their arrival, remnants from one such failed exploit—their voices joined with the many from inside forms in which they were not in command. They would lead the hunters to them...and would be dealt with swiftly and with painstaking precision.

Ronny would see to that.

A feathery smile parted his lips, his unblinking eyes turning to look down the long courtyard to where he knew them to be. The others, those trapped within, called to him, summoning him to them. It was only a matter of time now. Only a matter of time...

Ronny turned on his heels and began to walk, sensing those who had been chosen to be his horde falling in behind him.

The others, the multitudes of bodies standing everywhere, lining the sidewalks and the streets, began to move as one. Merging into lines that filtered into the middle of the street from every avenue and alley, they began their trek to the meteorite that had born them.

Raising his nose to the air, nostrils flaring, Ronny inhaled the night, passing the wonderfully sulfuric atmosphere across the fluttering feathers that lined his sinuses. He could smell his prey as well. Every sensory receptor was now fully primed for the hunt.

He was coming for them now.

He was coming.

5 | Exodus

I

"OhmyGodohmyGodohmyGod!" Jason blithered, rolling from his back to his hands and knees, and propelling himself forward to his feet. "He's alive! I saw him in the fire! Jesus Christ! He's alive!"

"Hurry!" William screamed. "Get away from him!"

None of them could bring themselves to move, just standing there beneath the shelter of the building, staring out at Jason's twisted features while he sprinted toward them. His eyes were so wide that it looked as though his eyelids had slipped right back into the sockets. Mouth contorted into a wide-mouthed, yet unvoiced scream, he ran so fast that he nearly outdistanced his churning legs and threw himself to the concrete.

That…thing out there…that zombie, that reanimated abomination, just stood there, frozen. It studied them, stalked them with those hollow, fluorescent eyes…unmoving, cast of stone…waiting…watching…and then finally raised its face back to the sky and allowed the rain to pour over its glistening features.

"Dad!" William snapped, tugging on his father's arm. "Dad?"

Brad shook his head to drag his focus from the man outside, looking down to William with the distraction and confusion of a man just waking from a long slumber.

"We need to go now," William said very slowly, enunciating each word carefully and precisely.

Brad scratched the growing stubble on his face and began to nod faster and faster.

"Yeah…" he said softly. "Yeah. I think maybe you're right."

"What is that?" Nancy screamed, lifting Tim from the gurney and pulling him tightly to her chest.

"Them," Tim whispered into her ear, his head lolling onto her shoulder.

She could feel his bony fingers tighten into the back of her sweatshirt, pinching the skin.

"Everyone!" Jason shouted, blowing through the front of the

building. "Get upstairs! We can lock the doors and—"

"No!" William screamed, breaking free from his father to run to Jason. "If we stay here we're going to die!"

"What do you propose then? Hmm? Just run off into the night? Where are we going to go?"

"Sanctuary."

Jason chuckled nervously, his head shaking and twitching like an arthritic hand.

"Sanctuary? And just what is that? This isn't the Middle Ages, kid! We can't just lock ourselves in a church and claim sanctuary!"

"It's in the moun—" He had to stop, nearly nipping the tip of his tongue. The voices in his head grew deafening, forcing out even his own thoughts and jumbling them into an incoherent mess to be battered around his skull. "—mountains…it's in the mountains."

"And how the hell are we supposed to get there? There are cars blocking every major road, we couldn't hope to get more than a block from this place!"

"We walk," William said. "But we have to go now!"

"If that gets us away from here," Cindy said, approaching Jason. "Then I'm all for it."

Trick looked directly at Brad, his gaze so focused it was like a laser penetrating Brad's face.

"You tell me right now," he said, huffing, lips curling tensely over his teeth. "You told me you thought this kid was psychic—"

"I never claimed he was—"

"Listen!" Trick screamed, shaking his head from side to side with an uncomfortable looking smile wrenching his mouth. "Do you believe? Do you think we should listen to what he says? No crap! No father defending his son garbage! I want it straight and I want it from your mouth! Do…you…believe… him?"

"Yes," Brad said, swallowing the knot of fear in his throat. "Yes. I think we should go wherever he says."

"Then we'd better get going," Trick said.

"I can't take Tim back out in that rain!" Nancy screamed. "I can't do it! He could catch pneumonia! For God's sake! Even a common cold could kill him right now!"

"Bundle him up really well," Cindy said, biting her lip to keep the panic from swelling through her words. "Wherever we go, we'll change the blankets when we get there. We've got a doctor right here with us—"

"No! I won't risk his life! I won't do it!" she railed, shaking her head furiously. "Who's to say whatever's out there is even dangerous? Maybe…maybe there's a gas leak or something and we're all just sharing the same hallucination! Maybe—"

"Mom," Tim whispered, waiting patiently for her to turn to him, to feel her warm breath on the side of his neck. "We need to go now...before it's too late."

"Timmy," she whined, lips pursing, tears wetting her cheeks, stealing away the fear and the rage. "We can't take you out there...not after all we've made it through. I can't just take you out in the rain just to...to lose you..."

Unable to raise his head, he kissed her on the shoulder.

"Have faith, Mom," he whispered. "I didn't live through everything I have just to die from a cold."

"I can't lose you," Nancy cried, hugging him tighter, her tears dripping from her cheekbone onto his exposed neck. "I don't know what I would do..."

"Come on," Cindy said, patiently taking Nancy by the elbow and leading her back to the center of the room with the others. "It's going to be all right."

"Nothing will ever be all right again," Nancy whimpered, allowing her sister to wipe the dampness from her puffy eyes with the corner of Tim's blanket.

Karen, who had fallen silent, plopped right down in the middle of the floor. She pawed at her eyes with the butts of her hands, pressing so hard that she let out a little squeak. They were in there. She could feel them. Squirming, slithering, poking into the delicate tissue with sharply forked tails. And she could hear them...so many of them, communicating in a singular voice so omnipotently thunderous that it sounded like the voice of God resonating in her skull. She wanted to silence it, to drive it from her head by running her fingers straight through her eardrums, but at the same time...she wanted nothing more than to hear it, to feel it, to become a part of it.

"Each of you grab one of those oxygen tanks," William commanded the men. "Cindy, help me stuff as much food as we can into our backpacks."

"What in the world could we possibly need these for?" Trick mused, though he heaved one of the heavy tanks into his arms all the same.

"Take whatever else you can think of right now," William said. "It's time to go."

He yanked the pack from his back and raced over to the broken vending machine. Stuffing whatever he could reach into his pack, he closed it and donned it again. Without even looking over his shoulder to make sure they were following, William strode right across the lobby, glass skittering away from his feet, and stepped out into the rain. Focusing on his feet to keep from looking at those people still standing there collecting the water on their already saturated forms, drawing it inward on those miniature feathers that covered them like fur, he rounded the corner of the building onto the street.

Footsteps slapped the standing water on the sidewalk behind him in their hurry to catch up, causing him to walk just that much faster to get them moving at a more acceptable pace. They doubted him. He could see it in each and every one of their faces there in the lobby...except for his father. His father believed in him. And regardless of what they thought, they were following him...and that was all that mattered now.

The light rail station passed on the left, the smashed train, no more than a single car that looked less like its chugging steam ancestors and more like a bus without wheels, lie on its side, halfway into the formerly glass-enclosed station. Those who had been trapped inside, pinned between the roof of the train and the rows of chairs, had dragged themselves from the building and were now standing side by side with the cab drivers out in the rain, arms raised in human crosses like all of the others. Bent and broken, bones stabbing through torn flesh, they stood sentient, not even bothering to look William's way when he passed. But he could hear them. The voices in his head cried out to them, urging them to awaken.

There was no panicked answer from them. Soon enough they would awaken. Soon enough they would be able to deal with William and the others.

Soon.

There were more of them. Everywhere. Lining the streets. Standing outside their wrecked cars, filling the balconies from the apartments high overhead. Like cactuses in a desert, they stood there, arms out, reveling silently in the rain that poured over their stoic bodies.

They needed to get away from the population centers. The further they were able to get from all of the minions before they awakened, the better their chances would be. William was sure he knew where to go, he could see it no more than a block ahead, beckoning to him, calling him toward it like a lighthouse leading a storm-bound ship to shore.

Feeling them behind him, sensing that the others were on his heels, William ran toward that distant mouth of darkness.

"Wait!" his father called from behind him, fearing he might lose his son in the darkness that grew in the absence of streetlights. Granted, the sun was slowly rising in the sky behind them, but ahead, it was still pitch black.

The street reached a T-intersection, terminating at a wide sidewalk. To the left was a tall building occupied by brokers and computer programmers who would never again see the insides of the suites they had paid through the nose for. The golden address numbers lie beneath a pile of crumbled mortar on the cement steps leading up to the revolving door, the light staining the dusty sky behind him glimmering from the shattered windowpanes. An old warehouse building towered over him from the right. Where once it had been used to process coal by black-faced men in dirty overalls, sending the fragmented pieces up a long conveyor to where they could be poured through a long arm into the waiting freight cars, it was now gutted and completely remodeled. Instead of iron walkways and processing chambers, it was now filled with luxury lofts that overlooked the Big Thompson River that ran along the western edge of downtown. Those who died within had migrated out to their cement balconies, lined with short columns and a wide parapet of gothic design minus only the perched gargoyles.

William ran down the long path between the buildings, the fallen leaves from the now bare crabapples to either side covering the wet walk and the hidden lawn beside. The sign identifying the designated path had been ripped from its splintered stump and tossed into the eagerly burbling river down the steep slope. A cement bridge led directly away, the bank dropping before him. The chain link walls that had channeled it flapped at the mercy of the wind, having been torn from the metal clips that moored them to the tall green railings that poked up from the rail every dozen feet or so. The bridge, the railings, even the tall concrete posts that supported it, were lined with crumbling cracks separating the cement in anticipation of collapsing into the river. But he had no intention of using the bridge. That would simply lead them across the stream and to another bridge crossing the highway. And beyond was nothing but a line of rooftops as far as he could see.

They needed to veer clear of any developments, for if they were right in the middle of even a moderately populated residential block when the bodies began to stir...

He shuddered at the thought.

Reaching the fenced edge of the bank leading down to the river, he turned to the right of the bridge and onto a thin path slanting downward to the widened riverbank, paralleling the engorged Big Thompson. The black water swelled well over the bank, dragging thick tree limbs and other tangles of refuse along the path. That artery of frigid water was so clogged with whatever the rain could drag through the storm-gates into it, that it flowed like the slush-riddled runoff of a high mountain stream. It dammed itself with woodwork to make a beaver envious, only to tear it right back down and wash it into another tangle further downstream.

William padded down the cement ramp, to the all but invisible path beneath the rising water. Doing his best to keep from walking right through it, he flirted up the rocky, landscaped bank, heading to the north.

"This isn't such a good idea," Brad said, catching up with his son. Water turned his pants black, all the way up to the shredded knees, clinging to his shins and draining a line of freezing water right down his calves, over his Achilles' and into his shoes. "If this storm causes a flash flood, it will blow down this channel like a tsunami and take all of us with it."

"This is how it has to be. We'll be easy targets if we're out in the open walking down the middle of the street."

"I just don't like the idea of risking anybody's life—"

"This is our chance! We need to keep close to the river as long as possible. We make them hunt for us, rather than strolling through their midst where we'd be outnumbered."

"So where are we going then?"

William slid his small hand into his father's.

"Home."

II

From everywhere they started to come, first singly, one by one. Those who had died off on their own, stranded in their cars on the foothills highways, in their secluded homes, the first to arrive. The others would be coming, and they would be coming en masse, but for now, it was up to the few to begin the work.

The thing that had once been Brian stood again at the lip of the crater as his formerly living doppleganger had done earlier in the night. He stared with inhuman eyes through the seared and blackened limbs of the bare trees on the far side of the cut, watching the amber stain of the sun in the eastern choked sky of dust, through the warping haze of heat produced by the embers smoldering in the trunks. The distant outline of downtown, black fingers rising defiantly from the earth, was framed against the otherwise pristinely flat horizon.

Enormous droplets of rain still pounded the earth all around, though by now it was of no practical use to them. The majority of the spores had already reached the ground, the last lingering, floating members filling the drops in decreasing concentration. Those who had already arrived filled the most practical life forms first. Let those who still fell from the sky inhabit those lesser creatures.

He didn't need to look to either side to know that they were there, just like him, shadowed forms lining the smoking rim of the freshly burrowed hole, looking into the distance to the source of all of the voices within their heads. The wispy ringed mouths of those that inhabited his skin reached out as far as they could from their pores, grasping, closing feathery hands over what little sunlight they could, drinking it in. Photosynthetic cells lining their circular mouths slowly turned moss green, stealing the energy from the rising, diffuse orb, and began converting it not just to energy, but to mass. Their bodies, the worm-like stems that planted them into the skin, swelled wider, tearing at the follicles that held them, quickly swallowing back down the blood that seeped out to replenish it in the host. They oozed of a waxy secretion that dripped down their stems and expanded on contact with the tattered edges of skin, sealing them closed again in much the same manner a tree heals its own wounds with sap.

Now, the universal voice commanded inside of their heads.

As one, they raised their hands before them, inspecting their palms. Those polyps stretched to their furthest limits from the skin on their fingertips, and then blew their feathers and died back to the pores, leaving miniature, hardened cones from which another clone rose, only to do the same. Several generations passed in a sparse few minutes, rising from the same holes as their predecessors, strengthening it, fortifying it, in much the same manner as a volcano grows with each subsequent eruption, adding the mass of the cooling lava. Brian's hands looked like the underbelly of a scavenged ship, thick with a nearly impenetrable crust of miniature barnacles that added a good quarter inch of calcified skeletal remains to the flimsy layer of God-given flesh. They hooked into claws, curling slightly inward and fixing the joints in place beneath a carbon exoskeleton like gloves.

The last of the hurriedly dying polyps poked their ringed mouths through the holes, their feathers faded from the autumnal glory of the changing leaves to a drab gray to match the base color of their crusted forefathers. A faint tinge of green highlighted the clusters of cells spotting the open mouths, those still capable of modifying energy from what little sunlight managed to poke through the churning dust that sealed off the atmosphere. Sucking in a great, final breath of the sulfuric air and charging their weakening photosynthetic cells one last time, their feathery openings rose and fluttered, and then dove right back down into their growing tubular domiciles.

Brian dropped his crusty, grayed claws from in front of his face to his sides and plunged down that first deep step. His hands clattered against the sides of his legs like wearing forked rakes from the hips of a gardener's belt.

He lumbered down the hill, the superheated layer of earth cracking like glass under his weight. The rain eroded channels through the dirt around his feet, descending down the slope until the heat made them evaporate around that deeply set funnel like the steam from a sauna. The others followed, sloping down the parabolic hole to meet at the center. At the bottom, the shadowed tunnel leading into the ground still issued miniature tentacles of smoke. The orange glow of heat from the meteorite was all but extinguished. Only thin yellow veins ringed the rocky surface from the dramatically cooled core.

Reaching the hole first, Brian paused to inspect the single-file line forming behind him, and then ducked his head and entered the black maw.

The polyps covering the remainder of his skin arose quickly from his pores, and then died back, covering the skin in that waxy secretion to protect it from the rising heat. Their replacements poked their still closed feathers from the pores like but a single human hair, garnering just enough of the modified air to maintain their basal functions. The coating over the skin blistered and bubbled, and though the skin beneath reddened like a cooking lobster, it remained intact.

Brian skirted the large celestial rock, extinguishing a couple of flames that rose from his assumed letter jacket with his forearm, and squeezed into the small gap between the meteorite and the hardened ground just past it. Bracing his feet against the stone, the rubber soles of his shoes slowly melting on the surface, he braced his left hand against the hard wall of earth, and raised his right arm into the air. He brought it down over and over with increasing speed like a cat striking at a mouse, clawing through the hard crust to find the softer dirt beyond.

The symbiotic flagellates pumped energy into his muscles, not only causing them to keep from tiring, but building their bulk at the same time. Scraping and scraping and scraping, he gouged clawed tracks into the rocky dirt, forming a pile beneath his leveraged feet. His face grew furiously red right up to the tips of his ears, his heart pounding a million miles an hour even though they chemically tried to slow it. He couldn't perspire as all of his pores were beyond clogged with those small parasites. His internal temperature rose to the point that it threatened his central nervous system, his brain. And after having lanced no more than a half-foot into the beginning of the tunnel, they had no choice but to brace his hands against the wall and pry his molten soles from the meteorite.

Brian turned and slipped back around the smoldering rock, passing his replacement and walking back out of the tunnel. He ducked his head to exit into the light; every feathery ring immediately popping right back out on the surface, though noticeably dulled in color. The line now nearly reached the top of the crater, each stoic face focused down at the hole in preparation of their designated task. Walking right past them, oblivious to the blood dripping from his crusted fingertips, though hurriedly and desperately slurped back up by the nest of polyps, he stomped up the slope and crested the lip.

He continued to walk straight ahead, stepping over the fallen trunks and skirting the small fires that still flickered from the piles of leaves against the base of the trees that had somehow remained standing through the explosion. Those greedy little mouths on his back grew longer, aggressively extending their apertures toward the aura of the sun behind, while those on his front flattened lazily against his chest in his shadow.

The pressure on his brain from the heat and overexertion was growing to the point that if he didn't cool down, and immediately, he would succumb to a massive stroke. That is, if his overworked, pounding heart didn't seize in a heart attack first. They couldn't stop him to cool him off. No amount of sitting in the shade could reduce his internal temperature so long as he was unable to sweat. There was really only one way to do it, but the distance was really taxing the limits of their endurance. It was one thing to inhabit a deceased form so long as the internal systems were in working condition: they could mend holes in blood vessels, even close up an opened windpipe. But if they lost the brain, it was like trying to control a marionette without the strings. And if his heart imploded first, no amount of cranial control could restart even such a rudimentary pump if all of the blood from the entire system filled the bloating insides.

The barren, blackened trees fell back to either side and he kicked through the sand on the bank, walking directly into the lake. The surface was a murky brown from the amount of dirt that had settled atop the layers of scum and algae, like a repulsive vinyl pool cover. He slipped through it, pushing his way past the floating body of a duck, stilled mid-quack with its blue tongue hanging uselessly from its browning bill atop the murky growth that had formerly sustained it. The feathers had been blasted from its bare drumsticks and wings, tufts even torn from its formerly brilliant green head. Small fluorescent feathers poked through in their stead, gradually yawning wide and tasting their first breaths.

Wading past his ankles and to his knees, he stopped and then fell forward with a splash. Hands held to his sides, he didn't even bother to brace himself. The cool water immediately began to lower his temperature, reducing the pressure exponentially with each passing second. No light penetrated the black water through the mat of detritus atop the stilled waves, allowing him to simply regenerate as though buried beneath the ground. His beating heart slowed to a normal rate; the swelling in his brain receding to its normal size and convoluted shape, no longer pressing from within on the limits of his skull.

Brian arose from the water, the entirety of his head covered in a mess of dirty swamp mire, and splashed back toward the bank. Water racing from his body, rolling over the shoes that were still in the process of being absorbed into his body mass, he slapped drenched footprints across the bank, thickening his feet with mud, and headed back toward the forest.

Another passed him on his way, doubled over from heat exhaustion, nearly dragging his clawed hands along the ground, stumbling forward, and splashed headfirst into the water. And there was yet another, lying crumpled on the ground, an older specimen that had been unable to survive the final leg of the trip to the miraculously cool water. The worm-like entities within wriggled from his skin, passing quickly from his now useless form and into the dirt beneath, as they couldn't survive long outside of the host they had hatched within. Their wait would be interminable: hiding beneath the dirt for their former accommodations to slip from the festering carcass and meld with the ground, giving them that last fleeting taste of life before eternally trapping them in the hardening ground.

Brian walked straight back through the forest, passing another overheated worker drone and following the path they were all slowly beating through the ashes and dust.

He encountered the end of the line before he even reached the edge of the crater, stopping in his tracks a foot behind the woman in front of him. He looked past the matted nest of brunette hair and patch of fuzzed-over, ripped scalp to the others making their way over the hillside like the advance of a front line in revolutionary days.

Shadows stretching far across the ground before them, merging into one line from the various other single-file lines leading inward from all across the Front Range to mask their numbers and showcase their ant-like organization, they rounded the rim of the hole and fell in behind him. There were hundreds of them there now, and before the sun reached its pinnacle overhead, there would be millions. They were efficient, methodical, and construction would continue unimpeded until the hive was done, no matter how many of them keeled over from overextending their flesh.

Brian stepped forward, following cue from the woman in front of him, her hair blowing free from its roots in clumps and fluttering off on the breeze. Another man, having finished his first round in the deepening tunnel, made it no more than a couple feet past Brian before collapsing onto the ground and expelling half of his body's total of fluids through his mouth on impact. Fleeing their fallen host, many of the polyps squirmed across the ground towards the feet of those standing in line, only to turn back and dive right into the dirt.

The line began to move more rapidly now. Step...pause. Step...pause.

Ahead, where the top of the far hill on the opposite side of the crater met with the skyline, a figure popped right up from the ground, coated in dirt. He walked all the way around the back of the line and toward his reward in the cool waters of the smarmy lake.

Brian was to the edge of the dark hole leading into the ground in no time. The steam from the vaporizing rain had all but ceased to exist, having reasonably cooled the meteorite, which now only produced an uncomfortably hot swell of tomb-like air from underground. Ducking his head, he followed the outline of the darkened form in front of him, passing the now black chunk of rock, walking easily past it. Where last there had been only six inches of his own claw marks scarred into the hardened wall, there was now a tunnel blowing dank, earthen breath in his face. He followed along for a good five feet before watching the silhouette in front of him veer to the left, while he turned to the right. The anxious polyps perked on his skin as they could taste the fresh air blowing in from outside, not only replenishing the sulfur they feared would be deprived by a good twenty feet of packed dirt overhead, but keeping the physical being cool enough that he would be able to work longer, harder.

Brian stopped behind another man, listening to the sound of his claws positively tearing through the ground like so many spaded shovels. The dirt flew at him, hammering all across the front of his body, but he didn't even notice. There was no need to pry the pebbles from his eyes or spit them out of his mouth, as those instincts were as dead as Brian himself. The being that he was now existed for no other purpose at this moment in time than to bend over and allow the exhausted man to step onto his shoulders and claw his way out through the hole of light above.

Standing fully erect, he approached the crumbling earth and raised both arms above his head, striking with each, one at a time like a windmill, carving directly through the softening ground, inching forward with each stroke until he was cleaving handfuls out at a time.

He stopped.

His arms fell to his sides and he cocked his head to the right.

He was needed elsewhere now. That was what the prevailing thought told him. The commune needed him to drop what he was doing right that moment and head above ground, without another moment of deliberation, hopping onto the back of the woman who knelt before him before he even turned around.

Stabbing his fingers into the dirt, he clung to the earthen wall. With his right hand he reached for the opposite wall and braced his feet between the two, propelling himself upward. He jumped toward the light, hands grabbing hold of the walls long enough to allow his feet to take hold and shove him upward again. Popping right up through the hole and into the scorched field of fried grasses and blackened scrub oak, he didn't follow the line leading back to the lip of the cut, but instead forked in quite the opposite direction, heading back toward where he had first arisen.

Intercept them, the voice repeated inside his cranium.

The fringes of the feathered polyps quivered with delight at the magnitude of the task that had been blessed upon them. But there was one thing that they were going to have to practice before they arrived if they were to obey the group will.

"Shannen," the voice grumbled past the unstrung vocal chords like a badly out of tune guitar. The sheer amounts of phlegm draped down the throat and coating the voice box made it sound like he was gurgling through water.

"Shannen," he said again, retching a gob of the foul mucous through his furred mouth and letting it dribble down his hairy chin. He croaked out a useless belch of air and tried again.

"Shannen."

III

The sun drew his churning shadow far across the asphalt in front of him, stretching it a good fifteen feet ahead as though he was chasing it, before being absorbed by the almighty shadow of the upcoming building to his right. His footsteps thudded heavily on the wet ground while he taxed the limits of his body, running faster and faster, all the while his tread echoing from the still corridor like that of a rampaging giant. Other footsteps joined the chorus until it sounded like a stampeding herd of bison tearing through the center of downtown.

Blocks passed in heaving breaths, sweat pouring in sloppy strands from his mouth in the form of saliva, like a panting dog. Every little fringed ring protruding from his skin stood erect, feathery shimmerings of auburn highlighting his dashing outline, strapping his clothing tighter against his skin until there was no way of determining where the flesh stopped and the cloth began. It was all the process of absorption, of melting the remnants of the suit beneath the brittle, dead exoskeletons of the forefathers slowly beginning to hide the skin. Only his joints were free from the crust that allowed but enough room for the pumping muscles within like an ancient suit of armor.

He was closing in on them. Closing in fast. But if he knew that, then surely so did those within the boy, and they had yet to determine if he could access the group mind.

Hurdling the hoods of wrecked cars barring his furious passage and shattering the bones in his feet running through the piles of crumbled brick and debris, he raged onward with a snarl fixed upon his tortured visage, oblivious to the pain, to everything but that one central thought...kill. He blasted through lines of those marching into the hills, parting before him without a glance, and then falling right back into rank in his wake.

His minions were hot on his heels, though he knew not how many. There would be no mercy any more than there would be pleasure derived from the hunt; they would simply descend upon them like an avalanche and tear them to shreds.

The voices of those trapped within the boy, those for whom time had passed in a stony grave, called to him, filling his head with their undulant cries. Baring his teeth, he homed in upon them, letting them guide him to their location so he could release them in a violent spray of blood. Those within, the millions of beings that communicated of singular voice, knew nothing of the concept of fear. It was of no concern to them that the body was well past its tested limits of endurance and in danger of exceeding its stress threshold. Too much heat, too much carbon dioxide produced with the lactose in the muscles, too much strain on the central nervous system. The body was close to expiring, but they were so close now.

They could taste the others on the air, so close, so close.

And even if it killed their host, they would force him on until he was upon them. It would be he who was the first to the slaughter. Damn the consequences. They would all die in service to the commune if that was their lot.

At the end of the street he could see it, that small gap between buildings leading off over the river where their prey had erroneously thought they could escape.

Ronny hit the path at a dead sprint, clearing the curb in a long stride that landed him five feet onto the path and somehow gaining momentum. Soaked, brown leaves flew from behind his heels. The bare, dead-looking trees passed to either side. Without breaking stride, he veered to the right before reaching the bridge, flying along the crest of the cement slope falling away into the river to his left. He tore through shrubbery that tried to tangle his feet, sending broken juniper limbs and scrub oak branches splintering into the air. A tall wall of chain link rose between the river and him, paralleling the flooded cement path below, but it wouldn't hinder him in the slightest once he reached his target.

The polyps on his toes, planted straight through the leather of his shoes and into the skin within, came alive with evolutionary fervor. The first of the fiery orange creatures died back to the flesh, leaving their calciferous horned exoskeletons pressing through the soft leather. The following generation swelled from the same holes, birthed in a moment through a process of replication, an identical clone of their predecessor, standing even further from the expanding crust before dying back themselves. Lifetimes passed while Ronny ran, the hardened exoskeletons of the deceased growing and growing until they had ripped right through the leather and forked in sharp points down toward the ground. In the span of a couple of blocks, they had converted his toes to claws, the sharpened tips slicing through the vegetation, stabbing into the sloppy earth to provide his tensing legs with that much more leverage to propel him forward. He was a two-legged lion, shredding through everything in his path, consumed by the hunt.

His fingertips did the same at his sides, growing sharp points from just the distal ends in his pumping fists, lancing right into the middle of his palms and between the lines of tendons and bones. Blood flew in arcs from his hands as he ran, the eager polyps drinking back as much as they possibly could and sealing the wound from within right around those nightmarishly sharp razors. Unlike the drones, the entirety of their hands converted to joint-less claws like hooks to serve their sole purpose of digging, Ronny's hands were still functional. His fingers could bend at the joints and he could still grapple and grasp, only now his fingertips were as sharp as knives to expedite the bloodletting.

Raising his right arm, he swung at the thick bark of a tall maple tree passing to the right with his newly grown claws, slicing directly through the bark in four parallel streaks so deep that the ensuing swell of sap was a brilliant orange-red.

Hardened patches formed along his cheekbones and over the ridge of his brow, framing his eyes now deeply set in a mask of brittle chitin, hiding them in the shadows generated by those two sunken orbs.

He was right upon them now! He could hear their voices in his head, taste the putrescence of their flesh like it was his own.

His feathery tongue pressed from his mouth and slathered across his lips. Claws clattering while he tensed his fists in anticipation, heart fluttering up into his chest, the time was nearly upon him.

Now, the voices screamed to him from inside the boy. *Nownownownownow!*

They were just on the other side of the fence from him, just down the slope at the edge of the river, trying to be quiet, to mask their footsteps, like they thought they had a prayer of hiding from him. Even if he couldn't hear their footfalls or their breathing, even if he couldn't directly see them, he could feel them, sense them, taste them. They were so close that he couldn't wait another second!

Three more direct strides forward, around the wide trunk of a leaf-less cottonwood, and he lunged to his left, slamming into the chain link fence. Claws raised, he threw two diagonal swings, slicing through the metal as though it were thread, cutting a large X right in the middle of the fence and throwing himself forward through it. The severed metal tore through the flesh covering his forearms, which he used to shield his head, though his scalp peeled back in long bloody lines as well.

He didn't even feel it.

Nothing mattered but the kill.

Planting squarely at the top of the cement slope, using those hooked talons to grab tight hold of the crusted dirt meeting the cement, he threw himself into the air above the river. He raised his arms out in front of him with those razor-honed claws ready to slice through so much flesh, falling from the sky like a powerful eagle plummeting toward the unsuspecting little mouse.

IV

They weren't going to make it.

William could feel them coming, feel them closing upon them like a Venus flytrap. The voices in his head thrilled at their visions of his demise, crying out for those who were descending upon them to tear him apart so they could take control of his physical being. He could hardly think through their revelry, hardly formulate a single coherent thought, yet he was rapidly running out of time to come up with a plan.

The roaring river beside him defied them to cross. They'd be swept downstream and tugged under to drown before they swam two strokes.

They were well north of downtown now, nearly to the highway that would lead them back up into the mountains and away from the city that was now positively crawling with this newly evolved species. But right now, William wasn't even sure if they would make it that far.

The others were beginning to lag, slowing with the rising of the river that forced them to walk along the slanted cement rise that turned their ankles and made balance a tedious prospect at best. Even his father had fallen a few strides behind, though he watched William like a hawk to make sure he didn't slip and tumble into the river. He cradled one of the large tanks across his chest, laboring slightly under the weight, but having a more difficult time grasping hold of the slippery, wet casing.

Shannen was right behind him, basking in the silence that isolated her with the thoughts she tried to force from her mind. Every now and then she let out a tortured sounding whine, and looked up with tear-streaked cheeks in hopes that the others hadn't heard, and then looked back to the ground. From the way she checked to the river from the corner of her eye, it almost looked like she was debating exactly what might happen were she to simply plunge like Ophelia into the cold water.

Jason had taken a turn carrying Tim. Nancy had reluctantly relinquished him only long enough to recover the strength that had nearly failed her when she slipped on the slope and nearly dropped herself and her son into the eager black river. Recuperation was slow as she was forced to carry the oxygen tank for Jason in exchange.

Cindy and Trick followed on their heels, the only two who openly conversed, though about nothing of importance. So long as they were talking, they weren't forced to think about what was happening.

Karen was the straggler, now a good dozen paces behind Trick, stumbling with the weight of the oxygen canister wrapped to her chest in her arms. Teetering back and forth, trying to maintain her balance though her equilibrium was shot, she fought to push the rising voices from her head. They were consuming her flesh now. She could feel them: wriggling beneath the skin, latching into every available part of her body. They were still sluggish however, held at bay by the oxygen pouring through her mouth and over her cotton-coated tongue. It wouldn't be long, however. The tank was appreciably lighter, but the way her strength was increasingly draining from her, she wasn't sure that she would even be able to carry one of the full tanks, should the others even be willing to relinquish it. They hoarded those things like a leprechaun's gold, and heaven forbid she even consider asking.

She could see the way they looked back at her, their contemptuous stares judging her like they had inherited the powers of God. None of them wanted her there. None of them. Not even that weird little boy who thought he could lead them out of their collective nightmare. He had another thing coming. That's what the voices were whispering into her ear. Yes, soon enough that boy, all of the others...they would be dead. But not her...not Karen. The voices assured her it would be so. She had a more divine destiny. She was special. And whether the others of her kind thought so or not, at least the parasites that wriggled in her guts and lined the insides of her ears and nose with their tickling little feathers, at least they recognized that she had something that none of the others did.

They would spare her. They promised her that. They would spare her, but the others were all lambs being led to the slaughter.

Karen swayed from side to side, fighting with her elusive balance, and then dropped to the ground. The tank clanged off of the ground but she managed to grab it before it ripped the mask completely from her mouth. Her pants tore from her knee as she skidded down the slope, causing a bitterly stinging abrasion. Wrapping the tank in her left arm, she pawed at the stinging wound, the salt from her skin only making it hurt that much worse.

She watched in awe as several dozen of those little worms that writhed in her insides rose to the surface and blossomed with little bouquets of orange and gold, covering the entirety of the scrape, sealing off the swelling droplets of blood that rose through the surface where the small pebbles had embedded themselves in her skin. They covered the whole patch with a bandage of brilliant moss, and before she knew it, the pain was gone.

Gently, she grazed her fingertips along it; those little flowers springing back into place the moment her touch passed.

She arose from the ground, brushing off the seat of her pants and began walking anew, this time unencumbered by the weight of her depressed feelings. Her muscles felt stronger, the oxygen deprivation that made them weary and rubbery was almost gone entirely.

She doubled her pace, hurrying along without the feeling that her ankles were going to snap from having to walk along that slant like the wicked little boy insisted.

From where he stood, watching her, William could tell that they nearly had a hold of Karen. He could see it burning in her eyes of coal, resonating from her rejuvenated flesh like a physical aura. And worst of all...worst of all he could hear them from inside of her, almost thumbing their little noses at him. They were tormenting him with it, for they knew as well as he what would happen when they usurped her body, and he could feel the great joy resonating from them.

He turned from her and to the river.

The others, those who were bearing down on them from the shadows of the buildings cast by the rising sun, they were his immediate concern. They were nearly upon them now.

Following the course of the frothing, white-capped waves, mounding immense piles of twisted metal and enormous limbs, upstream to the north, William could see just the outline of a bridge crossing the river at the next bend. The raging waters disappeared into the darkness beneath like flowing from the mouth of some great cement behemoth.

He turned and looked at Trick, more specifically, the large silver canister in his grasp, biting his lip contemplatively. The blue knob on top, the one just like the spigot for the hose attached to his house in the back yard, drew his attention. He remembered what had happened to it a couple of summers back. He had been sitting there on the swing in the backyard, balancing a glass of lemonade between his thighs and gliding back and forth just enough to occupy himself, but not to spill the cold, pulpy juice onto his shorts. There had been another man there, wearing a blue and white striped shirt with a patch on the chest with a raccoon and a squirrel above a handful of words...Rocky Mountain Animal Control. That was what the patch had read. And the man had been all the way up to the roof on that tall ladder of his, talking to William's father from the balcony. Both of them were focused on the glint of the silver trap mounted atop the roof from the sun. There was something inside of it...a squirrel: a frightened little mound of fur huddled against the back of the trap.

But it hadn't been the squirrel that had fascinated him that day. He had sat out there watching because it made him sad to think that this captured rodent was going to be stolen from its home, from the only life it had every known, and relocated to some park far away. Or so the man whose truck was also loaded to the gills with poisons promised.

It had been what transpired between the man removing the trap from the roof and tossing it into the back of his white company truck that interested William the most right now.

The man had climbed down that ladder, balancing himself with only one hand as he carried the trap by the handle in the other. William had just watched his father walk in through the sliding glass door above, no longer needing the raised vantage to inspect the process. Reaching the grass, the man set the trap down on the ground and yanked on the cord to the extension of his ladder, but for whatever reason, it stuck. Grumbling under his breath, the man jerked it again. Nothing. He gave it a solid kick and then tugged and tugged at the long yellow cord, until finally, with a snap, it gave and the upper half of the ladder slid down the track, far faster than the man had been prepared for. He jumped backward, throwing his arms out to his sides to make sure that none of his fingers got severed, tripping over the cage with the now deathly-terrified squirrel, and landing squarely on his rear end.

The extension aligned with the lower portion of the ladder with a bang like a gunshot, the impact making the entire works wobble. It toppled to the left, sliding along the back of the house with a scraping sound that left a large arc of carved wood through the finish. The top of the ladder followed the chiseled rainbow toward the ground, but before it could slam sideways into the spongy turf, that eight-foot metal rail hammered the handle to the water spigot mounted to the house.

With a ping, that little circular handle popped right from the metal and whizzed across the yard like a miniature Frisbee and into the trees. A stream of water sprayed from its stead, firing with such force and pressure that the geyser cleared the entire patch of lawn. The exterminator and Brad had shared a look that had led to both of them battling through the ferocious spray of ice-cold water to finally seal off the leak.

The whole episode, while at the time seeming insignificant, was one of the many signs that life had shown him to prepare him for the coming test.

Only this test was not simply pass/fail. This was life or death. There would be no make-up exam, no chance of evening out the grade with subsequent tests.

This was it.

He looked quickly from the tank in Trick's arms to the river, following the bank, hoping for…Yes!

William's eyes caught fire and he raced down the bank, splashing precariously through the water that rose over his ankles, the undertow threatening to lift him right from his feet and drag him along with it. Splashing closer and closer to the invisible edge of the bank and the ferocious waters beyond, he stopped right in front of a mess of debris caught along the rocky edge of the river like a carelessly assembled beaver dam. In the midst of the piled sticks and branches and muddy leaves, a car bumper stood upright. The green license plate, set against a white background to make it look like the silhouette of the mountains against the sky, hung from a single screw, swinging, pendulum-like, back and forth. The rain beat a tinny tune on the warped metal. Where once the steel had bowed gracefully to round the front of whatever model vehicle it had once been attached to, it was now crumpled and straightened from either the accident that had wrenched it from its moorings, or from being bounced along the boulders lining the bottom of the river. The rim was jagged and scraped; metal slivers curling upward like glistening, sharpened truffles.

He reached for one of them, wriggling it back and forth to snap it off, opening a bloody seam on his fingertip before finally prying it free. Slurping the fluid from the stinging laceration on his right forefinger, William positioned that hooked sliver of metal between his fingers and opened his mouth wide.

"What are you doing?" Brad gasped, starting forward quickly as he was unable to believe his eyes.

William rammed it forward into his mouth, sliding it between his molars until he felt the sharp point lance through the weak lining on the inside of his cheek. Wincing and stifling a shriek of pain, he forced his trembling hand to jerk forward, opening up a seam through the gummy membrane.

"William!" Brad shouted, dropping the canister onto the bank to tug the boy's hand from his mouth and pulling the metal from his grasp. Tossing it immediately behind him into the river, he knelt right down into the water and tilted his son's chin up to look inside.

Veins of blood outlined his little teeth, highlighting the papillae on his tongue.

"What in the world did you do that for?"

William threw his chin back to loose it from his father, and swallowed back a bitter, coppery mouthful of blood-infused saliva. With the tip of his tongue, he inspected the tattered edges that now curled inward from the wide flesh chasm. He felt them. Though there weren't nearly enough of them to infest his body as they now did all of the others, and they only appeared able to survive in the thin, damp, interior membranes like his eyelids, nostrils, and gums, he could feel their little ringed mouths. They were circled with what felt almost like microscopic eyelashes, filling the gap and pulling the edges closer together to heal the self-inflicted wound.

He stepped around his father and walked right back up to the bumper. Reaching into his mouth, he cupped his fingers and scraped his nails along his cheek, tearing painfully into that same wound, and fished out a thick, red, dripping mass. Immediately, he reached up and slathered the mess onto the crest of the bumper, splitting all four of his fingertips on the sharpened ridges. For just a fleeting second, the blink of an eye, he could see those little feathery orifices atop the mass of his own bloody tissue before they folded right up and slipped back into the blood.

"Everyone!" he yelled, matching lines of blood creeping from the corners of his mouth. "Follow me!"

He sprinted back up to the drier portion of the path and raced toward the tunnel ahead.

Each looked, somewhat dumbfounded, to the others before quickening their pace and following.

William reached the overpass first, running right into the darkness. He stumbled, the slope growing steeper, finally regaining his balance and running for easily another thirty strides before stepping into the slant of light that led the rain into the shadow, and turned.

The river raged by, now to his right, choppily slamming rising waves against the cement support columns like the vicious tide before a storm against the legs of a pier. To his left, the concrete embankment sloped upward to where it met with the road above. The small, black gap created formerly housing everything from pigeons and bats, to the homeless that slept out of the elements beneath abused blankets "borrowed" from the shelters, on those sharpened, crispy little black and white droppings that powdered under their weight. Unseen graffiti covered the rise, right down to the base, where a line of columns held the highway aloft over the washed out path he now stood on.

It would have to work.

Please, God. Let it work.

Their footsteps echoed from everywhere around him beneath that bridge, long before the first hints of their approaching silhouettes materialized from the pitch-black nothingness.

"Hurry!" he whispered, tapping his right foot nervously. "They're coming!"

"What are you do—" his father started.

"Shh!"

He debated just pulling the oxygen tank from his father's arms, but then watched Trick's shape come into focus. Time was now of the utmost essence. He not only needed what was in the man's arms, but what was in the right front pocket of his jeans.

He ran up to Trick and grabbed the tank, nearly toppling backward beneath its weight before regaining his equilibrium. Placing it, standing, onto the ground, he whirled in a circle, hurriedly looking for…for what? How was he going to do this? There had to be something close by he could use to…

Scurrying into the water, feeling the cold grasp of the Big Thompson wrapping tightly around his ankles, he grabbed the glistening top of a rock protruding from beneath. He felt all along the sides until his hands found the jagged bottom, nearly up to his elbows in the quickly flowing water. Skin peeling back from his fingertips, he heaved the stone from the mud, and juggled it in his grasp. Struggling back to where he had propped the tank, he lifted the rock and then drove it down right on top of the small blue knob. The stone ricocheted upward with a resonant clang.

"What are you doing?" Trick shouted.

Grunting, William raised it again and slammed it downward.

"Stop!" Trick spat, grabbing the boy's vibrating arm.

William shrugged it off and brought the rock up nearly to his chin, huffing, and groaned before hammering it down.

Pang!

The handle popped right off and shot up the embankment before rolling off into the darkness and spinning to a clattering halt. Oxygen hissed through the opening like so many snakes fighting to get out through that diminutive hole.

"Give me your lighter," William said.

"You're out of your freaking gourd," Trick said, taking a step back.

"Please!" William shrieked frantically. "Give me your lighter!"

Trick shook his head and retreated further, the movement of the air before him changing substantially from the sheer amount of force expelling that pressurized gas.

"There's no time to argue! Please! Give me—"

A scream interrupted William, an impossibly pained howl of agony drowning out even the deafening grumble of the river. All eyes peered through the darkness toward the distant opening where they had walked beneath the bridge.

"Now!" William shouted, breaking the silence left in the wake of the scream.

A bellowing roar erupted from downstream, assaulting them all with its sheer volume. It rumbled from the walls and inside of their very bones.

Trick reached a shaking hand into his pocket and fumbled to grasp the Bic. He pulled it out without a word and passed it to William. The pounding of footsteps echoed from the south.

"Everyone," William said, holding the lighter close to his face so that he could see it, see the track of the striking knob that would spark the flint, the little red lever to release the butane. "Run!"

V

Ronny hurdled through the air, expecting to see them standing down there, staring up at him in gratifying awe and amazement, no more than a second before he sunk his claws through their flesh and began tearing.

He was completely unprepared for what he found instead.

There was no one looking fearfully up at him, no target to align the tips of his claws with like sighting a deer down the barrel of a gun. Instead, there was a large slab of steel standing erect from a tangle of wooden debris...waiting for *him*. He tried to flip over in the air, tried to change his trajectory, but in the span of a heartbeat, he had no more time than to twist his torso. The shredded corner of the metal sliced right through his side beneath his raised arm, cutting so deep as to tear a separation through the intercostal muscles between a pair of ribs. It snagged between the bones, latching like a ratchet. His legs swung out in front of him, his impaled side suddenly ablaze with the pain that shattered both ribs to splintered fragments as though they had been made of glass. Popping upward, all he could see was the swollen, dusty belly of the clouds, before landing squarely on his back atop the wreckage of wood, his own screams piercing his ears.

The sharp edges of the haphazardly collected twigs stabbed right through his back, gouging through the flesh and prodding the muscles within.

Bodies flew past him, shadows passing across the sky like dark storm clouds, claws glinting in the first rays of sunlight, fixed snarls crunching their faces. They splashed into the river, and had but time enough to raise their startled heads above the choppy surface of the water before being dragged right back down with their open mouths filling their lungs with the river.

Gingerly reaching forward, Ronny grabbed hold of the steel spike that had nearly skewered him and pulled himself up from the bed of sticks. The sharpened tips slurped out from his skin, capped with the glistening blood that poured in lines down the knobby lengths. Wincing, his face crumpled tight like a fist, he brought himself to standing and limped back to the bank where he crouched, allowing the wounds to stretch and lengthen to their fullest so that those within him could hurry and begin sealing them off. He stared up the long path toward the darkness beneath the bridge ahead while the polyps started knitting his flesh back together using only their bodies to congeal in the sappy wounds.

"Now!" he heard the boy scream in that shrill little child's voice.

He buckled his head back in rage and roared up into the dawning sky, clawing at the cement with such magnified anger that he carved chunks right from the sidewalk. Pouncing forward like a jaguar from a tree, he hit the ground running. Dozens of others leapt from the embankment above, landing all around him like they were raining from the sky, thudding in heaps of humanity, before finding their balance and sprinting right behind him. Like a pack of snarling wolves, they charged forward, racing directly toward the darkness where each and every one of them now knew the boy to be. They could hear the voices from inside of the child, calling to them, spurring them on.

Pang! A metallic noise echoed from the darkness.

There had to be close to fifty of them, outnumbering their prey more than five to one. They'd be diced to flesh confetti before their bloodied parts even slapped to the ground. Just the thought of it urged them forward with renewed strength; talons gouging holes in the concrete, splashing clouds of water in their wake like water buffalo thundering across a forged river. Colors blazing from orange to fiery red, those little mouths covering Ronny's flesh quivered, vibrating their wispy eyelashes that ringed those bloodthirsty orifices, drawing every ounce of energy they could possibly steal from the choked sun before barreling beneath the bridge.

Excitement pinned Ronny's ears back, stretching his formerly pain-contorted mouth into a slobbering mockery of a smile that ripped his cheeks in half, widening his eyes to maddening crimson embers. He could already taste the pulsing spray of blood from their arteries, hear the slapping of the steaming fluids patterning the river there in the shadows, their dying screams cut short by severing claws to abruptly echo into the resonating nothingness of the darkened oblivion.

With his mind so intently focused on the visions of the massacre, he didn't see the first spark of light that blossomed from deep in the tunnel, momentarily illuminating the spectral outline of the small boy. Another spark, and this time the small gas-fueled flame showed them their target, highlighting his form with an angelic aura of light. Yellow light quivered, dancing up and down the embankment to their right, lining the sides of the tall cement support posts, highlighting the spider-webbed cracks that defied the fact that they could still even support the highway above.

Exploding with vigor and rage, Ronny leveraged himself forward and ran as fast as his pathetic flesh and muscle would allow, raising his claws up into the air in preparation of that first climactic slash that would gut the boy like a deer hanging by its heels from a tree. He focused on the boy's eyes, almost glowing as they stared down at that miniature little flame wavering from the lighter in his hand. Why was he just standing there? Why was he holding the flame? Did he intend to try to fight him with that little bit of fire that could barely scorch a spider, let alone a charging rhino? What was he doing? What was he —?

Ronny heard the faint hissing of compressed gas firing from the small hole in the tank as soon as he charged from the faded light and into the darkness. It was such a small sound next to the river, like a coiled serpent lazily basking in the tall grasses on the bank of the Amazon, but he could hear it all the same. The way his mind had focused on nothing but the kill, he didn't make the connection between the flame and the hissing gas until the boy lowered it in his cupped hand, outlining the large, reflecting tank positioned on the ground just to his right. The flame shivered in the wavering rift in reality caused by the gas before igniting with an explosive plume of flame that shot straight up into the cement rafters and pigeon crap-riddled water and gas pipes.

The boy jumped back from it, covering his face with his arms. The tower of flame burned bright blue atop the canister, blasting upward into a yellow spire that lapped at the underside of the highway, spreading sideways and creeping along the surface with combustible fingers of amber heat.

Ronny was close enough to see the reflection of the flame in the fear in the boy's eyes, the dotting of the sweltering perspiration on his forehead and red cheeks. A stretch of dirt covered the neck he was lining his arm up with the slice right through it. He could hear the others now, their fleeing footsteps echoing from above...

Above? They were crossing the bridge directly overhead. Had they all really sacrificed the boy to buy themselves time to escape?

No.

No, they hadn't. The all-consuming passion of the hunt had deafened them to the frightened pleas of warning from those still living in the boy. He had been so focused on his prey, on what he would do when they finally caught up with them and drew first blood, that he had closed his mind off to all but the massacre. Now, recognizing that something wasn't right, feeling it throbbing in his very blood, aching dully in every bone, it was all he could hear.

But it was too late now.

The boy raised his right foot and kicked the blazing tank, knocking it directly back onto its side with a loud clang that sent the flame out across the water to burn from its surface as though coated with a film of gasoline. It rolled down the slope, echoing like a bowling ball down a long smooth alley in preparation of striking the pins.

Ronny's face paled, his furry eyes widening in what could only be described as fear. Panic urged him forward, lengthening his strides, as well of those behind him.

Focused on the tank rolling pall mall down the cement path,

bouncing from the cracks in the concrete and bounding from the pebbles it hopped right over, firing the flame into the air before flattening it back over the snapping waves, he didn't see the boy turn tail and run. Heading up the embankment leading up from the tunnel and to the road overhead with those little legs churning, arms flailing, William disappeared out of sight entirely. Ronny could only see the rolling canister of billowing flame, feel the inevitability of what would happen were it to gain further momentum and slam into one of those tall concrete columns. The voices in his head, the communal voice goading him from afar, the voices of all of the others inhabiting his hunting party directly on his heels, all merged into one overriding command.

Stop the tank!

Madly dashing forward, he dove through the air, trying to grab it, to stop the impending collision with the already weakened and cracked pillar. His fingers grazed off the top of the smooth surface, and in the fraction of the time it took for his heart to pump blood through the valve from one atrium to the adjoining ventricle, the explosion of flame consumed his vision.

VI

Panting, heart fibrillating in his chest, William rose over the crest of the hill and darted down the sidewalk on the bridge, separated from the snarls of stalled traffic by a shoulder high cement barricade. Through the chain link wall paralleling him to the right, he could see the warping ribbons of heat rising from beneath, making the incoming river itself look like a fever-dreamed mirage.

The others were well ahead of him, leaving the bridge and running up the start of the hill that would eventually lead them into the mountains. Now no more than distant shapes casting long shadows across the asphalt, they darted between angled cars that had crashed up onto the sidewalk. All but his father that is, who was waiting right there in front of him with a fantastically frantic expression of panic on his face.

"Come on!" Brad yelled, snatching William from the ground and pulling him to his chest. He raced forward, fixing his eyes on the others to make sure that he reached them.

The bridge shuddered under foot, knocking him sideways against the chain-link rail, his shoulder bouncing back from it and nearly sending him careening in overcompensation over the retaining wall that separated them from the traffic, even before he heard the explosion.

It sounded like thunder in a bottle, a wrecking ball slamming through the wall directly above his head in his own living room. So loud, in fact, that it felt like someone had run up behind him and broken a two by four across the back of his skull. Flames blasted right up beside him, flirting in and out through the small diamond-shaped gaps in the metal rail, lapping at his right shoulder and cheek like a starving tiger's paws reaching through the bars of its cage. The heat baked his skin, immediately parching it.

He covered William's head, doubling over like a fullback preparing to charge through the line of scrimmage, and sped forward.

Dust exploded from behind, blasting past them and nearly sending them sprawling to the ground. The bridge leapt upward with the force of the explosion, before collapsing immediately back in on itself, bringing with it large, irregular shaped chunks of the very roadway they were trying to flee. Cars toppled downward with the asphalt that dropped from beneath them, their undercarriages scraping from the jaggedly fractured bridge, before free falling into the rising flames and the billowing clouds of black smoke and powdered concrete. Plumes of flame fired from beneath, carrying with them the burning limbs and sloppily charred flesh that splattered atop the river like so many fish leaping from the surface, and splashing onto the sidewalk in burning little piles of molten remains.

The whole bridge began to slant backward, crumbling in upon itself. The asphalt cracked in rugged seams ahead, quickly separating to cave into the river below. Tires squealed from the cars, adding the smell of burning rubber to the convulsive smoke from the explosion; locked wheels screaming while they were dragged down the increasing slope until skidding right off.

Brad focused on the others, who had now turned to face them, watching the entirety of the bridge collapse into the darkness, blasting smoke and debris straight up into the already clogged sky. He could see the direness of his plight in their paled expressions, their flailing arms, panicking, screaming to urge him on faster. The sidewalk fragmented before him.

William shrieked in his grasp, clinging painfully tighter while he watched the bridge collapsing over his father's shoulder, falling out of sight into the rising cloud and stealing the cars away with it. He could hear the terrified voices screaming in his head, immediately silenced, playing over and over against the backdrop of the fear in his own mind.

Brad raced from the edge of the bridge just before the last of it crumbled away from beneath his feet, throwing him forward to the ground. He rolled onto his shoulder, taking the brunt of the impact so that he didn't land right on top of William, driving him into the sidewalk. The fabric ripped from his exposed shoulder, the skin peeling back to flood with a rush of crimson from the expanse of shredded road rash, the side of his head bouncing from the ground before returning with a final thump.

Wailing in agony, he tried to roll to his back, impeded by the pack, and stared up into the hidden sky through pinched eyes squirting bitterly stinging tears onto his cheeks. The thickening plume of smoke melded with the dirt-clogged atmosphere overhead, widening before simply staining it a dull gray.

"Are you all right?" he cried through the pain, grabbing William's face between his hands and raising it before his own. His eyes darted all across the boy's face, searching for signs of life in his wet eyes.

William just nodded, dripping tears onto his father's cheek.

"I was so scared for you," Brad whimpered. Pinching his eyes shut, he kissed William on top of the head, leaving bloody lip-prints from his tattered, red-stained mouth as though he had been wearing lipstick.

"Me, too," William sobbed, his fingers tightening in the cloth under Brad and pulling him even closer.

"That was incredibly brave what you just did," Cindy said, crouching to stroke the matted hair on William's head. Gently, she excised him from Brad's ferocious hug and eased him to his feet.

Trick offered a hand to Brad and carefully pulled him upward.

"Are they all dead?" he asked, grimacing at the sight of the wound on Brad's shoulder and then looking to William for the answer.

"I think so," he managed to say through all of the noise inside his head. "How's Tim?"

"None the worse for wear, I hope," Jason said, having transferred him into Nancy's urgent grasp the moment they had safely crossed the bridge.

"We have to make sure that nothing happens to him," William said, walking unsteadily toward Nancy and placing his hand on Tim's shoulder. With the faint hint of a smile on his face, Tim opened his eyes long enough to look at William, and then closed them right back up. "Gotta keep holding on. Not much longer now."

"I know..." Tim whispered, nodding while he dragged his face up and down his mother's sweater.

"He needs to sleep," Nancy whispered, leaning her cheek atop his bald head and closing her eyes.

"Monster!" Karen cried, turning from where she stood at the edge of the cut, looking down toward the river. She'd been watching it like a hawk, waiting for any sign of movement. There was nothing down there resembling life but the splattered gobs of flesh and severed appendages, bleeding themselves dry into little pools of glistening fluid. She waited for a shifting in the piles of debris, begging silently for the sight of the powdered cement to cascade from atop them, for a single hand to reach for daylight from the rubble. But there was nothing. And as hard as she tried, she couldn't hear any of their voices in her head.

"You killed them all!" she screamed and ran right at William with her open hands stretched before her in preparation of wrapping around his little throat and squeezing the life right out of him.

Brad threw himself at her, grabbing hold of one of her arms and spinning her to the side while Jason fought through her swinging and pinned the other.

"Let me at him! I'll kill all of you if I have to!"

"Settle down!" Jason snapped, remembering how the orderlies back at the hospital had corralled the violent patients, bringing Karen's wrist back up behind her and pinning it against her shoulder blade.

She screamed at the sharp pain in her shoulder, but there was nothing she could do to shake him free. That arm was no longer of any use to her so she focused her energy on kicking her legs forward in hopes of landing one solid connection squarely in the middle of the boy's chest with enough force to collapse his ribs inward.

Trick stepped into the way, taking a solid kick to the thigh before wrangling her flailing legs and holding one to either side of his hips, gritting his teeth against the strain of trying to hold them there.

Suspended above the ground, she flopped and threw her body around like she was racked with the throes of an epileptic fit. Flopping and floundering, she bucked until it felt as though her shoulders were about to be ripped right out of the sockets.

She stopped.

Her form grew as limp as if they had been folding a big wad of melting taffy between them. From the bottoms of her eyes, she could see the tips of the feathery mouths lining the inside of her lower lashes, the ring of them forming right around the mask covering her mouth and leading up into the nest in her nostrils.

"Maybe we'd better part ways," Trick said, unable to look her in the suddenly far too docile eyes, like she had somehow been tranquilized.

"You'd leave me alone to die?" she whispered, raising the question with her brows, displaying the orange, furry growth poking from the corners of her eyes like algae from the still waters of a marsh.

"She's already dying," Jason said to the others. "Look at that stuff growing all over her face. We'd be taking a monumental risk if we were to bring her with us any further. And that oxygen won't last forever."

"Got news for you, chump," she said, shaking her head from side to side to display the severed end of the tube that dangled from her oxygen mask. "No more air for Kare-Kare."

A thin veil of blood rolled over her eyes, similarly pooling around the inner rim of her mask, dotting the plastic dome with each sputtering breath. Her chest buckled back and forth. Each attempt at a breath sounded like a high-pitched scream through her windpipe, filling with fluid.

"Christ!" Trick gasped, dropping her legs to the ground to kick harmlessly along the shoulder of the road, dragging lines like a snow angel into the gravel.

Jason and Brad pulled their hands quickly back as well for fear of whatever was happening to her transferring to them.

She flopped up and down, raising her head from the ground only to slam it back down repeatedly with a cracking sound. Loosing the mask from her face, it flopped haplessly around her neck, allowing her to convulsively spit sprays of blood into the air.

Rolling her eyes backward into her skull, her entire body growing rigid, she bared her bloody teeth, little polyps squiggling across them and slipping beneath the gums. She drew an enormous breath, her chest swelling like a balloon. Releasing it in a trilling scream, she quickly flipped over to all fours and scrambled toward William, kicking up clouds of dust from the gavel, thickening into mud on her scraped and bleeding knees.

With the last of her strength, she grabbed for him, wrapping a claw around his ankle. Brad leapt onto her back and rode her to the ground, grinding her face into the asphalt. His weight atop her squeezed the last of her air from her in a sickening, garbling belch, evacuating her bowels into her pants in the same final, jittery death rattle.

A stream of phlegm-thickened blood rolled from the corner of her mouth like raspberry syrup, dripping to the street. It snapped loose, the thin remaining strand recoiling to her lip and swelling with the next wave.

"She dead?" Jason shouted over William's hysterical crying.

"I think so," Brad said, rolling off of her and clasping his hand over his mouth and nose to keep from smelling the repugnant scent that rose from her.

Jason walked up and crouched beside her, his face wrinkling. He reached down to press his first two fingers against her carotid, and looked to the others, standing back, aghast, and gave a quick nod.

William screamed again and shook at his leg, trying to slip it out from the dead woman's clutches. Jerking it back, he freed it with a cracking of her joints, and then he suddenly quieted, lowering his brow. If she was dead, then maybe his vision wouldn't necessarily come to bear. Maybe she wasn't going to be able to kill his father after all.

He smiled, and threw himself on the gravel next to his father and hugged him.

"What should we do with her now?" Trick asked.

"If she's going to come back to life like the others, then maybe we'd better...I don't know," Cindy added, not wanting to finish the sentence.

"I don't want to touch her again," Brad said.

"We should lop her head off," Nancy said, drawing all eyes to her. "She can't come after us again if she doesn't have a head...can she?"

"What do you propose we use to do it?" Trick said, frightened by the words that had come out of his mouth. "I don't see anything lying around her that would be of much use."

"We could roll her down into the river," Jason said.

"What does the kid think?" Trick asked, kneeling in front of William and waiting for him to raise his head. "You're the man of the hour, kiddo. I think we're all of the opinion that you're about the only one here who has even the slightest clue as to what's going on. If you've got anything to add, feel free to pipe up."

William rose to his feet and looked from one face to the next. They were all looking at him, all holding the silence in wait for whatever he was going to say. It made him incredibly uncomfortable. He didn't care what they did with that hag. Douse her in gasoline and light her on fire, heck, they could tan her and make boots from her for all he cared. Just so long as she didn't come back to kill his dad. But they were right. They couldn't take any chances. The resolution needed to be swift and final.

"What do you think?" he asked Trick, who took a step back and recoiled at the first sign of doubt from the boy.

"I think any minute now my alarm clock's going to go off and I'm going to wake up in my nice warm bed in my own crappy little abode. You guys figure this one out."

"For lack of a better idea," Cindy said, looking to Trick for reassurance, "I say we do what the doctor suggested. Just roll her into the river and be done with it."

"I'm not a doctor," Jason said. "Not any more."

"I agree," Brad said, and William looked quickly to him. He

needed to know what his father thought. In the scope of his little world, his father was as all knowing and all seeing as God Himself. "A rolling stone gathers no moss, right?"

"Then we're decided," Cindy said.

"Wait!" William piped up.

He bent back down over Karen and pulled on the elastic strap holding the oxygen mask around her neck.

"Someone grab me a stick," he said, pulling the elastic taut.

Jason leaned over and picked one up from the ground and walked it over to William, who laced it between the parallel cords and started to turn. He wound it tighter and tighter, turning it like the propeller of one of those wooden toy airplanes. The more times he cranked it, the closer it got to her neck. He turned it until he was scraping the ends of the stick through the back of her hair and a necklace of bruises formed around it, pinching the skin so tightly that it ruptured in spots. With the last crank, he could feel the elastic threatening to give against the strain and knew it was time to cease. Slipping the end of the stick under the collar of her shirt, he stepped back and raised his hands to his sides to make sure it was going to stay and not quickly unwind.

The stick tugged tightly against her collar, but appeared to be reasonably well latched.

"All right," he said, unable to take his eyes off of the growing bruise that crept up her neck and toward the orange and gold fur growing out of the insides of her ears.

"Then we do this," Jason said, squaring his jaw and nodding, if only to convince himself. "On three."

He reached beneath her, his knuckles scraping on the gravel, and propped both hands under her right arm and against her chest. Brad crawled to his feet and sidled up beside him, similarly grabbing her underneath her bulbous belly. Cindy quickly scurried to the woman's feet and grabbed hold of her calves.

"Oh, that's just great," Trick said, puckering his features. "Leave me with that brown mess soaking through her pants. I'll remember this, you know. Next time we have to roll a dead body off of the road, I'm making sure it's mine. Let you all sniff my shorts."

"One," Jason said, chuckling despite himself.

They all tensed their hands to assure themselves that they had a firm hold.

"Two."

At once, they all drew a large breath in anticipation of the exertion.

"Three!" Jason blurted, grimacing, and he rolled the woman forward.

She slopped onto her back, flapping her lifeless arms onto the ground with a shuddering jiggle. They readjusted, getting beneath her once more, and flipped her again, this time rolling her onto her stomach at the very edge of the cement embankment leading down to the river. Repeating the process, all grunted and groaned. Her feet were the first thing to roll over, leading her hips and then finally her torso. She slid feet-first down the first third before snagging her heels and sending her head careening past her body, slamming her face onto the hard surface with an explosion of teeth that skittered down the slant before her. Dragging her face along the concrete, she splashed into the water.

Her entire rear end stood out of the river for a moment, before slowly subsiding beneath the surface of the churning water, her feet the last to submerge, like the stern of a sinking ship. They all stared at the soles of those formerly blinding-white leather sneakers, floating downstream, all the while sinking little by little into the blackness.

"Should we say something?" Cindy asked, feeling the twang of guilt.

"Something," Trick said, though it didn't even make him smile as he just stared at the dark water where last he had seen her.

"Don't you think we ought to say some sort of eulogy?"

Trick looked her right in the face; his features softening, and gave her a pleasant smile that under different circumstances would have been quite disarming.

"In case you haven't noticed, sweetheart," he said, still smiling, "God don't live here no more."

And with that he gave her a squeeze on the shoulder, and but a simple, curt nod, and headed back toward the road. Cindy just lowered her head.

"So where are we going now, oh great prophet?" Trick asked through a smirk.

"I wish you wouldn't talk to him like that," Brad said.

Cindy gave him a pop in the shoulder with her fist.

"What?" Trick said, throwing his arms up. "The kid's like Jimmy the Greek or something."

"Zorba," Nancy corrected.

"Zorba couldn't beat the spread week in, week out. My, my, my. What I wouldn't give to bounce that kid around on my knee come game day."

"Leave him alone," Cindy snapped.

Coming from anyone else, Trick might have come up with something snappy to put her back in her place, but there was something about her…the way she had spoken really almost hurt.

"Sorry," he said, checking her from the corner of his eye. "I get a little punchy when I'm...you know, running for my life and all. We still good, buddy?"

He offered a hand to William, who, rather than shaking it, held it like his father's.

"Still good," William said and smiled up at Trick.

"Are you going to make me ask again or are you ready to tell me?"

"West," William said. He started walking straight up the rising highway, dragging Brad and Trick with him.

"Anything more specific?"

"We're going to my house," he said, starting to walk faster. There was nothing but silence in his head for that one pristinely peaceful moment. "There's something we really need to get."

"Cryptic," Trick said, snorting, but fearing if he pushed the issue any further he might incur the wrath of the boy's father, or worse yet, Cindy. Even though she curled her thumb into her fist and punched like a girl, she could still pack a wallop.

With the scent of pine blowing down the highway, foretelling of what was to come, they walked down the middle of the highway with the futile rays of the sun on their backs.

Cindy wrapped her arms around her chest and shivered with the prickling of goosebumps rising from her shoulders. She rubbed at them and then looked, as Coloradoans did with the first sign of cold, to the mountains framed against the western sky ahead. Dark clouds sat atop the deep blue mountains, swelling like the tide preparing to crest over the break. The temperature had easily fallen a good dozen degrees, but it was July, and with all of the walking, that wasn't necessarily a bad thing. But if she didn't know better—and even her surgically scarred knee had been duped into believing it—it almost—

"Looks like snow," Brad said, finishing her thought and looking up into the storm.

The raindrops were smaller now, but still falling every bit as ferociously. It was like walking through the spray from a waterfall.

Nancy flipped the flap of the blanket all the way over Tim's head and leaned over to shield it with her own. The first hint of her breath blew back over her shoulder on the wind in a pale white mist.

Brad looked down to William, noting the reddened tip of the boy's nose and the paired plumes of exhaust gusting out, and then back to the horizon and the stockpiling clouds growing taller over the peaks.

"Snowmobiles," he whispered, squeezing his son's hand.

William looked up at him and beamed.

"I think I'm getting the hang of this, too."

6 | Nary a Shallow Grave

I

The rain had turned to driving sleet, lightening their packs as they were now wearing most everything within, soaking them straight through to the shivering bone before they were even out of town. It was almost a relief when it finally started to snow. None had thought to stop and revel in the dimming warmth of the sunlight, to feel its golden caress on their skin one last time before it became nothing more than a pale yellow aura through the thick layer of dust that stained the snow from white to gray.

Progress slowed with the weight of the accumulation clumping in the tread on their shoes, piling on their shoulders and atop the hats of those who were fortunate that William had the foresight to pack a little extra. Trick and Jason looked like hooded old monks with the snow blowing in through their flapping casks, melting just enough from their radiating heat to drip into thin, icy lines that crept down their necks and beneath their shirts. All were past the point of exhaustion, but so long as they were moving, they could produce heat. And so long as they could generate internal warmth, they wouldn't fall forward into one of the growing banks of snow that covered the cars and drifted at the sides of the highway, knowing that once they did, they just might never be able to arise.

The few needles remaining on the pine trees held handfuls of snow at the ends of the otherwise skeletal branches: bones blanched white by the interminable flakes. Knifing through them, unimpeded by the formerly thick foliage, the wind drove the snow sideways, dragging it straight through the foothills from the mountains for seemingly no other reason than to assault them with it. It was oddly surreal. There were no prints of any kind in the pristine gray layer. No car tracks packed the landscape in parallel lines. Not even the small dots left from a quickly hopping rabbit interrupted the unmarred serenity. The only signs of life were in the tracks falling quickly behind them, only to be filled by the snow and wiped clean from the face of the earth.

"Are we there yet?" Trick called from behind, having taken to saying it for its initial comic value like a child in the back seat of a car on a long road trip, but it had quickly worn thin.

"Soon," Brad said, looking up to the road and then quickly down to his feet again. He wiped the almost spontaneous accumulation of snow from his cheekbones, and tightened his arms over his chest to stifle a full-body shiver. "Next road we come across, take a left."

Powder kicked into the air from before their advance, crusting in a layer over their jeans all the way up to their knees. It was ankle deep even in the middle of the road where they were somewhat shielded by the now intermittently spaced cars, giving them but the most wonderfully transient respite from the wickedly cold wind.

Nancy hummed along her shivering breaths, pressing her cheek against Tim's forehead so she would notice immediately if it either began to cool off or heat with fever. She had zipped him up inside of her coat, melding their shared warmth, and thrown the blanket around the both of them like a long shawl, constantly reaching behind her to make sure that his feet were still tucked beneath. Only the back half of her head was shielded beneath the upper rise of the blanket, her bangs frosted into crisp, icy strands, the tips of which melted on her forehead and ran down her cheeks through the already smeared mascara.

William wore one of those ski masks with the three holes, having offered it to Tim first, but Nancy preferred to be able to feel her son's skin, to see his breath from his nostrils, to clearly identify his eyes should he open them. His lips puckered out of the rust-colored mouth hole since the fine hairs from the sewed seam tickled his lips and grew damp from his running nose if he didn't. It was capped with a white crown of snow, and a matching line right down the slant of his nose. He wore his dark blue ski jacket with his gloved hands shoved into the pockets.

Brad was relatively comfortable in his matching, blue Gortex coat, alternately warming his bitter red hands in his steaming breath and shoving them into the pockets. Shannen wore his gloves, as well as one of his long sleeved sweatshirts and his stocking cap. He had lent the interior lining of the waterproof jacket to Jason, who had pulled the thin retractable hood up over his head and walked with his hands in the pockets of his jeans.

Trick and Cindy trailed the others, sharing a blanket wrapped around the both of them as neither was wearing more than a double layer of sweatshirts. It clung to them like a second skin, sticking wetly atop them, but at least it kept the snow from coming into direct contact with their skin.

"I never would have thought I'd need my winter jacket when I left my house yesterday," Trick said. "I remember waking up in the middle of the afternoon in a lake of my own sweat. I guess I should consider myself lucky that I even bothered to put on any clothes at all."

"I suppose we should all consider ourselves fortunate then," Cindy said, smirking.

"It's just killing you, isn't it?"

"What?"

"Being under a blanket with me and knowing I'm fully clothed."

"I could always take back my blanket…"

"Sheesh! It was just a joke, darlin'."

"The joke would be if you weren't."

"Weren't what?"

"Fully clothed."

"That was kind of a stretch reaching back for that one, but it's nice to know you're still thinking about me in all my naked glory."

The mile marker stood from the side of the road, the numbered placard having been blown off and hidden beneath the snow. Only the reflective orange disk flashed in recognition, though half of it was obscured by a crusting of snow from the drift that rose halfway up the thin green post.

Brad walked around a parked car that could just as easily have been a bale of hay under that dome of snow, looking off into the trees to the mound that was his Cherokee. It didn't even look like the same road now. The long ponderosa pine branches that dangled across the mouth of the road were barren of needles, the removal of their weight causing the naked branches to rise high enough that he didn't have to worry about ducking to get beneath them. Without any tracks on the road, had he not known it was there, they could easily have walked right by. The packed snow simply slanted down from the hillside to the right, covering the road formerly cut from it as though it had never been. No trails of gray smoke rose into the sky from the wood burning stoves and fireplaces that generally gushed from the houses that lurked out of sight in the valley.

The only sound was the whistling wind stealing their pluming breath from their panting mouths. No larks or starlings called from the trees, though every now and then, they actually came across one: sitting there on a dead branch, staring down at them, watching them walk by without raising a cry in alarm or flapping from the tree and into the forest. In fact, with their patchy feathers and bare gray down peeking from their absence, it really didn't look like they were capable of flight any longer besides.

There had even been a single ground squirrel that had stared out from a rotting, termite-hollowed trunk, merely studying them from its haunches. It's gray tongue dangled out the side of it askew jaw, jaggedly broken teeth nowhere near fitting together as they should have. The fur on its right flank was matted with dirt, and its eyes were bright red like they had been caught by the flash of a camera.

"Beautiful area," Jason said, stepping in Brad's tracks, falling in behind William to follow them up the hidden gravel road. "It's like your own little world back here I'll bet."

"Yeah," Brad said, smiling. "Our own little world."

Rounding the first bend, William stared off to the left. He could barely see the gate framing the Abernathy's driveway beneath all of the accumulated snow. The house itself was invisible down the hillside now: the piled flakes on the roof matching those of the slope beyond. Were it not for that large boulder that had stopped after smashing through the aluminum rails, he might simply have walked by without being forced to look at it. But there it was...an enormous rock set right into the middle of the drive, and to the right...to the right that long, sharpened piece of metal shrapnel protruded like the razor-honed tip of an elk antler. His mind started to replay his vision at the beckoning of those within—

"Stop it!" William barked, pinching his eyes shut and pounding his temples with his fists. When he finally opened them and looked up, his father was staring back at him with a look of concern.

"Stop what?" he asked.

"Nothing, Dad," he answered, looking back to that long, accidentally formed sword, and then, fighting with the uncomfortable thoughts it engendered, back to his father.

"You'll tell me when you're ready?"

William tried to force a smile that probably ended up looking more like he was trying to keep from hurling.

"You know," Brad said, swatting the pile of snow from his son's head, "you can talk to me about anything, right?"

William just nodded.

That was the second time that his son had been drawn to the Abernathy's gate since they had left the house what now felt like a lifetime ago. There had even been that strange incident where he had helped William to pry that seemingly insignificant shred of metal outward. Something about this place was definitely troubling the boy, but it wasn't in his nature to try to beat it out of him. When the time was right, William would tell him of his own accord.

"Is this it?" Cindy asked, raising her hand to shield her eyes and staring through the sheeting snow down the invisible driveway.

"Not yet," Brad said. "Just a little further."

"Then let's just keep going," Nancy said. "I'd feel better if I could get Tim inside and out of the snow…if only for a few minutes."

"The sooner we get there, the sooner we can all be toasting our toes in front of a nice warm fi—" Brad started, but William cut him off with a tug on his sleeve.

"There's no time for that."

"I really think we'd all be better served to warm up for a while before we catch pneumonia."

"You were going to say fire," Trick jumped in. "I heard it plain as day. You can't say fire and then just take it back."

"They're still coming for us," William said, whirling in a circle to make sure that he had everyone's attention. "You do realize that, don't you? What did you think? Hmm? That was it? They're not going to stop! They're going to keep coming and coming until we're dead! All of us!"

They stood in silence.

"Thank you, little Mary Sunshine," Trick said, and then felt the wrath of Cindy's elbow against his ribs. "What?"

"We're ahead of them now, and I don't think that with this weather they're capable of moving any faster than we are, but it's not worth taking the chance."

"We need to dry off, son," Brad said, kneeling to look William right in the eyes, "or we're all going to die, anyway. That's our more immediate concern. I'm sure we can all agree to be quick, but I certainly believe that it's in our collective best interests to find a change of clothes and to warm up in front of the fireplace…at least for a minute."

"You don't understand, Dad!"

"Maybe in this case I understand better than you, William. We need to get dry, get warm, and get out of these wet clothes."

He could see in his father's eyes that there was no dissuading him, so he nodded reluctantly.

Brad smiled in return and gave William a sly wink, stood, and started tromping ahead through the virgin snow.

Sighing, William glanced one final time over his shoulder to the hooked metal spike brandished from atop the gate, and prayed that he would never have to see it again.

They all looked down while they walked, fitting their feet into the footprints already laid out for them so as not to worsen the feel of the packed snow rising up their pant legs over their socks and sealing against their bare skin. Occasionally they looked up, batting their lids from the large snowflakes that clung to them, only to ensure that they were still right behind the person in front of them before looking back down.

"Are we there yet?" Trick asked, looking up and blinking furiously from the cold needles of snow that stabbed into his eyeballs.

"Yeah," Brad said, pointing off toward the left where they could see but the back of a wood-sided house through the nest of naked pine trunks. "Right up there."

He had never in his entire life been so excited to see that house, envisioning it now from an entirely different perspective. Rather than looking at it and saying "Maybe I should have added a balcony there," or "It would have looked better from this vantage with cathedral ceilings," he saw it from a basic, practical perspective. It was four walls surrounding a room where there was a fireplace. There were warm clothes hanging in the closets exactly where he had left them, and there was something to quench his thirst other than the snowflakes he swallowed after melting on his tongue. And there was a bathroom.

He quickened his pace. This time, even the burning muscles in his legs didn't protest, but urged him on, kicking through the snow and breaking into a jog.

The broken stump of the mailbox marked the drive, which he headed straight down and toward the front door, already pulling the keys from the front pocket of his slacks with his numbed and shaking red fingers. Tucking them into his closed fist, he sped down the remainder of the driveway and pounded up the front steps to the door, priming the door key and shoving it into the lock. With a satisfying click, the deadbolt snapped back into its housing and he turned the knob.

Only slighter warmer air rushed through the opening door to greet him, though it was thick with the scent of the macaroni and cheese he had fashioned for dinner the night before. At the time, the noodles had been underdone and the cheese tasted like processed paste, but right now, it was just about the most divine smell he could ever imagine.

"Wipe your feet on the mat," he said, laughing his way through the foyer. The imported Grecian tiles were covered with a half-inch of snow atop decaying leaves and dirt.

William followed, stamping his feet and following his father up the steps to the main floor.

"Time to fire the cleaning lady," Trick said, stepping inside and looking around while he held the door first for Nancy, and then for Cindy. He traipsed through the debris with Shannen right behind.

"Right now it looks marvelous to me," Jason said, closing the door behind him and already starting to peel the jacket from the wet shirt beneath.

"Master bedroom's the second door on the left," Brad called, crouching in front of the fireplace and brushing the leaves and snow from atop the stacked cord of logs in the bronze basket. "Help yourself to whatever you want."

"I'll help you find some dry clothes for Tim," William said. He took Nancy by the elbow and guided her toward his room, across the hall from where all of the others were yanking the hangers from the closet and throwing all of the clothes onto the bed to divvy them up.

He flipped the light switch out of habit, but continued walking. Yellowing pine needles bristled from his bed like a porcupine under the thin sheet of snow that drifted through his window, tousling the curtains, before alighting on his comforter. A Wolverine action figure poked his head up from under the snow next to the square yellow top of a bulldozer. Kicking aside a football, he threw back the sliding doors of the closet and stepped inside.

"I think this sweater should fit," he said, yanking it from the swinging hanger and passing it to Nancy. "It's so hot it could bake a ham. That's why I never wore it, but that's what we're looking for, right? My grandma made it for me. My mom's mom."

"Where is your mother?" Nancy asked. For some reason she hadn't thought about it until now, and immediately regretted it once the words came out. The boy's mother obviously wasn't waiting for them in the kitchen to pass out glasses of lemonade and freshly baked cookies. "I'm sorry. I shouldn't have—"

"It's all right," William said, reaching all the way to the back for the coat he outgrew the prior year. "She died when I was born. I've had a while to get used to it. I once heard my dad say they had to give her an emergency c-section after she was already dead to get me out. Don't tell him I heard that though. Please."

"I'm so sorry," Nancy said, reaching down to tug the comforter off of the bed. She laid Tim down atop the sheet and started to unwrap the blanket she had swaddled him within.

"It's like those shrinks tell my dad, though. How could I really know what I'm missing if I never had it in the first place? When you're really quiet like I am, people tend to forget you're even there."

"I like your room," Tim whispered, the corners of his lips curling upward beneath his blackened sockets. His eyes rolled slowly from one torn poster on the wall to the next, eyeing the pushpins sticking from the wall like they were somehow every bit as fascinating as the pictures they had once held in place.

"Thanks," William said. "You should have seen it before."

"I'll bet it was pretty cool."

"Save your strength, Timmy," Nancy said, twisting the collar of the sweater over his head and sliding his hands into the sleeves for him.

"I want to—" he started before being abruptly cut off by a throng of hoarse coughing. "To talk. I want to talk to my friend."

Nancy forced a smile and nodded. The disease had robbed him of damn near everything in his life. His friends had stopped coming by long ago. Their parents felt the need to nervously try to justify it to her, but she understood far too well. She was a mother too, after all.

"When you used to talk to me at night," Tim said, his face glazing over placidly, "I used to imagine that you were lying on your back, just like me, watching the light of the moon on the ceiling. I'd think about why you kept telling me I was so important—"

"You're very important," William said, shyly shedding his own soaked layers in the shadows of the closet. He donned a t-shirt, and then a sweatshirt, and threw a sweater over the top of both.

"But it doesn't matter why," he said, trying to lift his weary legs to help his mother slide on the sweat pants she had pulled from the dresser. "Just that you thought I was special was enough. I've got a pretty good idea why, but I really don't feel like thinking about that much. It was just nice to talk to someone else."

"I'm always here to talk to, honey," Nancy said, rummaging for socks with another pair of sweat pants to add atop the others under her arm.

Tim coughed, wincing at the sharp pain in his stomach and trying desperately to stop.

"I know, Mom. It's just nice to talk to someone who doesn't start to cry when he looks at you, even if he can't see you."

"You know I don't mean to," she said, raising his feet to sit beneath them and begin layering the socks.

"Of course. And it's okay. It may sound kind of weird, but it would probably hurt my feelings if you didn't. You're my best friend in the world, after all."

Nancy stopped fidgeting with the socks, and looked him in the shadowed face. Her lower lip began to quiver.

"And you're mine, too," she said, unable to keep her voice from cracking. "You're mine, too."

She leaned down and kissed him on the forehead, wiping at her eyes to keep the tears from dripping onto his face.

"Fire's ready!" Brad shouted from down the hallway.

"How 'bout we finish dressing you in front of the fire?" Nancy said, slipping her hands beneath his armpits and cradling him to her chest.

"Sounds…good," Tim said, yawning. His eyelids fluttered, though he raised his eyebrows to try to keep them up.

"There'd better be S'mores!" Trick yelled, thundering out into the hall from the master.

"Forget that!" Cindy said, running right behind him. "What I wouldn't give for a pig on a spit!"

"Ah, the most underrated of the 'meat on a stick' genre. A woman after me own heart. Arr."

"I'd settle for a bologna sandwich," Shannen said, stepping into the hall. Catching a glimpse of the shadowed silhouettes in William's room, she stopped and stuck her head in. "You guys coming?"

"Yeah," William said, bashfully turning his back to her as he was standing there in his tightie-whities, preparing to don his long underwear. "Just a minute."

Nancy walked past him and slipped around Shannen in the doorway.

"I'll save you a seat by the fire," Shannen said, patting the doorframe and hurrying down the hall with the growing warmth melting the icicles from her hair and lashes.

William peeked out of the closet to make sure she was gone and then hurriedly jumped into a pair of jeans. He grabbed the last pair of sweatpants from the drawer and an armful of socks, and raced to join the others.

"All right," Brad said, swiping the soot and crumbled bark from his hands and rising from the floor. He knocked the box of wooden matches to the floor but didn't even bother to reach through the snow to pick them up. The wind blew unimpeded through the shattered remnants of the sliding glass door, battering them from the side with an onslaught of flakes. But not even that or the accumulation they knelt in was enough to keep them from pressing in on the fire and toasting their hands. "I'm going to change my clothes as well."

He looked from Trick to Jason, and then Cindy.

"If there are any left."

All three were heaped beneath multiple layers of haphazardly assembled clothing. Trick had capped off what looked to be a good dozen shirts by the thickness of him, with a blue sport jacket and a red and blue tie dangling loosely around his neck. He wore Brad's dress socks over his hands, yet shoved them into the crackling flame all the same. A white t-shirt was draped over his head, fixed into place by a Denver Broncos baseball cap tightened over it. The sleeves dangled beside either cheek, as he figured as soon as he got outside he could tie them in front of his face.

Cindy wore a similar makeshift turban, only opting for the blue and white mesh Disneyland cap to affix the shirt over her hair. She too wore socks on her hands, though of the white, sweat variety, and her blazer was buttoned shut in front and unaccessorized with something as impractical as a tie. She wore gray slacks despite the blue jacket, with the waistband of the baggy sweats beneath protruding out over the belt she had cinched so tightly to hold the multitude of ill-fitting pants that it dangled nearly all the way down to her knees.

Jason, on the other hand, fit perfectly into Brad's clothing and was easily able to comfortably fit a pair of jeans on under some navy slacks. He wore what he hoped was a waterproof jogging jacket, aqua-blue with a white Nike swoosh across the back, over a couple of sweaters and an old tan blazer with brown corduroy patches on the elbows. He had similarly draped an undershirt over his head, but as the others had used the more practical hats, he held his in place with a wide-brimmed, red and green wicker, novelty sombrero someone had obviously brought back from Mexico as a joke. But so long as it would keep his head dry, then it served its purpose.

"Could I help you find something dry to wear?" Brad asked Nancy, heading to the hallway. "I can't guarantee I've got anything that will fit you, but I'd be willing to bet it would feel a lot better than what you're wearing now."

"You okay for a minute?" Nancy asked Tim. He twitched his nose at the itch of the crust rimming his nostrils, but didn't say a word. His eyes darted back and forth under his closed lids as he sped off into a dream. Rising, she gently propped Tim on Cindy's lap and hurried to catch up before she found herself wearing some old Halloween costume or something of that nature.

"Keep in mind we're still in a hurry," William said, squeezing his thickly socked feet back into his boots.

"At this point I'd be willing to arm-wrestle God Himself if it would keep me in front of this fire a while longer," Trick said.

"Bizarre as that may sound," Jason said, tugging at the rim of the sombrero, the frayed edges growing increasingly distracting in front of his eyes, "I agree. The prospect of heading back out into that storm is positively daunting. Maybe it makes sense to hunker down here for a while and wait out the snow."

"It's not going to stop," William said, rising to wring the melted precipitation from his ski mask.

"Never?" Cindy asked, half in jest.

"So far as I can tell," William said, cringing against the ferocious, bitter cold of tugging that wet mask back over his face. "Never."

"Oh," Cindy whispered, knotting her brow in her loss for words.

"Come on, Dad!" William shouted down the hallway, already working his pruned fingers back into his damp gloves.

Shannen paced the back of the room, allowing the fire to warm her, but at the same time refusing to succumb to its almost serpentine wiles. If she were to sit down and allow it to intimately caress her freezing, desperate form, she'd be asleep before her eyelids even met. And in that sleep, the dreams were sure to come: dreams of dragging her dead boyfriend through the forest, of abandoning him right there on the side of the highway as if he had been no more significant than a torn sack of refuse. Specters of the corpses of her family surrounding such a beautifully set table with food they would never taste, still saving her a place right there beside them in their infinite, festering final feast.

She had to occupy herself, distract not only her weary body, but her sleepy mind as well, so she stared out into the night, through the flakes that blew brazenly through the remains of the glass door, past the ragged rim of the balcony and to the forest beneath.

Shadows clung to the trunks of the trees like stranded hunters awaiting the search and rescue mission that would never come, awaiting the release from their darkened coil by a sun unable to permeate the clouds.

William suddenly stood stiff, cocking his eyes upward into his head.

Unconsciously trying to nibble at her fingernails through the socks on her hands, Shannen allowed herself to stare dreamily into the shadows, feeling the intensifying weight of her eyelids threatening to close whether she liked it or not. Her head tilted peacefully to the left, and she started to sway, back and forth, though inside of her head she was still standing still. The shadows widened, drawing her gaze within, willing her to just join them in the darkness for but a moment, to allow her eyes to simply drip shut and wither into sleep. Their unvoiced argument was so compelling that she didn't realize that her eyes were closed until she snapped them open again when William screamed.

"They're here!"

Furiously batting her lids, Shannen fought to regain her grasp on consciousness. The shadows played before her like an old black and white reel melting on the projection bulb, shifting and metamorphosing like a living and breathing Rorschach card. A large white rabbit could have walked right out of the darkness, frittering as he checked his pocket watch, and she'd have willingly followed him down his hole. But when the shadows yawned and a figure stepped out into the clearing, it wasn't something so remotely plucked from her imagination, though it might as well have been.

"Dad!" William screamed, drawing the others from their positions on front of the flame to their feet. "They're here! We've got to go!

NOW!"

Her first reaction was to raise her fists to her face and rub her eyes, but even a moment inside of her head couldn't erase the vision. She stood there, still, blankly scrutinizing every little detail until—

Shannen gasped and stumbled backward from the doorway.

II

Through unseeing eyes, the being that once was Brian stared down at his feet.

At first exposure to the snow building atop the ground, death had been spontaneous. He had heard each and every one of those small voices cry out at once, sharply silenced by the intolerable cold. Their clones had arisen in their place, only to perform the same dying ritual, screaming until all within were deafened to their cries, leaving only their crusted, carbon remains to belie their terminal plight like so many barnacles crusted to the bottom of a ship. That shell grew thicker and thicker until it was more than a half-inch deep, shielding the shoe and the foot within, tapering up over the ankles and into the calves in twirled ribbons of crust like climbing ivy. The last of those to remain retracted all the way back into the hardened catacombs against the saved flesh, biding their time until the snow grew deeper—as they knew it would—and they were forced to similarly sacrifice their lives to save the physical domicile.

His feet looked like the snaggled paws of a stone lion perched atop a parapet, though they had lost all semblance of symmetry. No longer did they hold the shape of the creature that bore them, but blotted tracks through the snow that looked like irregularly shaped, shriveled clovers.

Even his face was hardened with generations of amassed exoskeletons to spare the skin beneath from exposure to the elements, allowing them to make the necessary alterations to the considerably meek host. Ridges of hardened chitin rose from the cheekbones and the brow, shielding the sunken, vulnerable optic sensors from both the weather and any sort of hostile advance. A hardened conical structure, much like a conch shell, replaced the withered flesh that was the ears over the auditory canals. They had widened the mouth, tearing back the skin of the cheeks and then fortifying it with their deadened masses to allow greater range of motion for the jawbones that could now easily pop in and out of joint like a python. And from the top of either side of his forehead, just beneath the hairline, large horns like those of a ram wrapped around the side of the head. Not just to be used as some sort of primitive weapon should the need arise, but to protect the contents of the skull, the precious brain that controlled every component of their stolen existence, from a potentially lethal blow.

For all intents and purposes, the human being that had once been the starting safety on the varsity squad and the love of Shannen's life, was no more. Even his own mother wouldn't have been able to recognize him, though that was of no consequence now as she slaved with all of the others beneath the ground. The only thing they had left…the only thing they had been able to leave for fear of the snowflakes killing them was the tattered letter jacket he still wore, though mountainous patches of carbon had arisen through the ripped seams.

The girl would recognize the jacket.

She would certainly recognize the voice.

And that was all of the distraction that they were going to need.

He could feel the others beside him, similarly hardened and crusted over to prevent the frostbite to the host's form that would lead to blackened tissue and, ultimately, necrosis. They scampered from behind one crumbling trunk to the next, shielding themselves from the barrage of flakes before darting back into the storm and to the next momentary haven. He could hear them in his head, hear them reveling in what was to come. It didn't matter that the others who had tried before them had failed, for this time they would succeed. They had learned from that first attempt, where they had been slain by fire and explosion, others pinned beneath the rubble. That information had been passed from those about to be blasted limb from limb into the communal memory. They would not make the same mistake twice. Unlike every other species they had ever encountered, for them, even death could be used as a learning experience.

Faint glints of light sparkled from the carpet of snow, glittering though there was no light in the choked sky to reflect. He tromped through, wary of the clouds of powder that blasted up from his feet, triggering the mass termination of those along his still, as of yet, ill-reinforced arms and chest. The others…they were fully converted, armored limbs fitting neatly into shielded joints to allow fluid range of motion, as if humans had been bred to armadillos. Like the snowflakes that threatened them with every advancing charge, no two were exactly alike. Some had horns resembling Brian's, though the arches were different, some even looping straight through the shoulders and poking out the front like spikes, while still others grew spines like those that grew down the back of an iguana over their reinforced scalps. There were those with parallel crests like ice skate blades protruding from their skulls. And still others with absolutely no horned growth whatsoever, just rugged crusting of no design as though biological tectonic plates had come together beneath the fissures in the cranium and forced craggy foothills to rise where once there had been hair.

Cocking his head back, he inhaled through rigidly fixed nostrils, savoring the night air, peeling apart each layer until he found what he knew would be there.

Smoke.

Through scores of eyes he scanned the treetops until he saw the distant plume of gray smoke drifting skyward, widening until it merged with the very layer of clouds overhead.

This time they would be wary. There could be no direct attack so long as their prey had control over the flame. They would have to be more cunning, masters of strategy. Yes, they would have to flush them like partridges from the sagebrush. And then they would be waiting to pluck them off, one by one.

He looked to his left, to the form crouched at the base of a halved pine trying to stay out of the wind's way. Without so much as a nod of agreement, it quickly sprinted away from him, fanning out into the forest to take post in encircling their encampment. To his right, the large form that had once been a female of the species grinned widely, exposing long knives of teeth that had grown over the existing enamel from the polyps that had given their lives from their mooring along the gum-line to create those devilishly sharp outcroppings. They fit together about as poorly as a jack-o-lantern left to close like a fist on the curb for the garbage man, but they hadn't been grown for aesthetics.

Brian walked slowly forward, taking his time until all of the others were in position. They would close in on them like a net through which not even the most slippery of minnows could escape. Fire would be eliminated from the equation entirely, and they outnumbered their prey, not to mention the fact that not one of them, not even the boy, had any idea that they were coming.

Not yet anyway.

The back of the house slowly took form from the darkness. An amber glow flickered from within, staining the walls and the railing on the deck with such an intense glow that not even the swarms of snowflakes could dampen it, like raging clouds of moths flapping at the fire. A silhouetted shadow formed in the shifting light framed by the shattered glass, standing there, still, staring off toward him.

He had to be careful. She had to see him, but not clearly. Yet at the same time she had to be able to easily identify him. So long as she could see the jacket, but not the physical changes occurring beneath, her eyes, her heart, would convince her of the rest. It would be her love that would provide that moment of indecision, that critical split-second that would prove to be all the time that they needed to attack.

He waited out of sight, the tense anticipation even blocking out the torturous pain of the rapidly accumulating snow. If she ran to him, he would gut her with those claws of his as easily as he had torn through the soft earth in the tunnels. If she hesitated—and he truly liked the thought of this even more—then he would run her down and tear her apart with all of the savage ferocity of a lion hauling down a limping wildebeest.

Without words, the others announced that they were in position.

Brian took a step forward, allowing the light from the balcony overhead to filter across the front of his jacket, while masking his face with shadow.

He couldn't see the spark of recognition in her eyes, but from the way she straightened right up, he could positively tell that she had not only seen him, but had recognized him. His claws clacked eagerly against the hard plates that covered his thighs. The polyps inside of his mouth squirmed anxiously, popping out from his tongue so thickly that he could hardly contain it in his mouth in their zest to taste her blood.

"Shannen," he forced through the rusted vocal chords, softly enough so that only she could hear.

The corners of his mouth drew back all the way beneath his earlobes, spreading the plates that had formed over his lips. Jaggedly sharpened triangular teeth, like those of a shark, parted in a demonic grin.

"Shan—"

III

"—nen," the voice drifted up to her from below as if moaned by the whistling wind itself.

She clapped both hands over her mouth and shook her head violently from side to side. Brian was dead. She knew that with every bit of surety. She had left him there at the side of the road...but there was no mistaking the fact that right now he was standing down there beneath the balcony calling up to her like Romeo preparing to serenade his Juliet.

"The garage!" Brad shouted, running into the living room from the bedroom, stomping into the hurriedly donned boots and quickly tugging his jacket back on.

Nancy sprinted in right behind him, ripping Tim out of Cindy's grasp even as she rose with him.

"Grab the oxygen tanks!" William cried.

Trick and Jason slowed to scoop up the large metal canisters, clutching them to their chests, and darted after the others.

"Hurry!" William screamed, tugging at the back of Shannen's jacket. "We've got to go right now!"

She just turned to him with this blank look of bewilderment paling her face, lowering her brow, and then slowly turned right back to the darkness through the broken glass.

"It's not him!" William trilled, grabbing her by the wrist and yanking her until she stumbled after him, still unable to remove her eyes from what she saw down there in the shadows. "They're using his body! Just like the others! They're using his body to fool you into thinking he's still alive!"

"Alive..." she whispered.

William could hear the clatter of disengaging locks and then the jangle of chains being dragged across the fiberglass hoods before clattering into piles on the ground.

He jerked at her wrist until it felt like he was going to crack her bones, and then let go. Whirling, he dashed right up to the fire and reached into the smoke and flame. His fingers wrapped around a piece of wood and he pulled it out, brandishing it above his head like a mighty torch, the fire rising a good foot above the half-consumed log.

He sprinted through the remains of the sliding glass door and heaved the branch over the broken railing, arcing it through the sheets of driving snow and toward the shadows where the creature lurked.

The thing roared and leapt backward, the flame staining its face with that golden glow. There was nothing left of those features even remotely reminiscent of how they had looked during life. It could just as easily have been a stone gargoyle standing out there in the shadows.

The flame landed in the snow with a hiss, immediately extinguishing.

"No," she whispered.

"Come on!" William cried. "There's nothing you can do for him!"

Seizing hold of her wrist again, he jerked her from the window, only this time her legs were no longer rooted into the snow-covered carpet and she stumbled along behind him, watching in terror as that creature emerged quickly from the shadows and darted out of sight beneath the deck.

William dragged her across the living room and down the short hallway leading to the garage, just in time to hear the clatter of the runners from one of the snowmobiles hitting the concrete over the metallic grumble of the trailer shuddering back into place.

"Hurry!" he screamed, leaping down the pair of stairs with the thudding echo of his small feet.

The garage door was still open, as they had left it when they had driven the Cherokee out and into the night on its final journey, allowing clouds of snow to blast inward from the wailing wind. He could see their darkened silhouettes. Nancy cradled Tim to her breast on the back of one of the snowmobiles, her fingers knitted into the back of her sister's jacket. Cindy had her arms wrapped around Trick's waist, lodging the tank between her chest and his back, ducking her head to the side of it in preparation.

"Go!" Brad shouted, shoving the matching black snowmobile forward from the concrete and into the standing snow where the Jeep had once been.

Trick twisted his fists around the handles and brought the engine to life with a scream. He revved it several times like a bull snorting at the gates while William shoved Shannen forward onto the second SnowJet. She draped her arms around Jason's waist, and just leaned forward onto his back, resting her tear-stained cheek onto the nylon fabric of his jacket.

William climbed on behind her and reached around her to lace his fingers tightly together.

"Hold on!" Brad shouted, jumping on in front of Jason, who shifted the tank of oxygen to his right arm and grabbed hold of Brad's jacket with his left.

The engine fired to life, spewing black smoke from the twin tailpipes and causing the whole works to shake.

Shannen mewled and tightened her grip.

"Go straight!" William screamed over the roaring of the engine. "Dad! Whatever you do, don't head down the road!"

He could only hope his father had heard him. The snowmobile lurched forward, grabbing hold of the snow and then firing like a bullet out into the darkness.

Trick guided the second snowmobile into the tracks of the first, fixing his sight solely on the small red taillight that flirted in and out of the snow. It had been so long since he had driven one of these things. The motor shook and whinnied, threatening to buck until he eased back off the throttle, settling the beast, and shot it straight out and away from the house with a loud buzz.

Shadowed forms blew past to either side, taking several sprinting strides to try to keep up but winding up left in the sprays of snow that kicked up from behind the runners. Brad couldn't even bring himself to look at them. He had to stay focused on the road ahead. The only light was the thin halogen beam that bounced up and down from beneath the handlebars, clogged with falling snow nearly back to the bulb.

They sped straight toward the end of the driveway, marking the street by the stump of the mailbox.

A shadow stood directly in their path, the dim beam from the headlight illuminating a large letter C on the front left breast of the jacket. Hooked claws slowly rose from the shadow's side until its arms stood straight out to either side. A flash of red glinted from those deep-set eyes, barely visible from the shadows formed by the massively obtrusive bone structure surrounding them.

Brad cranked the handles to the right, careful not to turn so quickly as to roll the blasted snowmobile and scatter its passengers across the snow. Its turning radius was so small that he had to give a little on the gas and slow the machine.

The shadow roared and leapt forward through the air like a jaguar. Shannen screamed and Brad twisted the throttle again, kicking them forward with a lurch. Her former boyfriend sailed right past her left ear, his snaggled claws tearing a tangle right out of her hair, and, had she not immediately tightened her grip around Jason, nearly cleaving her right off the seat and plunging her backward into the snow.

"Holy sh—" Trick spat, jerking hard on the handles to keep from slamming into the creature that appeared out of the first snowmobile's wake like a phantom from the blowing snow. The snowmobile slid sideways, bucking and skipping like a flat stone from the choppy surface of a lake, before finally slowing. The runners trailing the skid rose from the snow, threatening to roll right over. "Hold on!"

Before the snowmobile even skidded to a halt, the creature in the letter jacket was upon them. It reared right up on its ugly haunches and leapt over all of them while the snowmobile skidded beneath, striking with its claws to snare Cindy's jacket and yank her right off of the seat.

She landed squarely on her back, knocking her breath from her chest into the cloud of flakes that blew upward from the impact. The tank clanged to the gravel beside her, immediately vanishing into the deep snow. Eyes lolling skyward, she clutched at her chest and rolled slowly from side to side, trying desperately to suck in the air. She could hear the others screaming for her, shouting for her to get up and get back on the snowmobile, but their cries sounded so distant, like the lingering residue of a dream.

A tall shadow towered over her, the flakes angling past and swirling around the dark form.

Driving her hands into the snow, she tried to propel herself backward, kicking with her heels though it accomplished little more than carving grooves into the hidden dirt road.

The shadow raised both hands above its head, forked claws framed against the bleak sky.

Other sets of footsteps padded closer, dark shapes churning into focus to either side of the one looming above her.

"No," she sputtered through the last of her breath. "Please."

It felt as though someone had lowered an enormous boulder right down on her chest.

Scraping at the gravel, clawing through the snow, she dragged herself slowly from the shadow, though with a single step it could match her most fevered efforts.

The creature's whole form tensed, its mouth widening into a torturous, macabre display of ferociously sharpened teeth.

Cindy looked quickly from the corner of her eye to the right where Trick was only now throwing himself over the side of the snowmobile and racing toward her.

"Run!" he shouted to her, kicking through the mass of accumulation that was now nearly to the middle of his shins.

But she couldn't run. She couldn't even get up. Her chest throbbed so terribly that she couldn't even begin to nip enough of the air to taste its bitter dampness on her tongue. All she could do was continue to scrape at the ground and drag herself away from the monster.

Her left hand butted into something beneath the snow, and she had but time enough to roll to the side and grab it before the beast let out a tremendous roar that split the night itself.

Its claws sliced through the air.

With the last of her strength, Cindy raised the object she had cleaved from the snow up above her chest. She turned her head to the side and closed her eyes, praying that whatever it was she held above her was strong enough to withstand the impact from the claws and keep them from tearing right through her flesh.

Brian's eyes, filled with those greedy red mouths, flashed for the last time from within the now deeply set sockets. He could already feel the give of her feeble skin parting for his hooked fingers, the spray of pulsating blood that would splash up from her and coat his entire front. The voices in his mind railed with the thrill of victory, growing to a furious pitch as his claws lanced through the night toward—

There was no time to recoil, no time to even formulate the thought to send its urgent message to the striking appendages. In that one fateful fraction of a second, they all, every transient mind linked to the collective being, knew fear.

His right hand hammered the oxygen tank a split second before his left. The hardened claws made first a loud pinging sound upon collision, and then a guttural wrenching sound as they tore right through the metal casing.

Pressurized gas fired out through the slanting gashes, firing ribbons of shredded metal right into his face. There was only time to open his mouth to scream before the gust of oxygen hammered his face. It filtered through all of the small catacombs that formed the maze of his thickened exoskeleton. No matter how quickly they receded deeper into their host's tissue, or how fervently they tried to close their gaping mouths in time, those polyps all drew a deep inhalation of the toxic oxygen. They immediately shriveled right up and fired out a clone that would never draw its first breath.

Brian teetered there, swaying drunkenly back and forth, his fingers still buried in the metal.

Snowflakes blasted up into the air at the force of the expulsion.

The other monsters, those who had closed in from all sides to wet their claws in her flesh and revel in the savory first slashes of pulsing blood, shrieked in inhuman horror, throwing themselves backward and away from the swelling cloud of oxygen. Rarefied gas raced through their savagely gaping mouths and directly up their nostrils, passing effortlessly through the permeable membranes and into their brains. Millions of voices cried out at once, but were abruptly cut short.

The hardened collection of dozens of generations crusted over the human form beneath began to crack immediately, the oxygen spontaneously breaking down the structural components and turning it to dust before the bodies even slammed onto the tundra. Clouds of snowflakes and fragmented chitin plumed into the air from the fallen bodies, crumbling off like dry, caked mud and littering the top of the snow. The all-too-naked flesh beneath poked out from under the jagged fragments that had managed to stay attached, a sickly pale gray. The flesh no longer appeared to have any semblance of its former luster and elasticity, taking on the curdling appearance of cellophane stretched across warm oatmeal. Useless eyelids settled in like limp flags draped over the now hollow sockets; formerly rigid cartilage in the ears and nose had withered to nothing, allowing the flaps of skin to simply drape down the cheeks.

Cindy's breath returned with a vengeance and she screamed with all of her might.

Brian still wobbled over her, his hands lodged in the jagged tears in the metal that now drew the blood from his fingers while he rocked back and forth at her beckoning.

Hands trembling, Cindy tried to shake him free, but only succeeded in making it appear as though he was about to drop right on top of her. The crusted layers on his face were already beginning to crack and separate like chiseled mounds of sandstone, dropping down onto her chest and clattering from the tank that now hissed its last dry breath and fell silent.

Panic sunk into her veins and she threw the tank to the right while she scurried out from beneath it to the left.

Brian toppled forward, pulled by the weight of the falling tank, and slammed face-first into the snow. His face shattered like a China doll, his nautilus-like horns fragmenting off and dropping beneath the piling flakes. The letter jacket hovered in place for a moment before settling back down atop the flattened remains of the body beneath. His fluids spilled right out and into the ground, raising steam into the air and melting the snow back from his frail, lifeless corpse in an expanding, wet amoeba shape.

"Get it off! Get it off!" Cindy screamed, frantically brushing at the crumbs that stuck to her from her face all the way down to her legs.

"You're all right!" Trick called. He took her by the shoulders and swung her around so that their eyes met, and spoke softly, soothingly. "You're all right now."

Brad zipped up to them on the SnowJet, pausing only long enough to wipe the crystallized snow and ice from around his eyes, and then from the Plexiglas shield in front of him.

"There are more of them out there!" he shouted, pointing off to the left toward the end of the street at a group of shadows that raced headlong toward them. "We can't beat them all!"

Shannen looked helplessly to the ground where Brian's jacket was already beginning to disappear beneath a layer of snowflakes. She studied the small notches in the snow where his fingers had made their final descent and watched the last of his warmth converted to heat, rising in one final wave of steam. The snow was stained red in a ring all around him, the edges of the accumulation collapsing inward from the fluids that eroded its packed base.

Brad thrummed the throttle and zoomed back toward the street. Shannen looked longingly back over her shoulder until she could no longer even see the jacket atop the snow, and finally turned forward and fixed her eyes stoically over Jason's shoulder and onto the flakes swarming the headlamp.

"Come on!" Trick barked, grabbing Cindy by the hand and racing toward his snowmobile. He hopped on and wrapped his freezing hands, dampened and icy beneath with sweat, around the handles and immediately felt Cindy's hands drape around his waist. Dropping his right hand atop hers, he gave her a quick squeeze of reassurance and then threw it right back into position and forced the engine to growl. "Ladies and gentlemen, keep your heads and hands inside the vehicle at all times," he said, forcing the jet into gear with a rumble. "It's going to be a bumpy ride."

The SnowJet launched forward with Trick fighting to see through the blinding snow, batting his eyelids from the flakes assaulting them like a sandstorm. As soon as he caught the first glimpse of the wan red glow from the other taillight, he locked onto it like a cruise missile and drove toward it.

Brad's speeder crossed the street and bounced through the gully on the far side, nearly throwing them all from it, before catching and firing up the hillside. He couldn't see anything but the barren tops of the trees over the steep rise, the headlight staring purposelessly up into the night sky. Clumps of scrub oak, buried beneath the branch-breaking weight of the piled snow, blew by to either side. Only the sharpened tips of the yucca plants broke through the otherwise pristine plain.

The SnowJet flew over the crest of the hill, bounding from the ground hard enough to slam his head forward into the plastic shield.

The headlight flashed across what looked at first to be a line of tree trunks directly in their way, but they didn't look quite right. There was something about them...

"Christ!" Brad spat, jerking the handles to the right before he slammed into the line of people standing there atop the hill...waiting for them.

Shannen screamed and dug her nails into Jason's stomach, pressing her face into his back.

Trick was nearly to the top of the hill himself when he saw the flash of Brad's headlight flare from above and point quickly off to the right. He adjusted his course to follow, slicing an angle up the steep incline not knowing what had caused the sudden alteration in direction, and not really wanting to find out either.

"No!" William screamed, pulling tightly against Shannen's back and leaning over her shoulder to try to make his words audible to his father over the roar of the engine. "Don't go this way! Please! Don't go this way!"

Maybe it was the horrendously loud throng of the motor, or the fact that he was both trying to simultaneously watch the road in front, and the shadowed figures that raced toward him from the side, but he probably wouldn't even have heard the boy if he were shouting through a bullhorn right into his ear. Naked and sharpened branches reached out for them, tearing at their clothing and trying to snag their flesh and gouge out their eyes from the underbrush he steered directly through. There was no room for cleverness, no room for error. He couldn't risk trying to slalom through the tree trunks or wind around the all but invisible clumps of foliage and end up dumping them all out onto the snow and stalling the motor. With the rate those creatures were moving, and the angles they had chosen in anticipation, it was going to be a tight squeeze getting them through there regardless. All he could do was pin the gas and pray.

A branch ripped free from its trunk and clattered across the windshield just before they slammed through a bank of snow and into the air. An explosion of powder blasted over the windshield, blinding Brad and caking the Plexiglas. The whole snowmobile leaned to the right as they had been launched at an angle to the hillside. The headlight first focused on the snowflakes above the nothingness, quickly blending into the gray mat of their accumulated brethren on the road below.

The snowmobile slammed into the road, nearly tearing the front rudder right off. It bowed as far as the monster spring would allow, forcing the whole works to hop into the air like a frightened cottontail, before hammering the ground again with a spray of frozen slush and flakes.

"Come on, baby," Brad muttered, listening to the protests of the grumbling motor before it switched over to the familiar hum and sped down the middle of the street toward the highway.

"No!" William screamed, nearly crawling over the top of Shannen. "Turn around! Please, Daddy! TURN AROUND!"

A light flashed across them from behind, spreading their long shadows across the snow before them. Trick skidded the SnowJet into their tracks and fell into tow directly behind.

The last of the silhouettes atop the crest of the hill faded behind them, but Brad didn't let up. He was going to run that engine hot and heavy until it either got them out of there or died trying.

"No! Listen to me!"

For just a moment Brad thought he heard his son wailing from behind, but rationalized it as nothing but his imagination. It could have been the wind or another underlying sound beneath the hum of the motor for all he knew. And even if it had been William, whatever he had to say could wait until he got them far enough away that it wouldn't be risking their lives to slow.

"You have to listen to me! Please, Dad! You can't go straight! Get off of the road! Go left! Go right! Go anywhere else but straight!"

Focused on the road, which was nearly invisible itself were it not for the faint remaining impressions of the tracks they had made walking up the street to the house, Brad wound with the curves, navigating the roundabout road through the forest. Black trees, capped by mercilessly piling snow, pressed in from either side, hiding the darkness beyond and who knew what else. Each turn sent his imagination into overdrive. He pictured one of those armored creatures darting out from the darkness and hurdling toward them on the road, expecting to find another line of them just standing there in the middle of the road, barring all passage where there was no room to either side to swerve off into the forest.

"Please!" William sobbed, frozen lines of tears shimmering on his cheeks. "You have to stop! Turn! Please God...just don't go...straight..."

Shannen turned to look at him, noting the redness in his cheeks in contrast to the stark pallor. He had pulled the mask from his face and crumpled it into his right hand to ensure that nothing was interfering with his speech, his words. With that same hand he was trying to swipe at his father's shoulder over Jason, nearly standing up to try to attract Brad's attention.

"Tell Brad to stop!" Shannen whirled and yelled into Jason's ear.

Jason half-turned to look questioningly to her over his shoulder.

"William says to stop!"

Jason's eyes darted to the boy who looked like he was about to crawl right out of his skin. He was blubbering hysterically, oozing fluids from every possible orifice.

With the image of unimaginable fear in the boy's face, Jason quickly turned and brought his lips right up to Brad's ear.

"Stop!" he shouted at the top of his lungs.

"We're almost to the highway!" Brad called back over his shoulder. "Just another quarter mile and we'll be able to make better time up into the mountains!"

"Your kid says to stop!" he screamed again.

Brad's brow furrowed and he hurriedly glanced back over his shoulder.

William was crying and screaming to him, slapping at him madly with his hat, nearly standing to the point that if they hit a bump he'd be tossed right from the seat and into the snow. Never in his entire life had he seen his son so frantic, so...terrified.

"Now, Dad! Please! Please! Stop now!"

His eyes turned back to the road in slow motion while his hand gently released the throttle. The trees to the right opened into a gap where he could see but the snow-coated top of an aluminum rail and a large white-capped boulder leaning against it, framed against the pitch darkness.

His heart dropped and he became intimately aware of everything around him.

William's panic.

The boulder.

The gate.

The long sliver of metal glinting from atop the rail.

Slowly, he shook his head to chasten himself.

A thin smile etched his lips.

At least now it will be quick, William's words echoed in his head.

And his eyes dripped shut.

"No!" William screamed, his mortified, sharpened voice slashing through the night.

IV

She crouched beneath the overburdened, invisibly needled branches of a blue spruce, barely able to see more than a sliver of the night through the nearly impregnable blind. Clawed fingers impatiently dragging slices through the dirt and crumpled, browning detritus to her sides, she didn't dare steer her vision from the road for even a second. They were coming…as she knew they would, as the voices had told her they would be.

They were able to see into the future to some extent, though really, it was more like foreseeing all possible futures and determining which was the most likely. That was the gift of the pseudo-divine network of billions of shared minds, though in their self-professed omnipotence, they were allowing ego to obscure their vision. So enthralled with their own amassed might, so overconfident were they becoming, that it skewed their perspective. Rather than looking ahead to verify the outcome of their plans, that brash impudence insisted that overlying numbers, superior strength, and the combined mental omniscience of a deity would avail. Why should they focus all of their energy into squashing such insignificant gnats, when their primary focus was where it should be, after all: building the hive. It was like the Holy Roman Empire pausing to consider a line of ants on its way to world domination; hardly worth wasting the time for thought. But they needed to be crushed all the same, ground by armored heel into the dirt.

The boy especially.

He shared their blessing of precognition by happenstance, a fluke of nature that allowed him not only to survive their infestation, but to peer into their otherwise guarded thoughts. While they focused solely on the big picture, building their fortress from the ravaged trunks from the forest, he inspected the individual trees. In the grand scheme, something as trivial as his own survival mattered for naught to them, but to him, it was paramount. Maybe he could see scattered glimpses into the future, but as they knew the outcome, as they always knew the outcome, they really didn't even need to look.

Without the boy, the others would be lost.

She could feel him, hear those trapped within his diminutive frame calling out to her for release, begging to be freed from their mortal prison so they could take the form of something they could control, rather than being held hostage within.

The distant sound of the buzz of an approaching engine brought her to her haunches, her plated legs tensing in anticipation.

The body once belonging to Karen Fletcher fought the urge to peel back the foliage in front of her. It was all she could do to keep from betraying her presence. She lusted for death, wanting nothing more than to tear down that hillside and wait there in the middle of the road. But she didn't. The element of surprise would be crucial. She cleared her mind of all thought, silencing the multitude of voices in her head and focusing through the silently falling snow on that faint droning motor.

They had left her for dead, and maybe the part of her that had once been the human Karen would have been able to forgive them, but the minion that now controlled her could not. While their individual lives were of little consequence, each was important to the hive, and it took that personally.

They had awakened, trapped beneath the destroyed bridge. She had washed downstream, lodging her ample waist between two large chunks of mortar. The current had managed to keep her head above water, repeatedly bouncing it off of the debris until she had a bruise on her forehead that looked like hamburger. It had taken them close to an hour to drag her out of there, crawling through bowed, rusted rebar and fractured cement, through mounds of fragmented asphalt and demolished cars. The skin had peeled all the way from her fingertips, exposing the bloodied, bony stumps beneath, her fingernails flagging limply back over her first knuckles. It was all they could do to plant their roots and hold that flesh together as it wanted nothing more than to succumb to the will of the water and slip free from the bone in adipose clumps. They could barely draw enough air for sustenance through those waterlogged lungs, coughing and spewing out mouthfuls of the vile, dirty water. By the time they had dragged her to shore and flopped her down on that steep cement embankment, her body was all but useless to them. Had they not begun the die-back process when they had, fitting her with a suit of carbonized armor, her flesh might just have melted away and been useless to them. As it was now, it was no more substantive than a jellyfish in a plaster cast, held together despite itself.

So long as the internal organs were functional and the brain could still be made to command them, then the rest of it didn't matter. Let her blackening flesh slough from her yellowed gobs of cottage cheese beneath. Let the pressure from the water absorbed into her brain cause a painful death of hydrocephalus. Let her slowly bleed out through her exposed vascular webwork, seeping through the seams of her self-generated armor. None of it mattered now…for she was about to draw first blood.

The others, those who had been unable to successfully ambush the prey that now sped toward her, ran toward her in the distance, calling out to her, telling her what she already knew.

They were coming.

The host's heart pounded in her chest, fibrillating faster and faster until it felt as though it just might combust with anticipation. Spikes grew from the backs of her gray, crusted arms, similarly sending up spires atop each shoulder. Two long horns, originating not from her temples as did the majority of the others, but from the rear of her head, hooked over the crest of her hardened scalp, forking out in front of her like those of a bull. Her narrow, slanted eyes stared out from beneath those jaggedly sharpened points, the ice coating her forehead melting around them like tears from those blood-red organs, sunken deeply into the recesses of her cranium.

Dust crumbled from her mouth when she smiled, drawing the corners of her torn cheeks all the way back to her jaw socket, exposing all of her teeth, all twenty-eight of those bared, overgrown teeth sharpened to fit together like a bear trap. Useless saliva poured over her lower lip, stretching as far as it could reach toward the ground before pausing, and snapping free to splat onto the detritus.

The buzzing sound grew louder, vibrating the weighted branches, dropping cascading showers of flakes atop her head.

Patience.

The sound grew louder still until it sounded like twin bees pollinating her eardrums, humming right there against her timpanic membrane.

She carefully reached one clawed hand forward, resting it on the branch in front of her and slowly pressing it to the left just enough to free her line of sight. Her right hand forked into the ground, her bent legs eagerly poised against the ground like a sprinter preparing to explode from the blocks.

    A faint aura of light appeared from the right, little more than highlighting the snowflakes swirling within it at the edge of her sight like so many swarming locusts.

    Her left foot started to tap anxiously.

    The blossom of light grew larger and larger until it focused into a long, single beam drawing a halogen circle on the snow, heading directly toward the road beneath her. The bracket holding the lamp wobbled up and down, making the sphere of light look like a basketball cast from the sun bouncing down the center of the road.

    Patience.

    She turned her eyes from the approaching SnowJet just long enough to study the road directly below her position. It widened into a gated drive just before taking a sharp turn to the right, bottlenecking into the trees that packed the side of the road so tightly that there was no possible way they could veer into the forest to avoid her. And there was no way they could steer down that driveway with the aluminum rails locked together with chain and a padlock, and that monstrous boulder planted right in the center of it.

    She quickly turned back to the approaching vehicle, now framed to darkened silhouette by another headlight behind them. There were four distinct shapes atop it. The first was huddled down behind the windshield, ducking his face to keep it out of the stabbing wind, while the two in the middle were simply human lumps of flesh pressed against his back. The one in the rear, whom she quickly identified as the boy, was standing up, trying to signal to the driver. He was screaming, panicking.

    He knew.

    Stifling a predatory roar of rage, she held to the brush.

    It was too soon. Just a little further.

    The driver turned to face the boy, and immediately the trilling buzz of the motor started to fade.

    No! Just a little further.

    The rapid advance of the light across the blowing snow began to slow.

    She couldn't wait any longer. The boy knew she was there and she couldn't allow him to alter their course.

    It had to be now.

    Her legs drove from the earth, firing her out from beneath the shielded canopy of the spruce and into the air over the road with the swirling snowflakes.

V

Brad barely had the time to turn to his left and tilt his gaze upward.

That enormous black shape dropped right out of the sky like an anvil, landing on the shoulder of the road on two feet and then dropping to all fours to use the force of its leverage to spring forward. It cut right through the snowfall, knifing directly toward him through the air. He didn't even get a chance to draw a final breath to scream, didn't even have a split second to twist the throttle, before it hammered him directly beneath his left arm. Two powerfully large arms wrapped around his chest and cleaved him from the seat, slamming him into the ground and driving him into a slide through the snow.

"No!" William screamed, throwing himself off of the snowmobile and into the powder. He scrambled to find his feet, shoving himself up from the accumulation that covered even his bare face.

Brad groaned as his ribs splintered beneath the weight of the creature, gushing a mouthful of thick blood past his lips in a single geyser. He flailed to struggle out from beneath it, but he couldn't see anything with the mound of snow covering his eyes, his flapping arms only adding to the effect by throwing clouds of snow back above him. It felt like he had been tackled by an avalanche of stones, the hard exoskeleton pressing through his flesh and into the bone with such painful ferocity that each one felt as though it was going to snap. He tried to sputter a cry for help through his fluid-filled mouth, but succeeded only in spraying the snow around him with droplets of crimson.

Those arms, like he had been sealed within a vise, squeezed again and raised him from the ground.

He hammered with his fists down on the creature's back, his torso lodged between the pair of monstrous horns, narrowly averting being speared right there atop its head.

"Go!" he shouted, wincing terribly at the pain that spewed steaming fluid past his lips and down the thing's rocky posterior.

"No!" William screamed, dashing through the snow that rose up over his knees. Progress was maddeningly slow. The distance to his father appeared insurmountable, as though no matter how fast he ran he would never be able to get there in time.

Karen buckled back and bellowed a thunderous roar into the sky.

"Please, God!" William screamed, tripping and falling forward into the deep snow and pushing himself immediately back to his feet through the mist of powder.

The beast released its hold on Brad for a brief moment, following his sides up to his broken ribcage with its hands, and then quickly tightened its grip.

Brad screamed, bucking up from the creature's head with the terrible pain. The wickedly broken shards of bone carved into his insides, tearing through the paper-thin membranes of his lungs and stabbing into anything soft enough to allow it to pass through.

She raised him above her head like a mother holding up a child to swing him in the sunlight, and then jerked him quickly toward her, driving one of those long horns straight through his midsection.

"Dad!" William screamed, throwing himself forward with as much velocity as his little legs could generate. His father's rag-doll form flopped over her head and draped down her back with a splash of blood that immediately melted a hole through the snow. "NO!"

"Mother of God..." Trick gasped, finally catching up with the first SnowJet. He had noticed the snowmobile starting to slow, but it wasn't until he saw the large black form fire straight across the seat and toss Brad into the snow, sending the snowmobile careening off to the left into the bank, that he knew why. And now, staring at Brad's impaled form dangling limply from the creature's head, he hadn't the slightest clue of what to do.

Brad raised his jittery head just enough to look to William, their eyes locking one final time. He wasn't dead: the gored horn lancing right through the side of his stomach just inside of his oblique muscle, pouring blood down his back.

"Daddy!" William cried, running up to his father and taking him by the hand.

"Out of the way, kid!" Trick yelled, solidly fixing his lips and letting the engine have the gas. The snowmobile shot forward toward Karen. Using that lone headlamp like sighting a rifle, Trick aimed the front rudder right toward her legs.

"Go on..." Brad retched, dribbling a line of crimson past his lips.

"No," William whined, refusing to relinquish his father's hand.

"I...love you." He tried to feign a smile though his agonized eyes were tightly stretched from the pain. The corners of his lips quivered. "Go..."

Karen tossed her head back, trying to slide Brad free from her horn. She roared into the night with furor enough to loose snow from the branches on the trees surrounding them. Brad's fingers snapped out of William's grasp.

"Dad!" William screamed, desperately reaching for his father's hand.

The light from the speeding snowmobile blinded him from his right, stretching his kneeling shadow a good fifteen feet across the snow, his grasping arm reaching off infinitely across the road before bending up and over the stalled boulder.

"Move!" Trick yelled, wildly waving his arm at William, eyeing down his target. She was dauntingly enormous, as though her mass had nearly doubled. She stood more than six feet tall and looked to be cut directly from the stony ridges along the foothills. He never would have recognized her were it not for the constrictive length of clear plastic tubing dangling down her back with that oxygen mask still attached, the plates of armor merely forming around it.

"Everyone!" Trick shouted as loud as he could so that the others could hopefully hear him over the engine. "Hold on tight!"

"Help!" William screamed, rising to his feet and reaching up for his father.

Pressing his thighs against the seat and squeezing the handlebars tight, Trick ducked his head down and braced for impact. Cindy's arms wrapped so hard around his stomach that he could barely breathe.

The tip of the front runner swatted the creature's ankle, bending to the left a heartbeat before the side of the snowmobile hammered her across the back of the thighs. Glass from the shattering headlight flew overhead to the tune of the horrendous crack that quickly buckled in the windshield and rapidly spider-webbed outward. Fiberglass splintered and cracked along the side of the machine, the right rudder bending awkwardly backward against her leg and nearly tearing right off.

Karen's head snapped backward with the impact. Overcompensating for nearly having her legs clipped right out from beneath her, she threw herself forward. Her arms flapped in vain, snatching for anything to catch herself on, to regain her balance, but Brad's weight atop her head already had her off-kilter.

"NO!" William screamed, racing through the blinding white wake from the SnowJet that skidded past him down the street.

Karen fell forward directly toward the aluminum gate, reaching out to try to catch herself on the upper rail. Her hands met with the ice-coated metal, and slipped right off. Her inertia carried her forward, slamming her head downward toward the gate.

That long sliver of metal drove easily through Brad's back, passing just to the left of his spine and spearing straight through his heart. With a crack, it gored straight through Karen's cranium.

Brad flopped back immediately, folding lifelessly back over the rail like a towel draped over a rod. His warm blood spread along the top of the rail, steaming as it melted through the ice and dripped down to the rail beneath before patterning the snow.

Karen's entire body twitched like she had an electrical current running through her. Feet carving into the dirt road, she scraped and dug to pull herself backward, arms slashing through the air at her sides.

"Come on, William!" Jason shouted, racing up behind the boy and wrapping his arms around his small chest. He lifted him from the ground and attempted to whirl the boy back to the snowmobile, but William flopped and struggled, slipping through his grasp and falling into a heap on the ground. Before Jason could so much as bend over to sweep the boy up again, William was racing back toward his father.

With a roar of rage, Karen planted her sharpened heels into the ground and grabbed hold of the rail. In one labored motion, she slid her head from the piece of metal, leaving a thick trail of blood to drain down onto Brad's chest. She wobbled in place for a moment, the bitter wind forcing her to stagger from side to side to maintain her balance, and then slowly turned to face William.

She took a single step toward him, her head bobbling from side to side on her rubber neck, the crumbling shell first growing wide fissures and then disintegrating around her black throat. Hovering, she raised her tremendously shaking claws to her sides, and then fell forward.

Her horns drove straight into the ground, her neck snapping with a loud crack. Fragments of gray coating splintered from her skull and spread out across the snow, her body slamming limply into the powder, expelling a cloud of snowflakes back into the sky.

William sprinted past her and to the fence, wrapping his father's legs to his chest and trying to leverage him upward, to pull him back off of the spike.

"The others are coming!" Trick shouted, watching the shadows form from the darkness at the distant end of the road where they had come from. He gunned the motor to make sure it was still going to go, and looked nervously to Jason.

"We've got to go!" Jason yelled, slipping his arm between Brad's legs and William's chest. This time he squeezed the boy tight enough to pry him away.

"Dad!" William screamed, trying to catch his father's legs before they flopped back into place.

"We can't help him now!"

"Daddy!"

Tears streamed from William's eyes. He had no control over his trembling body. He couldn't think, couldn't breathe. His world had come to an end in the blink of an eye.

The whole scene had played out before him exactly as he had

envisioned it. He had thought he would be able to change it; thought that had engendered hope.

"He didn't suffer," Jason whispered into William's ear for lack of anything more comforting to say. He passed William off into Shannen's grasp and hopped onto the front of the snowmobile.

The engine still idled, rumbling the seat beneath them.

With a twist of the throttle, the SnowJet darted forward with a lurch and then stopped. He did it again and the snowmobile rocketed into the snow.

"We can't leave him!" William screamed, fighting through Shannen's arms to try to crawl back over her shoulder. He reached out, wailing.

"You have to be strong, William," Shannen said, hugging him to her to stabilize her tenuous balance on the seat. "He would have wanted you to go on."

"I don't want to be strong! I don't want to go on!" he screamed. "I want my daddy!"

He watched his father, propped there like a scarecrow loosed by a windstorm, until he faded into the blackness behind the driving snow, and dropped his head onto Shannen's shoulder.

She could feel him shuddering against her chest, and knew exactly how he felt as she too had lost both of her parents, and like William, felt absolutely alone.

"It's going to be all right," she whispered into his ear. "It may not feel like it now, but you'll see. Everything is going to work out."

He raised his head from her shoulder just enough that she could feel the warmth of his breath on the fine hairs lining her ear.

"Nothing will ever be all right again," he said, and then dropped his head right back onto her shoulder and held her tight.

She kissed him atop the blowing hair on his head, and looked up over Jason's shoulder, watching the snow stretch out before the yellow glare of the headlight. They didn't even slow to make the turn, nearly capsizing to the right as they turned quickly onto the highway and headed straight toward the mountains, now invisible through the thick flakes, blowing directly into their faces. She could barely hear the second snowmobile behind them until it caught up and rode their tail.

She couldn't help but wonder, as they sped toward the unknown, cloaked in shadow and darkness, if maybe William was right.

7 | Sanctuary

I

Jason blinked his red-striated eyes against the interminable snow that accosted him over the windshield, letting them linger shut just a little bit longer each time, requiring that much more effort to tear them back open through the already congealing, golden gobs of sleep. His mouth hung open of its own accord, though by the time he sensed it and closed it up, it was beyond blanched and parched. It was so dry that swallowing a single strand of the thin mucous that trailed down the back of his throat was like choking back a walnut whole. The feeling was slowly returning to his socked hands, making him appreciate the numbness he had been so eager to abandon. Knuckles both burning and freezing simultaneously, he felt like the skin was peeling away to expose the electric nerve endings atop the bare white bones of his knuckles. The wind tore straight through the mesh of holes in the cotton, and even at arm's length he could see that the skin beneath was about as red as a trout's gills, and about the same consistency. The basal need for shelter superseded even the hunger that grumbled and wrung the acid from his stomach, and the prodigious need for some fluid to quench his tattered throat.

But the thought of stopping the snowmobiles longer than it took to fill the gas tanks and the portable red cans terrified him even more than just riding off to his death at the helm like the captain of a skeleton crew.

How many hours had it been now since they had last seen any sign of those creatures, since they had rounded that last bend, leaving the demons to slash through their frosty wake? Since they had abandoned the child's father without so much as a word, let alone a proper burial? How many miles?

Time bled into an endless stream, like the channel they rode through the center of, following the pristine white of the unmarred snow, keeping the trees as far as they possibly could to either side. Nothing looked familiar. The blizzarding snow packed the faces of the mile markers and road signs with a crusted blanket of gray ice.

Where once the valley they cut through must have been magnificent, now it more closely resembled that of the shadow of death. The river to their right only occasionally poked through the ice and snow; flowing brown and marred, rather than crystal blue. The pockets of aspens leading up the increasingly steep foothills to either side were stripped of all foliage. The pines, firs, and spruces that filled every available gap were now defined by the shadows between and beneath them, that impenetrable darkness where once deer and elk had foraged for bark and berries. They stood beaten and nearly bare, like so many mongrel dogs, patchy with the amounts of fur ripped from their scabbed flesh.

Jason closed his eyes again, only this time, allowing them to stay that way until he unconsciously began to lose grip on the throttle and the engine began to slow.

William was still wrapped around Shannen, as he had been for however many miles, and though she winced when she stretched out her cramped and uncomfortable legs to untie the knots in the muscles, she was comforted by the simple fact that she had someone to hold on to. She just tucked her face down into his shoulder and reveled in the shared body heat between their torsos, dozing in and out until the bitter stab of the frost and wind through her scalp roused her with sharpened needles. She didn't even care to rummage through the pocket of candy bars she had filled at the last gas station. All of them felt somehow tainted by the spatters of blood from whatever customer had left the streaks and smears on the polished white floor before arising from the dead to answer the call of the others.

Her lips stretched, splitting about thin red seams, the tatters of dried skin peeling up to the bright red, chafed rings around her mouth as she tried to swallow the sparse droplets of fluid produced by her dry, useless tongue. Debating the merits of risking the giardia to slurp from the oddly appetizing looking stream, she cradled the back of William's head, combing through the icy knots in his hair with her fingers before cupping his fluorescent red left ear and pressing his right to her cheek to warm them. She too, allowed her eyes to drip closed at the urging of the aching within her skull, listening to William's sputtering breaths in her ear.

By the time either realized they were sleeping, the motor was barely idling at the side of the road, tilted up onto the steep cut rising from the shoulder on the far side of a car buried beneath feet of snow.

"What happened?" Shannen rasped, and tried to clear her parched throat.

"How long have I been out?" Jason gasped, immediately jumping up from the seat and whirling around in surprise.

"Relax," Trick said from behind a tree just up the slope. Steam poured from the bark and the melting snow beneath. "I think we could all use a little break."

It took close to a full minute from him to re-cinch the layers of pants and slide down the slope into the knee-deep snow.

"We should keep moving," Jason said, doing what he could to pry the tangles of sleep from his frosted lashes with his sock-clad knuckle.

"It's easier to do that when you're awake," Cindy said with a smirk, skidding down the frozen turf through Trick's tracks.

"What I wouldn't give for a steaming hot mug of coffee."

"There's something steaming and hot up there," Trick said, having to raise his eyebrows to keep a straight face. "It looks a lot more like cider though, but you're welcome to it if you want."

"It's not that I don't appreciate the offer…"

"Beggars can't be choosers, m'man."

"Uck! Are you two almost through?" Cindy gagged.

"We should start thinking about finding some shelter before nightfall," Nancy said without opening her eyes. She was stretched out on the seat of the snowmobile with Tim asleep on her chest. "I don't think any of us want to risk this kind of weather at night."

"We need to get out of this valley then," Trick said, pivoting in place to eye the crest of the rise way up to either side through the sheeting snow. "I'm not comfortable here. It just doesn't feel right, you know? Like it would be the perfect place for an ambush or something."

"I'm with you on that one," Jason said, suddenly well aware of just how steep the mountains were that rose to either side, and how pathetically thin their channel was growing. His shredded lip slipped between his teeth and he gnawed on it to work through the swelling feeling of claustrophobia.

"Sanctuary," William whispered, coughing through a windpipe so dry it felt like it had closed in upon itself and sealed together.

"Any more specific instructions? Or would you have us driving through these hills until we found a church inside of a damned Texaco—" Trick started, but William cut him off by merely raising his right hand from around Shannen and pointing past him.

Trick turned and walked a dozen paces toward the green highway sign, the entirety of its face crystallized and covered by a sheath of frost. Raising a socked hand, he curled his fingernails under and chiseled at the ice until chips powdered and cracked away.

"Oh." He had cleared away the first five letters of the word, and now resumed the task of chipping away the remainder. "Sanctuary. Three miles," he read, gesturing to the sign like Vanna White for all to see.

"What's in Sanctuary, William?" Nancy asked, parting her closed lids.

Only the wind interrupted the silence, tossing snarls of flakes through their midst, while all waited for the boy to answer.

"Home," he said softly. "For now...home."

"Sounds good," Trick said, for the first time, perhaps in his life, his voice bereft of sarcasm. "What say we get going then?"

Jason answered—sidling up to the handlebars—with a rev of the engine.

Nancy sat up, making room for Trick to climb back behind the wheel, and her sister to slide in between. Cindy leaned her head against his back, holding him tightly around the waist. He reached back over his shoulder and stroked the side of her face for a moment before stealing his hand back to fix it on the gears.

Sanctuary. 3 miles.

Steadying his eyes on the wobbling slant of light arcing from the headlight, the assault of flakes slashing through it, Jason inched the snowmobile forward until it started gaining momentum, and then launched it into the unflinching darkness mottled only by the faintest hint of the wearily hiding sun. There was no way of knowing what lie around the next curve, let alone three miles deeper into the valley. He didn't know if he would ever again see his apartment, ever again know the normalcy of his former life. The only thing he knew with any sort of certainty was that nothing would ever be the same again.

He glanced back over his shoulder to make sure that his shadow, the other snowmobile cloaked in darkness, was right there, and cranked the throttle. The high-pitched buzz seared the solitary night.

Jason ducked his head behind the plastic shield and accelerated toward his fate.

II

William opened his eyes from the fleetingly transitory respite of the unheralded sleep, blinking back the exhaustion that streaked his reddened eyes and the flakes alighting atop.

The trees peeled back to either side, the ground beneath them rising and falling like they were skipping over moguls. Wooden rails from splintering fence posts passed in a long parallel line, holding the naked forest at bay. Falling away behind, the road vanished into the whiteout like the memory of his former life.

"You awake?" Shannen whispered into his ear.

He raised his head and nodded, wiping the frozen drool first from her shoulder, and then from across his cheek.

"We're here."

William craned his head over his shoulder to look toward the headlight. A weather-beaten barn passed to the right where the fence terminated, baled hay mounded beneath the snow that drifted through the opened doors. Invisible beneath an enormous lump of snow, an abandoned tractor interrupted the otherwise desolate field.

The headlight veered slightly to the right to guide them through a gap in the fence in front of them where the upper, graying, twin rail had snapped and fallen under the snow. An old white farmhouse, the paint peeling in curls from the warping paneling, a relic from a time long since forgotten, blew past, the absence of life betrayed by the hauntingly black holes of the shattered windows like the eyes in a bull's skull on a windswept plain.

Forging the first tracks through the virgin white, they buzzed forward through the hidden pasture and dropped into a gully, only to arise on the other side in the middle of a road. Bending to the right, Jason steered down the center.

Shadowed storefronts materialized in the distance like the rocky walls of a canyon closing in on the road, framed by the skeletal limbs of oak trees that were taller than any of them.

Easing back from the throttle, Jason slowed the SnowJet, bringing it to a grinding, rumbling stop in the middle of the road. There was a sign to the right, a green placard with white lettering held aloft by nothing more elaborate than a single metal rail. Killing the engine, he climbed off and scuffed through the knee-deep snow to the placard.

Trick pulled beside William and watched Jason, letting the engine growling between his legs shudder to a halt. He sighed, billowing a plume of steam, and reached back to rouse Cindy with a gentle stroke of his sock-clad hand across her forehead.

"Time to wake up," he said, staring briefly at her intoxicatingly blue eyes behind those fluttering lashes, and then turned to Jason, who had by now nearly scraped all of the ice from the sign.

"Welcome to Sanctuary," it read. "Elevation 7700 Feet." And then in smaller letters, scrawled in cursive. "We've Been Expecting You."

"We made it!" Trick whooped, leaping into the air and grabbing Cindy by her hands. She squealed, but allowed him to cleave her from her seat and swing her in a circle.

Jason knelt and wadded a ball of snow and launched it toward Trick, laughing.

"We're here, baby," Nancy whispered to Tim, smiling not just with her lips, but with her shining eyes when he raised his head from her shoulder.

"Yeah," he said in an almost impossibly quiet voice. "I knew we'd make it."

"Come on, William," Shannen said, bucking him to the seat and stepping down into the snow. "Let's round up some firewood. I don't know about you, but I could stand a little warmth."

"In a minute," he said, feigning a smile.

Let them celebrate this small victory. Let them revel in it for the moment, because the next storm was brewing on the horizon, every bit as daunting as the one that would continue dumping snow until they all but forgot the sun had existed at all.

Soon.

Soon they would no longer be able to run from the others, and not even this little town lost in the mountains would be safe.

Soon they would be forced to turn and fight, to take their stand or face extinction.

Let them have this one moment where the excitement staved off the fear. There weren't to be many more like this.

William knew that far too well, for he had seen it in his visions, but worse, he could feel them coming. And they would never relent.

And bad as everything felt now, it was only going to get worse.

Soon.

Soon...the hive would be complete.

8/26/03

About the Author

Michael McBride lives in Westminster, Colorado, in the shadow of the Rocky Mountains with his wife, Danielle, and their three perfect children. *Species* is his first published novel. To learn more about Michael and his upcoming works, please visit his website at www.mcbridehorror.com. He would also love to hear from his fans. Comments and questions may be addressed to michael@mcbridehorror.com.

5/13/07 Sunday 9:08 pm

Printed in the United States
40414LVS00002BA/229-237

9 780974 768045